SEASONS OF SOLDARK

LIZ DELTON

Seasons of Soldark
Novella Collection
Liz Delton

Copyright © 2023 Liz Delton
ISBN: 978-1-954663-15-2
Paperback

Character illustrations, and corner art by Amy Marchant
Cover design by Deranged Doctor Design
Map by Angeline Trevena

Tourmaline & Quartz Publishing LLC
P. O. Box 193, North Granby, CT 06060
www.TourmalineandQuartzPublishing.com

SEASONS OF SOLDARK

Read this collection of cozy steampunk novellas in any order. Each one tells a tale of a different character from Soldark, in a different season.

The spring, the summer,
The chiding autumn, angry winter, change
Their wonted liveries, and the mazed world,
By their increase, now knows not which is which.

-A MIDSUMMER NIGHT'S DREAM, WILLIAM SHAKESPEARE

WELCOME TO

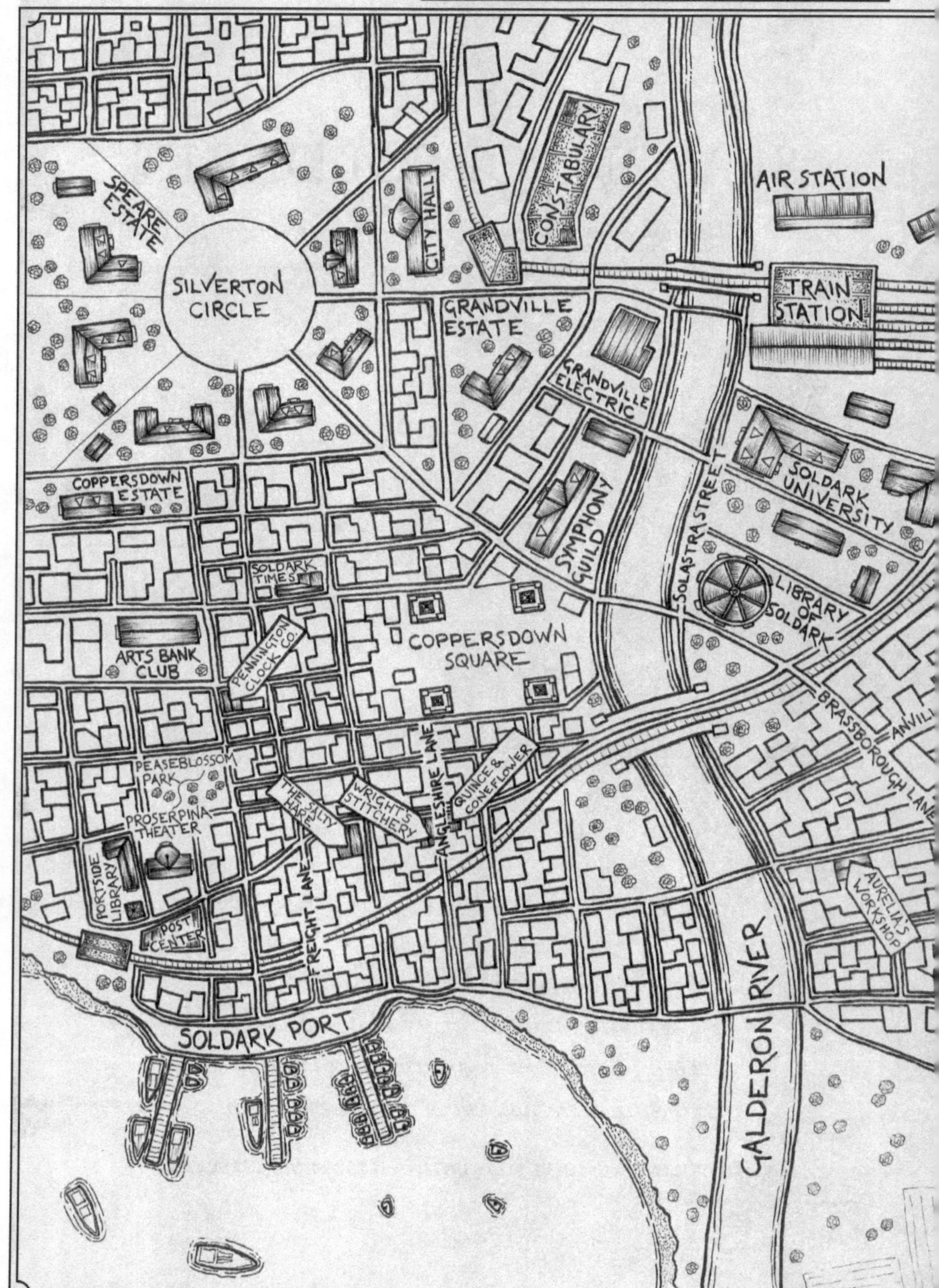
SPEARE ESTATE
SILVERTON CIRCLE
CITY HALL
CONSTABULARY
AIR STATION
TRAIN STATION
GRANDVILLE ESTATE
GRANDVILLE ELECTRIC
COPPERSDOWN ESTATE
SOLDARK TIMES
SYMPHONY GUILD
SOLDARK UNIVERSITY
SOLASTRA STREET
LIBRARY OF SOLDARK
ARTS BANK CLUB
PENNINGTON CLOCK CO.
COPPERSDOWN SQUARE
BRASSBOROUGH LANE
ANVIL
PEASEBLOSSOM PARK
PROSERPINA THEATER
WRIGHTS STITCHERY
ANGLESHIRE LANE
QUINCE & CONEFLOWER
THE SALTY HARE
PORTSIDE LIBRARY
POST CENTER
FREIGHT LANE
AURELIA'S WORKSHOP
CALDERON RIVER
SOLDARK PORT

SOLDARK 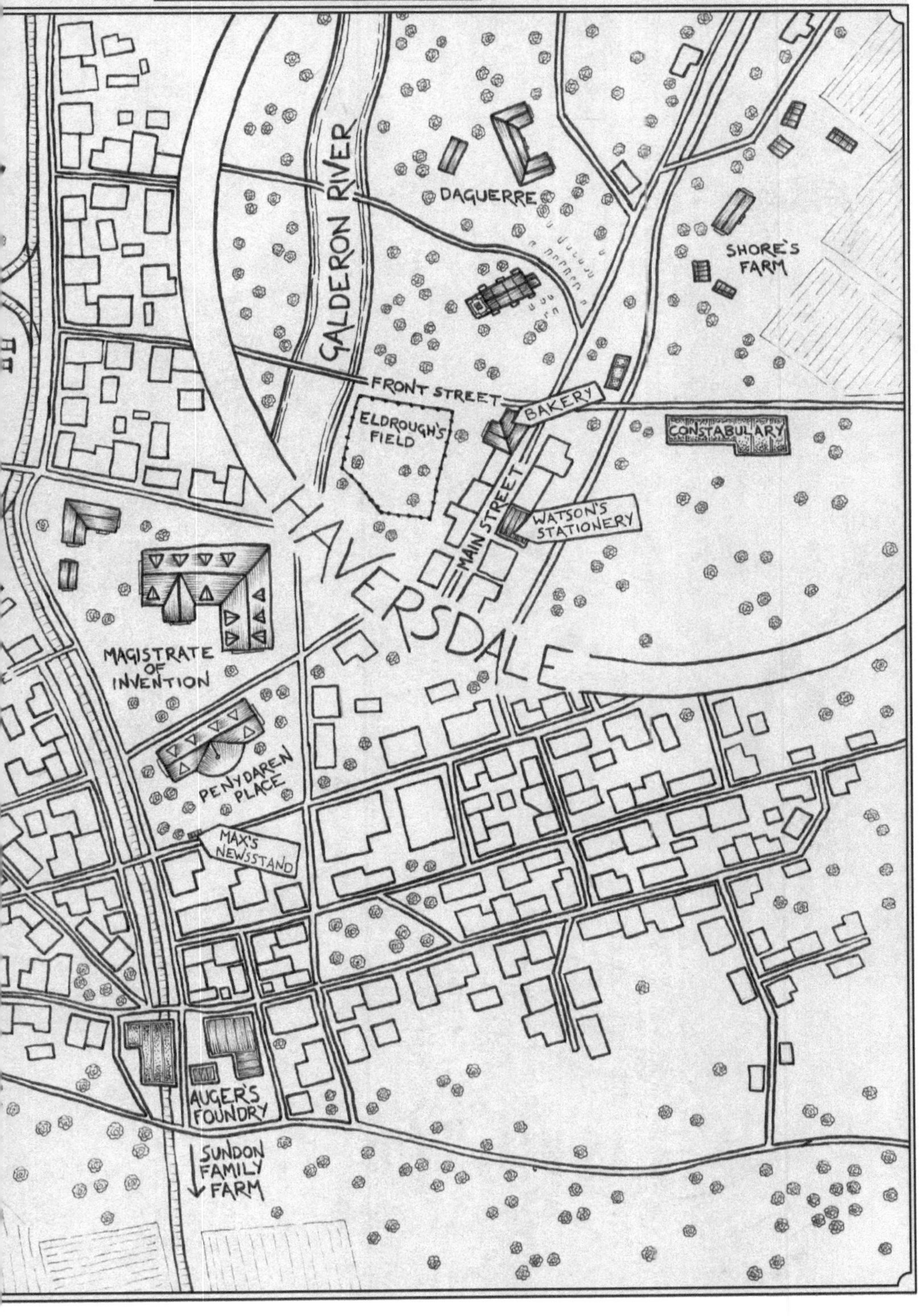
CALDERON RIVER
DAGUERRE
SHORE'S FARM
FRONT STREET
ELDROUGH'S FIELD
BAKERY
CONSTABULARY
MAIN STREET
WATSON'S STATIONERY
HAVERSDALE
MAGISTRATE OF INVENTION
PENYDAREN PLACE
MAX'S NEWSSTAND
AUGER'S FOUNDRY
SUNDON FAMILY FARM

SPECTACLE
OF THE
SPRING QUEEN

MAE WRIGHT

I

As she stood on the dock beside the steamship, Mae Wright reached up to pull off her fur scarf. She adjusted the white hat pinned neatly to her curls, which she had dyed pink to celebrate her new venture. They matched her traveling dress, which was dark pink with white trim, and brought out a little color in her pale cheeks.

She shifted her hold on Bobbin, her mini Goldendoodle, as she unwound the suddenly stifling scarf.

"Well, I suppose it *is* spring, Bobbin," she muttered, "just not the type of spring we're used to." She threw another glance at the wood and iron gangplank to the steamship she'd spent the last two weeks on and adjusted Bobbin more securely on her hip as she waited.

She filled her lungs with the crisp air of the Soldark harbor and was thrilled that the air didn't burn her lungs with cold like it did back in Corsich. She eyed the red and gold sunrise over the ocean as she exhaled in relief.

"Well, this is our home now," she said brightly to Bobbin as she tucked the scarf into the small suitcase she'd lived out of for the past two weeks. "The warmth does have its benefits."

She tore her gaze from the ship—she was still waiting for her trunks to be unloaded—and glanced toward the varied cityscape spreading out from the port. Though she had never set foot in Soldark, she now owned a small shop in the merchant district; the building had landed in her lap by way of her second cousin's will.

A whiff of smoked meat on the salty air reached her, making her mouth water. Her stomach immediately responded as if it had only just realized it was on stationary land and no longer roiling about on the ocean. She was eyeing what she thought was the source of the smell—a small pub down on the corner of the harbor—when the ship's captain walked toward her. *Finally*, she thought, smiling up at him. Once she had her trunks, she could find her new shop, her new home. She was quite looking forward to properly bathing and getting out of her traveling dress.

The first mate followed the captain, his head tucked down

and his hands behind his back.

Mae tilted her head, wondering if there was a problem. Over the course of her trip, she hadn't once spoken to the captain, though she had spent as much time outside of her quarters as she could, unable to stand the cramped space for any longer than necessary. Her queasy stomach, however, often demanded she retreat to the privacy of her commode.

"My apologies, madam," the captain said, his voice surprisingly quiet for a man who commanded an entire steamship, "but we've searched the hold—myself included—and your trunks are not aboard."

Mae's stomach fell as though she were still on the ship amid stormy seas, something the steamship had encountered several times. She clutched Bobbin to her chest, and he wriggled. "Well, I suppose I'll have to manage somehow," she said automatically. "What do you think happened to them? Are they still in Corsich?"

She dug her hand into her pocket and pulled out her coin purse, glad she had kept it on her person. "At least I have my coin purse," she said, trying to look at the bright side. Then the realization sank in. "How am I supposed to open my seamstress shop without my equipment? My fabrics?" She gasped. "My clothes!"

She looked down at her dress, trimmed in fur and made from as many layers of thick cotton flannel as could easily be stitched together. Even without her scarf, she was still sweating. She only had one other traveling dress, and it was the exact same style as this one, only with a more muted blue and gray color scheme. Her suitcase only contained the few essentials she had needed while on the steamship.

The captain frowned politely. "The port master in Corsich will have kept them safe in his office, I assure you. This does happen...on occasion," he added somewhat reluctantly. "We can retrieve it at no cost to you, of course."

Mae nodded. She would just have to make do, like she always did. It wasn't as though she had expected moving to a new city and opening her own business would be easy. But starting out without all her clothes...

Squeezing her coin purse, she wondered how much of her startup money she would have to spend merely clothing herself until—

"Wait. When will they arrive?"

A brisk wind ruffled her dress and hair, blissfully cooling the sweat on her neck.

The captain looked over at the first mate, who shrunk in on himself even further. "Seven weeks, six if we're—"

"Seven weeks!" Mae yelped. Just as she did, a steamship disembarked at the next dock, letting out a piercing whistle from the bridge.

At the shrill sound, Bobbin contorted himself out of her grasp in terror.

"No!" she shrieked, losing hold of him. They were too

close to the edge of the dock!

Something fell out of her other hand as she blindly tightened her hold on Bobbin before he could leap from her hands. She clutched him safely against her chest, burying her face in his curly gold coat. "Oh, Bobbin," Mae muttered, her heart racing. She hastily stepped away from the edge of the dock, the dark waters churning menacingly below as the wake of the departing steamship slapped waves against the massive dock posts.

As the shock wore off, she became aware of a strange sound—like something metallic rolling on the dock—and noticed that both the captain and the first mate were on their hands and knees at the edge of the dock, scrambling for coins.

Her coins.

Her coin purse was gone, and the tiny bubbles emerging from the water below indicated exactly where it had fallen.

She took another step back from the edge, not wanting to lose Bobbin...or anything else.

What did she even have left? Bobbin was safe, that much was important. She herself was safe and intact. Beyond that...

Her scarf. A bar of soap and a toothbrush. An extra shift for sleeping in. Two novels. Half a scone wrapped in a napkin. And...

"I'm sorry, madam," the captain said in a choked voice, holding out four copper coins they had scrounged from the planks of the dock.

Mae took them with shaking fingers.

Four coppers?

Her automatic urge to smile and say "It's all right" faltered and died before she could speak. Would it be all right? How would she make do with almost nothing?

Not even a single gold coin?

And she had to wait seven weeks for her things!

Her knees wobbled, so she re-secured her hold on Bobbin. The sounds of the harbor grew louder, overwhelming her. The slap of the waves on the dock posts. The shouts of the port master to the deckhands. A far away whistle—thankfully, this one didn't bother Bobbin.

The captain was speaking again.

"Sorry, what did you say?" She shook her head to clear it.

"I'm so sorry, madam," the captain said, frowning. "I was saying, we could offer you passage back to Corsich, so you aren't stranded here without money or belongings, and you can take the return trip with your trunks. There would be no charge."

She bit the inside of her lip, gnawing at the skin. "Seven more weeks on the ship?"

"Six, if we're lucky," the first mate added, though this failed to cheer her.

Six or seven more weeks in the same two dresses, with no money—no, she would get her trunks eventually, which contained another purse with half her finances. She had deemed it prudent to split it up for this very type of misfortune...except she hadn't predicted *both* coin purses would become inaccessible.

Still, she didn't think she could spend even one more week back on the ship. Though the steamships were well-equipped with amenities these days, nothing in the world could fully dampen the effects of the rolling sea. Not for the first time, she regretted not booking an airship, which would have been quicker and smoother, but the extra cost had deterred her. She had been saving up for so long, even before she had inherited the shop. And now, half of her gold lay at the bottom of the bay, the hungry tides of which had probably already swept her savings away.

Mae rubbed the remaining coins together in her fingers. Four coppers.

She would have to make do.

"You know what, Captain?" she said, forcing a smile to her face. "I think I'll take my chances here. I'm sure I can find some work in a shop or something until my things arrive."

Saying it out loud strengthened her, and she lifted her head, eyeing the streets that led out of the harbor. Solid land. New faces. And fresh food, if she could get her hands on some more money. With her sewing skills, that shouldn't be a problem.

"Where will you stay?" the captain asked, his face wrinkling in worry. "I can't very well leave you here with nothing." He patted his pockets absently. "And, well, I don't have any—"

"I have a shop," she said, gaining more confidence in her decision. "It's empty, but I'm sure it'll suffice. Now I'll have plenty of time to get my bearings in Soldark before I open it."

The captain's face visibly relaxed. "Ah, good. Where shall we deliver your trunks when we return?"

"Wright's Stitchery, on Angleshire Lane."

II

"As I said, the previous owner didn't live over the shop," Howard said apologetically as he opened the door to the apartment above the shop.

"Right," Mae said, surveying the room. Her correspondence with Howard Glass, the solicitor who executed her late cousin's will, had included a detailed floorplan of the property, but those papers were secure in her trunk back in Corsich...along with all of her other business plans, not to mention her sewing machine, fabrics, threads, and notions.

The room was completely empty save for a cold and sooty fireplace, which Mae walked over to inspect. The grate needed cleaning, and the whole thing could use a good sweep, but it looked serviceable.

"I'm afraid he never upgraded the living quarters to steam heat," Howard said, clutching his bowler cap with both hands, "but once we fire up the boiler in the basement, the shop will be nice and toasty."

"Oh, it's plenty warm enough," Mae said brightly. "I'd be at home in a snowstorm." She bent over to set Bobbin down, but he wriggled and refused to put his feet on the floor. Writing this behavior off as fear of a new environment after two long weeks of oddities in his routine, she straightened and hugged him a little closer. She went over to the window, which was coated in thick dust and grime. The window overlooked an alley, but also gave a good view of the other shops for a few blocks and a slice of saffron-colored sky.

"Yes, of course," Howard said, "but the nights here are still terribly cold." His thin frame visibly shivered as if the mere mention of cold nights had chilled him.

She hitched up her smile once more. "I'll sleep in the shop if the heat doesn't rise up to warm this floor, but it's fine. It's wonderful, actually." She had intended on renting furniture when she arrived, but she would make do for now.

Howard's mustache twitched as he returned her smile. "Of course. Now, I already had the water company turn your water on, so you're all set there..."

She poked her head in the remaining rooms as he filled her in on the status of the property. Her heart sank a little at the barrenness of the rooms, which didn't surprise her, after the correspondence she had shared with Howard during the months since learning of her inheritance. What troubled her was her missing funds, which she had planned to use to purchase furniture the moment she landed in Soldark. The small kitchen contained only a few odds and ends in the cabinets, and the single bedroom and the front room held only dust. She wished she had taken Howard up on his offer to assist in the purchase of furniture prior to her arrival, but she had wanted to pick out the items herself.

She still couldn't believe this place was *hers* though. She had never met her distant cousin Petyr, but he had spent summers with Mae's mother when they were children, and evidently had no one else to pass his estate to. Mae's mother had been quite touched after processing the grim news of her cousin's passing, and they were both thrilled at the idea of Mae taking over the shop premises.

It had been a dream come true, after all her saving and planning for her own seamstress shop. And in Soldark, no less! She would just have to make do with the rough start and hope her trunks would come early.

Bobbin still in her arms, she followed Howard back down to the shop. "I never knew my late cousin," she admitted. "He was a jeweler, you said?"

"Quite a respectable one, at that," Howard said. "I was sad to hear of his passing. He closed up and stopped selling to the public a long time ago, though he never fully retired. He would take appointments for friends or longtime customers. Why, I'm sure he was working on custom jewelry for his closest patrons up until the end."

Mae gazed around the empty shop with pride.

She pictured where she would stand mannequins in the front windows, dressed in her latest styles, with fabric swatches on top of the jewelry cases. Perhaps her selection of fine buttons and snaps could be displayed too. She would spend most of her time in the workroom in back, which was just big enough for her sewing machine and all her notions.

The solicitor showed her the basement and demonstrated how to turn the boiler on, which would feed steam into vents throughout the shop. Mae hoped the warmth would rise high enough to heat the apartment. Perhaps after her shop began to make a profit, she would have vents run up to the living quarters. She certainly wouldn't want Bobbin getting too cold in the winter.

After Howard gave her his calling card, should she ever need legal or estate advice, she bid him farewell, accepting the shop keys from him with a little thrill. Glancing down at Bobbin, she said, "Well, let's get started, shall we?"

Bobbin only let her put him down after the shop floor had been swept.

Mae sighed in frustration and relief, sweating profusely after having swept the floor while holding him the entire time. Every time she had tried to put him down, he retracted his legs, forcing her to heave him back up with a sigh and sling him on her hip while she awkwardly held the broom. He finally got down and trotted around the clean shop, happily unaware of his mistress's exasperation. A chuckle bubbled from her lips, and she absently brushed dog hairs from her corseted torso. "I know it's a new place," she remarked, "but the floor's nothing to be afraid of. Or was it the scare at the dock?"

She let Bobbin explore the newly dirt-free floor while she trudged upstairs to wash up and drink some water using a cup and pitcher she found. Petyr had left a few items in the cupboards in the small kitchen. She located a shallow bowl and filled it with water for Bobbin, whom she found nosing around some crates in the workroom.

Starving, she sat down on one of the crates and pulled the scone out of her pocket, unwrapping it from her embroidered handkerchief. After one look at it, she offered it to Bobbin instead, who gratefully accepted it, scattering crumbs all over the floor by her feet. She chuckled. Although she had been back on land for a few hours now, she couldn't stomach the food from the steamship; even the smell reminded her of the rolling sea.

"I'm glad we didn't get back on the ship," she told Bobbin, rising to her feet to grab the broom once more. "But we're going to need to find work soon—four coppers will only buy a few meals if we're lucky."

In the end, Mae didn't need to sweep again, since Bobbin

licked the crumbs off the workroom floor. Instead, she took the broom upstairs to rid the second floor of dirt so that Bobbin could roam freely. As she wondered where his newfound hatred of dirty floors came from, she held her handkerchief to her nose as the broom kicked up what seemed like years' worth of soot and dust.

By the time she finished, she was famished. Bobbin resisted any attempt of hers to keep him in the shop—including laying her fur scarf on the workroom floor as a makeshift dog bed—so she tucked him under her arm and locked the shop door behind her. She was unable to resist stepping a few feet back and admiring the shop front before embarking on her journey for an affordable dinner for two.

"We'll need a sign," she muttered to Bobbin, glancing up at the wrought iron arm jutting out over the door, where she pictured the quaint wooden sign she could hang from hooks. The shop windows would need cleaning, but that wouldn't be difficult. The paint was serviceable, though she couldn't quite say what color it was originally. At least it wasn't chipping, even along the window panes. She nodded and headed down the lane, heading vaguely in the direction of the harbor.

Somewhat revived by the fresh air and the coolness brought about by the sinking sun, she decided to explore a bit, keeping an eye out for job postings or inexpensive food. At the very least, she should be able to get work in a seamstress shop, even if they only had a lowly position. If she was stuck sewing buttons and hems endlessly, it would only be for a few weeks.

As she caught a glance of the port down Freight Lane, she made a mental note to inquire at the port master's office to see if someone could search the ocean floor where she had dropped her purse. She had assumed it was too deep, or the current too swift, but it was worth asking, wasn't it? Right now, she needed to focus on getting a meal and a job, and she was fairly certain she would soon collapse without the former.

As the streetlamps flickered to life, their gas flames dancing in the twilight, she spotted a friendly-looking ordinary. Mae looked at the sign above the door, which boasted a painted rabbit with a block of something white on its head. Mae hefted Bobbin securely on her side, where he fit perfectly in the curve of her corset, and she stepped inside.

It was far from what she would call *ordinary*, a portrait of another rabbit hanging prominently above the bar, with a grimace on its face this time. *What is this place called? The Judgmental Rabbit?* Mae wondered with a smirk as she approached the barwoman. There were stuffed rabbits mounted on the wall, and all manner of paintings of people from airship pilots to inkslingers standing before a printing press.

"'Ello there," the woman said, reaching up to touch her cap.

Mae was the only customer at the bar, and only a handful

of patrons occupied the benches lining the ordinary, thoroughly focused on their meals or cups.

Hitching Bobbin up again, Mae gave the woman her best smile and said, "Good evening. Have you any knowledge of seamstresses in town looking for help?"

The woman frowned. "Help, you say? Oh, aye. I might know of one thing or another…" The woman trailed off, picking up a mug as if in suggestion.

"Oh! Um, I could also use something to eat. What do you recommend? My budget is—er—tight. Hence the need for work." She wished she had led with the food question first.

"Soup's fresh and cheap, as you like. Half a copper each."

"Perfect, I'll take two—if you don't mind." She gestured to Bobbin.

The woman's expression warmed for the first time, and she said, "I'll do you one better—chef'll give 'im just the meat and vegetables plus a hunk of bread for ya both. Sound all right?"

"Sounds heavenly," Mae said, sliding one of her four coppers across the bar with extra care.

When the woman came back not five minutes later with two steaming bowls, Mae all but melted into the barstool, much like the pats of butter pooling on the bread slices.

Keeping an eye on Bobbin as he neatly ate from his bowl on the floor, Mae lost track of time, realizing how hungry she had been when her stomach was finally full. The gas lamps looked brighter, and a few more patrons had filtered in.

"As for work," the barwoman said when she came over to collect their empty bowls, "you'll want to check the boards outside the post center. It's right around the corner from the Proserpina and the Portside Library." She flung her arm in the general direction behind the bar.

Thanking the barwoman profusely, Mae headed back onto the streets. Before finding the post center, however, Mae decided to turn right for the harbor. If there was any chance someone might find her coin purse, she needed to ask sooner rather than later. She hefted Bobbin onto her hip and strode off with the wind in her face.

"Sorry, ma'am," the port master said when she asked. "Couldn't send anyone under today. Me second hand man sailed with the *Fisherman's Folly* this mornin', and I ain't got no other help today. Maybe tomorrow or the next day."

"Really?" she asked, some hope still kindling.

He shrugged, thick shoulders inching up under a worn wool sweater. "Can't make any promises, though. The tide does as it pleases, you know."

She forced a smile. "I thank you for trying. The *Riveter* lost my luggage too."

He shook his balding head. "A shame, ma'am. Captain Jeffries told me so when he asked about your purse."

"Yes, well, I'll manage. I don't suppose you know of any seamstress work? I just need—"

For the second time, Bobbin wriggled in a herculean effort out of her grip at the sound of a piercing steam whistle coming from an outgoing ship. *Not again!*

III

"Bobbin!" she cried. Likely terrified, he sped away through the foot traffic on the street lining the port, and Mae raced after him. She thanked her stars he hadn't almost fallen into the ocean this time.

"Where are you going?" she demanded, gasping for air. Hoping Bobbin would make for the shop, she darted between a small crowd that had gathered along the street where the post center was supposed to be. But she didn't have time to even glance around for the noticeboard. She spotted Bobbin's gold tail wagging furiously as he sprinted down the crowded lane.

She couldn't lose him too.

Mae held up her skirts and soldiered on, glad his short legs didn't give him much of an advantage. However, weaving through the people was proving a difficult task for *her*. She certainly didn't want to create a bad impression—anyone here could be a future employer or client. She bumped a man's elbow and smiled in his direction, not even looking as she said, "Sorry! Lost my dog!"

Hustling on, she saw Bobbin turn down a dark lane. Her breath heaving and constrained by her corset, she followed, thoroughly ready to be done with this forsaken day of bad luck.

The streetlamps were dim, and Mae noticed another tavern ahead, with a few people hanging about outside. Bobbin must have followed the smell of food into the alley, but then lost his courage and turned back toward her hurrying footsteps.

"Oh, thank goodness," she said breathlessly. Indeed, she could scarcely breathe with her corset poking into her torso from all sides. Stiff-backed, she stooped down to scoop him up.

Just then, she noticed someone outside the tavern approaching her, lurching far too close for the smell coming off him. She took a shaky step backward, her chest heaving.

"Hey there, miss," the man growled, coming even closer. He leered at her behind a scraggly beard and stale breath.

"Excuse me," she said and tried to turn.

The foul-breathed man grabbed her arm, and she pulled away, as hard as she could. She needed to get out of this alley, *now!* The sound of fabric tearing rent the air. She staggered away from him, back toward the main street. Her sleeve was ripped, but she had broken free.

A new person stood in the mouth of the alley, a dapper gentleman. She glanced back and forth between the tavern-lurker and the gentleman.

"Ah, there you are," the newcomer said. "Come."

Thinking her chances with this gentleman were leagues better than with the foul-breathed tavern lurker, she accepted his arm. He led her out of the alley and back onto the brightly lit street.

Her vision blurred amid her shallow breaths and racing heart. The corset had stolen her breath, and she really wanted to sit down. The next thing she knew, she was being led up a set of grand stairs into an equally grand building. She blinked, realizing her breath was still too shallow to function properly. She held up her palm that was still clutched under the man's arm, and they paused inside the foyer.

There was a wild assortment of people about, men and women dressed so oddly she blinked heavily and shook her head to clear it. A woman in an all-white ballgown, wings on her back. And was that...a satyr? She tried to take a deep breath, but the steel boning was relentless.

"Rehearsal at ten tomorrow, Des?" the satyr asked her rescuer.

The man called Des nodded, longish black hair falling into his eyes.

"Madam Rosnah's still in the dressing room," the man in the satyr costume said. "She probably has some smelling salts..." He trailed off, nodding in Mae's direction.

It *was* a costume, Mae realized. She could now see that the hooves were attached to tight leather boots, and the hairy legs were merely tight-fitting pants.

"You weren't going out in your costume, were you, Robyn?" Des said as he led a still-stunned Mae forward.

"'Course not, Des!" the satyr replied shiftily, then followed Mae and Des into what Mae was slowly realizing was a theater.

She really shouldn't have run so far in her corset.

Her rescuer—Des—was clearly thinking along the same lines. "You must not be from Soldark," he said in his deep baritone.

Something deep in her stomach tingled. "How do you know that?"

"That is the tightest corset I've ever seen."

"Seen many corsets, have you?" she wheezed.

They were walking down the aisle of the grand theater—small though it was, the architecture was marvelous. She had never seen something so beautiful. The stage itself was made from glossy dark wood, the velvet curtains of the finest scarlet material. The satyr sauntered ahead of them, clip-clopping into the dark shadows up front.

"I have, as a matter of fact," Des said as they slowly neared the stage. "Fashions of all kinds come through the theater." He gestured to a black side door she hadn't noticed. She finally got a good look at him, now that they were alone and she wasn't fighting for air. He was much taller than she, with a well-tailored black suit that fit his slender frame perfectly. His handsome face and gray eyes were mostly thrown into shadow from his black locks, which, at their longest, barely brushed his shoulders. A thin black beard caressed his face, darkening his jawlines. He held himself almost in a military fashion as he waited for her to calm herself, with his hands clasped behind his back and his legs straight.

"I—" she began. What was she even doing here? She should just go back to the shop to revive herself. "I think I'm fine now."

"Suit yourself," he said with a slight shrug, "but Madam Rosnah's sure to have some smelling salts that might revive your senses or, at the very least, can point you to a reputable seamstress to fix your dress."

She glanced down at the tear that ran from her elbow to her wrist. "Seamstress?" Mae said, hope rising. "All right then," she agreed, and let him guide her through the threshold into the blackened hallway.

"Sorry about the dark," Des's deep voice came from behind her. "There's a railing on the right, but your eyes should adjust soon."

"Aren't there any lights in here?" she said, shifting Bobbin to the other side so she could find the railing. Bobbin whined a little, and she lightly caressed his fur.

"Not a one. Can't have any light bleeding through the side doors when a show is on. I got sick of touring actors accidentally turning on the hallway light, so I took it out."

"Oh," she said.

"Hold on," he said, lightly touching her shoulder. "Let me get the door for you. It sticks."

She paused, shrinking against the railing to the side, and she felt him move in front of her. The next thing she heard was a switch flipping, and she blinked at the flare of light coming from the cozy room ahead. Gathering her senses and her heavy skirts, she stepped over the threshold.

An elaborate black and gold chaise lounge took up most of one wall, among mismatched wingback chairs that looked like they had seen better days. Reading materials were draped across side tables and arms of chairs. It looked like a waiting room of some kind. The faint scent of perfume lingered in the air, and Bobbin sneezed.

"The dressing rooms are just through there," the man said, pointing to the only other door.

"Thank you," she said.

"It is no trouble at all," he replied. "We just finished rehearsal."

She paused at the doorframe, facing him. She was struck by just how tall he was. His eyes were guarded by strands of obsidian hair. "No, I meant to say, thank you for what happened in the alley, for—"

"Ah, yes," he said, with a little bow of his head. "Where *are* you from?" he asked suddenly.

"Corsich."

His gaze on her turned appraising. "Indeed? We once had a troupe of trapeze artists from Corsich, but not many actors treading the boards."

She cocked her head. "I don't think Corsich has many theaters, now that I think of it." She looked around the cozy room. "In fact, I can't think of a single one. When I saw *Son of Swan*, we had to go to Mercantia."

"*Son of Swan*? You don't seem like the type of lady to attend such a dark comedy."

She straightened. "Why do you say that?" she demanded. "And for your information, I found it quite clever. I thought about Markus Jessen's monologue at the end for quite some time."

"Then you must have enjoyed it indeed. The purpose of art is to make people think."

She turned to look for the dressing rooms with a huff, confused by his statements. Did he think her stupid? Too poorly cultured to understand why people enjoyed theater?

Faced with a corridor of closed doors, she slowed down and was shocked when Bobbin tried to get down. "Really? Here?" she muttered with a glance at the questionable wood floor that looked dirtier than her shop floor. "You little scoundrel."

With a furtive look back at the man called Des, she asked, "Can I put him down here? He's well behaved." *Or was until we got to Soldark*, she thought grimly, but she wasn't about to tell him that.

"Go ahead. He can't escape here. I assume that's why you ran into that alley?"

She set down Bobbin and nodded, still shaken by her ordeal. Bobbin immediately got to work sampling the plethora of smells in the narrow hallway. The backstage of the theater was a stark contrast to the front. Mae thought the floors could use replacing, not to mention the bare light bulbs that dangled precariously from the cracked ceiling.

Des bowed his head a little, gesturing down the hall. "Madam Rosnah's dressing room is the second door on the left."

The door in question was closed like the rest, so she allowed Des to squeeze by her to knock. Bobbin dutifully stayed nearby, and Mae gave her little dog a tired smile. She couldn't wait to curl up in her shop with Bobbin and finally end this miserable day. But she was beginning to feel hope that her detour to the theater would help in some way.

The door swung open, revealing an older woman. "Hadrian Desmond!" the woman shrieked in pleasure. "To what do I owe the honor? Normally, you're locked away in your office this time of night. I would have kept my hair on."

Mae peeked into the room to see a lush red wig on a stand amid piles of dresses, feather boas, and stacks of paper. The perfume that had been faint in the cozy room came at her in full force, and Bobbin sneezed again. The woman's hair was cut in a short style that no doubt fit well under a wig cap, though it was also dyed a shade of red that couldn't quite compete with the wig on the stand.

The woman looked past Des, and her eyes widened. "Now, who is this? You're not replacing me as Fiona, are you?" She gasped dramatically. "But I'm perfect for the role!"

Mae could tell she jested by the saucy glint in her eye, so she smiled at the woman. "Mr. Desmond rescued me from a fraught situation in an alley when my dog ran away. I was overcome by the ordeal, and he brought me here."

Madam Rosnah's thinning eyebrows disappeared into her hair. "Really, Des?" she drawled with intense interest.

The man in question remained stoic. "She was faint, and Robyn said you had smelling salts. And she requires your assistance in finding a seamstress in the city."

"Who exactly are you, my dear?" Madam Rosnah said, reaching forward and pulling Mae into the cramped room. "Des, why don't you properly introduce the poor woman?"

His polite expression cracked as if in realization. "I'm sorry. I don't actually know—"

"Oh, you," Madam Rosnah said, swatting away Des's

hand, and sticking out her own for Mae to shake. The woman's bony grip was surprisingly strong. "Madam Lyre Rosnah," she said with relish. "Famed actress of the illustrious Proserpina Theater. So pleased to make your acquaintance, my mystery woman our Des deigned to rescue off the streets of Soldark."

Mae felt her cheeks flame, but the woman's light-hearted ribbing and fanciful description made her chuckle involuntarily.

"Mae Wright." Madam Rosnah looked expectant, and so Mae thought for a second. "Ah...not as much *famed* as...*fastidious* seamstress of the forthcoming Wright's Stitchery on Angleshire Lane."

Madam Rosnah grinned indulgently at Mae's playing along, and Mae warmed a little. She took a shallow breath that, thankfully, felt less painful.

"Seamstress?" Madam Rosnah questioned. "I thought you said she was *in need of* a seamstress, Des, not that she *was* one."

"No, it's true," Mae interrupted. "I *am* in need of one. I arrived in Soldark with almost nothing," she said, and hastily explained her situation.

"Oh, you poor dear!" Madam Rosnah exclaimed. "We *must* get you some new clothes. Des, do you have the key to the costume closet?"

IV

"Oh, I couldn't possibly!" Mae insisted. She wasn't here for their charity—but then, what *was* she here for? She glanced at Des. He was staring intently at her, and his hand went to his waistcoat pocket.

Madam Rosnah was already pushing Mae out of the dressing room and into the narrow corridor, hustling past Des. Bobbin followed at their heels.

The actress went on. "It's nothing, right, Des? I bet Lady Walldrick's morning dress from *The Copper Rose* would do just fine. And you won't need that oppressive corset anymore, my dear."

Mae looked down at her waist. "I never thought the styles would be so different here," she admitted. "This silhouette is what all the ladies are wearing in Corsich."

"Pfft," Madam Rosnah chided. "Stuck up ladies without a taste for entertainment."

"Lyre," Des growled.

"Not *you*, dear," Madam Rosnah told Mae. "I didn't mean you."

"Of course," Mae muttered in confusion. Though her first impression of the actress was that she liked her, Madam Rosnah didn't know a stitch about Mae. *Was* Mae some stuck-up uncultured lady? Certainly, she didn't know enough about Soldark fashion. She should have done more research on clothing styles before she left. Or did they change faster here than in Corsich?

She let Madam Rosnah lead her to the costume closet, which turned out not to be a closet as much as a storage room as big as her whole shop, both floors combined. Rows upon rows of somewhat musty-smelling outfits hung on metal rails. Madam Rosnah expertly pushed aside hangers, looking for just the right thing.

Des swept into the room like a shadow behind them in his all-black suit.

"I can't see a thing," Madam Rosnah said. "Des, get the other light, will you?"

The director sighed and flipped the big brass switch over by the door, forcing Mae to step farther into the room. His towering presence behind her didn't go unnoticed, and his dislike for the room's bright light didn't escape her attention either. He lurked as far as he could in the shadows of the doorway.

"Don't worry about Des," Madam Rosnah said, coming forward and yanking on Mae's hand to pull her into the maze of costumes. "A good director can usually be found in the shadows, if you know what I mean."

Mae didn't. She turned her attention back to the clothes. Her nose wrinkled at the slight smell, then she stopped herself. They were helping her without knowing a thing about her. The clothes could be aired out, surely. She had seen an airing cabinet in the back room of the jewelry shop where she could let them hang overnight.

But something gnawed at her as Madam Rosnah pulled out a couple of dresses and slung them over a velvet pouf chair at the end of one aisle. "I'm sorry," Mae, said, shaking her head. "I can't take these clothes. I told you, I don't have any money. It's not like I can repay you."

Madam Rosnah *tsked* and kept holding up dresses to Mae's frame to judge their size, then piled them on the chair.

"I should just go," Mae said. "I'm quite recovered from the incident now. You probably have work to do, and it's late."

"There," Madam Rosnah said, laying a fifth dress on the pile with a flourish. "These should fit you for now," she went on, ignoring Mae's words.

"But I can't—" Mae repeated.

"You can," Des said, drawing out of the shadows at last.

The bare bulb hanging from the ceiling cast shadows over his eyes, but his all-black outfit was thrown into the spotlight. The fabric was of even higher quality than Mae had originally estimated. Fine details were embroidered at the cuffs of his shirt, and dark silver threads were woven into his finely tailored waistcoat. "You could work for them, if you like."

"Work? Here?" Mae repeated, her eyebrows stitching together. "But I don't—"

"Who do you think maintains all these costumes?" Des said. "We are in need of a new costumer for the run of *Fortune Defines Us*, and if we get into the spring festival, we'll definitely need a talented seamstress."

"But I know nothing about costumes," Mae said. Her hand involuntarily reached out to the nearest rack to run her fingers along a beautiful blue skirt that reminded her of butterfly wings.

"You don't have to!" Madam Rosnah said, her face lighting up. "It's just modifications and repairs. You could do that, right?"

Mae glanced back and forth between Des and the actress.

A quiet yip from the hallway drew her attention to little Bobbin, standing patiently in the doorway. Her stomach churning inexplicably, she nodded, and agreed. "I can do that."

After Madam Rosnah had Mae try on all five dresses and two more skirts she had found, Mae was yawning uncontrollably. Des disappeared while the two women retreated to a large-but-somehow-still-cozy room which had long counters running along one wall. In the center of the room stood what looked like a wooden dining table, but from the small cabinet perched in its center full of sewing notions, Mae assumed it was used for spreading out fabrics for cutting and draping. A rack full of strange looking costumes stood by the door, and in one corner of the room, hanging precariously from the ceiling, were swaths of fabric arranged like a changing booth.

From behind the curtain, she outfitted herself into the simplest dress of the lot. It was dark pink—her favorite color—and had minimal frills compared to some of the other costumes she had seen. Madam Rosnah said it was usually used for background characters, but Mae didn't care what character it belonged to. It was light and airy, and she could finally breathe, thanks to the light stays sewn into the bust. She wasn't sweating along her collar anymore either, and the reprieve of removing her traveling dress was deeply relieving. She swatted at her new skirt, flicking away imaginary dust. Mae called, "I think this is more than enough to be getting on with."

When no one answered her, Mae poked her head out from

the changing area. Madam Rosnah had disappeared, and Mae was alone in the room. She *thought* she had heard Des call it the costume shop, so it was safe to assume this was where the costumes were altered. And the sewing machine and serger on the back counter were a dead giveaway.

She checked that she was decent and swept aside the curtain. Wandering over to a tall cabinet by the sewing machines, she quietly pulled the doors open, wanting to see what she would have to work with. A multitude of drawers and compartments met her eyes, and she ran her fingers along their peeling paper labels. *Thread. Zippers. Eye-hooks. Corset bones.*

Bobbin, from the comfortable chair by the changing area, gave a small yelp. Mae turned around.

Des stood in the doorway, a scroll of paper in his hand.

"Oh," Mae said, closing the cabinet doors with a snap. "Sorry, I just thought I should—"

"It is all yours to work with now," he said. "The costume shop, all the costumes in the closet. Here. This is your contract. I usually have basic contracts on hand—the turnover in the theater is astounding, you might know—" He held out the scroll.

She glanced down at her comfortable borrowed dress and the serviceable room with all its equipment—even a small office in the corner—and made her decision. She took a step forward and accepted the paper.

It detailed her role as the Proserpina's costumer in exchange for the clothing she would borrow for the duration of her employment. She would also receive a small weekly stipend. The date the contract expired happened to coincide with the date she estimated she would receive her trunks back, which worked out perfectly. She nodded, skimming the rest. That was all she needed, really, just enough work to get on her feet until her belongings arrived. How hard could it be to mend a few costumes?

He handed her a heavy black pen.

"That looks in order," Mae said, stealing a quick glance at the director's face. It was difficult to read his expression. He looked so serious, save for his eyes, which held a bright energy under the shadows cast by his falling hair. She couldn't tell whether he was glad to hire her or not, but that wasn't going to stop her. He *had* rescued her on the street, after all. And besides, it was only for six weeks.

After she had signed it and Des gave her a secondary copy for her own records, Madam Rosnah bustled in carrying a wicker basket stuffed with food. Mae's mouth watered at the smell of the pastries inside. She even spied some fresh fruit, something that had quickly dwindled in her steamship rations. And there were meat pies, which Bobbin would like.

"For you, Miss Costumer," Madam Rosnah said. "Georgie always brings leftovers to rehearsal from the cafe she works at during the day."

"Yes, please take them," Des urged unexpectedly. "There's always too much, and we can never eat it all before it goes stale. We're always throwing leftovers out."

"Oh, sure," Mae said, hastily reaching out and taking the offering. She didn't have many coins left, and she wasn't sure when she would first get paid. She would have to consult her contract when she got back home...

A thump from the hallway made them all turn their heads. The actor Mae had seen earlier in the vestibule stumbled into the costume shop, his eyes widening at the sight of the three people standing there.

"Oh," the actor said.

"Robyn," Des growled.

Robyn stumbled over to the chair in the corner. Bobbin vacated it immediately. The actor sank down to remove his satyr hoof boots, ducking his mop of chestnut brown hair which was rakishly tousled. He looked around nineteen or twenty, probably only about five years younger than her.

"This is the second time this month," Des said, towering over the actor.

Robyn kept his head down, and Mae wondered what exactly was going on. This *was* her place of work now, after all.

"I was careful," Robyn said, "but someone at the Salty Hare tripped over—"

"I don't care how careful you are," Des said. "Costumes

are *not* to be taken from the theater. But you don't have to answer to me about it anymore. We have a new costumer."

It took Mae a moment to take stock of the issue as Robyn looked up at her.

Madam Rosnah came to Mae's rescue. "Robyn, this is Mae Wright, the newest member of the Proserpina. And you'll have to answer to her if you take your costumes from the theater again."

Oh. Mae glanced at the satyr shoes, one heel dangling precariously from the rest. "Shoes?" she said blankly. "But I don't—"

"You do," said Des. "It's all in the contract. Looks like it'll be your first assignment tomorrow. And we'll need them by rehearsal, as Robyn still needs to get used to them on set."

Shoes? She had never mended a shoe before in her life! How had she missed that? She chastised herself for not reading the contract more thoroughly. Anger at Des bubbled up, but she only had herself to blame. She glanced down at Robyn and demanded, "Hand them here."

He did so with fumbling fingers.

"And you," she told Des. "The key to the costume closet."

Madam Rosnah grinned. "Lady Wright is in the house."

After hearing the full details of the back-alley incident, Madam Rosnah insisted someone walk Mae home.

"No, I'll be fine," Mae argued weakly as she gathered up her borrowed dresses, though she was certain Des's solemn presence would ward off any trouble on the streets. She had already asked too much of them.

"I can walk with you," Robyn offered, poking his head into the costumer's room. He had his regular plain leather shoes on now along with a brown newsie cap. "I'm only heading to my boyfriend Theo's."

"I'll escort you," Des said, looming behind him. At this, Robyn touched his cap and ducked away.

"Oh, I don't want to put you out—"

"Nonsense," he said. "It's late. No one should be out walking in Soldark alone at this time of night, when they don't know the city streets well enough."

Mae bobbed her head in acceptance. She didn't want to admit she barely knew how to get back to her shop, but if she had to choose between embarrassing herself further in front of the handsome theater director or stumbling across more unsavory characters in the streets, she would choose the former.

His hand looked large and inviting as he held it out to her, and some sort of uproar took place in her stomach. The thought of putting her hand in his froze her to the spot for a good moment. Finally, she heaved her stack of dresses into his arms instead, earning a cackle from Madam Rosnah as the actress retreated to her dressing room once more.

Des accepted the load with dignity. Mae offered a blushing smile in return and then scooped up a sleepy Bobbin and the basket of food. At least, she wouldn't have to spend her money on food for a little while. Unless she got sick of pastries and fruit, anyway.

She let Des lead the way out of the theater, through the cozy room with the mismatched armchairs, then the long dark corridor, and finally into the main part of the theater. The ceiling and rafters were nearly invisible in the darkness. A single light shone down on the empty stage.

The quiet pressed down upon her in the large space, and she blurted, "I'm sorry, I should be able to get back by myself. You're probably very busy."

Des let her walk up the aisle between the red velvet seats ahead of him, following behind her amid the swish of the dresses in his arms.

"It's no bother." His voice rumbled, and the hairs on the back of her neck tingled. She resisted turning her head to steal a glance at him.

They continued in silence, across the foyer, through the double doors, down the steps, and onto the sidewalk. Mae looked up and down the empty street, hesitating for a second, and then turned right.

A lone auto drove by, but other than that, the streets were

empty. She wasn't sure *what* time it was, but it was certainly long after dinnertime.

To her annoyance, Des continued to walk behind her, even though the sidewalk was wide enough for three or four people to walk abreast. They continued on this way the entirety of the street, until they reached the corner of Freight Lane, where she gained her bearings once more. The streetlamps were helpful, brightening the streets enough to see by, but offering long stretches of darkness in between. She quickened her pace through the darkness, despite the presence of her reserved escort.

She threw him an irritated look. Why had he insisted on walking her home if he wouldn't even walk beside her? She should have accepted Robyn's offer; the actor would have been good conversation, she was sure. But Des had withdrawn into a stoic façade.

Did Des regret his decision to hire her? Did he think she was some stuck-up uncultured woman from Corsich? Well, she would certainly show him. She vowed to arrive early tomorrow to inspect Robyn's shoes and have them ready before the rehearsal. She had taught herself how to bone a corset with no instruction, after all.

"I can take it from here," she offered again, sniffing the harbor breeze with her chin held high. It was clear he didn't want to walk beside her, so why walk her home at all?

"No, I insist," he said, holding his free hand out to indicate she lead on.

"Then walk beside me, why don't you?" she demanded, unable to keep the annoyance out of her voice.

His eyes crinkled in confusion, and he blinked. "I'm sorry," he said, his tone sounding genuine. "I thought it best to walk behind you, to keep an eye out."

Mae cocked her head to the side in surprise. "Are the streets really that dangerous here?" She pulled Bobbin closer to her chest.

"After your earlier encounter, I simply thought you would feel safer."

"I see," she said, though she wasn't certain she did.

A warm feeling settled in her stomach as he stepped up beside her and they continued on without further mention of it. Now that he was next to her, she noticed him surveying the streets with a keen eye, particularly eyeing the dark alleys they passed.

She continued to steal glances at the director until they reached her shop on Angleshire Lane—after only one wrong turn on her part. He had been generous and kind back at the theater, but it seemed his natural facial expression was one of seriousness. She was amazed at how well he got along with the boisterous actors with his reserved demeanor.

She turned to face him at the door. "I want to thank you again," she said, pulling out her key, "not only for the job, but for the dresses. You really didn't have to do that."

He bowed his head a little. "It was my pleasure, and the Proserpina has an extensive wardrobe. Though, I do expect you to live up to your name."

At her quizzical look, he quoted, "*The Fastidious Seamstress of Angleshire Lane*." A hint of a wink graced his expression.

A grin burst forth from her lips, and she bid Des goodnight. As soon as she was behind her closed shop door and the deadbolt rammed home, he raised a hand in farewell and turned back down the street. She watched him until his black coat whipped around the corner.

She surveyed her shop with a mixture of excitement and nerves for the next day. She had proper clothes and a new job to tide her over. Things were finally looking up.

V

When Mae awoke in cold darkness on her apartment floor, confusion set in, chasing away all the excitement from the night before. Her windows were pitch black. What had woken her? Bobbin whined in his sleep at her side, and she realized he was shivering. The fire had gone out.

Her solicitor had been right; Soldark spring nights *were* cold. She pulled her scarf from atop her suitcase and draped it over Bobbin. Padding over to attend to the fire, she cursed as she stepped on something sharp.

She hopped over to the fireplace on one foot, suddenly *very* awake from the sharp pain in her heel. She had to fumble about in the dark to find the poker, unable to even see her foot and whatever had stabbed her. She let out a whoop when the coals came back to life, glad she wouldn't have to fumble with the matches in pitch black.

After feeding the coals some tinder, waiting for the fire to catch, and then adding a few fat pieces of firewood, Mae examined the bottom of her foot, which was bleeding from a small puncture. She hissed as she poked at it. Whatever had stabbed her was still stuck in there.

Lighting a candle, Mae limped to the washroom to examine the wound further. Her cousin hadn't put electrical wiring into the apartment either, though her shop and much of the street seemed to use it. By the flickering candlelight in the cramped commode, she pulled out the tiny metal fragment using her fingernails.

It was a thin shard of silver. She must have missed it while sweeping. Tears threatened, tightening her chest, but she forced them back down.

Then she clucked softly in realization, wondering if this was why Bobbin hadn't wanted to walk on the floors. Perhaps his keen eyes had seen the metal shards, which she now feared were all over the building. Her cousin had been a jeweler, after all. It could have been tracked up here from the workshop. And it wasn't as if Petyr had been lying on the floor or walking around barefoot as she had done.

The fire was crackling merrily when she returned to her room, and after roughly bandaging up her foot and slipping her shoes back on, she stood by the fire warming her hands. Her shoulders shook with the chill.

The promise of the other dresses in the airing cabinet drew her downstairs. Surely the smell had aired out in the few hours she had slept. She could use several of them as blankets for her and Bobbin until the fire warmed the room back up. Though she was surprised the steam heat from the shop hadn't risen to warm the upstairs at all.

She found out the reason for that as soon as she got downstairs. Icy cold air hit her face, and her heart sank, chest constricting again.

Unsure what to do or think, she strode over to the airing cabinet to retrieve one of the dresses, slinging it over her shoulders like an ungainly scarf. It was chilly from the night air, but it would warm up, and the musty smell had mostly dissipated. She left the other dresses in the cabinet to air out with the help of the holes in the wall that let in outside air.

A second thought made her snap open the cabinet again to grab another dress, which she hastily ran upstairs to drape around Bobbin. Next, she descended all the way to the basement, half-limping to avoid walking on her right heel.

Her worst fears were confirmed: the boiler had shut off. And it wouldn't turn back on.

She closed her eyes in anguish. "Why?" she demanded of no one in particular. Why had she been cursed with such bad luck the moment she stepped foot in Soldark? Finally ready to pursue her dream of opening her own shop—and in Soldark, no less!—and she was struck with one misfortune after another.

"I should have gotten back on that steamship and gone home," she muttered as she tentatively opened the fuel door and checked the gauges as Howard had shown her.

She would have to contact Howard in the morning and ask him to recommend a repairman. Though how she would pay them, she didn't know.

After poking around for what must have been half an hour, she admitted defeat and trudged back up to the apartment. Glancing at the basket of food Madam Rosnah had given her, she smiled a little as she cuddled close to Bobbin, not just for warmth. At least she would receive some kind of pay from the Proserpina. She would just have to work hard, that was all. *As if I would have done anything else*, she thought to herself sleepily as she drifted off.

As soon as the dawn light trickled in through the windows, Mae stuffed her borrowed pockets with as much food as would fit, and set out for the Proserpina. She and Bobbin had awoken shivering, and the drafty fireplace was again cold.

"I think it's warmer outside!" she exclaimed to Bobbin in surprise as she locked up the shop and headed down the lane. She was wearing the borrowed cream-colored dress, which fit even better than the one she wore yesterday and also had built-in stays. There were little flower details on the cuffs and bottom hem, and delicate lace poked out from the sleeves and bodice. She was lucky her black short-heeled shoes went with everything, because they were all she had. *Well, maybe not all.* She smirked a little, remembering the whole wall of shoes she had spied in the costume closet...

The gifted food restored them both. She tossed Bobbin the final piece of his meat pie, which he expertly caught in his mouth mid-step. Mae took a deep breath as she finished her pomegranate muffin, enjoying the freedom the new-to-her dress afforded. Full bellies and high hopes that a day's work would shove her worries from her head, she mounted the steps of the theater with increasing worry.

What if it was locked? How would she get in? She couldn't hang about like a vagrant waiting for someone to open the doors. And she didn't want to go back to the shop, wallowing in the cold and worrying about shards of metal on the floor. She had spotted more sinister-looking sparkles in the dawn light, confirming her suspicions that they were all over the shop.

The Proserpina loomed above her, glorious in the morning light. The sight brought a smile to her tired face. Two columns held up a gilt marquee at the top of the stairs, and the rust-red building looked newly painted. The mullioned windows on two levels glinted in the morning sun, though most of them looked like they were darkened from the inside. As her luck had predicted, the doors were locked.

Bobbin hopped down from her arms, and Mae peered through the glass, using her cupped hands to shade out the sunlight. The theater was dark inside, save for the single light shining down on the stage. She checked the other doors along the front for good measure, though the effort proved fruitless.

Bobbin huffed and trotted down the steps onto the sidewalk. Mae eyed him warily. "And where are you going?" she asked, in no mood for another chase.

He yipped playfully, his back legs dancing, as though encouraging her to join him. She sighed, shaking her head with a reluctant smirk as she hopped down the steps.

The morning sunlight twinkled above the roofs of the nearby buildings, and her smile grew warmer despite her predicament. It was hard to worry about vagrants and thieves in such inviting light. She had to look at the positives. She and Bobbin had food in their bellies and plenty more at the shop, and she had a job—if only she could get in...

Her little dog trotted down the sidewalk, and she followed curiously. She really wanted an early start on Robyn's shoes, and she wasn't sure what time the actors started rehearsal. It hadn't been in the contract—which she had read thoroughly by firelight before falling asleep last night.

When Bobbin turned down a narrow alley next to the theater, she paused. She could see clearly that it was empty, none of the buildings on either side boasting doorways large enough to harbor any criminals. Lifting her chin, she followed Bobbin down the narrow corridor. A door on the side wrenched itself open.

The shriek died in her throat before it could make it out of her mouth, when she recognized the red-haired person who yanked her inside by a bony hand.

"Shh," the actress said. "If you wake Des, there'll be hell to pay."

Mae nodded mutely, and Madam Rosnah shut the back door quietly after Bobbin came in, tail wagging.

"Tea?" Madam Rosnah offered, sashaying down the narrow hallway, which Mae recognized as the one that led to the dressing rooms. Mae and Bobbin followed her to a room she hadn't seen the night before, which looked like a kitchen, with three worn cafe tables and a few rickety chairs grouped around them.

"This is our break room," Madam Rosnah explained in a hushed voice. She headed to the small stove and removed a steaming kettle. "There's more of those pastries in the cupboard. Help us eat them up before they go stale—Georgie brings leftovers from the cafe all the time."

Mae poked her head in the cupboard and extracted a chocolate croissant from a bulging wax paper bag. Mae glanced over at the cafe tables and saw a half-eaten croissant on a plate, so she searched the cupboards for her own dish.

A few minutes later, she was inhaling the blissful steam

coming off her cup of tea. The two women sat at one of the tables, which Madam Rosnah explained the actors had found in the alley behind a restaurant a few years ago.

"This is cozy," Mae said, sipping her tea to wash down the bite of buttery croissant she had just taken. "How come you're here so early? If you don't mind my asking."

"Not at all!" Madam Rosnah said, brushing her fingers off on a napkin. "I always run lines in the morning when the theater is empty—started doing it for a show a while back. Des finally gave me my own key when I promised I'd have tea ready for him when he got up. Been doing it for years now."

"Does he—Des—live in the theater?"

"Oh, yes. In apartments on the lower level."

Mae's brain lurched into thought, wondering where he might be sleeping at this very moment. She was surprised at the intensity of her curiosity.

"And what are you doing here so early, my dear?" Madam Rosnah asked. "Come to work on the shoes?"

Mae nodded, and hastily changed the subject. "How long have you been a part of this theater?" It seemed like Madam Rosnah was close with Des, and she didn't want him finding out she didn't know what she was doing. She was *supposed* to be a skilled seamstress, after all. Though that implied nothing about being a cobbler, she needed this job.

"Oh, twenty years or so. I can't remember anymore," the actress said.

"Twenty years? And has Des always—I mean, is he—"

Madam Rosnah chuckled quietly. "Oh no, he's not *that* old, my dear, and not nearly as ancient and distinguished as me." She sat up straighter and stuck out her chin, causing Mae to laugh abruptly. Apparently, this was the correct response, because Madam Rosnah grinned at her, despite all the warmth inflaming Mae's cheeks.

"He bought the theater about ten years ago, after his army service ended," Madam Rosnah said.

Mae nodded slowly. Now that Madam Rosnah had mentioned it, she could see he did have a military bearing in the way he stood and the way he had walked her down the street last night, watching her back.

"Not a bad price for it, either," Madam Rosnah went on, "although it was practically falling apart. He's been trying to bring it back to its former glory ever since."

"It does look beautiful," Mae said, thinking back to the façade and the velvet curtains on the stage.

"Well, yes, the *public space* is coming along nicely—how else would we get butts in the chairs?"

Mae snorted into her tea, then she set it down in a fit of giggles. She vowed not to do any tea drinking until Madam Rosnah was done talking. She didn't want any coming out her nose.

"But the rehearsal space—and much of the backstage— still needs to be refurbished. He did the seats first and then the marquee outside to draw people in."

"Wow," Mae said, "It must have been a lot of work. Maybe I should take notes for when I open my shop!"

Madam Rosnah got up to pour herself another cup of tea. Mae waved her off when the actress wordlessly offered her more. "That's right. When do you plan on opening?"

Mae looked down at her lap briefly, then straightened. "Seven or eight weeks, I expect. Once my trunks arrive, I can start getting things in order."

"Ah, yes. What bad luck—for you, anyway. It's wonderful luck for the Proserpina that you landed in our laps!"

A smile crept up Mae's face. "I'm glad I can help."

"Now, quit avoiding the subject, and let's talk about those shoes."

VI

Ten minutes later, they ensconced themselves in the costume shop, the shoes in question sitting on the large table between them.

"I've never worked on shoes before," Mae finally admitted.

"Well, yes, I thought as much," Madam Rosnah said with half a wink, "by the look on your face when Robyn stumbled in last night. That roustabout. I couldn't get him to stop taking costumes out either." She picked up the offending shoe and clucked. The broken heel dangled by a sad strip of leather.

"What do you mean?" Mae asked.

"I was filling in as the costumer, my dear. And I'm quite glad to be rid of the temporary title."

"Oh," Mae said as things clicked into place; Madam

Rosnah had seemed rather familiar with the costume closet.

Madam Rosnah turned her back and went over to the wall of cupboards, poking in and out of the bins and drawers there. "And of course, you seemed like a perfect fit for the role. Des doesn't rescue too many beautiful ladies off the street, you know. Renowned seamstresses, at that."

Beautiful? That wasn't why Des had rescued her, was it? Heat flooded Mae's cheeks, and she seized the shoe. "Thank you," she mumbled. "Although, I wouldn't say *renowned*. Not yet, anyway."

Madam Rosnah came back over with a small jar of glue.

Mae studied the broken heel and pursed her lips. Tentatively, she got up and looked into the cabinet herself, where she found a large curved needle that she suspected was for upholstery and incredibly thick thread, likely intended for upholstery as well.

The shoes were high-heeled brown leather boots that had been reworked to include a hoof instead of a heel. Mae wasn't sure what the hoof was made of, but she was quite sure it wasn't real and only modeled after the real thing. Or, she hoped so, at any rate. The top of the boot was covered in coarse hair, presumably to match the hairy satyr pants Mae had seen Robyn wearing the night before.

"What's this play about anyway?" Mae asked.

"Love, like most stories," Madam Rosnah said with a wink, "and the inevitable heartbreak. Here, pull off the heel, and we can scrape off the old glue."

As they got to work scraping the glue, the actress explained the play. She mostly spoke from the perspective of her own character, Fiona, who made several valiant attempts to get two young people to fall in love—"through Fiona's cunning, guile, and sharp wits"—and she valiantly admitted to not being the main character.

With a careful brush, Mae set some fresh glue on the heel. Next, she took the upholstery needle and thread and began the arduous task of sewing the hoof on as an added precaution.

"We've got one more week of rehearsals before the show opens," Madam Rosnah told her. "And they'll need to last all ten weeks of the show's run."

"Ouch!" Mae yanked her left hand away from the heel, having stabbed herself with the force of pushing the needle through the tough material. Madam Rosnah looked up from her script, which she had produced sometime during the repair to peruse the lines she had meant to practice this morning.

"Oh, dear," the actress said. "I'll run and get Amelie's kit. It's up in the booth."

Mae looked down at her finger in alarm, but it was only a little blood. "All right. Thanks," she said softly as Madam Rosnah departed.

With no idea what or where the booth was, or who Amelie might be, Mae pulled out her handkerchief to blot the flow, not wanting to get blood on her borrowed dress or the satyr shoes. She stared at her repair job, scrunching up her nose. She had only gotten in a few stitches, but she wasn't impressed with their appearance. She wasn't used to working with this material, her most comparable experience being with linen or heavy wool.

Her stitches were neat and even, but Mae worried they might be visible to the audience. Did it matter? She pursed her lips. It mattered to her. She rose to her feet and headed over to the cabinets on the far wall searching for something suitable.

A few minutes later, she awkwardly held up a scrap of leather to the intersection of the boot and its hoof heel, covering the stitches. The leather had a jagged tuft on the end that hung down, matching the rough satyr look.

"That looks even better than before," a voice came from the door.

Bobbin raised his head, and Mae turned around, spotting Des in the doorway.

"Oh, hello," Mae said, giving him a timid smile.

"Have you seen Madam Rosnah?" Des asked.

"Yes, she just ran to...to the booth to get something for me. I pricked my thumb."

He took a long step into the room toward her. "Ah." He looked around a bit frantically. "We should really keep a kit in here. I bet Amelie would have something, but she's not due to arrive until ten."

"Yes," Mae said, "Madam Rosnah said she was going to check Amelie's kit."

Des nodded. "Good, good." He blinked long and slow, then shook his head. She noticed his hair was a little less well-kempt than yesterday, but he stood straight-backed, and his clothes were just as fine as before. He glanced around and said, "I don't suppose you know whether... Did Madam Rosnah make..."

"There's tea ready," Mae said, hiding a small smile. "It's in the pot with a tea cozy."

"Good," he said again. "Good. Well, I'll leave you to..."

"Thanks," she said, watching him lurch from the room.

"He's certainly not a morning person," she whispered to Bobbin, who gave a little whine of agreement.

Mae chuckled and checked her finger, which had stopped bleeding. She shrugged and got back to her stitches, no longer self-conscious about them since she was going to cover them up. By the time Madam Rosnah had returned, Mae was done with the stitching and was halfway through applying the leather with a light layer of glue.

"Oooh!" the actress fawned. "That looks marvelous, dear! Here you go. It took me a while to find it. Her injury kit was in a separate box than her regular kit."

"What are all the kits for?" Mae asked, going through the contents of the small leather pack. She removed a thin strip of fabric for a bandage, and a small bottle neatly labeled

"*ALCOHOL*" with which to wipe the wound.

Madam Rosnah's eyes lit up. "I keep forgetting, dear, you're not theater folk. Amelie's the stage manager, so she's responsible for running the show behind the scenes. She's got a whole kit in case anyone needs anything—and I mean *anything*. Bandages, of course. Tweezers. Matches. Pencils. All kinds of tape. I once saw her pull out a set of binoculars." She chuckled.

"Des wandered in, looking for his tea," Mae said as she finished cleaning her tiny wound. Then she glanced down at her foot, which hadn't bothered her all morning. "Oh, I should probably..." she trailed off. Madam Rosnah gave her a curious expression. "I stepped on a shard of something metal this morning in my shop," Mae explained. "My cousin ran a jewelry store, you see, and I didn't actually clean the wound, and I—"

"Oh, *do* feel comfortable, dear! You *must* take care of yourself. You don't want to get lockjaw from metal poisoning."

"I hadn't even thought of that," Mae said, reaching down and yanking off her shoe. "Oh, that's much easier to do without a corset on," she said, eliciting a chuckle from Madam Rosnah. The stays built into the borrowed dress were the most comfortable thing she had ever worn for support. She would have to make a pattern so she could put them in the dresses she made for her shop.

Before she could get her shoe back on, someone darkened the doorway to the costume shop. Mae's stomach dropped to the floor. Des was the only other person in the theater. She ducked her head.

"All fixed?" an eager voice asked, surprising her. "Though I'm not sure they'll fit *you*. Your feet are much smaller than mine."

Waves of relief flooded Mae's body as she looked up to see Robyn standing there, his hair tousled and his loose white shirt half tucked in. She thought she might have perished from embarrassment had it had been Des. She hastily shoved her foot back into her stocking, then into the shoe, breathing an exasperated sigh. "I wasn't trying it on," she assured him. "But also, no. It's not quite finished yet."

"And we don't need an audience," Madam Rosnah drawled when he lingered in the doorway. "She'll put them in your dressing room when they're ready."

"Thank you," Mae told the actress after Robyn left to go run his lines. Mae was no actress; an audience was the last thing she needed—though Madam Rosnah's company was comforting and helpful.

It didn't take long to finish gluing the leather over the stitches after that.

"There," Mae said, setting down the repaired shoe next to the matching one. Except it *wasn't* matching. The other shoe that Robyn hadn't broken was now missing a strip of leather, not to mention the extra fortitude from the stitching, which she was rather sure Robyn needed. "Right," she muttered to herself, grabbing the second shoe and testing the heel. The original glue seemed sturdy, so she set to work adding the stitches and leather.

By the time they truly matched, it was almost time for rehearsal. People were moving about in the hallway with increasing frequency, calling to each other from different dressing rooms—at one point she even thought she heard a baby cry—and finally, a loud call. "FIVE MINUTES!"

Mae jumped. She picked up the shoes and headed into the hallway, nearly colliding with someone.

"FIVE—Oh, sorry. Who are you?" the woman asked bluntly. Her black hair was styled in a severe bun atop her head, and she was a few inches shorter than Mae.

Mae bobbed her head and said, "Mae Wright. I'm the new costumer."

"Good. I'm Amelie, the stage manager," she said quickly, and then added, "Can you fix this?"

Mae looked down and noticed a pair of costume wings in Amelie's hands. They were made with bent wire covered in tulle, with little straps to secure the wings onto someone's shoulders. Her mouth hung open for a second, and then she saw that one strap was hanging by a thread.

"Sure."

The rest of the day was filled with more of the same.

Despite the actors being "in rehearsal," they moved around the theater and dressing rooms a lot, requiring all sorts of adjustments to their costumes. It was late afternoon when she finally answered her stomach's growling pleas and wandered into the kitchen to snag a leftover pastry.

She helped herself to a crumpet, though it was a little dry without any butter, and after poking her head into the costume shop to offer one to Bobbin, she wandered down the hallway. It had been quiet for some time now. The dressing rooms were empty, and from her brief glances inside, it looked like people's personal effects were still here. Were they finally rehearsing?

The green room, as Madam Rosnah called it, was empty of everything but scripts draped over chairs. Apparently, it was essentially a waiting room for the actors as they readied to go on stage. Mae pressed her ear to the door that led to the stage, and it swung open a little when she touched it. Gingerly she opened it the rest of the way and crept down the long dark corridor, ears pricking for any sound. The darkness and quiet wrapped around her like a soft blanket after the hectic morning she had spent mending the oddest assortment of clothing items she had ever seen. The shoulder strap on a magnificent red tulle dress. A metallic belt that had lost a snap. The satyr shoes had only been the tip of the sewing needle.

Ahead, a voice came from the stage. "Must I?" the unfamiliar voice asked. "Must I shrink in on myself, and reject all that burns like a fire inside of me? Must I reject my very inner being, just to for—fortify? *Line!*"

Mae wrinkled her brow and peeked out the door at the end of the dark hallway. She couldn't see the stage, and only two people sat in the auditorium, dead center. One was Des, the other was the woman named Amelie, who looked down at the script in her lap, and shouted, "Just to fortify your own."

Des held up his hand and called, "Let's take ten for dinner, and we'll come back to the top of Lady Comay's monologue. *Ten* only, Robyn," he repeated.

"I know, I know," Robyn said in a sing-song voice, materializing on the opposite side of the theater, wearing a completely different costume than he'd had on when Mae had last seen him. Actors began heading her way, so instead of getting trampled in the dark, she swiftly exited the hallway and entered the theater.

Since she had already been *on* a sort of break, she wasn't sure what to do with herself. Amelie must have sensed this and seized the opportunity to pull Mae over.

"Good," the stage manager said. "I wanted to talk to you. Fabulous work on the repairs. Madam Rosnah could only do so much in her free time getting the costumes sorted. It's about time Des hired someone."

Mae hid a smile as Des glowered good-naturedly at Amelie. "Yes, well, I was waiting for the right person," he said with a glint in his eye, "and we have an expert seamstress now."

Her heartbeat raced inexplicably, and Mae glanced back at Amelie.

Amelie went on. "Oh, Mae, about the quick changes—"

"The what?" Mae said as politely as she could.

Des came to her rescue—as was becoming a habit of his, apparently—and said, "Mae has never worked in a theater before, so you'll need explain a little more."

Amelie's mouth popped open, but she quickly recovered. "Oh! So, when the actors need to change costumes, er, really quickly. Those kind of quick changes."

Mae grinned. "I see now. What about them?"

"Well, Georgie wants a privacy booth on stage left, and Robyn says his satyr pants are too tight to get off between act one and act two—"

"And the clothes rack needs to be repaired," Des added. "But I'll have the set designer fix that, and Mae, you can just oversee it when they move the costumes. Amelie, why don't you put it all in notes at the end of the night? There's bound to be more, and Miss Wright can get started again in the morning."

"Will do," Amelie said, picking up her large script book. "I'd better go grab some food." She shouldered a heavy bag and went off backstage in pursuit of dinner.

Which left Mae alone in the dimly lit theater with Des.

"Sorry. Hold on," he said, pulling a notepad from a vest pocket and scribbling in it for a minute. "I just thought of something else I need to talk to Charlie—our set designer—about. Anyway, you don't have to stay for the rest of the run-through. I don't normally keep the costumer in house all day when we have these long rehearsals, and I see you've done plenty of the costume repairs we were sorely in need of. I'm sure you want to get back to your shop. Would you like me to escort you home again? I can extend the dinner break. I'm sure no one would complain," he added with half a grin.

"Oh," Mae said, heart dropping. The shop was the *last* place she wanted to get back to, with its metal shards and broken boiler—the boiler! Her eyes widened. She had forgotten all about it! "Actually, I do have some business to attend to," she said reluctantly.

Her stomach sank as she glanced up at the doors that led outside. The streetlamps were on, and it was already dark. Surely Howard didn't keep office hours this late. There was no chance of her boiler getting fixed tonight. What had she been thinking? She had gotten caught up in all the theater activity, and now it was too late.

Something must have shown on her face, because Des asked, "What is it? Is something wrong?"

"Um," Mae hedged, not wanting to heap more of her complaints upon him. She sure had a lot of them lately.

But surely, as a business owner, he would know someone who could fix a boiler. She could call on them in the morning, and only have one more cold night to deal with. She would just have to get up a few times to rebuild the fire. "Well...I just remembered I needed to engage a repairman for my boiler. I don't suppose you could recommend someone?"

Des dragged a hand across his stubbled chin. "A repairman? Well, yes, I know someone... What's wrong with your heat?"

Mae pressed her lips together, but she was unable to come up with a convincing reply that didn't sound as if she had no heat and had completely forgotten about the situation all day until now.

"I...don't have any," she finally admitted.

"You don't have heat."

"It's not an issue," she said, swallowing the lump that suddenly formed in her throat. Her chest constricted for a moment, but she tightened her hold on her emotions. She had to make do. "I have a fireplace in the apartment that works okay. I'm sure I can contact the repairman tomorrow. Do you have a card?"

He narrowed his eyes and shook his head. "I'll check my office. But the temperature's supposed to drop for the next couple of days. You didn't hear?"

"I—" the words died in her throat as she thought back to that drafty fireplace, which she'd had to get up and stoke back to life *twice* last night.

Des looked her over, then nodded. "You can stay at the theater."

"What? No, I couldn't possibly!"

"It's quite all right. Do you know how many times Robyn has crashed here?"

Her face flamed. "But—you don't even know me. You've given me too much already, the clothes—"

"Which you're working for."

"—the food—"

"Which was free and would go to waste—"

"But I..." She thought of the cozy costume shop and access to a kitchen. The early morning company of Madam Rosnah. A place where Bobbin could walk around safely.

"Then don't pay me," she said, sticking out her chin, as a plan formed. "If you let me stay here while it gets fixed, I won't need the wages." She could get by on pastries for a few days while her boiler was fixed.

Des thought about it, his gaze sliding over her shoulder toward the main theater doors and outside. He crossed his arms over his chest. "Half. I'll cut your wages in half. You deserve full pay for the work I've seen, but if you insist on being—if you insist," he amended, with a subtle bow of his head.

She swallowed past the lump in her throat, immense relief washing over her. Suddenly she became very thankful for how warm the theater was, even in this large open space. And then her face warmed at the thought of Des living here too. His apartments were on the lower level. Surely, he wasn't suggesting...

Her heart thumping loudly, she opened her mouth to speak.

Des pulled out his notepad again and marked something down. "I think we have some cots in the back of the costume closet; we could set one up in the office in the costume shop, if you like."

"Oh," she said, sudden heat rushing to her face. What had she been thinking? A respectable man like Des never would have offered a place in his own apartment! "That would be perfect, actually."

VII

Des asked Robyn to escort Mae to her shop so she could grab her things. Apparently, Robyn wouldn't be needed on stage for several scenes, and the actor was only too giddy to get another break. He had dutifully changed out of his costume by the time she was ready to go.

"My boyfriend Theo lives with his dad just a few streets over, so I'm in this area a lot," he said as she unlocked the shop. "He's a constable—his dad, I mean. Theo's studying at the university. Sewing, actually; you'd get along well! Anyway, you've got a great location. Lots of foot traffic, and the neighborhood's nice."

"Good," she said. "I just need to grab a few things, and we can head back. Oh, and watch your step." She warned him about the bits of metal she had found, and before long, she found herself regaling him with the full tale of all her woes since landing in Soldark. Robyn was easy to talk to, and he didn't make her feel self-conscious about her complaints. If anything, he validated them.

"That's awful!" he exclaimed as he followed her about—much like Bobbin would, had he not stayed back at the warm theater. She didn't begrudge her dog for staying in the warmth after last night's ordeal.

They were in the basement now, where she checked the boiler one last time. It was stone cold.

"I know," Mae said with a huff. "And I'm sorry. I don't fancy myself a complainer, but I find that's all I have to talk about lately."

Robyn's hands darted out and landed on her shoulders. "Mae! Bad luck isn't your fault. And I find complaining makes me feel better about things, anyway. When you get to share it with someone, it feels less big."

The smile that rose on her face felt good. "Thanks, Robyn." Then she turned and headed upstairs again. "I have one last thing I should do. I don't want the pipes freezing."

After setting all the faucets to drip, she re-packed her traveling suitcase, having only taken out a few toiletries last night. Her Corsich-style traveling dress would have to go in the airing cabinet until she had time to launder it.

"What'd you leave the water running for?" Robyn asked as

they stepped outside and she locked up.

"If there's water moving in the pipes," she said, her teeth chattering as the cold air hit her, "it's less likely to freeze. If it's moving, you see." Des had been right; the temperature had dropped significantly during the brief time they'd been inside.

"Oh," he said, impressed. "That's a trick, isn't it."

They hastened back to the theater, with Robyn carrying Mae's borrowed dresses, and Mae holding her suitcase. The air grew colder as each minute passed, and Mae's breath clouded before her. She was beginning to wish she'd had time to launder her warm traveling dress, with its many layers suitable even for a Corsich winter. She also still needed to repair the rip in the sleeve.

Once they raced inside the back door of the Proserpina, it didn't take long for the chill to leave. Warmth met them as soon as they stepped inside. Mae definitely needed to contact whoever serviced the boiler here; clearly, they knew what they were doing.

Robyn sped off for his dressing room, and Mae settled into the costume shop, her new home. Instead of being embarrassed that she was forced to rely yet again on Des's charity, an unexpected thrill coursed through her. Camping out in the Proserpina for a day or two would be an adventure, and surely a much livelier one than sleeping on the floor of her shop with only Bobbin for company. She had lived with her parents all her life and hadn't considered what it would be like to live alone in a new city.

Even though Des had told her she needn't work the rest of the night, she found herself attending to the miscellaneous costumes left out on her sewing table that were in obvious need of repair. What else was she to do? She didn't want to go digging around in the costume closet for the cot, particularly if the rehearsal was still going full swing. She would wait before lugging a cot down the hallway herself—with her luck, she'd bang the walls and disrupt the actors.

Eventually, she ran out of things to mend and spent a little time familiarizing herself with all of the supplies and notions in the cabinets. The Proserpina was well stocked, and Mae was impressed with the sewing machine in the corner; even *she* didn't own a Thomas' patent sewing machine. Perhaps when she had her shop up and running, she would invest in one with her first profits. The Thomas' had over twenty stitch styles (whereas her own had three) and after using it a few times, she found the quality of the stitches impeccable, and it didn't jam once.

Finally, she found herself drifting toward the green room, which was again empty. All was quiet, and it was quite late— just how late did these rehearsals go?—but she had nothing else to do, so she crept down the hallway toward the stage.

"Must I reject my very inner being, just to fortify your own?" the woman on stage was saying. Mae realized she had come down in the same place as last time. Quietly, she slipped out the door and into the auditorium. She snuck a look at Des and Amelie, but they were both completely focused on the girl on stage. Mae sank into the nearest seat and tried to make herself inconspicuous.

The actress wore a beautiful white tulle ballgown and a majestic curly blonde wig, though Mae could tell she was naturally blonde from her almost white eyebrows. She was petite yet curvy and had a kind face. Mae suspected this actress was the one whose wings she'd mended earlier, and she wondered when the wings would come into the play.

The woman was completely alone on stage and was apparently speaking to herself. Suddenly, she sank to the floor and beat it with her fist. "Gods! If I must transform myself in order to live this life, it will be on mine own terms! This life is mine and mine own!"

Mae leaned forward. The woman seemed near tears.

Silence pressed in on the entire theater. Mae was on the edge of her chair.

Then, from the heavens—or, she supposed, the space above the stage—the white wings descended on nearly invisible thread. It was almost flawless; they paused only briefly on their journey down. Mae had to imagine that someone backstage was lowering them.

Finally, the wings reached the actress, and in a practiced motion, she slipped the straps on. It ruined the moment a little, Mae thought, frowning. *I wonder if I could make the wings attach more seamlessly.*

She enjoyed the final moments of the play as the now-winged woman towered over Robyn and delivered a succinct monologue. Robyn played it well and, at first, dismissed the woman's transformation—which Mae assumed was supposed to be metaphorical, though with the satyr costume in use earlier, perhaps it *was* literal. She was looking forward to talking about it later with Madam Rosnah, anyway.

At last, the actors all assembled on stage for brief bows. Des led the applause while Mae cheerfully joined in. Robyn grinned at her, and the other actor's smiles seemed to brighten at seeing the third audience member at their performance.

"Thanks, everyone," Amelie called, "Nine o'clock sharp tomorrow for full technical!"

"Georgie and Robyn, a few notes before you go," Des said. The rest of the actors hastily headed backstage, divesting themselves of costume pieces as they went.

Robyn groaned, and Georgie, the blonde lead, stepped to the edge of the stage. "But Des—my mother will be so cross..."

Des closed his eyes and pinched his nose. "Fine. Go. I'll have Amelie write up your notes—but please arrive half an hour early so we can go over them."

Georgie squealed and ran off, hastily yanking off her wings. With a snort, Mae realized why the straps on the wings had looked as if they'd been mended once or twice before.

Robyn turned heel and headed backstage too.

"Not you, Robyn."

"Des," Robyn whined, "I have to get home too."

"You don't have a small child to attend to."

"Theo can be just as needy sometimes, I promise you."

Des ignored the joke and continued, "Unless you'd like to get here at eight o'clock?"

"No, no. Now's fine!"

Mae chuckled and headed back down the long dark hallway. In the green room, she spotted Amelie spread out with her large script book and sheaves of blank paper. "Good night," Mae called.

"Night," the stage manager said distractedly, thumbing through papers. "Notes in the morning."

"Got it. Thanks," Mae replied, finding herself looking forward to it. This work was *nothing* like sitting in a quiet shop mending broken buttons or hemming women's dresses. The fact that her contract was only six weeks made her a little melancholy about the idea of leaving the Proserpina. But she was supposed to be running her own shop, wasn't she?

VIII

She spent the night in what felt like a warm cocoon of joy, bundled up in the small office in the costume shop. She barely wanted to move from her cot upon waking.

Madam Rosnah, before departing the night before, had shown her where they kept clean towels, and Mae had used several of them as blankets. After emerging from her cot, she made use of the full bathing room down the hall and freshened herself up. Madam Rosnah had said the actors sometimes needed to wash off intense makeup...or fake blood and gore from the plays with more gruesome scenes. The commode wasn't anything nice—it was probably still on Des's renovation list—but it had running water, towels, soap, and a mirror. All she needed, really.

For the first time since leaving Corsich, she felt at ease. No rocking ship, no cold shop, and the fact that she had lost her money and trunks suddenly didn't feel so dire.

The first item on her own clumsily written to-do list was to call a repairman about her boiler, but that would have to wait until Des awoke, and was presumably awake *enough* to do business with her. She would wait until he'd had his morning tea.

Bobbin had made himself cozy on her cot and opted to sleep in while Mae tidied up the costume shop again, looking forward to another pleasant morning with Madam Rosnah. She busied herself arranging the thread, sorting through fabrics, and untangling a spool of lace, but the actress didn't show. Eventually, Mae gave up waiting and headed to the kitchen where she found yet another bag of food from Georgie's cafe, this one also containing fruit. As she took a bunch of grapes and a lemon scone, she decided to start the tea herself.

It wasn't Madam Rosnah who arrived first, but Des. He paced into the room with heavy steps, and had she not been looking at the door directly as she sipped her tea, she would have missed the expression of pure joy that lit up his face upon smelling the steam that pervaded the room.

"Ah," he said with a spreading smile when he spotted her. "I had thought I'd have to make do on my own." He opened a cupboard and without hesitation grabbed a black mug on the top right.

"How come?" Mae asked. "Where's Madam Rosnah this morning?"

"Now that we're in full tech, all the actors are supposed to have their lines memorized. So, no need for running them."

"Oh, I see," Mae said, a little put out. There went her idea of jolly morning breakfasts. But now that Des was here...

Her stomach fluttered. It was just the two of them in the whole theater. She watched him brush his black hair from his face as he brought his cup of tea over to the dining area.

Were her hands this warm because they were wrapped like vices around her teacup? Surely her heart shouldn't be racing so fast; she was merely sitting in a chair, after all. What was wrong with her? They were both adults; it wasn't improper to be alone together. And Des's apartments were on another level, for goodness' sake. So why was she acting so strangely?

He sat down at her table, inches from her, and she quickly blurted out, "Do you have the card for your repairman? The Proserpina is so warm; you must have a good boiler." She was babbling.

"Yes. Up in my office," he said. When she glanced up into his eyes, her thoughts took a strange turn, and she suddenly wondered, *Why did he help me that night in the alley?* He seemed so reserved, so aloof. Why had he rescued *her* of all people? Did he think her pretty, like Madam Rosnah had said?

Unable to remember what they were talking about, she said, "I enjoyed the end of the play last night, though I think I need to see the whole thing for context."

A chuckle rumbled up from his chest. "Yes, you really should. I'll have Amelie get you your own script, though, if you want to read it in the meantime."

"That would be lovely! And, actually, I had an idea for Georgie's wings."

He winced. "Yes, I need to go over the transformation monologue with her this morning. The stagehands need a little more practice on the drop too."

"No, it wasn't that," she said. "It was the straps. They looked so cumbersome. I was thinking about it last night in my office. What if we do away with the straps, and replace them with...magnets, so they attach as soon as they get close enough?"

He put down his mug and stared at her.

"Or not," she added hastily.

"That is brilliant, Mae."

She looked down at her hands. "I mean, it's just magnets. Plus, I probably wouldn't have to mend the straps again next time she rips them off," she added with a small smirk.

A genuine laugh boomed out of him. "Brilliant," he said again. "Artistic *and* practical. Make any changes to the costumes as you see fit. You have full rein, Mae."

"Oh, I-I," she stuttered, "Thank you, Des."

"Until Friday, anyway," he added. "Once the show opens, I don't like any changes, unless something *really* doesn't work...or breaks."

"Right," she said, nodding. "That makes sense. There might be a few other things I want to update that I saw last night." Her voice raised at the end, not quite a question.

Another smile graced his face. "As I said, you're the costumer."

Warmth spread from her chest, and she glanced down at her tea.

"I should probably get that card for you," he said, pushing his chair back. "He has a repair shop not two streets over. We can do without you for a few hours, while you take care of your business."

"Really? Are you sure?" She'd had plenty of odd jobs in shops back in Corsich while she saved up for her own shop, and never had one of her bosses let her have an extra-long lunch break when she was sick or needed to run important errands. Working in this theater was completely different than anything she had ever experienced before.

"Of course."

"I'm really not used to theater life," she admitted. "The hours are strange, and everyone here has been so"—her breath hitched as he looked at her—"incredibly helpful. Including you. Thank you. Again."

He stood and headed out the door as he gave her a sidelong glance and said, "Well, the time might come when I need a favor from you. Who knows."

Alone, Mae took a deep breath and regained her head. That last look had sent tingles down her spine. Was he flirting with her? *No, no.* She shook her head. That was ridiculous. He must be referring to her sewing skills or her idea for the wing magnets.

The sound of a baby crying made her jump from her seat.

"Shh!" a girl hushed. Georgie bustled into the kitchen holding a chubby baby. She beelined for the cupboards and made a grab for the bag of food. She withdrew a muffin and broke off a piece for the baby.

"Milk, milk, where's the milk," Georgie muttered to herself, whirling around. "Oh, hello!"

"Hello there," Mae said, giving her a little wave. The baby was munching on the piece of muffin and looked content with his head resting on Georgie's shoulder. Mae had a hard time telling children's ages, but this one could hold onto his own food at least.

Georgie flitted about the small kitchen space, making her own tea with milk and honey. "My mother had to run an errand, *of course*, the morning Des called me in early." Then her tone changed, "Nana will be back for you soon, little Isaac, won't she?"

Mae smiled at them. "Are your wings in your dressing room? I'm going to alter them so they fasten on easier—with magnets, actually."

"Really?" Georgie said, interested. "That'll be loads easier!

And yes, they're hanging from the back of the door, I think." With her baby on her hip, half a muffin in the hand wrapped around the baby, and a mug of tea in the other hand, Georgie bustled from the room with a hasty goodbye.

The wings weren't on the back of the door, but Mae found them tossed onto a chair in the corner easily enough. She brought them back down the hall to the costume shop, where she noticed a piece of paper tacked to the board outside her door. It looked like a list of notes about all the costumes from yesterday's rehearsal.

"Wow," Mae muttered. Amelie's handwriting was immaculate, and each note was detailed enough that Mae knew exactly what it meant. She read the notes about the quick-change curtain and Robyn's pants; there were also a few new problems she would have to put some thought into.

But first, the wings. She knew they didn't come into the play until the very last scene, but she would also have to rig them up to whatever mechanism the stagehands used to lower them onto the stage, and probably do that while the stage was clear *before* rehearsal.

She spread the wings on her big table and examined the back where the straps were attached, trying to figure out where to put the magnets so that they would perch properly on Georgie's back. But after rummaging around in all the cupboards, she came back to the table empty-handed. "I suppose magnets aren't often used in costumes," she muttered to herself. From the little office, Bobbin perked his head up at her voice, and gave her a doggy smile. She grinned back at him, happily curled up on her cot.

"What else could I use?" she thought aloud, tapping her fingers on the table. She shook her head. Nothing would work as quickly and seamlessly as magnets, so she headed out into the hallway to find Des. He had given her free rein after all and approved of the magnet idea. He could point her to some or arrange for their purchase.

Her steps slowed as she realized he was probably working with Georgie. Her feet brought her right to Madam Rosnah's dressing room, and she grinned seeing the actress ensconced there, donning her red wig.

"I missed you for tea this morning!" Mae said. "I only had Des for company."

"I'm so glad Des offered to put you up, what with your heating issues. He treats us theater folk like family. But you mustn't let his cloudy demeanor darken your day." Madam Rosnah winked at her.

Mae chuckled. "He wasn't that cloudy, I must admit."

"Perhaps you'll bring the sunshine out," Madam Rosnah said, adding some red lipstick with a flourish.

"I was wondering, do you know where I could get some small magnets? I need some for a costume, and there weren't any in the shop..."

"Oh, you should ask Charlie, I bet they have some in the

scene shop."

After getting very specific directions, Mae headed behind what Madam Rosnah told her was "stage right," the opposite side of the stage where the green room was located. She discovered the backstage hallways formed a sort of U around the main stage, and the scene shop's location mirrored that of the costume shop.

Her boots scuffed on sawdust the moment she entered, and she glanced around, wondering if she had found the wrong room. All she could see were woodworking supplies, boards, and a freestanding set of stairs in the middle of the room leading nowhere. "Hello?" she called tentatively.

The set of stairs swiveled around slightly, and she lurched away, only to discover the person pushing the stairs—which were on wheels.

"Oh, hi," the person said, pocketing a tape measure in their half apron. Their short hair was combed back and set into a sort of pompadour, and their arms were muscled enough to tell Mae they were the one who handled all this woodworking.

"Is this the scene shop?" Mae asked, glancing at the staircase. The stairs were dark wood with intricate carvings at the top and bottom, with fine golden details and metalwork. Or at least they *looked* that way. As she got closer, she realized the metalwork wasn't metal at all, but merely some sort of painted clay; the same as the carved wood details.

"Sure is. I'm Charlie, the set designer."

"Perfect!" Mae said, pulling her attention back. "Sorry. I'm new to the theater. I'm the costumer."

Charlie's face lit up, and they ran a hand through their hair. "Good. We needed somebody. Was there something you needed, or just looking around?"

"Yes—something I needed. Um... Do you have any magnets?" she asked, then circled her thumb and forefinger tightly. "About this big?"

Charlie frowned in thought. "Let me see. For a costume?"

Mae nodded, and Charlie disappeared around the freestanding staircase. Mae wandered over to it. "What's this for?" she couldn't help but ask.

Bangs came from the back wall, where a line of metal tool cases stood. Charlie's shop, it seemed, wasn't as organized as the costume shop, though Mae had the previous costumer to thank for that. "Oh, it was left over from *Conwell's Contrast*. Not sure what we're going to do with it, but I'm not going to disassemble it yet."

"I see."

"There we go!" Charlie called. "I knew I had some."

Mae's face lit up. "That's perfect!"

Magnets in hand, Mae quickly headed back to the costume shop to rig up the wings. Two magnets for the wings, two for Georgie's dress, and two for the wires that lowered them. That way, they would be evenly balanced and not flop around on

Georgie's back. But she still needed to see the wire system to determine if she could hang two magnets from it.

She headed to the green room and crept down the hallway toward the theater, not wanting to interrupt the note session.

The auditorium and stage were empty. Somehow scenery had been set up on the stage since last night, whenever someone had had time to set up two walls, three columns, and what looked like a fake fountain.

Hands on her hips in the center aisle, Mae surveyed the theater, wondering where Des's office might be. She didn't want to go poking around on the stage for the wing wire, and she still needed that contact card for the repairman.

She didn't have to go searching, however. A door closed at the back of the theater with a snap, and Des was soon striding down the center aisle toward her. A slow grin crept across his face as he approached, and he said, "Looks like I get to call in that favor after all."

IX

"Oh?" Mae asked, her breath quickening.

"The Proserpina has secured a place in the Soldark spring festival—I only just got the telegram."

Mae tried to nod appreciatively, even though she had no idea what he was talking about.

Apparently, he could tell. "Apologies. We've been trying to win the spring festival for years, but always miss out. I didn't think they'd even let us in this year after last year's debacle. It was—" he stopped himself, pinching the bridge of his nose. "Anyway, it's a parade of sorts, a festival to celebrate spring, and they choose winners in four categories: food, music, float design, and costumes. With you on board, I think we have a real fighting chance."

Mae couldn't help but respond with a smile. "So, the

Proserpina needs a winning costume. What do you win?"

"Enough money to run several seasons of shows without having to worry about ticket sales." His stoic mask melted away as his eyes lit up. "I can finally renovate the backstage. We can develop new plays, focus on the art..." He shifted on his feet as if embarrassed, then his gaze flitted down to her hands. "I had to borrow from the bankers for the façade renovations, and ticket sales are really only keeping our heads above water. One bad show run, and we'll sink."

Mae bit her lip in concern. She knew what that was like. Though practically penniless at the moment, she wouldn't have had the money for a shop premises in Soldark without her inheritance.

Des clasped his hands behind his back. "So, will you do it? It's in six weeks."

She pursed her lips. "Well..." she said, stomach lurching as her thoughts whirred. "I had hoped to have my trunks by then, and I might need the extra time for my shop. But since I lost half my startup money... what would you say to splitting the winnings?"

He looked over her face, a hand absently going to his short beard. Then he nodded. "On my word. But I warn you, it could be a lot of hard work for no payout."

She mustered a smile. "Isn't that what makes it fun? The uncertainty?"

A raised eyebrow was his only response.

But her spirits had risen, and she merely found his expression amusing. "Very well. It's a deal, then. What do I need to do?"

"We can talk about it after *Fortune* opens. These long tech days can be gruesome, and it'll be easier to think once we're up and running this weekend. But for the festival, we must embody spring, and we usually give a nod to whatever show we're running, to drum up business, if nothing else. I'll give you a copy of the acceptance letter and see if I can find a flyer for the festival."

"That would be helpful," she said, thinking six weeks wasn't really that much time. A door shut and she saw Amelie walk in, clutching her massive script book. The rehearsal was supposed to start at mid-morning and last until almost midnight. According to the schedule that Amelie had given her, the days leading up to opening night were twelve hours long. "Oh! Do you have that card for your repairman?"

"Yes, of course. Sorry," Des said, ducking his head. "I'll go fetch it. We'll talk more about the festival after the show opens."

He disappeared into the shadows at the back of the auditorium as Amelie approached and brought up a few pressing items from the list she had left. "If you could, take care of Robyn's pants first," the stage manager said. "We'll be running the scene shifts between acts today and the timing will be important."

Mae nodded. "Right. Des is letting me run an errand, but I'll take care of that as soon as I get back. Oh! I wanted to ask you about Georgie's wings—how do they drop from the ceiling?" It was all so much to keep track of. Perhaps she should get her own little notebook like Des had.

She glanced toward where Des had disappeared, but he must still be in his office, so she followed Amelie over to the side of stage left where the mechanism to drop the wings was attached to the wall.

"Magnets?" Amelie said, frowning thoughtfully after Mae explained. "That should be much smoother. And you should be able to attach it to the cable just fine. Although, you said there were two?"

"Perhaps a small rod to space them apart?" Mae mused.

By the time they had worked out what Mae would need to do, Des returned. He pressed a card into her hand. "Thank you," she said, sneaking a glance into his eyes. Surprisingly, he gave her a small smile, and then his fingers slipped from hers. Her breath caught as he stepped away, and she quickly headed down the long aisle to the front doors.

Her mind was racing all the way. Des's hand lingering in hers as he passed her the card and the subsequent jolt through her senses. The promise he had made to give her half the winnings from the festival... She was still a little shocked he had agreed so quickly, but perhaps after their devastating loss last year, he was desperate to win.

Was his interest in her merely for her skills? That was what he had hired her for, was it not? That was surely the reason he wanted her help on the festival and why he had allowed her to stay here and borrow dresses. For her skills. It wasn't as if he knew anything about her. They had only passed a few moments together over tea that morning.

She huffed and stiff-armed the theater's front door open, then looked down at the address on the card. Des had said it was only two streets over. She thought she had seen Dougherty Street on her way from the port, so she headed that direction in the mid-morning light.

Soldark was awash with activity; people lined up at newsstands to get their morning papers, men and women rushed about their shopping, and sailors and travelers bustled around in the vicinity of the port. She shot a glance in the direction of the harbor. She wondered if they would ever retrieve her money. She was sure it was long gone by now.

That festival prize money would go a long way toward rebuilding her shop finances. She still had plenty of materials and equipment she needed to buy—even passing over the idea of upgrading to a Thomas' sewing machine—things she had planned on waiting to get until she was set up in the premises. Not to mention the money she had originally budgeted to purchase furniture upon landing in Soldark.

Her cozy little office at the Proserpina was heavenly, but only until her boiler was fixed.

As she eyed the street sign for Dougherty Street, she vowed to win that festival contest. But a small part of her mourned the impending loss of her work at the Proserpina, a place that was growing more and more like a family each day. And with Des at the heart of it, she wasn't sure she wanted her work to end, even if he had only hired her for her skills.

"All right, everyone. Take five!" Amelie called.

The cast dispersed from the stage as quickly as possible, hastening off to relax in the green room, or more likely, to grab a snack in the kitchen.

Mae took advantage of the empty stage to head over to stage left to lower the wire, wings tucked under her arm. Amelie had shown her how to use the gearbox earlier, and after a moment's confusion, she got it figured out again. She cranked the gears until the wire hung about stomach-height in the center of the stage. She had completed most of her tasks for the day, including adjustments to Robyn's tight pants, and had watched the run-through from the auditorium, following along with her new copy of the script. It was fascinating, though this run-through was particularly frustrating to watch since they kept stopping to adjust the lighting or work on the actors' movement around the scenery.

She headed to center stage and attached a very thin metal

bar to the wing wire—another item she had gotten from Charlie in the scene shop. As she did, she glanced over at the theater doors. She was waiting for the repairman, Christoph, to check in with an update about her boiler. She had left her shop keys with him this morning, and he had promised to take a look this afternoon. But it was just about five o'clock, and she was beginning to wonder if she would hear back at all today. Luckily, she didn't need anything from her shop—since Christoph still had her keys—and even more luckily, she had nothing valuable in the shop to worry about.

"There," she said, pulling on the little metal bar she had attached. It seemed sturdy enough. A little thrill ran through her as she lifted the wings up to the bar. The sudden *click* as the sets of magnets snapped together was enough to elevate her spirits from her boiler troubles for the moment.

Amelie strode back into the space holding a jeweled walking cane—a prop, Mae assumed—and a chocolate croissant. "Ah, the new wing attachment! We can have Georgie try it out as soon as we get back from break, in case you need to make more adjustments."

"That would be perfect," Mae said. "Do you want me to leave them down, then?"

Amelie nodded. "So, there's a set of magnets in her dress too?"

"Yes, I did those first. They're already in there."

"Perfect," Amelie said. "And I saw the quick-change booth

on stage left. It looks amazing. Do you think you could do another—"

The front theater doors opened, and a newly-familiar man walked in—Christoph. "Oh," Mae said, "Sorry, it's about my shop, hold on—"

"Sure," Amelie said, pulling out a pocket watch. "I'd better go round up the actors. They're always slow on the last break before dinner. But we have an hour and a half to go before then."

Mae grinned at Amelie and headed along the short flight of stairs leading down from the stage to meet Christoph, who was lingering in the lobby.

"Hello," she called uncertainly. She couldn't tell the verdict of her boiler's assessment from his ruddy face, but suddenly butterflies were jumping in her stomach. What if the cost was too much? The repairman had agreed that she could pay him on a payment plan after she got her wages from the opening of *Fortune*, but still...

Christoph touched the tip of his cap in greeting and rustled in his pockets for a sheet of paper, which he held out to her. "I'm sorry, miss. I even went to Randolph's on Locust Street, but they don't have the parts right now. I can fix it, but it's going to be a few weeks before the new deaerator and valves come in from Fragall."

An unpleasant swoop went through her stomach. Weeks? She tried to ignore the wobble in her knees, but as she glanced at the actors assembling on the stage in their previous places, she took a deep breath. It wasn't so bad, after all. Truth be told, she was enjoying her stay at the theater far more than her cold and increasingly unfriendly shop. Now she just had to make sure Des would be all right with her staying longer. She glanced at the director settled into his chair in the front center of the auditorium, in deep conversation with one of the actors.

But if she created something magnificent for the spring festival, she had a feeling he wouldn't mind.

After thanking Christoph and taking her keys back—he reassured her that he would install the new parts as soon as they arrived—Mae went back to watch Georgie try out the wing magnets.

The actress's squeal of delight was worth far more than the satisfaction that her idea had worked. With a grin, Mae headed back to the costume shop to tackle a few more problems she could *actually* control.

X

The cold snap lasted three days as the production of *Fortune Defines Us* readied for opening weekend. During this time, Mae let out Robyn's satyr pants a second time, put up another quick-change booth on stage right, hemmed Madam Rosnah's red tulle confection of a dress—a massive undertaking—and worked down an extensive list of other costume repairs that Amelie supplied or Mae herself decided were necessary.

At this point, she was fairly certain she had seen the entire play, though not in order and never all at once. She hoped, once the show opened, she could get a better feel for it, which she could use to influence the costume for the spring festival. The prize money was becoming more and more important to her with the impending boiler repair to pay for. Christoph had left a slip with an estimate for the parts and repair costs, and she wasn't sure how she was going to afford any of the supplies or furnishings for the shop. She was on the verge of begging Des for a more permanent job but didn't want to come across as any more desperate than she already seemed. The other day, however, when she had approached him about possibly staying in the theater longer than expected, he had merely nodded, though that slight action had sent the butterflies in her stomach fluttering. Was she imagining how his eyes seemed to light up with a gray intensity as he looked at her?

She shook her head and took a sip of her morning tea. Ensconced in the costume shop, darning a hole in one of Robyn's shirts—the poor dear had begged her to fix one of his own shirts—she was full of nervous excitement for the evening to come. She had finished all her tasks for *Fortune*, and was glad to have some downtime before anyone arrived for the day.

Tonight was opening night at the Proserpina, and finally, all of their hard work would be presented to the public. There had been countless run-throughs until all present were bleary-eyed and fatigued, working relentlessly into the late hours of the night. There had been countless adjustments to the lighting, the scenery, and the props. Mae had been flabbergasted when she poked her head backstage one night to watch the stagehands at work; they turned cranks which moved the set walls or flew in one piece of scenery or another.

The gear which moved the wings up and down was merely a drop in the bucket compared to the rest of the stage magic. Mae was looking forward to watching the show from the auditorium, all in one go. But tonight, she would remain in her costume shop, on hand in case help was needed with the costumes...or anything else.

The theater was quiet, since the actors were finished rehearsing. Everything was ready. But there was one thing Mae couldn't quite stop thinking about. Des was composed and organized when it came to discussing *Fortune*, but anytime she approached him about the spring festival, he told her they could discuss it later. Perhaps he was more worried about *Fortune* opening than she had realized. Or maybe, the fate of the festival was too overwhelming to think about with everything else going on. She had studied the flyer and telegram copy he gave her but was no closer to coming up with a concept.

If she were to create an award-winning costume from scratch, she would need time to plan it out. When she had sewn her first wedding gown for a well-to-do family back in Corsich, she had planned the garment for well over two months before finally taking scissors to fabric.

I'll confront him after the opening when everyone's—

A massive *BOOM* sounded overhead, and she leapt from her chair. It wasn't an ordinary sound, like when one of the columns had fallen over on the stage. The sound continued, rattling and rumbling like thunder on the stage above. Mae covered her head instinctively and lurched to the costume shop door, Bobbin at her heels. What was going on?

It kept coming.

Panicked, she looked up and down the hall, but saw nothing amiss. The terrifying rumble continued, and she could feel a vibration humming through the walls. She should get out. Now.

She glanced in the direction of the back door, but then remembered she wasn't the only person in the building. She thought the door to Des's apartments was by the back door, so she scooped up Bobbin and ran that way.

Just as she reached the heavy wooden door that led downstairs, it swung open, almost hitting her. "Oh!" she yelped. Des grabbed her by the arms.

"Are you all right?" he demanded, frantic eyes searching her face and then pulling her close.

She looked up at him and realized his arms were shaking. "I am." She gasped. "Are you?"

The rumbling had finally stopped, but Mae still braced herself for more.

"I'm—fine," he said tightly. He still looked terrified though, and she wasn't sure what scared her more—Des's fear or whatever had made that noise. Finally, he let go of her. Her arms were warm where he had touched her, and she suddenly wished he hadn't let go.

"It sounds like the roof fell in," she whispered.

Des took a ragged breath, deep and slow. "I don't think it's as bad as that," he said, shaking his head.

"How do you know?"

He took the moment to shut his door, and she took a step back so she wasn't crowding him. The fright still had her heart racing, and she patted Bobbin's head in relief.

"I know this theater inside and out," he said. "That was the thunder run going off, unfortunately. I'm sorry it...gave you such a fright."

"The *what*?"

"Here," he said, "I need to assess the damage—do you want to come with me?"

"Um, sure," she said hesitantly.

"I'm sorry," he said, "You still look frightened. Would you rather wait down here?"

"No," she said hastily. "Do you think it's that bad? Or do you want a cup of tea first?" By now, she knew what he was like first thing in the morning.

Des chuckled darkly. "I'm quite awake after all that. Here, I'll show you the thunder run. I just hope nothing fell through the grid and damaged the stage."

Mae had never been up on the catwalk before. She was quite content to watch the stagehands adjust the lights or the fly wires from the floor. Des went up the ladder first. Bobbin had hopped from her arms once they entered the theater and saw everything was intact, and he gave her hand a lick before trotting backstage, probably to cozy back up on her cot for a morning nap.

Hand over hand, she climbed up the black metal ladder on stage right. At the top, Des held out a hand for her. She swallowed the lump in her throat and reached for him. A tiny thrill ran up her spine when he didn't let go, instead gripping her arm more fully as they walked along the narrow metal walkway suspended midair. It was one of many walkways, a crisscrossing path that hung above the entire stage. It wasn't as high as she expected, and it felt sturdy, but she was thankful for Des's arm entwined around hers. More than *thankful*, she was awash in a strange mixture of excitement and uncertainty at his touch.

"Here. This is the bottom of the thunder run. Ah…I thought so."

He was pointing to a section in the ceiling where heavy metal tracks held what looked like a dozen cannonballs. Mae supposed the tracks ran up through the ceiling over the auditorium.

"What is it for, exactly?"

Des turned to look at her, his eyes lighting up as he cocked a smile. It seemed that he had mostly recovered from his shock. "Thunder, of course."

She tilted her head politely. "Oh?"

He pointed at the balls in the track. "They start up over

the lobby and run down the tracks, making it sound and feel like thunder for the audience. We don't use them for every show, but I suppose I should have Charlie service them more often. It seems, the mechanism went off by itself. From the sound of it, I thought they had fallen out of the track and onto the stage."

Mae chuckled. "It did sound like cannonballs had pervaded the theater."

He pressed his lips together, tight. "Yes, well, I've seen that before, and I'd rather not again. I'll get Charlie up here as soon as they get in."

Mae was suddenly aware of how close they were standing in the cramped space and said softly, "What do you mean, you've seen that before?" She was glad he was holding her elbow, for her hands had begun to sweat awkwardly.

A sigh heaved from his chest, though Mae could tell he hadn't done it consciously, and she probably wouldn't have noticed if she weren't inches from him in the darkened space.

"I served in Aprica...during the war. It was... a long time ago, but sometimes it feels like I'm still living it."

"Oh," she said. "Is-is that why you were familiar with Corsich?" Aprica shared a border with half of Corsich and had undergone a nasty civil war a decade or so ago. Soldark had sent aid, she remembered, but she had only been about fifteen at the time. Des must have been...what? Eighteen?

"It is," he said stiffly. "I'll never forget the needless

destruction. It's the reason I bought the theater when I came back home. I wanted to create things, to give people something of beauty, pure enjoyment, even if just for a few hours of their day." He was silent for a moment, then his forehead wrinkled, eyes cast down. He began to pull away, shutting down, trying to put his professional mask back in place.

She didn't let him. She grabbed his other arm tightly, too, holding him as he had held her in the back hallway when she had been frightened. She felt tiny, her comfort insignificant in the face of such remembered trauma. She didn't know what he had been through, but it didn't matter. Everyone carried their own darkness in their own way.

Des didn't move. Her breath became so shallow she wasn't sure she was taking in air anymore. Had she crossed a line? His dark hair covered his face, and she couldn't see his expression in the shadows of the catwalk.

Finally, his chest moved as he took in a deep breath. His hand came up to her face and brushed a pink curl aside, his fingers lightly brushing her cheek. She looked up into his eyes right as he said, "Thank you."

XI

The stage was set, the props in their proper places, the costumes functional and clean. Georgie's mother would keep little Isaac overnight, and Robyn's boyfriend had come early to bring flowers to his dressing room. Mae stood in the doorway of her costume shop with a smile plastered to her face.

"Ten minutes!" Amelie called into each room as she strode down the hallway. "Ten minutes 'til curtain!"

A live wire of excitement ran through Mae. But all she had to do tonight was sit and wait. Her job was done, unless there was a wardrobe malfunction during the show, and she had done her best to ensure there wouldn't be any.

The chatter of people in the theater above was new and exciting. Mae was too nervous to even sneak down the hallway for a peek at the audience, as some of the actors had already done. Robyn had reported that journalists from the *Soldark Times* and the *Sunbelt Chronicle* were out there and even half the Grandville family, who ran most of Soldark's electricity. Mae hadn't realized what a big deal opening night would be, and wondered if the popularity of the show would keep up for its ten-week run.

It made sense that the spring festival costume needed to draw publicity to the show, to keep people coming to see it during the run. But that all depended on how the show was received on opening night. She crossed her fingers as Amelie ushered the last actor into the green room to prepare for the opening scene.

Madam Rosnah, who wasn't needed until scene two, sashayed out of her dressing room in her simple brown dress for act one. Not a hair was out of place on her red wig, and her makeup was without reproach. Mae grinned at her.

"Happy opening, my dear," Madam Rosnah said, squeezing one of Mae's hands. "You've done wonderfully."

"Thank you," Mae said, ducking her head. "You as well."

"I've been at Des all week to hire you on after *Fortune* closes. We can't lose someone as talented as you. Are you sure you want to leave us to open that shop of yours?" she added with a wink.

Mae bit her lip. The noises in the theater had stopped, and the lone creak of the floorboards on stage as an actor named

Walker delivered the opening monologue. It had begun.

"Well, who knows," Mae said with a sigh. "I can't even pay for the boiler to be fixed yet, and there's all the things I need to buy for the shop. I only packed the essentials, you see—I intended on buying as much here as I could for the convenience," she added sourly. "A fat lot of convenience any of this venture has been. I'm just lucky I found the Proserpina."

Madam Rosnah nodded. "And we're very lucky Des scooped you up off the street. We'll have to hound him to keep you on. It's not like he has anyone lined up for *Flight of Daguerre*."

"Oh? What's that?"

"A new play by a journalist in town, if you can believe it. About a famous airship pilot. You probably haven't heard of the Daguerre, have you?"

"Can't say that I have. When does that start?"

"Not for a while. We haven't even gotten the script yet."

A scream came from the stage. Madam Rosnah nodded and said, "That's my cue! See you in act three. Maybe we can pester Des at the after-party about your contract."

Mae watched Madam Rosnah head for the green room with a small smile on her lips. She had no intention of pestering Des for anything and was unsure where she stood with the director at the moment. After the intense moment of closeness upon the catwalk—which both lasted an eternity and was too brief—Des had guided her by the elbow to the ladder. Ever since they stepped back on the ground, he had been his usual professional self.

Still worried she had crossed a line, she kept to herself as much as she could. There was no way she would force herself upon him by demanding he extend her contract. She should be thankful she was already engaged for the spring festival and leave it at that. Though a small part of her wished that Madam Rosnah could convince him to let her stay forever, the reasonable part of her argued that she had her own shop to take care of.

The after-party would be held at the Salty Hare, the tavern she had encountered on her first day in Soldark. Having found a small envelope on her sewing table around midday with her first wages, she was quite looking forward to spending some money and not having to subsist entirely on increasingly stale baked goods and leftover fruit. And she quite thought a celebration was in order for all her work on the play.

The usual traffic of actors in and out of their dressing rooms commenced, as actors who had time between scenes freshened up their makeup or changed costumes. Even though she knew all the actors had memorized their lines, she spotted Robyn pacing the hallway at one point reading his script, likely out of nerves. No one came rushing to Mae for anything, and for the first time, she was quite bored in her little haven.

She found herself sneaking out the back door of the theater

toward the end of the play. She walked around the front of the building and into the back of the auditorium just in time for Georgie's closing scene.

As Mae stood in the shadows at the back of the theater, excitement surged through her as she realized the other figure standing there was none other than Des. But it was already too late, and she glanced up at him with a timid smile. He nodded in response, focused on the stage.

She was happy to see she hadn't missed Georgie's transformation. Her heart leapt as the wings lowered seamlessly—the stagehands had practiced a lot—and the gasp the audience let out when the wings attached to Georgie almost like magic sent an unfamiliar wave of euphoria through Mae.

This must be what it's like for the actors, she thought. The appreciation of an audience fueling your art. She let out a quiet sigh and found herself smiling through Georgie's final scene as a winged beauty.

When the curtains closed and the audience surged to their feet amid the applause, Mae risked a look at Des. He glanced at her as well, and the euphoria spread from her chest to her toes. Breath heaving with excitement, she opened her mouth to say something. But before she could speak, the audience was suddenly moving, picking up their things and exiting their rows. The lights came on in the house, and she and the director were revealed from their shadowy viewing spot. Theater-goers began to approach Des, whose towering height and all-black suit made him quite recognizable

Some even came up to Mae, shaking her hand with excitement. She had no idea how anyone knew she worked for the theater, besides the fact that she was standing next to the director. Perhaps Robyn was to blame for her notoriety. She knew he'd helped spread the word about the show, pinning up posters on street corners, and chatting it up in every eatery and shop he could find. And her name was in the small paper program each audience member clutched, although costumer was listed at the very end with the names of the crew.

The next hour was a blur. Shaking hands with strangers in the auditorium, then finally excusing herself to go backstage and arrange the costumes amid the giddy actors. One sleeve needed mending, but it was a minor seam rip. She sorted out the costumes that needed washing—the lights on stage were hot, and no one wanted to wear a sweaty costume tomorrow night—and soon everyone was packing up for the after-party.

"Coming, Mae?" Robyn asked. "Charlie's already gone and reserved a corner for us!"

At the Salty Hare, when she opened the envelope that held her wages to pay for a small glass of Soldark mead, she gasped.

Des had paid her full wages. Her gaze locked on the director who stood with his back to her at the end of the bar, speaking to the barwoman. Her cheeks flamed. Why had he done that? She was only supposed to be getting half for living in the theater since she was essentially homeless. And she was certain it had been intentional. Des wasn't the type to make such a mistake.

She paid for her drink, picked it up, and headed toward him, untouched by the mead but with warmth surging through her.

"Congratulations," she said as she reached him. He turned, holding a tray of mugs. She cocked her head at him when she realized they were all filled with water. He gave her a conspiratorial smirk.

"Need to make sure everyone makes it to the theater tomorrow," he told her, handing her one. "Including you."

A cup in each hand, she followed him. "I think you made a mistake. On my wages."

"No mistake," he said, handing water to Robyn and his boyfriend.

"I think you did."

He turned and locked eyes with her. "I assure you, I didn't."

"But—"

"Your work was exquisite, Mae. You went leagues above and beyond my expectations. The details, the skill, the innovation—I couldn't pay you any less, your living situation notwithstanding."

Her chest swelled like a great balloon. "I—"

"Just say thank you."

"Thank you."

Madam Rosnah slipped a hand over and took a mug of water with a nod of thanks.

Des went on, "Besides, I know you need that money for your shop. You're going to do great things there."

The balloon in her chest deflated. "Right. Right."

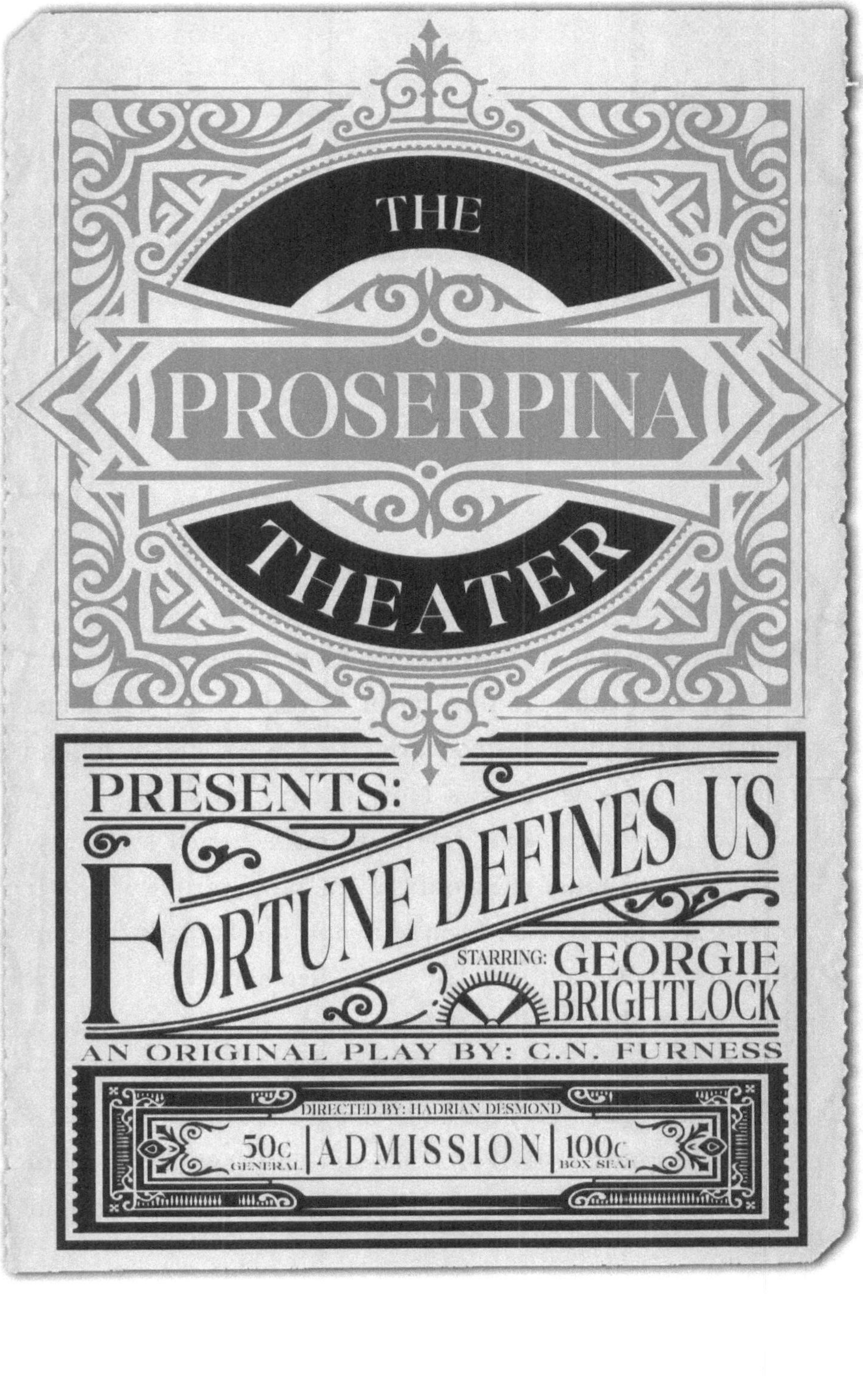

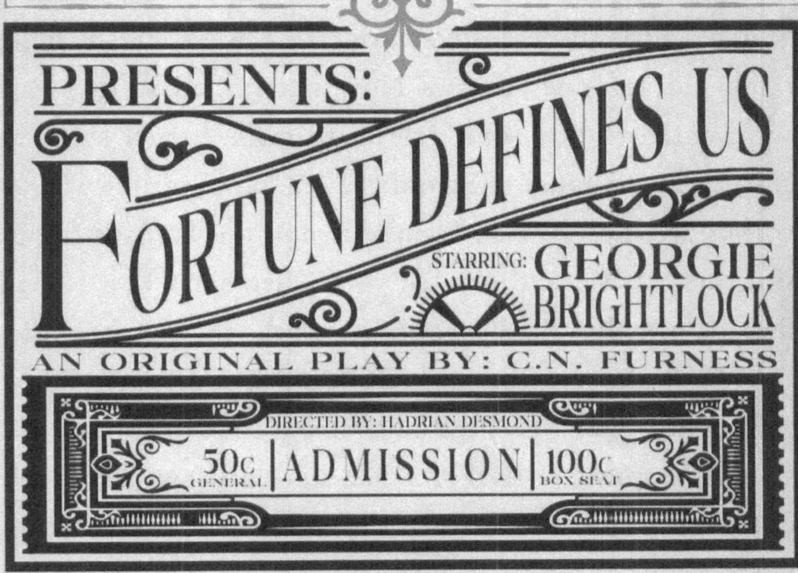

THE
PROSERPINA
THEATER
PRESENTS:
FORTUNE DEFINES US
STARRING: GEORGIE BRIGHTLOCK
AN ORIGINAL PLAY BY: C.N. FURNESS
DIRECTED BY: HADRIAN DESMOND
50c GENERAL
ADMISSION
100c BOX SEAT

XII

Opening weekend came and went in a blur. Mae didn't have much to do now that the show was up and running. She spent her time cleaning up the costume shop, which had gotten a little disorganized during tech week, and sketching out her ideas for new dresses. Now that she had her first wages, she wanted to buy some fabrics to make herself some new clothes. Even though she would have a full wardrobe when her trunks arrived, she had been studying the Soldark fashions since her arrival and wanted to try her hand at a few new designs. She also, finally, got to watch the show in its entirety.

When the crowds started thinning not even halfway through the play run, Mae knew it was time to approach Des about the spring festival. She had started a few sketches, but abandoned them halfway through, rudderless without direction. And every time she saw Des in passing, her stomach fluttered with nerves at the thought of approaching him. Since opening night, she had taken to having breakfast and tea in her own office, though she left a pot in a tea cozy for when Des finally ascended from his apartments.

It wasn't that she had been avoiding him. *But I am,* she thought. *I can't keep staying here and working here. I have my own business to attend to. And he knows it. That's why he paid me full wages. That's why he's been distant. He wants me to succeed—just not* here.

The parts for her boiler had been delayed, and when Christoph told her, Mae had experienced a surge of guilt at how happy she was. When she asked Des if she could stay longer, he had granted her all the time she needed. It filled her with joy, not only because of the unlivable qualities of her shop, but if she were being honest with herself, she didn't want to leave the Proserpina at all.

She sought Des in his office at the back of the auditorium on Saturday morning. It was only two weeks until the spring festival, and it was now or never. She rapped sharply on Des's office door and heard a chair move.

Suddenly, he was standing in the doorway. She swallowed the lump in her throat. "We need to talk about the spring festival. Do you have a-a vision of some kind? I'm having difficulty coming up with a concept."

Des nodded, sighing heavily. "Yes, you're right. It's only

two weeks away." He glanced back at his desk, which was a comical contrast of messy and tidy. The desktop itself was strewn with papers, which Des had clearly been working on, but the perimeter of the desk held paper trays that were neatly organized with labels in his own handwriting.

"I can finish that later. Is here good?" He gestured to the auditorium seats.

"How about the costume shop? I should get some paper and pencils."

She began with sketches. A freshly sharpened graphite pencil scratching on the paper brought her a modicum of ease in his presence. Seeing him lounging in the chair at her sewing table, one ankle perched on the opposite knee, had brought heat to her neck and hands.

But she knew her place. She was a talented seamstress, not a costume designer, not a real one, anyway. And though she had finally admitted to herself her feelings toward Des were more than the platonic relationship should be between a director and his employee, she didn't think he felt the same. She had simply caught him in a moment of weakness on the catwalk and crossed a line.

He described the festival, the Proserpina's floats from previous years, and the winning entries. "Honestly, Mae, I must apologize," he said abruptly.

Her heart leapt into her throat.

"I shouldn't have waited so long to begin on the festival

preparations."

"Oh." She could have sunk into the floor.

"I was so sure we wouldn't get in after the debacle last year—something broke on the costume, and the actor stumbled on a scene wire right in front of the judge's table, pulling down half the scenery—so when I got the news, I didn't know what to do. At the time I entered, we didn't even have a costume designer."

"It's...fine. We can figure it out. There's plenty of time."

Except two weeks didn't seem like plenty of time. And yet, after all the miraculous costume adjustments she had accomplished over the last month, she had a wild courage in her own skills she had never encountered before. Sometime between hemming an actor's pants two minutes before they had to be on stage and hefting a steam drill to hang a support frame for a changing curtain, she had gained a new confidence.

And she owed it all to the man who had whisked her off the street and into the depths of this beautiful theater.

"I've been studying *Fortune*, since I finally saw the whole play the other week," she said, deciding to take charge of the situation. "I think the heart of it is at the end, with Lady Comay's speech about transformation."

"Of course," he agreed, nodding thoughtfully.

"And the essence of spring is also about transformation. Well..." She thought for a few minutes about what she had seen in the scene shop and the costume closet. How she could bring it all together to embody *transformation*. "I think I might have an idea for how to win *two* categories."

A week and a half later, she, Des, and Charlie stood in the scene shop admiring the set of stairs Mae had noticed on her first trip into the room. Charlie had been more than happy to put the staircase to use, bemoaning the fact that they hadn't used the thing in four shows and how it was only taking up space in the shop.

It was now transformed, though it still wasn't quite finished. The bottom of the steps had been painted shades of black and gray, to signify the depths of winter, which faded into pure white at the very top. The gold details remained like glittering veins in the darkness. At least, that's how Mae hoped it looked.

"The top needs something," Des remarked.

"Of course," Mae said, a finger over her lips. "I'm still working out how it will tie in with the costume piece." She had spent the greater part of the past week repurposing several costumes into the one for the festival. She'd tried sketching it out, but in the end, she had ended up cutting and sewing without a pattern. The dress now hung on a mannequin in the costume shop, but it wasn't quite done either.

"Well, the float is street-worthy now," Charlie said with an almost maniacal grin as they gestured to the wheel-and-gear contraption they had built in order for the stairs to become mobile. "I don't think it'll fit on the stage like this ever again, but it'll be worth it. Can you imagine the look on the judge's faces?"

Mae thought the base looked like a cross between an auto and a train car that were squashed beneath the large staircase, but from everything she had seen of Charlie's sets, she was confident it was functional. She nodded.

This was the sixth week of the *Fortune* run, with only three days to go until the spring festival.

Mae was certain her trunks would arrive from Corsich any day now, and things were about to transform in her life. She tried not to think about leaving the Proserpina and had thrown herself into the spring festival costume. She and Des saw each other in passing, and she snuck glances at him out of the corner of her eye, but she feared that moment on the catwalk was as close as she would get with the stoic director. Time was running out, and she hadn't had the courage to try and pierce his stubbornly dark armor again.

She had spent some of her earnings on fabric, and sewn a few new dresses for herself, an activity that filled the long hours. During the day, she and Des were the only people in the building, though he mostly stayed in his apartments until the actors started arriving for the evening shows.

All the while, *Fortune* continued to suffer from declining audiences. She knew everyone hoped the festival would bring in more patrons, so the show could finish with a bang. And she, more than anyone, was hopeful for the winnings the festival might bring them. Christoph had begun work on her boiler, only to run into a water issue—probably from the deep freeze the shop had suffered. As a result, he'd had to contract a plumber. Her bill was running up.

"I'll be back an hour before curtain," Mae assured Des after they finished surveying the staircase float.

"Checking on the shop?" he asked quietly.

She nodded as they headed through the back corridor of the theater together. It had become a weekly occurrence, mostly to assure herself that nothing else was amiss, and to check her post box.

"Not long now, before you'll be directing an opening of your own," Des said.

Mae didn't answer, mumbling "Mm-hmm" in agreement. With each passing week of *Fortune*, her guilt and worry grew heavier. But hadn't it been her dream since she was a girl to open up her own seamstress shop? Hadn't she worked and saved for years for the funds to do so? If it hadn't been for the generosity of her second cousin's will, she would still be in Corsich, saving up for her own premises.

The truth was, the Proserpina had changed her. Her dream of quietly planning fanciful garments for rich Soldark society no longer excited her as it once had. Yet an inner voice argued with her. *How can you throw away the dreams that you worked so hard for all these years? What about all the sketches and the sample dresses you've already created? What of all that hard work?* She didn't know what to do anymore.

She bid Des goodbye as she popped her head in the costume shop for her keys. "Coming?" she asked Bobbin, who perked his head up from her cot in the back. He remained there, and she smirked, turning to head out the back door.

The fresh spring air revived her, burying her mixed emotions about the future a little deeper. She took her time strolling to the shop, enjoying the cool air on her face, a light breeze blowing in from the harbor. She wondered whether she should check in at the port master's office to see whether the *Riveter* was due to return soon, though the prospect of unpacking her sewing equipment in her empty shop had lost its luster in the glamor and glitter of theater life.

The shop looked the same as ever. Christoph had left some tools in the basement—he now had his own set of keys—and the water was completely shut off, making the place unlivable even though the nights weren't nearly as cold as they had been when the boiler broke.

As she locked back up, her mind drifting back to the festival costume—which still needed a special something—her gaze landed on the florist shop across the street. She cocked her head and smiled. Checking for passing autos, she ran across the narrow cobbled street to Quince & Coneflower.

A bell tinkled merrily upon her entry, and Mae was greeted by a kind-faced girl with wide eyes and short brassy hair. Mae described what she needed to the girl, whose face lit up.

"I've always wanted to enter the spring festival," the girl gushed, "but all we do is flowers. I wouldn't know about all the costumes and floats and stuff, but I'm sure we can help you get whatever you need!"

The girl scratched out some numbers on a small receipt and handed it to her. Mae was glancing around the shop as the girl wrote, and her gaze settled on the stairs—leading to an apartment, no doubt. She thought of the barren staircase float. "Actually, we're going to need a lot more flowers than that."

Her flower order completed—charged to the Proserpina, of course—she stepped back out into the fresh air with a newfound excitement. The flowers wouldn't be delivered until Friday, so they would be fresh, and they would still have time to set them up for Saturday morning. She would sketch up where they would be placed on the dress and stairs in the meantime.

As she turned to head back to the theater, she noticed a familiar man heading for the door of her shop, and she paused. Was that the first mate of the *Riveter*?

She darted across the street toward him, and he looked up. "Ah! Miss Wright, I thought this was the place."

Her stomach was in turmoil, and she braced herself—her luck had been good lately, but the sight of the first mate brought back all the memories of her first few days in Soldark, and she couldn't help but wince as she waited for bad news.

"Your trunks, miss," he said. "They're at the harbor. But I wanted to check in with you before I had them brought over by courier. The captain sends his deepest apologies. And— you'll be glad to hear, the port master secured this—"

He withdrew her red velvet coin purse from a deep inner pocket of his coat. It clanked heavily as he placed it in her hand. She froze. "H-How?"

The first mate shrugged. "I think he said it took a week to get down there to check—the current's not that aggressive this time of spring, you see—but they hadn't your address on file, so they had to wait until the *Riveter* came back in."

Her mouth popped open. All this time, her money had been sitting in the port master's office? She had been so content and busy at the Proserpina, she had neglected to check with the port master since that first day! *I guess I didn't have time to give him my address when Bobbin ran off...*

She clutched the purse to herself in a state of shock.

Between what was in her trunks and her coin purse, she now had all the money she needed to fix the boiler and the water and furnish her shop. She didn't need the prize money from the festival, after all.

After profusely thanking the first mate and agreeing upon a time to meet the courier with the trunks, she headed back to the theater in a daze.

The curtain call came and went, and she sat in the costume shop, staring at the dress she had transformed for the festival. A cup of cold tea—courtesy of Madam Rosnah, though it had been delivered hot—sat on the sewing table before her, amid the sketches of the dress and staircase. She had planned on sketching the flowers onto the drawings, so when they were delivered, others could help her place them. The pink, white, and blue dress hung proudly on the mannequin with swaths of matching tulle flowing from the skirts and little butterfly fascinators—that Mae had borrowed from a few hats in the costume closet—on the shoulders.

She had already fitted the costume on Georgie but hadn't yet shown the actress the final part that really brought it together: the butterfly wings. She hadn't shown anyone, in fact. Mostly because they weren't ready yet. There was still something missing from the wings, something that the added flowers wouldn't solve. She just hadn't figured it out yet.

The theme of transformation had easily drawn her mind to a butterfly back when she and Des were brainstorming. The butterfly made a fitting correlation between the play and spring. They had the *theme* part down, but the execution was still lacking...something. And of course, the stairs signified the transformation out of winter, rising from the dark depths into a flower-filled oasis—that was the idea, anyway. But she still needed to figure out something else to add to the wings.

Though the coin purse she had locked in her office desk

had presented her with a solution to all her problems, she had no intention of leaving the Proserpina until she had finished what she came to do—even if her contract was ending soon. They would do the rest of the run without her; the costume repairs had dulled to a minimum anyway, and Madam Rosnah would probably end up covering again. She was sure Des had only given her the contract for six weeks to coincide with her luggage returning, and it made sense, on a business level. Now, she just had to help them win the spring festival, and her time here would be done.

The Proserpina needed that prize money and notoriety, if Des's dreams were to come true. And even if those dreams didn't involve her working for the theater, she would still follow through. She had given up hope that another contract would suddenly materialize in her costume shop one day. And why would it? She had plans for her shop; Des knew that.

No flowers were sketched that evening.

The next day, she made a pot of tea for Des and then headed to her shop on Angleshire Lane to wait for the courier with her trunks. She let herself in and stalked about the empty shop in agitation. Should she just ask Des for a job? Would she really give up on owning her own shop?

Heaving a sigh, she bumped into a crate in the backroom and knocked the lid off. She found the likely source of the slivers of metal that littered the floor—which she hadn't had time or energy to clean up yet. The crate was packed with various bits of copper wire, different sized gears, and thin metal plating: the remains of her cousin's jewelry supplies. Another box held different sized clips and magnets. She cocked her head, thoroughly curious about the type of jewelry her cousin had made, when a thought struck her.

The magnets reminded her of Georgie's tulle wings, which were still a hit whenever her onstage transformation took place. The festival wings were going to be stationary, but what if... What if Mae used the copper and gears and magnets to make the festival butterfly wings really transform... What if...

A sharp rap on the door drew her attention to the front, where two lads from the harbor were waiting for her.

She signed for her trunks, not even bothering to look inside them after they stored them in the workroom and asked, "Can you transport another crate for me?"

XIII

She set to work as soon as the jewelry crate was delivered to the theater that afternoon. When fully extended, the butterfly wings took up the entire sewing table. She had repurposed them from a beautiful blue skirt with a dye pattern that looked almost like a watercolor painting with black piping along the edges. Adding more black piping to define the veins of the wings, even she was impressed with the final product. But mere flowers weren't going to pull the wings together. No, what she needed was *transformation*.

Barely noticing as Amelie called the actors to the stage, Mae took inventory of Petyr's jewelry supplies. She quickly realized she would need some tools and headed to the scene shop to ask Charlie.

The scenic artist smirked as they loaded up Mae with

everything she needed—Mae was regularly borrowing tools from their shop, but as long as she returned everything, Charlie didn't seem to mind.

It was intermission by the time she set metal to fabric. By some luck, the black piping she had used was just the right size for the copper wire to snake through, giving the wings more structure. But she used it sparingly because she didn't want *too* much structure.

Eventually, the actors filtered back downstairs after the play was over amid applause, and Mae took a step back to admire her work.

"Beautiful," said a voice from the doorway. Mae turned to see Des hovering on the threshold.

"And that's not all," she said with a grin. "I got the metal pieces from my shop—my cousin was a jeweler. I don't know if I ever told you that."

"I see," Des said, moving next to her to admire the wings.

Her heart raced; she hadn't been this close to him since that morning on the catwalk. Afraid she was going to blurt something out about extending her contract or say something even more embarrassing, she abruptly said, "They recovered my coin purse. And my trunks have been delivered."

He stepped back, and she thought she saw his gray eyes darken, though his hair had swung in front of his face a little. "Good news."

"Indeed," she said.

He paused for a moment, then cleared his throat. "Well, I expect this will be done by Saturday morning?"

She swallowed...hard. "Yes," she said, through gritted teeth, "and I've got flowers coming for the staircase tomorrow, so we'll have the day to assemble them."

"Good. The Saturday crowd for the play should be big, no matter how the festival goes."

Nodding, she clasped her fingers together painfully.

"I daresay you must be itching to get your shop up and running, though, Mae." His smile looked forced from the way his cheeks had sunken in. "Now that you have everything you need."

"I—" A lump had formed in her throat.

A baby's wail interrupted them, and Georgie's mother bustled down the hallway to the dressing rooms with little Isaac in her arms. Des turned and headed out of the room, leaving Mae alone, still staring down at the blue butterfly wings.

Why hadn't she said something? Des wanted her out of the theater—she was supposed to be starting her new life now, wasn't she? She paced around the room, irritating Bobbin, who kept lifting his head every time she walked by the office door. The shop or the theater? Des or her dream? Did Des even *want* her here?

Madam Rosnah bustled into the costume shop, and Mae burst into tears. After enveloping Mae in a perfumed hug,

Madam Rosnah retreated and brought back a bottle of sherry. They ensconced themselves in Mae's office with the door closed. Mae chuckled weakly as Madam Rosnah poured the sherry into two mugs from the kitchen. Most of the other actors had gone now, and the place was quiet.

"What is it, my dear?" Madam Rosnah asked. "Has something happened?"

"N-not really, no. I just…I just don't know what to do," she said in a near whisper. Her chest heaved with the pressure of holding in the sobs she knew wanted to escape in force, but she wouldn't let them.

Madam Rosnah patted her knee. They both sat on the cot; Bobbin had retreated under the desk as soon as the two women had intruded on his cozy abode.

Mae sipped her sherry and cried in silence, the actress occasionally patting her back. Mae found it reassuring, particularly because she didn't have to explain herself. Because she *couldn't* explain herself.

Since landing in Soldark, she had been beset with bad luck. And the only place she had found comfort was the Proserpina. She had carved out her own niche here, using her sewing skills in ways she'd never imagined. The Proserpina had changed her. She had found beauty in the work, found family in the cast and crew. And it was all because of Des.

His protectiveness, rescuing her from the alley. His kindness, offering her the job and clothing. His serious demeanor was endearing, yet she longed to discover his true feelings. He had opened up to her once, but now seemed to be shutting her out.

In his haste to ensure Mae followed her dreams, he failed to see that maybe what she wanted had changed—*she* had changed.

Did she want to go back to the life she had originally planned? Should she try to fit herself into her neat little shop with her neat little plans? Alone? She wasn't sure she could.

Lady Comay's final monologue entered her mind then. She had heard it over a dozen times at this point. *If I must transform myself in order to live this life, it will be on mine own terms! This life is mine and mine own!*

Mae hiccupped and straightened up, her tears dried. Madam Rosnah looked at her sadly, but she didn't pry. The fact was, Mae had transformed whether she had intended to or not. And she would live on her own terms.

The flowers arrived in a cascade of magnolias, violets, and ranunculus of all colors, bursting out of simple woven baskets. The flower girl, who introduced herself as Marigold, stared in awe from the door of the scene shop where she made the delivery—in what must have taken several trips, since she was alone and on foot. The staircase had been moved closer to the massive barn doors that opened out onto the street.

After Madam Rosnah had wished her goodnight the previous evening, Mae had set colored chalk to paper and finally drawn how she wanted the flowers on the staircase, reserving two dozen white and pink ranunculus for the dress. The rest would go to the staircase.

"Good luck," Marigold called after Mae had signed the receipt.

"Don't let the actors hear you saying that," Mae said with a slight wince. She had made that mistake once, and after a brief scolding from Madam Rosnah, hadn't done it again.

"Oh, right," Marigold said with a chuckle. "Break a leg? I can't wait to see it tomorrow!"

Mae looked up to the top of the barren staircase. "Me too."

She got to work right away, and was soon joined by Madam Rosnah, who had volunteered to help. "I don't have an eye for it, but if you tell me where to put them, I'll put them."

Mae had hoped to see Des darkening the doorway of the scene shop, but by midday, only Charlie and Amelie had joined them.

Not only did the flowers have to be put in the right spots, but they had to be attached securely enough that the wheeled contraption bumping along the cobblestone streets wouldn't shake them off the minute they rolled it outside. Charlie had supplied spools of thin gold-colored wire for the job, which matched the details at the bottom of the stairs and was soft enough not to damage the flower stems. Since there was still a show that night, Amelie was the first to leave, her duties requiring her presence long before curtain call.

"This is great," Mae said to the others. She surveyed the gold entwined flowers of white, yellow, and varying shades of pink covering the top of the stairs and growing more sparse towards the bottom until only a single pink ranunculus resided on the bottom-most black step.

They all dispersed, heading for their various stations for the top of the show. Madam Rosnah walked with Mae as far as the costume shop. The actress gave her hand a squeeze and said, "It's wonderful, my dear. We shall win every category."

Mae burst into a fit of laughter. "Even the food one?"

Madam Rosnah's eyes widened in her usual demeanor, "Of course, my dear. Flowers are edible, are they not?"

Shaking her head, Mae faced her final project: the wings.

Tuning out the bustle of the actors was second nature to her by now, and she only lifted her head from her work when Robyn came in with an apologetic look, holding up a satyr shoe.

She gave him a motherly look of exasperation, set down her pliers, and took the shoes from him. "How long until you need to go back on?" she asked while examining the shoe.

"It's the next scene," he said. "I'm sorry, I don't know how it happened!"

"Oh, it's nothing," Mae said, striding over to her large cabinet and taking out the glue. "It's only the strip of leather coming loose. The shoe wasn't wobbling, right?" She gave the heel a good jerk, but it seemed intact.

Robyn watched eagerly as she applied the glue and pressed the leather back in place.

"Just try not to catch it on anything. The glue might still be fragile!" she called after him as he darted down the hallway a moment later. She had dealt with plenty of last-minute repairs between scenes over the play's run. She got back to work on the festival costume until she was interrupted once more.

The butterfly wings were almost done, and the magnets, the gold gears, and most of the decorative pieces were in place. She was positioning a few more metal plates when Amelie rushed into the room holding a ragged blanket.

Or...what *looked like* a ragged blanket. "It got caught in a fly line," Amelie gushed, waving the remains of the white tulle wings at her.

Mae's jaw dropped as she reached for them. The fabric was ripped, the wire completely bent out of shape, and oil from the fly gears had marred the entire thing.

Heart racing, Mae looked around the shop. "How much time?" she asked.

"Intermission's just started. I went backstage to double-check the fly lines for act two, when I saw this up on the catwalk."

Des bolted into the room, and his gaze landed on the mangled remains. For the first time since their curt parting yesterday, Mae met his eyes. He looked at her with such intensity, she lost her breath for a second. And just like that, she knew what to do.

"Well, good thing we have another pair of wings right here."

The room was silent for a moment.

"A-Are you sure?" Amelie asked, gazing at the beautiful blue wings in wonder. "They could get caught in another fly line—they're much bigger, and we won't have tested it."

Des's cool mask of professionalism slid into place, but his eyes still retained their intensity. She knew how much rode on these wings for him. A chance to pursue his dreams without worry. A chance for art to be art—and not reliant upon getting the right number of ticket-buyers in seats. A chance for him to create beauty for people to enjoy, even if it was only for a few hours.

But they meant even more to her. They were her way of repaying his kindness. Her way of transforming someone *else's* life for the better. Mostly, they were a thank you...and a whisper of something more.

And she would make sure they remained that way.

XIV

Up on the catwalk, Mae held her breath as she and Daniels, the stagehand who normally ran the wing line, crouched above center stage—right over where Georgie had just begun her monologue.

Mae clutched the wings tightly around the black and gold piping up top, the safest place to touch them. She was glad she had sewn magnets into the butterfly wings earlier—though they were for a different purpose—and she only had just enough time to rig a new bar from which to hold the big wings for lowering.

Daniels, when they quickly brought him in on the plan down in the costume shop, had hastened up to remove the gear box which normally ran the wing line. The gear box now lay on the floor of the catwalk between them, the line retracted inside of it, the new magnet bar ready and waiting for the wings.

"Must I reject my very inner being, just to fortify your own?" Georgie's words floated up from the stage.

Mae lifted the wings over the railing of the catwalk, and Daniels fed the magnet bar through the rails. *Snap.* The wings were attached. Mae's heart thought of leaping out of her chest as she let go, relying entirely on the magnets now. It held, hovering just under the catwalk platform.

"Gods!" Georgie exclaimed. "If I must transform myself in order to live this life, it will be on mine own terms! This life is mine and mine own!" Something leapt in Mae's chest.

Daniels reached for the crank on the gearbox, and Mae shifted closer to him, reaching out to hold the gear box steady as he turned it. Smoothly, slowly, the blue and gold wings lowered. Mae wanted to close her eyes lest she see them fall, but she couldn't look away.

The audience gasped in wonder. Whispers flitted through the theater like an awestruck breeze. Georgie, to her credit, didn't falter or show surprise of any kind. The wings clipped on, and she completed her scene, though perhaps her movements were a little more careful than normal.

Her final speech sent chills up and down Mae's back at the profoundness of it all.

She and Daniels remained crouched on the catwalk until after the curtain fell, not wanting to risk disturbing the performance once their job had been completed. Daniels clutched his heart in wonder as the crowd cheered, and he let her descend the ladder first, which she was only glad to do.

Just as Mae reached the bottom of the ladder, someone grabbed her arm and pulled her toward the stage. It was Des. Her lips parted, and she only had a second to register his hand on her arm before she was standing center stage, the entire crowd and cast applauding, looking at *her*.

Georgie, grinning from ear to ear, came over and took her other hand. Together, she and Des raised her hands high in the air, and they bowed as one. Under the bright lights, the butterfly wings were glorious, with hints of metal glinting every time Georgie moved.

When Des finally tugged her arm toward stage right, she was only too glad to follow him. She grinned and somehow found herself close against him in the dark.

"I've half a mind to never let you leave the Proserpina," he said, a rare smirk tugging up the corner of his mouth. She fixed him with a look, only able to see half his face in the light reflecting off the stage. Equal measures of hope and fear surged in her chest.

The patrons were exiting, the actors descending to their dressing rooms, and there was movement and chaos everywhere, except in this little corner of closeness.

"Why don't you?" she breathed back.

He pulled away, his hands on her shoulders, and his hair

falling into his face. "I can't—your shop." He shook his head. "I can't do that to you. That shop is the reason you're here. It's everything you've worked for—"

"I can do both. There's no reason I can't do both. I can open the shop and run it in the mornings when there's no rehearsal, and I can be here for shows and repairs. I can live in both worlds." This realization hadn't actually crystalized until this very moment.

His hands slipped, sliding down closer to her elbows. His head dipped, throwing his eyes into shadow. "I...that's..."

And without worrying about anything in the world, she reached a hand up to raise his chin so that she could see his eyes.

That seemed to change something in him. "I didn't want you to go."

The words rumbled right through her, to her very bones, amid the chatter of the far-off crowd, the lights buzzing above them, and the hot darkness backstage. Still gripping his chin, she pushed herself up on her toes and brought her lips gently to his. "I didn't want to go."

XV

The smell of tea drew Mae to the kitchen before dawn. Awoken by nerves, she had rushed to the sewing table to check the wings once more, but nothing had happened to them since she had closed her eyes last night. Bobbin followed at her heels, just as eager for breakfast as she was. Mae couldn't wait to tell Madam Rosnah that she was becoming a permanent fixture at the Proserpina.

Only it wasn't the vivacious actress standing at the kettle. It was Des.

Her stomach fluttered at the sight of him, and she remembered that moment of warmth backstage as she gazed into his eyes. He merely lifted the teapot in a question, and she nodded in answer, hiding a smirk.

"Nerves," he said, as an explanation for his early rising.

"And yet on the show's opening day, you slept as late as you usually do," she replied.

He cut her a look out of the corner of his eyes. "This is different."

"Indeed."

She had never had a more enjoyable breakfast, though it was mostly spent in companionable silence while exchanging stolen glances.

An hour later, the float stood ready by the open scene shop door, an argument taking place in front of it.

"I won't do it," Georgie said.

Mae held out the wings. "Take them. Turn around. We have to put them on now or we'll miss the parade entirely!" Her gaze darted to the large brass clock on the wall. "Help me," she pleaded to Des and Madam Rosnah.

Des surveyed her and crossed his arms over his chest with an annoying smile on his face. If she didn't know better, Georgie's insisting on *Mae* wearing the wings had been with his blessing.

"Georgie!" Mae hissed. "I'm not wearing them!"

The actress crossed her arms too. "You deserve this, Mae. As recognition for your beautiful work! And that save last night at the eleventh hour! You deserve a *medal* for sun's sake! The least I can do is step aside and let you wear the wings."

Mae pinched the bridge of her nose. "But Georgie, I want *you* to wear them. I've never wanted to be on stage, in the lights. I'm not the one who wears the expensive dresses, the confections I make out of tulle. Believe me, the joy I felt watching the audience applaud you all last night—and every other night for that matter—meant more because I had *caused* it. Because I had brought that joy. I don't need to be in the spotlight. *You* are the spring queen."

Des finally rescued her. "I think that's reason enough, Georgie. Put on the wings now."

Georgie frowned. "If you're sure."

"I'm sure," Mae said. "Besides, I want to see the wings in action, and I can't do that if I'm wearing them. You know what to do?"

Georgie turned her back to allow Mae to adhere the wings on with a clip of magnets. "I do."

"Then let's show them our queen of spring rising from the depths of winter," Mae said.

All the actors assembled in Coppersdown Square where the floats were to pass by the judging stand. Robyn had volunteered to walk with the float in case Charlie needed any help with the half-auto half-train car contraption driving the staircase.

A huge grin lit up Mae's face as she saw the Proserpina's entry coming down the street. The crowd gasped at the sight of the staircase—an actual staircase!—rolling down the street toward them. The bottom of the steps was at the front, where

Georgie now stood, waving at the crowd. Upon seeing the judge's table, the actress turned around and started walking up the steps. The wings hung limply at her back, though they fluttered a beautiful blue and gold in the light breeze.

Mae shared a look of glee with Des. Madam Rosnah, who had donned a large red hat with a swath of white tulle and bird figures on it, clutched Mae's arm with her bony fingers.

Upon reaching the flowery top of the steps, Georgie stopped and half turned to look at the square. The wings still facing the judge's table, Georgie subtly reached up to pull on the wire that Mae had rigged at the bottom of the wings.

Through a series of wires and magnets, the wings snapped open, revealing their full beauty. They transformed from limp and fluttering to a display of watercolor blues lined in black, glinting with gold and gears in the morning light. Perhaps Mae had a knack for the type of jewelry her cousin had made after all.

Cheers circulated through the crowd, filling Mae with that same euphoria she felt last night. *She* had done this. This was her work, creating all this beauty. And she had shared it with hundreds of people.

But there was only one person whose opinion she really cared about at that moment. She glanced up at Des, who gave her a rare grin, and said, "Beautiful." His gaze didn't leave her face.

Her cheeks warmed, and it was she who looked away first,

her cheeks reddening at the attention.

They watched the rest of the floats with mounting anticipation. Madam Rosnah kept up a running commentary of criticism of each float that passed—"How did Lawson's get into the festival? What does MacElhenry think a golden cow has to do with spring? Pshaw! No one wants to think of tannery when they think of spring!"

Mae, on the other hand, was completely content. Many of the other floats were beautiful, but deep down, she knew the Proserpina's was the most beautiful. She just hoped the judges thought that way too.

By noon, the floats had finished parading by the judge's table, and Mae had wandered over to a food stand to work off her nerves. She bypassed the pastries—she'd had quite her fill over the past month—and bought a pack of tea sandwiches and some coffee for her and Des. Madam Rosnah had found Robyn, and the two of them were regaling Robyn's boyfriend with the tale of what happened with the wings last night.

Georgie finally joined them, the floats long gone. The butterfly wings were limp once more, and Georgie's curly hair was a little tousled from the flower crown she wore. A nervous energy pervaded the crowd—or was it just those surrounding Mae? She glanced at Des out of the corner of her eye and did something she never would have believed herself capable of— she reached out and slipped her fingers into his hand. She saw his chest rise and fall, and he squeezed her hand back. Mae could barely hear the announcer. Every last bit of energy had suddenly focused itself on her hand.

The crowd roared, and Georgie was shouting. Next thing she knew, Des was dragging her up to the judge's stand, Georgie ahead of them. In a blur, she tried to focus on the judges. "… awarded for two categories. Costume, by designer Mae Wright, and Float—also by Mae Wright—of the Proserpina Theater!"

Two? She tried to control her face—she was in front of hundreds of people. For sun's sake! How did actors do this? She nodded, she shook hands, she watched as Georgie pulled the wire and spread the wings once again to the frantic applause of the audience.

Des pushed her forward, and the judges presented her with two thick pieces of paper—the award money. With shaking fingers, she accepted them, clutching the papers as hard as she could so as not to drop them. The relief she experienced when Des led her off the platform and into the shade of the nearest newsstand was palpable. She focused on the one thing she could, and immediately handed Des the checks, not wanting to lose them in all the fervor. He shook his head, and handed one back.

"I believe you're going to need this if you want your own Thomas' sewing machine. I'm afraid I can't allow you to sew on sub-par machines even in your own shop—if you're to represent the Proserpina in public."

Her chest swelled as she took it, folded it, and slipped it securely in her bodice. Georgie and the others were off celebrating, and it was just the two of them in the shadow of the newsstand.

"Well," Des said, holding out his arm. "Would you like to spend an afternoon outside of the dim and dusty theater for once and join me in the sun for a picnic by the river?"

Her eyelids fluttered in surprise, and she took his arm. "A picnic?"

"It's the first official day of spring," he said simply. "I *do* get outside sometimes. And I believe we have much to celebrate before you begin your new double-life."

"I would love to."

THE END

THE
MECHANICAL
MASQUERADE

VERITY PENNINGTON

I

When the chimes of a dozen clocks began tolling four o'clock, Verity Pennington threw down her dusting cloth and untied her apron, tossing it onto the shop counter.

Her father waved from his workbench as she left the shop amid the clamor of the chiming clocks, all of which were perfectly tuned to the correct time—the trademark precision of a Pennington clock.

Out on the busy downtown streets of Soldark, Verity wasn't the only person headed toward Silverton Circle, the wealthiest neighborhood in the city. Her particular destination was the Speare estate. When she arrived ten minutes later, sweating slightly from her haste and the afternoon sun, a small crowd had already gathered there, peering at a small flyer pinned to the closed gate. Even though she wasn't close enough to read it yet, Verity admired the beauty of the calligraphy from a distance.

In the warm summer air, she waited, poking her head around the people in front of her, balancing on her tiptoes. She wasn't very tall, so she could only catch glimpses of the flyer from between people as they all jostled forward to read it.

Of course, they had posted the flyer hours ago, but Verity's father didn't care so much what the theme of the Speares' annual Midsummer Masquerade was, and she'd had to wait until she had finished working for the day.

Finally, with a small amount of gentle pushing—encouraging hands, really—she made it to the front, where she happened to bump shoulders with a wide-eyed girl with short brassy hair, her best friend, Marigold Quince.

They grinned at each other, Marigold's summer freckles stretching over her flat nose.

"Your father didn't let you out early?" Marigold teased, her eyes hungrily reading the announcement.

"You know it," Verity said, quickly skimming the words done in beautiful calligraphy. *"Forbidden garden?"* she whispered in awe.

Marigold nodded eagerly. "I heard a rumor at the flower shop this afternoon," she said, "but I couldn't know until I saw it for myself, and of course, Mother wouldn't let me out early either."

"About time they picked the theme," a woman behind them said, fanning herself with a rust-red lace fan. "I'll need to see my dressmaker right away," she announced seemingly to herself, but really to everyone who could hear.

"Do you think the Fawney Fair will have anything?" one girl shrilled, eyes wide in panic.

"Not if we don't get there tonight!" her companion answered as they bustled off, clutching each other's arms and squealing in excitement.

"I hear there's a sculptor from Helenia attending," the boy next to Marigold said, his face shining with sweat in the summer sun, a smudge of charcoal on his nose.

"That's nothing," a girl piped up, a newsie cap perched jauntily on her head as she jotted in a notebook, "Lady Tania has booked the top violinists from the Symphony Guild..."

Verity and Marigold shifted aside so others could see and found a clear spot in the shade of an old oak tree which stood on the Speare grounds behind the iron fence. The effect of the cool shade was almost immediate.

Marigold put both hands on the fence and peered inside the lush green grounds with a sigh. "Three more days." She gasped. "Three more days!"

"I know," Verity said, grinning. "Do you think your mask will be ready in time?"

"It'll have to be," Marigold said. "I've been working on it when the flower shop's not busy. And it already fits the

forbidden garden look, so that's lucky, but maybe it needs some baby's breath…" She began to rattle off the various flowers she had already used, complete with the special varnish that preserved the flowers, some of which she had painted gold.

Verity's mind drifted to her desk drawer where her mother's old mask sat, half of the jewels missing and the gold trim coming off in places. She bit her lip, gazing onto the Speare grounds without trying to look too nosy. In three days, they would walk through those gates. Perhaps they would stop at the marble fountain, the cherub and fawn spouting water into the serene pool; perhaps they would throw a copper in and make a wish. They would walk across the perfectly manicured lawns, the warm summer night air bathing their skin, fireflies hovering in the gardens like strung lights. And they would walk into the mansion just like everyone else.

And maybe, just maybe, Verity would find what she was looking for.

Her stomach sank as she thought back to the contents of her desk drawer. "I don't know if I'll get in," she confessed.

Marigold made a scandalized noise and grabbed Verity's arm. "What? Why not?" she demanded.

"I haven't had any time to work on my mask. It's barely functional, let alone going to fit the theme. You saw what the flyer said."

Any and all wishing to attend must don the masque of the

forbidden garden, or risk being forbidden from the garden.

"I'm sure you can get it ready in time. This is the best chance we've *ever* had at getting in," Marigold said, her eyes bright.

"True," Verity agreed. "They always have the oddest stipulations." *Meant for keeping out the riffraff,* she thought, gazing at the mansion behind the iron fence, and averting her eyes from her friend. "I was kind of hoping the theme would be busy clockmaker's daughters, you know, something easy..."

Marigold snorted. "Why don't you ask your father to help you spruce it up?"

"If *I've* been busy, do you think he's been sitting around playing dress up with me?" Verity shook her head. "No, but I'll ask my mother. It was her mother's mask, anyway. I'm sure she'll give me a hand. None of her clients have babies due soon. And she just finished painting the interior of the oak grandfather clock for Mr. Grandville, so maybe she'll have time..."

"Never enough *time,*" Marigold giggled. "And you'd think your family would have an abundance." Her gaze slyly slid to Verity, who gave her a perfunctory chuckle.

"Good one," Verity deadpanned, and Marigold gave her a mock bow.

Somewhere close by, they heard a clock strike the half hour, and Marigold jolted away from the fence as if shocked. "I better get home. Make sure you ask your mother to help you with the mask—we *have to* get in this year." She paused, then took a step toward Verity. "I mean it. It's my last chance."

"Wait, what? What are you talking about?"

Marigold looked down at the pristine cobblestones, huffed, and said, "We're moving. Leaving Soldark in a few weeks. We'll still be in the Galderon Republic, just... not here. I didn't–I didn't want to tell you. Now it feels like it's really happening."

Verity's mouth popped open. "What?" she demanded, eyes suddenly stinging. "What about the flower shop? What about you? What about—" She had been about to say *me*, but realized just in time that even though she had known Marigold all her life, she was just another cog in the works of Marigold's life. And a minor cog compared to Marigold's entire family.

"Well, maybe we'll open up another shop in Corbright. That's what Mother wants to do anyway—she says Corbright is perfect for it, mountains of lavender and fields and fields of sunlilies. She grew up there, you know—that's why we're moving there, to be with her family."

"Oh," Verity managed to say, trying and failing to imagine her life without her closest friend. No more trips to the Coppersdown holiday market together; no more racing each other after work to find the best coffee cart in town; no more listening to Marigold chatter about different varieties of the same flowers or gossiping about the events the flower shop catered to. No more Marigold.

Marigold looked at her with a mix of anticipation and apology, her mouth slightly open.

"Sunlilies, you say?" Verity said eventually.

Her friend nodded, a small smile forming. "Fields of them. They get more sun than Soldark I hear, so—"

"Is that even possible?" Verity scoffed, making an attempt at her usual ribbing.

Marigold shrugged. "Well, it's still in the solarbelt. If they have the variegated sunlilies, I hear those are really only grown in the sunniest climates, and we don't have them here, so—"

"Fine," Verity said with a genuine grin. "You'll have to send me drawings of them in the post. Or pressings."

"Of course," Marigold said, then glanced over her shoulder. "I better get home. We're supposed to be packing, otherwise, I'd offer to help with your mask, though I know nothing about gold and gems. Just petals and stems." She paused, eyeing Verity.

"Clever," Verity snorted, then laughed despite the bad rhyme.

"You *will* ask your mother, right?"

"I will," Verity said firmly. "We'll get through those gates, I promise."

Marigold threw her arms around her, and Verity was overwhelmed with the scent of a thousand flowers; her nose twitched as she repressed a sneeze.

"See you tomorrow for coffee?" Verity asked as she pulled

155

away.

"Wouldn't miss it," Marigold said. "Wait! Maybe if my parents will give me a break from packing tomorrow, we could check at the Fawney Fair for something to complete your mask?"

Verity bit the inside of her lip. "Maybe," she hedged, not wanting to voice her fears that every bit of clothing, jewelry, or accessory would be bought up tonight—the first night of the fair. "Yeah, maybe," she said in a falsely bright voice.

"I better go," Marigold said. "Tomorrow then!" She waved as she skipped down the street, her taupe dress fluttering in her wake, the scent of a dozen flower fields flowing behind her.

Feeling as if she were missing some vital part of herself— an arm, or her clothes or something—Verity patted her pockets and touched her hair, the black strands wrangled into a braid that only went to the nape of her neck. She heaved a sigh and stared at the Speare grounds until the next chiming of the clock jolted her out of her reverie. Four weeks and Marigold would be gone. They had known each other since they were babies, more than seventeen years now. Verity's mother had helped deliver all the Quince children, including Marigold. What would Verity do without her?

After skirting around the crowd still flowing to and from the flyer at the Speare gates, Verity glanced up at the sun, still visible over the houses and buildings. She took one last glance at the Speare grounds, vowing that she would walk through those gates in three days' time, for Marigold's sake, if anything.

But the other thing she wanted to see behind those gates might not be as simple to contrive as a gold and wire mask.

II

Though she wanted to curl up on her settee and read long into the night, Verity went straight to find her mother in the sitting room when she got home. However, the sitting room where her mother always had her afternoon tea was empty. As Verity checked the empty clock shop, she heard a muffled crash from the attic. She rushed through the cramped but tidy house, darting around a side table holding a brass dragon figure—which held a clock in its mouth—on her way to the stairs.

"Mother?" she called, and just as she reached the landing, floorboards creaking underfoot, a pair of sensible leather shoes poked out from the hatch leading to the attic.

"Oh, there you are darling," her mother called. "Can you—" One of her shoes slipped off, and Verity rushed to return it to its rightful place.

"Thanks," her mother said, finding the ladder with both feet. When she finally stood firmly on the landing, she removed a small fabric-covered box from where she held it between her teeth and opened it up to show Verity.

A beautiful brooch in the shape of the end of a peacock feather sat in the box, emeralds twinkling in the sunlight filtering in through the upstairs windows. "It's beautiful," Verity said, reaching out to touch it, then pulling her hand back. "What's it for? What was it doing up there?"

"It was your grandmother's, and it's for you. I heard about the Midsummer ball when Hermia came to drop off a book just now, and it made me think of this."

"Oh," Verity fiddled with a fistful of her skirt, unsurprised that their neighbor had already found out about the ball theme. "I meant to ask you about that. Can you help me with the mask? I need to make it fit the theme, otherwise they won't let me in." She couldn't help the pleading note in her voice. The plea reminded her of *why* she needed to get in with Marigold, and her eyes stung with tears she wouldn't let out.

Her mother pushed the box into her hands with a sly grin. "Well, of course. That's what this is for."

"But I need—well, I don't really know what I need," Verity began. "You're the artistic one."

Chuckling, her mother said, "Well, here's a start." She pulled a pair of delicate pliers out of the apron she always wore

during the day—either working in the house or helping paint and varnish in the shop—and plucked the box out of Verity's hand. Before Verity realized what her mother was doing, she had removed the biggest emerald from the brooch.

"But—"

Her mother held up the emerald in the narrow beam of light slanting through the upstairs hallway. "Your grandmother wouldn't mind. She hated this brooch. And she loved you." She put a brief hand on Verity's cheek.

Verity's eyes pricked again, but she focused on the emerald shining in the sunlight. "It's perfect. And maybe...maybe the little ones could fill in where the other gems came out?"

"I'm sure they can," her mother agreed. "Let's take this to the workshop, shall we? The lighting's better there. Go get the mask."

Inexpressible relief flooded through her as she rushed through the house and finally emerged into the workshop a minute later, the unfinished mask in both hands like a gutted golden fish. A smile rose to her lips as she spotted her mother sitting at Father's workbench, the sun setting through the big window beside it. Her mother had turned on the electric lamp over the workbench and was already removing the small gemstones, emeralds, and amethysts littering the clean workspace.

"What are the blue ones?" Verity asked as she wandered over, watching her mother work.

"Sapphires. There. That should be enough, shouldn't it?"

Verity placed the mask on the brightly lit workbench and counted the cavities where gems needed to go. "Yes, that'll do—"

Urgent knocking at the front door caused them both to whirl around.

"I'll get it," her mother said. "I didn't think we had any...but maybe someone's early..." she muttered on her way to the door.

Verity touched the loose stones gently, hearing frantic words at the front door which drowned out the gentle ticking of the clocks all around her. Her stomach sank. Her mother was being called away on midwife duties. She knew it. The familiar cadence of the person's pleas at the door had all the markers of one such visit.

A few minutes later, her mother bustled back into the room, tying on her midwife's apron now. "I have to—"

"I know," Verity said with a sad smile.

"Mrs. Laudry's baby's come early," her mother said with a frown. "And she's having a time of it. I need to get over there."

"Of course," Verity said, pushing the mask away from the edge of the workbench where she had left it. "Do you need help? Do you want me to come?"

Her mother shook her head, patting her pockets absentmindedly. "No, no. I'll send for Audrie. I know attending births isn't your favorite." No, it wasn't her

favorite; she had attended one—out of curiosity—and it had been her last.

Verity went over and gave her mother a hug, pinning her arms with her hands still in her pockets. "Good luck. *Somebody* needs to help bring babies into the world. And I'm glad it's you. You're wonderful at it."

A kiss on her forehead made Verity let go. She waved as her mother left, hastening behind little Kerry Laudry who had come to fetch her, hands wringing, brow furrowed. The door slammed, leaving Verity with only the sound of ticking clocks to keep her company.

Wondering where her father had gone, she turned toward the workbench and sighed, a few light steps bringing her toward the half-finished mask. The gems her mother had pried from the brooch now sat in a small brass dish her father used for keeping fine clock parts from getting lost while he was in the middle of a project. The gems glittered green and purple and blue in the light from the overhead lamp and the dying sunlight, and she couldn't wait to put them on her mask. She pulled out a pair of long tweezers, wire cutters, and a spool of gold wire and got to work.

Set the gem, twist the wire, then *snip* and twist some more. *Hidden garden*. The colors were perfect.

She had never seen her grandmother wear this brooch, but the golden mask had been worn to dozens of Midsummer balls by both her mother and grandmother, back when it was easier to get in. Now, with Lady Tania running the show, every year was more and more tricky to enter. One year, the theme had been exotic animals. And if you didn't bring one that matched your attire, you didn't get in. It was all over the papers when a solas fox got loose and ripped a woman's gown.

"I still can't believe they waited this long for the theme," she muttered, squinting in the electric light spilling from the lamp overhead. She placed an enormous emerald in the center of the mask and set to work securing it.

She had no eye for design, but the cogs and gears, the nuts and bolts and wires, were as easy as breathing, and she had filled all the open cavities with gemstones in no time. Her father was still out, and she wondered if he was making a clock delivery. She knew she might not see her mother for quite some time; she had once attended a birth that had lasted for three days.

She held the mask up to admire her work.

The gems twinkled in the light, casting emerald and sapphire reflections on the workshop walls. They were beautiful.

But they wouldn't be enough. Verity had seen plenty of getups from Midsummer balls in years past, and with her shimmery gold hand-me-down dress—from one of Marigold's sisters no less—she knew her mask would need to be better than this to gain entry. Even this close to the ball, many other patrons were rich enough to pay for custom masks from the silver and goldsmiths. It would be stiff competition for a clockmaker's daughter with a hand-me-down mask to boot.

Verity didn't doubt for a second the quality of Marigold's mask—she was a genius when it came to floral arrangements—and she had been working on it for weeks.

But she knew Marigold. If Verity couldn't get in, Marigold wouldn't go either.

They had to get in. No matter what. She knew little about Corbright, but she knew it was at the other end of the solarbelt, and it would likely be a long time before she ever saw Marigold again, unless Verity somehow got enough money for a ride on an airship.

They had to get in.

A snatch of singing outside caused her to snap her head up to look out the window, where a few electric lamps buzzed in their ornate black casings on the posts that lined Spindle Street. Grandville Electric had recently replaced all the gas lamps on their street; their steam plants powered almost the whole city. Verity was still getting used to the steady, yellow light pooling in spheres around the lamps.

A group of boys was heading north down the cobblestones, and Verity thought she saw the twinkling lights of Peaseblossom Park just around the corner. Deciding, she nodded once and flipped the big brass switch to turn off the electric lamp over the workbench, throwing the workshop into the semi-darkness of twilight. The lights down the street seemed to grow brighter, and she carefully wrapped the mask in a piece of cloth and tucked it into a small leather bag hanging from a post by her father's desk.

If her mother couldn't help her anymore, and her father wasn't here, she would just have to go to the fair by herself. She felt a little guilty going without Marigold, but she was more likely to find something on the first night of the fair than the second, and she had a few extra coppers from her shop wages. She hitched the bag on her shoulder and headed out into the street, carefully locking the shop door behind her with a big brass key.

Her stomach tingled with nerves the closer she got to the fair. What if *he* was there?

Just the thought of the artist she had seen at last year's fair made her face flush with heat. Of course, in honor of last year's masquerade, he had worn a mask the entire time he had presented his beautiful clockwork tree, complete with leaves that swayed in a false wind, but it was the beauty of his invention that had drawn her in. And the sound of his voice behind his black and gold butterfly mask had been like honey, just as golden as his eyes.

She was sure he would be at the Midsummer ball this year. He had been invited last year; all the upcoming artists were. The Speare family loved to showcase other people's creations, judging them much like they judged the people who entered their mansion. But in the artists' case, there was a glorious prize: a year of paid sponsorship from the Speares. A full year of being paid to create their own art. An invaluable prize for many. Surely the artist she had met would merit such a prize with his nearly magical clockwork tree.

And if Verity was determined to get into the ball this year, well, who knew when she would get another chance to meet him?

The idea that he might be at the fair again was what made her stomach start doing flips the moment she stepped into Peaseblossom Park. She knew nothing about him, his name, whether he was in the artist's union, or anything. She had tried to find out who he was, casually asking at the newscart, or attending some of the artist's showcases during the year—the ones that didn't charge entry fees, anyway. But an entire year had gone by with no sight or whisper of him.

Suddenly, she was glad she was going to the fair alone. She hadn't even told Marigold about him or the night she had met his eyes under his simple butterfly mask last year as he spoke of the beauty of nature and clockwork. She was sure he had been looking right at her, pinning her to the spot as he spoke, causing her heart to surge from her chest.

Would he remember her?

"Now's my chance to find out," she muttered, holding her head up high to look at all the booths lined up across the park.

Once a year, the Fawney Fair transformed the park into a twinkling bazaar, complete with electric string lights that were

looped around the lampposts and across the park like a net of glowing stars. The smell of food assailed her, and she couldn't tell whether it was the baker's tent with buttery crescents or the newscart parked on the corner with cinnamon scones that tempted her more. She shook her head. *No, I should look for something for my mask, not beautiful artists or delicious food.*

Though her mouth was watering for the latter, she began to wander around the park, glancing into vendor's stalls. The ones that were most crowded seemed like the right places to look—except one peek into the jeweler's tent she passed and the price cards posted there made her balk. She backed away and continued on.

The vendors must have raised their prices when they heard the news, she thought, mentally counting the coppers clinking in her deep skirt pocket. The jeweled mask in the bag bounced gently against her thigh, but instead of the light feeling of carefully-tooled gold, it now felt like a heavy weight she couldn't get rid of. As she studied the other tents—carpenters with carved figurines, a cheesemonger from Densine offering samples on toothpicks, a rival flower shop of the Quince's— she cursed the Speares for waiting so long to announce the ball's theme.

And she cursed herself for waiting so long. She should have just repaired the mask a month ago when her mother had dug the relic out of the attic. Or she could have bought another simpler mask. The prices weren't so bad then. But with her work in the shop and helping upkeep the house, she had assumed she could wait until the theme was announced and still have time.

Time.

Marigold's earlier jest gained new relevance and Verity let it sting like a pinched nerve.

Fairgoers who weren't intent on gaining entry to the ball—or who were already set with their garments and accessories—passed by, some enjoying odd-looking ice in a paper cone Verity had never seen before. Just as she was admiring one such orange and white confection, she ran smack dab into someone.

"Father?" she said in disbelief, pulling away and recognizing him, just as tall as her—not very—his mustache oiled and his hair oddly ruffled. He also had a wild look in his eyes that she rarely saw.

"Verity!" he said in relief, running his hands down the leather work apron he still wore. "Are you all right?"

"Why, yes, what's—"

"There was a break-in at the shop."

"*What?* When?"

"A few hours ago or more; you weren't there, were you? I left to go deliver the grandfather clock to the Grandvilles, and when I came back, you and your mother were gone, and so—"

"No, I wasn't there," Verity said, her nerves buzzing. Her fingers went to the mask in her bag and words flew out of her mouth. "Mother was in the attic when I got home. She didn't say anything about it. And I've been in the shop since she left for a birth. Maybe it was while she was in the attic? I know you can't hear the shop door from up there..."

He placed both hands on her arms and closed his eyes briefly. "Oh, good. Well, at least you two are safe. She's at a birth, you say? But I didn't think she had any—"

"Mrs. Laudry is early."

"Ah. All right then." He pulled away and twisted one end of his mustache in agitation.

"What was taken, do you know?" she asked, already feeling violated that someone unwelcome had been in their space, their home.

He shook his head slowly in disbelief. "My plans. For the steam train clock, you know the one? With the magnetic system I came up with, and the tracks, and everything—"

"Oh, yes. Oh, *no*, Father, I'm so sorry. Here, let's go back home." She glanced at the booths she hadn't visited and pressed her lips together. She still might have more time tomorrow.

But her father was shaking his head, also looking around the fair. "No. He's here, or he might be."

"The person who broke in? How do you know?"

His mustache twitched as he frowned and he strode off toward a brightly lit corner of the park, where Verity had once seen a beautiful mechanical tree...

"I know because I told him of the plans ages ago. A novice inventor, more like an artist with mechanical leanings. I thought he was just interested. And of course, I hadn't worked it all out back then. He must have waited." As her father muttered, they paced over to the exact spot where Verity had seen the beautiful tree at last year's fair, and her heart turned ice cold and slid somewhere near her knees.

But the tree wasn't there, nor was the man with the voice like honey who had made it.

"It wasn't..." Verity trailed off in a whisper.

"He was here last year," her father said firmly.

Verity closed her eyes briefly, thinking back to the masked inventor, soliloquizing on the beauty of his mechanics. Of course, her father had spoken to him, one creator to another. Everyone came to the Fawney Fair during the summer. But would the mysterious artist really break into their shop a year later and steal his plans for a clock that had a moving train car? Why would someone go to such lengths to do such a thing? Her recollections of the man seemed to tarnish in an instant.

Someone might very well take that risk in order to impress the Speares and win their favor and sponsorship.

"I think I know where he'll be," Verity said to her father as she steered him out of the fair and back towards Spindle Street.

"And you can help me get in."

III

"He'll be there."

The bell over the shop door hadn't even finished ringing as her father stepped in with his announcement the next morning.

Verity lifted her head from where she was marking Mrs. Ellington's clock repair order in the ledger; the woman herself was unpacking the small heirloom clock carefully from a small crate. Verity's stomach flipped at her father's news, and she gritted her teeth as she talked through Mrs. Ellington's order and finally ushered her out of the shop, promising that her great-grandfather's clock would be back in working order in no time. Surprisingly, her father bolted the door after bidding Mrs. Ellington goodbye and pulled the shade down. It was only midday. Verity wasn't about to complain though—she hadn't even had a second to glance at her mask, let alone brainstorm any further ways to make it incomparable enough to gain entry to the ball.

"How do you know?" she asked, flipping the ledger shut and sliding it closer to the giant black and gold register that sat at the end of the counter. Dust motes rose in the air, curling in a sunbeam amid the ticking of the clocks.

"Come," he said, motioning her back to the workshop. She looked at the register and shrugged.

"I went down to the artist's union first thing—no, wait. I went to the constable's first," he amended, perching on the stool at his workbench. She settled into the more comfortable chair by the shelves, where all the clock parts sat in neatly labeled boxes. "But they said I had no proof they'd been stolen, and without so much as a name... And then, the artist's union didn't know who he was either. And trust me, with his mechanical tree at the fair last year, they would have known. They *should* have known. How is he not in the union?"

Verity pressed her lips tight. The mechanical tree *was* unforgettable.

"Well, after that, I went to Hazard's to pick up some parts—that mantle clock for the Tremaines needs a strange sized buffer spring—and I decided to mention it to old Mr. Hazard." His eyes lit up then. "He knew him, sold him parts here and there. Name's William Risewell. And he's been buying parts lately for something big. Told Hazard last week it was for the Midsummer ball."

Verity nodded, her insides simmering sickeningly. She hadn't wanted to believe it was him. But her father had told her last night, after Verity had made him some supper and he went to bed early, shaken, that he hadn't told a soul about the steam train clock, besides this mysterious inventor—this Risewell person.

She had wanted to believe that her father had merely misplaced the plans, until she saw the scratches on the back door where the thief's lockpicks had scraped. She shuddered, feeling violated all over again. She had trouble getting to sleep last night, imagining she was hearing the thief's picks scraping the door and intruding footsteps on the floorboards.

"Then it's settled. I'll confront him at the ball," Verity said, her heart wrenching. She hadn't wanted to admit it was the same man with the beautiful honey voice, but who could mistake that tree? "I'll call him out in front of the Speares for stealing your plans. You don't think he's presenting something like your steam train clock, do you?"

Her father shook his head, then twisted one end of his mustache. "I doubt it. The mechanisms could be used for a million things. And though the clock is... valuable, it's not impressive enough to win such a contest." He dropped his hand into his lap and stared down his nose at her. "Are you sure about this?"

"I'm sure," she said, sitting up straighter. "I have to go to the ball—Marigold is moving, and I won't get another chance to go with her. We've been trying to get in for *years*."

He pulled his glasses from his shirtfront pocket and polished them on his hem before putting them on. "Well, then. We better get to work on that mask of yours."

She nodded, getting the mask down from the top shelf where she had kept it safe above all the clock parts. "I added these gemstones, but it's still a little boring. You know how elaborate these things can be. The papers probably don't even do them justice. I just don't know what I could do to make it something special."

He looked at her with a smile. "Hidden garden, you said? Hidden?"

She gasped. "What, do you think we could hide the gems somehow? But how would I..."

Picking something small out of the dish on his workbench, he held up a clock gear between two fingers, and Verity grinned at him.

Just before four, when they would normally close, a sharp knock rang out from the front door of the shop, causing Verity to wrench her neck up from where she had curled over the mask, attempting to line up an hour wheel with a locking wheel she had already secured. Her father pulled his nose out of the box of discarded parts he was perusing, sniffed, then went to answer the shop door.

She knew it wasn't her mother—even if she had lost her key, she would have knocked on the back door. They had received a visit from little Kerry Laudry that morning to announce the safe birth of her baby brother and to pick up a few of Mother's necessities since she would stay the night again to help the family with the new baby.

Before Verity could get the wheels to mesh correctly, her father returned with a very tall and thick gentleman, shiny copper buttons protruding down the front of his black constable's overcoat, his matching helmet under one arm blazing with the coppery badge of the city of Soldark. Verity drew her gaze from the truncheon at his belt and got to her feet.

"Officer Credge is here about the missing plans," her father said, puffing out his chest and looking around the workshop. "Here, let me show you where I kept them."

"Afternoon," Officer Credge acknowledged Verity with a nod, then ambled over to where her father stood waiting beside his desk. The officer looked nonplussed at the assortment of papers scattered there, but said, "Erm, and how exactly—I mean, *when* did you notice these plans were missing?"

As her father launched into the tale of his return from delivering the grandfather clock and finding the back door slightly ajar, Officer Credge wandered around the shop, taking in the contents. Verity saw a notepad in the man's top pocket, but he didn't even pull it out to make notes. When he came by the workbench, she gave him a tentative smile, her fingers seizing the mask for something to do.

"Ah," he exclaimed, eyes twinkling in interest, the first genuine emotion Verity had seen on him. "Attending the ball tomorrow evening, are we?"

She beamed, angling the mask toward him so he could see it better. "Hopefully. It's still a work in progress, but we'll have it ready in time."

"Mmph," he said with an approving nod. "And these gears here...?" He twiddled a finger in their direction.

"You've heard the theme, right?" she said. "Well, once we get the going train and the balance wheel all set, these gears will move the gold filigree to hide and reveal the gemstones—*hidden garden*, don't you think?"

He gave her a small smile. "Fascinating. My son and his partner will be attending—they're not sure they'll get in either, but I'm confident. My son's skills with fabric are second to none. You should see the quality of these masks. But they won't listen to me."

Verity nodded with a small smile. "I understand the fear all too well."

"Right," Officer Credge said, turning back to her father and whipping out his notebook. "The constabulary sent me because there've been a few other break-ins reported matching your description, Mr. Pennington. Would you please show me the door you say the thief used?”

A wedge of a pencil crammed in his thick fingers, Credge took notes as her father showed him the scratches on the lock. Verity’s heart lifted, glad it seemed they were finally being taken seriously.

“And I think I know the name of the thief,” her father concluded as they came back into the workshop after studying the alley out back. “A Mr. Risewell. I met him last year at the Fawney Fair and told him all about these particular plans.”

Credge nodded, his thick gray mustache bristling as he bit his lip. “Aye, and do you have any proof of this meeting? How can you know it was him?”

Her father had come over by the workbench and Verity squeezed his hand. “I can’t. I mean, I don’t know for sure. But that’s the name of the inventor I told—and he was the only one outside the family that knew of those plans. And I—well, it was my only copy. They weren’t complete, you see. And the clock in question was under contract.” His voice trembled.

Verity sat straight up on her stool and noticed her father’s gaze drop to the floor.

“Mr. Frederick Grandville bought first rights to the design—his father introduced me when we were refurbishing the family’s grandfather clock, you see. And the son wanted the steam train clock as a gift for his wife. And if the thief goes and sells the plans, or even makes the clock, well it—it was a large sum.” He gulped.

Trying to contain her dismay, Verity looked up at Officer Credge, who had stopped writing in his notebook and was now studying some of the clocks around them. Unfinished, or in the middle of repairs, they ranged from traditional clocks to the outlandishly-lavish timepieces the Penningtons were known for. Mrs. Ellington's heirloom clock sat in its crate on the large table in the center of the workshop, the work order peeking out from under the crate. Gears turned, second hands ticked, and pendulums swung to a steady rhythm. The designs were all original—some might even say peculiar, but that was what drew more people to the shop. The stained glass lamp built on the face of a clock, which turned the lamp on at the time you set it to. The round mantle clock with a crow behind it, whose feathers covered up the clock at intervals, their movements ticking along with the time.

"I see," Credge said, taking his helmet out from under his arm, then reached out to shake hands with her father. "I can't promise we can pursue this Mr. Risewell person, but with the other break-ins, we've got more of a chance than just your single report. The thief is bound to have left other clues at the other sites, or someone will have seen something."

"Will you let us know?" Verity said, standing and wrapping her arms around her middle.

He glanced at the nearest timepiece. "I'll try. I won't be visiting the other sites until tomorrow, though, and then nearly all the constabulary will be on the clock patrolling up at Silverton Circle, you know," he nodded toward her mask on the workbench. "We can't go in the grounds unless invited, but that part of the city sees too much traffic from the ball for us to leave it unattended. And they've never seen fit to invite the constabulary."

Verity clenched her teeth, nodding. "What if he's at the ball?" she blurted. "If he stole all these plans right before the ball, don't you think he'll have an invention there?"

His mustache tilted to the side as he frowned. "I suppose, but it'll be tough convincing the magistrate, and he certainly wouldn't let us march into the ball on such hearsay."

"I see," she said, burying the rest of the words she wanted to say.

Then I'll just have to find him myself.

IV

As soon as Officer Credge departed, Verity leveled her father with a look. "The steam train clock?"

He leveled a look right back at her. "I told your mother about the deal."

"How much did he pay?"

"Enough to pay for a few years' worth of rent on the shop...or to expand next door even."

For a second, Verity's thoughts drifted to having a slightly larger bedroom, one that might fit a proper wardrobe and that wasn't filled with the sound of chiming clocks on the hour from the shop directly below.

"And do we... erm... still have this money?" she said, twisting her hands together.

He blustered, "Of course! What do you think I would have

done with it? Gambled on the races? Sunspots, Verity. It's at the bank."

"Sorry," she said, holding up her palms. "I just wouldn't want to be in debt to the Grandvilles. I mean, they own half the city..."

"They just power it," he amended, "and they're plenty nice. They love the work we've done for them over the years. And the son was enamored with the idea of the steam train..." He huffed, clearly thinking back to his stolen plans.

Verity crossed her arms. "I can't believe that inventor would steal them," she said, shaking her head. "You know, I saw him too. At the fair—" heat flooded her cheeks at the idea of that night under the glowing lights last summer when he met her gaze. The rogue.

She gasped. "The fair—I was supposed to go with Marigold tonight!"

She glanced at the rabbit clock above the window—whose ears twitched with the second hand, the face clutched in his golden paws—and shot to her feet. "I still have time, I'd better—"

"Go," her father said with a grin. "I'll finish up your starting movement. Maybe Marigold can help you find something... erm... more..."

She grimaced, unsure herself what *more* meant, but knew Marigold was probably her last hope in that matter.

The air outside was cool against her skin as she walked

briskly to Peaseblossom Park, the lilting sound of a fiddler drawing her closer to the fair. She spied the musician on the small wooden stage in the nearest corner of the park, and smiled, temporarily forgetting her woes for a minute as the rapid notes surrounded her. Just as she was about to turn and look for Marigold, two kids walked by holding those shaved ice cones she had seen last night. She narrowed her eyes, mouth watering, and called to their retreating backs, "Hey, where'd you get those?"

They pointed to the newscart sitting under the bright circle of light under a streetlamp on Howarth Lane. She stuck her fingers in her pocket and pulled out her coppers as she approached the long line.

"Verity!"

She whirled to see Marigold approaching, a sunny yellow dress with white lacing clinging to her torso in the gentle heat that still lingered. Verity grinned, feeling like the sun had returned.

"I was worried when you didn't meet me for coffee this afternoon," Marigold said, joining her in line.

Shaking her head, Verity said, "I'm so sorry. A lot's been going on. I'll tell you about it after we get out of this line." Her gaze slid to the other people waiting for shaved ice cones, mere feet away. She didn't want to be overheard by anyone who might know this Mr. Risewell if she hoped to catch him admitting his guilt tomorrow at the ball.

"Then tell me about your mask," Marigold insisted as they moved up in line. "Your mother has been helping you, yes?"

"No. Well, a little." She told Marigold all about the gems from her mother, and the clockwork she had been working on with her father all day. "But there's just something missing," she concluded as they reached the front of the line.

The newscart operator pointed at a small placard which listed a dozen flavors of the shaved ice, and Verity had to make a fast decision. "Lemon," she blurted, avoiding looking too closely at the headlines of the newspapers on display, most of which conjectured about the Midsummer ball. Every time she thought of the ball, her stomach twisted into knots at the thought of not being allowed in with Marigold and at confronting the thief—or worse, not even finding him.

"Nothing for me," Marigold told the newsie.

"She'll have lemon too," Verity said firmly, handing over the coppers and receiving two paper cones. "I need your help with my mask now. Can't have you operating on an empty stomach."

Marigold grinned sheepishly, self-consciously running her hand along her yellow skirt where her pocket was. "Thanks," she said, taking the cone from Verity as they wandered back into the park together. "I'm saving up all I can for Corbright."

"I thought that might have been it," Verity said, then looked down at her ice cone. "Well?"

It was like a cold explosion of sweet and tart on her

tongue—like ice made from lemonade, but smooth. It immediately made the hot stickiness at the back of her neck where her braid sat more tolerable. Marigold's eyes were wide as she tried hers, too, and together they finished the cones without saying a word, listening to the distant sound of the lone fiddler. For a few moments, all felt normal.

There was a lot Verity wanted to say. *I don't want you to go. I'll miss you. What will I do without you?* But she kept silent long after the remains of the ice had turned to melted sugar water at the bottom of their cones. Finally, Marigold said, "Do you want to look at the stalls?"

Verity sighed. "Sure, but I don't know if they'll have anything that would help. I confess, I came last night and the prices were outrageous...if there's even anything left—"

"I saw," Marigold said as they started walking down the lane between tents. "I wanted to buy some souvenir of my last fair, but alas..." she trailed off, glancing at the stall where they were selling music boxes, without even a price tag in sight—never a good sign, Verity thought.

"How is your mask?" Verity said, wanting to change the subject. "Did you add the baby's breath?"

"No, I went with Forget-Me-Nots. They match the Clematis far better—" she stopped, her breath catching. "Sunspots, Verity, I'm going to miss you."

Verity halted, and grabbed Marigold's arm, pulling her in for a hug. "I'll miss you too," she muttered into Marigold's shoulder, getting a whiff of her usual perfume of a thousand flowers. "I'll write you every day."

Marigold snorted through her tears, pulling back. "Don't you dare. You know I can't bear to let a letter go unanswered—and I will not be hunching over my writing desk at all hours of the day."

Chuckling, they resumed their walk, Verity wiping her eyes on the back of her hands. "Fine. I know you'll be out in the fields, picking those sunlilies, right?"

"Right. Father showed me a drawing of the variegation I was telling you about—oh, and they come on these darling little vines—" she gasped and stopped in her tracks, nearly bumping into a woman carrying a sleeping toddler like a sack of potatoes from a long day at the fair.

"What?"

"Vines!" Marigold repeated.

"Yes, I heard you, they're darling—"

"No! On your mask, Ver!"

Verity's mouth formed an O of surprise. "That could fit under the gold filigree, if they were flush with the gems and the rest of the mechanisms," she said in a rush. "But how—"

"I have some—we have some back at the flower shop. But I'll need to soak them in the varnish, for seven or eight hours at least, otherwise they'll be wilted by the time we get to the gates—"

Verity squealed and jumped up and down—neither of

which she was normally taken to, but the excitement of the ball, her emotions high at Marigold's solution, and the rush from the ice cone sent her bouncing on her toes. "You know, I wanted to ask you for some flowers, but I didn't think they would fit under the gold or the gears."

"I better get back then," Marigold said with a grin. "I have just a little varnish left...and I'll take a few snips from the Creeping Wire Vine, and they'll be ready just in time!"

With equal excitement, they bid each other goodbye, and Verity passed back through the fair on her way to Spindle Street. The small electric bulbs overhead glowed brightly, the fiddler had switched to a quieter yet happy tune, and a current of joy ran through her. Her mask was sorted out, and though she would miss Marigold dearly, she didn't feel as saddened by her impending departure as she had before. It was likely due to the fact that the Midsummer ball was even more within their reach than before.

As she passed the corner where Risewell had displayed his mechanical tree, she stopped for a second, wondering if she really had the guts to confront him about the stolen plans. She shook her head, knowing that the money sitting in the family bank account would be as good as stolen should they not recover those plans. Her father had worked so hard for that sum—her mother, too, helping dream up the theme for the clock that her father had then worked out the unique magnetic gear assembly for. And with that money, they could do so much, *be* so much. Maybe Verity could even purchase an airship ticket to visit Marigold...

She shook herself and headed onto Howarth Lane, seeing the newscart operator packing up–closing hatches, flipping latches, and taking down his shaved ice sign. Verity smiled at him, then had an idea.

"Excuse me?" she said, waving him down.

"Yes?"

"Do you come to the Fawney Fair every year?"

He nodded. "Wouldn't miss it. Just wish I had gotten this shaved ice contraption figured out sooner."

She smiled, still feeling a hint of lemon on her lips. "Do you remember a gentleman from last year exhibiting a mechanical tree? He was just there—" She pointed.

"Oh, sure," he said, tugging on the tip of his cap. "Fascinating sculpture. We talked about the mechanics for quite some time."

"Do you remember who he was? I... erm... loved the sculpture, too, but didn't get a chance to ask him about it."

He crossed his arms, leaning both elbows on the counter. "Hmm, you know, I don't remember his name, but I did ask him whether he had any inventors in his family—you know, the skill of the tree was remarkable, I just knew he had to—but I was wrong. He's some relation of the Speares, can you imagine that!"

V

Verity insisted on opening the shop the next morning. "There's no reason not to," she argued with her father over a breakfast of eggs and toast. She smiled as she squeezed a lemon into her tea, thinking of last night. Of course, she didn't want to think about *all* of last night and the revelation she had learned about Risewell.

"Marigold won't be along until this afternoon with the vines, and we've got plenty of work to do," she said.

"You're a tough boss," her father said, cleaning up their plates. "But I suppose you're right. There's nothing we can do now except wait. I don't suppose we'll even hear from Officer Credge until tomorrow at the earliest, what with them patrolling the area for the ball. Best stay busy."

She finished her lemony tea and headed into the shop, tying on her work apron over her skirts and smoothing her black lace collar. The morning began as any other, but with a tangible feel of excitement in the air, even from the customers. They had their normal influx of people bringing in repairs and a few well-off patrons out for a day of shopping who were browsing the timepieces. All the while, a fresh summer breeze came through the door Verity had propped open, bringing her a taste of the Midsummer air.

Tonight.

The fresh air rallied her spirits like never before. By the time Marigold arrived amid the three o'clock chimes, Verity was ready. Her father gave her a nod toward the back room, and the two girls scurried off, a delicate paper box clutched in Marigold's hands.

Verity pried off the lid when they set it out on the workbench, the clockwork on the mask complete, with a few wheels exposed here and there to show the movement—a trademark of Pennington clocks and no surprise to Verity. She picked it up, grinning, and turned the gear on the right side of the mask.

The movement started, and several gold filigree leaves began to move, finally revealing the gemstones beneath. Marigold gasped and brought her hands to her mouth as she watched with rapt attention. Verity looked back down at the mask. Slowly, the gears continued to turn, and everything moved back into place, leaving it just a decorative gold. It continued its movement, revealing and hiding, and would do so until the movement wore out. The going train initiated by the single gear turn would run for half an hour or more. A few turns, and it would run all night.

"They have to let you in with that," Marigold said, her eyes still wide. "That's amazing."

Verity's face warmed, and she pulled the box of vines toward her. "It was my father's idea, and he helped me with the wheels..." she trailed off, gazing into the small box, her eyes lighting on the tiny vines inside. "I didn't think there'd be flowers," she said, curious. "They're so tiny."

A sly grin came across Marigold's face. "I had a few extra Forget-Me-Nots already varnished. I glued them on this morning."

An answering grin on her face, Verity delicately lifted one strand up to the afternoon sunlight shining in through the window. "They'll do perfectly."

Armed with her long-nosed tweezers, gold wire, and wire cutters, Verity got to work. With the clockwork addition, there wasn't much room for error with the vines, so she wove them wherever there was space. Glad she didn't have to think about what the artistic impact of her design would be, she placed them where she could, securing them with miniscule amounts of wire concealed under the leaves. She didn't mind Marigold watching over her shoulder until her friend asked,

"Why were you late to the fair yesterday, anyway? Did you say something was going on?"

Verity stiffened, snipping a piece of gold wire slightly too short. She brushed the useless wire into a discard tray and started over. "Oh, well, yes. Father couldn't find some plans for a very important clock is all." Her heart raced like someone had wound her up too tight. Why was she lying to Marigold?

One thought about Risewell's relation to the Speares, and Verity's impending accusations made her face warm. Would the patrolling constables detain her for harassing the exhibiting artists? Would the Speares kick her out for defaming one of their relations?

She didn't want to entangle Marigold or cheapen their time getting into the ball together. But perhaps she could tell a little of the truth...

"Listen, there's this inventor I want to try to meet," Verity said, clipping the end of the final vine in place. "I met him last year at the Fawney Fair, and he's supposed to be exhibiting at the Midsummer ball this year."

"Oh?" Marigold said, one corner of her mouth quirking up in a smile. "And who is this mystery inventor, and why have you never mentioned him? Ohh, that's so beautiful," she crooned.

Verity held up the completed mask, the rays of the setting sun shining through the open eye cavities as she lifted it up to the window. "Huh," Verity said in surprise. "I did it."

191

Marigold swatted her playfully on the shoulder. "Of course, you did! And it's amazing."

"Well, I had the best help, as you know," said Verity. "It'd still be a pathetic slab of gold filigree without you and my parents' contributions."

"And your work," Marigold chimed in. "Don't pretend like it was all us. You're the one who put it all together. I know you say you have no artistic eye, but *look*, Verity, *look* at it. Don't you want to try it on? Do you have a mirror?"

Verity chuckled nervously. "Not in here, no."

"The one in the hall then. Let's go. And don't think I forgot about this inventor of yours. You'll have to tell me about him on our way to the ball later."

They bustled out of the workshop, nearly tripping on their way down the hall to find the mirror at the bottom of the stairs that led up to the house proper. Verity could only hope that the distraction of her trying on the mask would help her avoid talking too much about Risewell. Marigold hadn't gone to the Fawney Fair with her last year, and part of Verity had wondered if the man's attention to her had all been her imagination, so she'd kept it a secret.

And now her memories of that encounter with him had been tarnished since the break-in, and she was sure Marigold would sense something was off.

Before they reached the mirror, the bells over the door in the shop jingled and a familiar laugh rang out, accompanying

the sound of the bells.

"That's Mother," Verity exclaimed, changing course, the mask in her hands.

"Oh, hello, Verity, Marigold," her mother said when they came into the shop. "Oh, *Verity*, did you do that?"

Both her mother and father—who had been sitting behind the register reading a copy of the *Afternoon Soldark Times*—bustled over to look, exclaiming at the sight of the mask.

Verity couldn't help her smile. She had done it. Sure, everyone had helped her in one way or another, but it wouldn't have happened without her.

Their admiration over the mask was interrupted by a sudden crescendo of noise as all the clocks in the shop began their hourly chorus. Verity grimaced good-naturedly at Marigold, whose eyebrows rose halfway up her forehead.

"I better get back home," Marigold said. "I promised my mother and little Delia I'd get dressed there so they could see." She frowned at Verity. "Sorry, otherwise I would have brought my dress and mask here. I'll meet you in Silverton Circle?"

Verity nodded, a thrill jolting her stomach at the very idea. "We'll walk through the gates together," she said, looking down at the mask and suddenly thinking she could do *anything* wearing something so beautiful.

VI

"Too plain. Go home."

The two Speare cousins at the gate waved away yet another girl in line in front of Verity and Marigold. The girl's companion awaited his fate next. The boy in question held up his hand and shook his head, leaving to catch his friend instead of attempting entry. Verity smiled as she watched him catch up with the girl, though Verity's stomach was twisted into a knot it might take days to undo.

And it didn't help that she hadn't eaten since breakfast.

There were still a few people in front of them. The next pair of boys got in, their matching masks each made with exquisitely sewn fabric and decorated with jade and gold fabric leaves, but each with a unique pattern. The knot in Verity's stomach loosened slightly. Surely her and Marigold's masks were just as good as those.

She glanced over at Marigold, who looked like she was about to be sick, and squeezed her friend's hand. Marigold returned her gaze with a wobbly smile, and suddenly, it was their turn. The man in front of them had just been turned away. His retreating footsteps seemed unnaturally loud as Verity stepped up to the gate.

"Hmm," the long-nosed woman on Verity's side said, gazing at her mask through the eyes of her own—a gaudy purple and emerald jeweled concoction. The woman's eyes narrowed in distaste, and she opened her mouth, the jewels on her mask glinting in the lamplight, and Verity suddenly remembered—

"Wait! That's not all—" She reached up and turned the gear. *How could I have forgotten?* Her stomach, instead of painfully twisted, now seemed to have disappeared altogether as she waited for the clockwork wheels to move and fully reveal her creation. The hollow pit where her stomach used to be ached something fierce. What if it didn't work?

She had tested it a few times this afternoon between donning the shimmery gold dress with the lace-up bodice, and taming her hair in a more civilized braid, but this was the longest she had worn the mask so far—what if something had gotten jostled?

"Ahh," the woman said, her eyes lighting up. "Yes, yes, go!" She flapped her beringed hand toward the entrance.

Heart soaring, Verity turned to Marigold, whose judge had been distracted by Verity's clockwork display. He closed his mouth and turned back to study Marigold's floral confection. The light blue Forget-Me-Nots highlighted the small gaps between the larger flowers on the asymmetrical mask.

Verity took one step into the grounds and crossed her fingers behind her back.

While the man contemplated, Verity's mind raced. What if Marigold didn't get in?

Verity still had to find Risewell. He had been a ghost all last year, and this was likely her only chance at finding him. Would Marigold ever forgive her for going without her? She really should have told Marigold about the thief.

Could Verity go through with it without Marigold?

The red-haired Speare cousin tilted his head, then put a hand on his chin, shifting his full-face mask slightly. His mask was a literal take on the hidden garden theme, complete with gold-brushed doors that were half open, revealing a base of greenery inside. But his mask held no movement, like hers did. His eyes were hidden among the leaves, and Verity couldn't tell if they were normally green or if they only looked that way next to the leaves.

"Pass," he said in a bored tone.

All the breath seemed to get sucked out of Verity's lungs. Marigold's gaze dropped and she started to turn away, but then the man said, "No, I mean *pass*. You may *pass through*.

Sorry. Poor choice of words." He looked like he meant it and offered her a small bow as he held out a hand.

"Oh!" Marigold exclaimed. "Oh, thank you!"

Verity grabbed Marigold's hand in a rush of adrenaline and pulled her friend over the threshold. Together, they danced a few feet away before dissolving into hysterical giggles, careful to keep quiet enough that the cousins wouldn't hear. They had moved on to the next group hoping to enter, a quiet bunch of girls who Verity recognized from the factory down the street from her. She bit her lip as the man rejected the first girl.

"Slow down," Marigold said, grabbing her arm again. "I want to savor everything!"

"Sorry. I just don't want to savor any more rejections from the gate," Verity muttered.

"Yes, you're right," Marigold agreed quietly. "It's not fair."

More guilt assailed Verity as Marigold lapsed into silence. "Well, there's nothing we can do about that, is there?" she said bracingly. "We worked hard, and well, here we are. Look at that shrubbery! Are those... erm... carnations?"

Marigold snorted, eyeing the perfectly manicured hedges they walked beside. "No, they're camellias. And you're right. We finally made it! We're in!"

They gushed over the fountain—real marble, they decided—each flipping a copper into the pool before moving

on. Verity made a vague wish for a successful night, not wanting to be selfish with her wish and leave out anything to do with Marigold. As they got closer to the mansion, the sound of violins met their ears. A delicate and lively tune invited them inside.

Two people stood at the door, simple gold masks covering their eyes, and for a second, Verity worried they were there to further judge them. But the man and woman completely ignored them, staring straight out into the night, their posture immaculate, their black and white uniforms pristine. They passed through the doors without a word.

"The house staff, do you think?" Marigold whispered, turning to look back at them as they wandered through the decadent foyer.

"Oh, yes, that hadn't even crossed my mind." Heat grew at her cheeks, but she wasn't sure if it was from the warmth of the hall and so many people crowded inside, or something else. She had to quash the urge to go back outside, where the cool summer air caressed her skin, and there weren't so many people.

A wave of apprehension flooded Verity as she took in the hall, suddenly feeling quite out of her element. Guests decked out in priceless finery milled about, munching on small delicacies, laughing, and admiring the artwork.

No, artwork wasn't the right term, Verity decided. The pieces adorning the walls and various pedestals throughout the entryway were masterpieces. She suddenly wished her father were here to admire the many metallic sculptures—the most impressive being a golden phoenix in the center of the foyer, made from what looked like odds and ends but shaped into a majestic fiery bird. Verity drew closer, sidling around a man in a green feather mask offering drinks.

The phoenix stood perhaps a foot over her own head. What looked like real rubies adorned its tail, which moved subtly, the gems glinting in the bright electric light like flickering flames. One glance up revealed a chandelier of hundreds of tiny bulbs, throwing light in all directions of the foyer, making the phoenix's citrine eyes glint. Bolts and gears, rods and pins, all plated or painted in gold formed the creature's head. It was incredible—and Verity's respect for the Speares grew slightly. That they valued this creature that was made from scraps, discarded materials. And that the artist could take so many materials—almost worthless by themselves—and create something so exquisite...

"Amazing, isn't it?" Marigold said.

"An understatement," Verity agreed.

"Here, try one of these." Marigold shoved a puffed pastry into her hand; it turned out to be filled with some kind of pear compote. "I'm going to find more—I'm starving. Did you see where the man in the green feathers went?"

Verity shook her head, chuckling. "No, but I could do with some more food myself. In there, do you think?"

They made their way through the revelers to the ballroom, where tables laden with food lined one side of the enormous hall. But before Verity could hasten to the food tables, her eyes were drawn upward, causing her feet to halt in their tracks.

She had heard stories about the elaborate decorations at past Midsummer balls, but seeing it firsthand was like comparing a lick of frosting to eating an entire cake. It was intoxicating.

Great big swaths of semi-transparent green fabric swept down from the ceiling, hanging at intervals down to the floor. Purple and turquoise fabrics lined the ceiling, crossed in a pattern to reveal the large globe lights hanging there. What looked like real vines trailed among the fabric, some twisting down the walls and around sconces. Verity had to force herself to look down and over at Marigold who had also stopped. They giggled nervously at one another and darted between a couple heading for the dance floor.

"I don't care what I eat. I just need something," Verity muttered to Marigold, who giggled again. Verity smiled as she assembled a plate full of delicious-looking food and quickly drew away to a nearby alcove. "I still can't believe we're here," she said as they ate. Verity barely knew what she was eating, only that it was the best food she had ever tasted.

Marigold gasped, and Verity whipped her head up. Her friend was pointing to an alcove swathed in translucent purple fabric where a human-looking mechanical figure was propped against a wall. Verity furrowed her brow.

"Is that..."

"A dancer," Marigold whispered. As soon as she said the word, it clicked in Verity's head. The figure was clearly modeled as a person, but that was where the resemblance stopped. Formed with metal and clockwork, the figure had a smooth metal face—though it wore a simple gold mask with metal leaves worked into it. The limbs were slightly longer than seemed fitting, and instead of feet it had casters at the ends of the legs.

"One of the exhibitors' maybe?" Verity said, studying it. She took an unconscious step as if to get in for a closer look.

"Must be. I do hope we'll get to see it dance!"

Verity grinned. "I'm sure we will. We'll make the most of tonight, I promise."

Nodding, Marigold finished off a tiny cherry tart. Verity didn't say anything further, not wanting to bring up Marigold's impending move and cast any more shadows on the night. But she could feel it between them, hovering there like an unwanted ghost. Their last night of revelry together. After tonight, Marigold would no doubt be consumed with packing, and between the two of them working in the shops, they weren't likely to have time for merriment.

And besides, they were finally *here*, at the Speare estate. The newscarts would be littered with headlines from tonight's festivities, and for once, Verity wouldn't have to scour them for all the details—wouldn't have to live through words on paper.

Just as she was sampling a beef turnover of some kind with a marvelous sauce, she caught a glance out of one of the large floor-to-ceiling windows.

A tree, glinting silver in the waning light outside, with twinkling lights adorning its branches.

The beef in her mouth turned to sand. She struggled to swallow it, gulping, as she glared out the window. It had to be him.

Mechanically she moved her jaw, working her mouth until the now-tasteless food was gone. She cleared her throat awkwardly, her eyes bulging slightly as she gazed at the tree. That must be him.

Still trying to clear her throat, Verity set her plate on a side table as Marigold flagged down a butler carrying a tray of some kind of purple iced beverage. She handed a small stemmed glass to Verity, who sipped its contents gratefully and avoided looking at the window at all costs.

"Mm. What is this? It's amazing!" Her throat cleared, and she sampled the drink some more.

"Lavender lemonade," Marigold said, taking a sip from her own glass. "It's heavenly."

Verity nodded, savoring the taste on her tongue and taking little sips, even though she wanted to down the whole glass. It instantly brought coolness to her skin somehow. The heat of

the day hadn't quite dissipated from inside the mansion, and as a wisp of a breeze came from the window, Verity shivered.

"Oh, look, it's her," Marigold said in a hushed voice, gazing over at a sudden disturbance in the crowd. A thin and graceful woman with her hair done high upon her head was making her way through the crowd, a small bevy of hangers-on following at a close distance. From what Verity had seen in the papers, she knew this must be Lady Tania.

A constellation of tiny lights twinkled from her mask, which was made from silver-tipped leaves and black lace. The twinkling lights and leaves didn't stop at her mask, though, but were worked through the whole dress, a purple and teal affair, with black ribbons lacing up her corset. Verity blinked at her for a while as she moved about the room. She did have a certain air to her, the way she walked, the way her shoulders thrown back demanded respect, and yet the happy chortles and toothy smiles she gave seemed genuine.

Verity glanced back at Marigold. "Hey, why don't you go find out about the mechanical dancer?" she asked, gesturing to the alcove with her empty glass. "I'm just going to... erm... pop outside for some fresh air. I'm melting."

"Oh, good idea. I'll find out when they're supposed to exhibit. Here, give me that," Marigold said, taking the lemonade glass and setting it on a passing butler's empty tray.

Verity chuckled and watched Marigold skip away to inspect the mechanical dancer—and immediately engage the

203

two boys standing nearby in conversation. From their intricate fabric masks, Verity recognized them as the ones who came into the ball right before them. She set her jaw and turned around, marching toward the side door near which she had seen the tree. It opened out onto a large balcony which spanned the entire ballroom, with stairs leading off onto the lawns from the center. Artists and their creations lined the stone pathway. She narrowed her eyes and started down the stairs, glaring at the tree.

It was shorter than she remembered. The dim yellow lights adorning the branches drew her down as her nerves jangled. She was beginning to regret not telling Marigold about her alternate reason for attending the Midsummer ball, but if she could just find the thief and take care of it now, then she'd have all night to celebrate with her friend.

A figure dashed past her on the stairs, stalking away from someone standing in the shadows beside the tree. But there was something about that figure now going up the stairs...

She whirled around, recognizing the same mask with the subtle butterfly markings done in black and gold. She followed as he bolted up the steps, sure it was him.

Now what did she do? The sudden memory of his relation to the Speares chose that moment to resurface, and she rushed up the stairs before he could get too close to the doors. The last thing she wanted to do was confront him inside the ballroom with everyone so close and crowded. And she certainly didn't want to get in trouble with the Speares and have her night with Marigold ruined.

She caught up with him at the top step. Steeling herself, she reached out and grabbed his shirtsleeve. He spun around, his face unreadable under his mask.

"Oh, my apologies," he said, turning to go.

"No, I'm sorry—for grabbing you, that is," she said, suddenly realizing how close he was to her, and she immediately wondered what his face looked like beneath the black and gold butterfly mask.

"Ah, can I help you with something?" he said, and she thought he was looking over her shoulder back at the tree.

She frowned, sudden ire rushing up, setting her chest aflame. She tamped down the first accusation that came to her lips, and instead nodded at the tree. "It's marvelous," she said. "I saw you last year at the Fawney Fair, you know. My father did too."

"Oh?" he said, visibly drawing a breath. "Well, yes. I was there with–with my tree."

Was it her imagination, or did he look a little nervous?

Sudden inspiration took her, and she leaned in closer. "Oh, yes, he's a clockmaker," she whispered, eyes narrowed. This close and she could smell mechanical grease and a scent of something fruity like grapes coming off of him. "He was quite interested in your tree. Quite interested." She arched her brows at him, staring into his eyes for any sign of guilt or recognition. This way, she wasn't accusing him of anything—nothing she said could be construed as problematic by the Speares.

He lifted his chin, eyes narrowed at her. "I see. Well, I must be going," he said abruptly. He pulled away from her, darting up the remaining stairs and striding across the balcony before Verity knew what was happening.

She scoffed as he disappeared into the ballroom.

Well, that hadn't gone quite as planned, she thought.

VII

She huffed, turning about, unsure of what to do with herself. She could pursue him into the ballroom, but that was where Lady Tania was, and if it got ugly, Verity certainly didn't want to cause a scene in front of everyone. She truly hoped it wouldn't get ugly. She didn't want her name showing up in the *Soldark Times* tomorrow.

Disgraced Clockmaker's Daughter Accosts Artist...

She pursed her lips and faced the mechanical tree.

It stood on a simple platform next to the stone pathway, alongside several other large exhibits. Momentarily distracted by the sound of water coming from the one next to the tree—where water spilled from what looked like hundreds of small metal basins, moving up and down in an obviously musical way. She couldn't help looking at it as she approached the tree, noting the different sized basins, even with different thicknesses of metal, where the water spilled from one to another and wooden cogs conducted the movement. *No, no. Stop getting distracted*, she told herself.

She stood on the stone path, just at the edge of where the tree branches reached. She wanted to get closer, but something held her back. The lights built into the branches glowed dimly, like a hundred fireflies had chosen to land on the tree all at once. It was smaller than she remembered, though it had been a year since seeing it at the fair. And right now, it was as still as a statue; before she had seen its leaves and branches gently moving as if swaying on a breeze. Perhaps it needed its inventor to start the display. She glanced angrily over her shoulder, regretting not following him into the ballroom and wondering if Marigold was beginning to notice her long absence.

"That's some mask," someone behind her said.

She turned, spotting a man a few years older than her wearing a mask of simple overlapping gold plates shaped like leaves. *He must have been invited to exhibit*, she thought. *He never would have gotten in here with that mask otherwise.*

"Thank you," she said, smiling as he stared at her face. He wore a foppishly embroidered yellow waistcoat, a silver pocket watch chain looping out of his pocket.

"It must have cost a fortune," he said. "It fits the theme

perfectly, I must say. Who did you commission on such short notice?"

"Oh," she said, heat rushing to her cheeks. "I... erm... I made it myself, with some help—"

He made a sound that was almost a gasp, and he bowed his head at her. "It's genius, and the precision of the clockwork is so smooth."

Her smile grew, and she resisted the urge to reach up and touch it. She knew the works were still running, could feel the gentle movement of the gold filigree as it hid and revealed the delicate flowers, gems, and vines.

He bowed his head once more and said, "My apologies, miss, I haven't introduced myself. Reginald Winch, at your service."

"Verity Pennington," she said, extending her hand.

"Delighted," he said, shaking it at once. He glanced up at the tree and cocked his head down the stone path. "I was just about to tour the gardens to clear my head—would you care to join me?"

For a second, she thought of Marigold alone in the ballroom—except she wasn't alone, she was probably chatting with the inventor of the mechanical dancer or making new friends among the guests, something she frequently did with ease. Risewell could wait. She had plenty of time to corner him again.

And besides, Verity was allowed to have a little fun

tonight, wasn't she? And maybe this man knew something about Risewell.

"Sure," she agreed, though she didn't take his proffered hand, but instead walked beside him. He didn't seem offended, but she wasn't comfortable touching the stranger just yet, even if he was pleasant and—she had to admit—quite good-looking, despite his overdone waistcoat.

"So, what's it like being one of the exhibitors?" she asked as they approached a well-tended rose garden. She inhaled deeply, enjoying the scent of the flowers and the cooling night air. Tiny glass lamps lined the path, encased in wrought iron leaves.

"Oh, it's flattering, to be sure, to have so many people admire your work," he said, gesturing down a path behind a small group of friends who were taking in the garden air with their glasses of lavender lemonade.

"I'm sure it is," she said. "Do you... know many of the other inventors?"

"Not really," he said with a breath, shaking his head. "I'm quite on the outside of the inventor's circles. Which does make it difficult to make an impression these days."

Verity frowned. "Well, you made it here! And if the Speares judge your exhibit to be the winner, then, you'll be thrust into the center of the limelight."

A servant stood stock-still at the edge of the rose garden, holding an empty tray. The friends carousing ahead of them

deposited their empty glasses with him, before whispering excitedly at the edge of a hedge and disappearing through an opening, wrought iron gates thrown wide.

Her companion had lapsed into silence, and she snuck a glance at his face. His eyes were drawn in what looked like sadness, the emotion validated when he spoke next. "I doubt I will win their favor. I..." he trailed off. "Do you want to go into the hedge maze? That is, if you feel comfortable. I wouldn't want to presume. But I hear there is a fascinating fox sculpture in the center."

The shouts and laughs from the group of friends who had already passed through the gates rang out in the night. Verity eyed the twinkle lights above the hedges with curiosity. She should really be out here with *her* friend, not this handsome stranger.

"I'm sorry, Mr. Winch," she said, meaning it, "but I really shouldn't. It's not that I don't want to. But perhaps we can go later. I'm afraid I've left my friend in the ballroom too long alone, and we came here together."

He gave her a polite frown as two boys went around them and into the maze. "Alas," he said, "I was hoping to get your expert opinion on something. Perhaps I can walk you back to the ballroom, then?"

"Oh," she said, her cheeks flaming. "Of course."

"And please, call me Reg, or Reginald, if you prefer."

He offered her his arm, and this time she took it, a light

211

heat flaring out from her chest at his touch. "Reg," she said. She gazed at him out of the corner of her eye. He did look quite handsome, under his simple metal mask. But the foppish waistcoat, which she now noticed was lined in yellow lace, was not her style at all. Perhaps he had just worn it to attract attention to his exhibit.

"You are something of an expert at clockwork, yes?" he asked, motioning to her mask.

"I wouldn't say expert—my father is, though, and I have learned quite a bit from him."

"Well," his voice dropped, the melancholy expression back on his face. "I'm having trouble with my sculpture. One of the mechanisms—I had grand plans for it—and now the whole thing is nearly useless. They'll never pick me," he added.

"Oh, well, I could take a look at it," she said. They were back on the stone path, and the now-hated mechanical tree was in sight. She glanced at the stairs leading up to the ballroom balcony. "How about this," she said. "I'll go and check in with my friend—she'd probably love to meet you anyway—and then, if I can help, I will." She wasn't sure when she would find time to confront Risewell, but the night was still quite young. She had plenty of time.

"You're a blessing!" Reg said, his eyes lighting up.

She smiled, her cheeks bumping into the curves of the mask. "I'll find you in a little while!" she called, bounding up the stairs.

She found Marigold almost immediately, her face flushed with excitement as she approached Verity. "Come, you must see! I found the inventor of the mechanical dancer! It's fascinating!"

Verity grinned, glad her friend had been happily occupied during Verity's poor attempt at accosting Risewell and talking to Reg. She would have to ask if he knew Risewell when she found him later.

She allowed Marigold to drag her over to the corner under an overhanging balcony where the dancer perched, mechanical limbs splayed in an artistic manner, her metal hands both reaching for the sky. Beside it, a man in a simple black suit, busy digging in a small toolbox on the ground.

"I told you I'd find her!" Marigold said brightly.

He turned, revealing the simple gold and black butterfly mask.

VIII

"You!" Verity shouted at Risewell. "I mean, *you*," she said, much quieter, spotting Lady Tania halfway across the ballroom, tittering at someone in a mask covered in black lilies and gold roses.

She couldn't read his expression through his mask, but he took half a step back.

"Yes?" he asked. "You're the one who... erm... accosted me on the balcony, aren't you?"

"Verity," Marigold hissed. "You accosted him? Why? What happened?"

"This is—" she gaped, realizing she had never told Marigold. "I was going to tell you, but with you leaving Soldark and everything, I forgot, and then I didn't want to ruin the ball for you—"

"If you'll excuse me," Risewell said, twiddling a screwdriver in their direction, "I've got some work to do here."

"No," Verity said. "You're not going anywhere."

"Verity!" Marigold said, drawing closer and whispering, "Why are you being so mean to him?"

Verity sputtered, "I... well... listen. Our shop was broken into. Father's plans for the steam train clock were stolen. It was him," she said, pointing. Marigold gasped. She wished she could see the full look on Risewell's face. His gaze darted to the door leading to the balcony and back.

"Excuse me?" he said, dropping the screwdriver down into the toolbox on the floor.

"I know it was you," Verity continued. "You were at the Fawney Fair with your tree last year." She jerked her thumb toward the balcony. "My father spoke to you about it. And you were the only one who knew about the plans for his steam train clock. I *need* those plans back."

He narrowed his eyes at her, then, finally, shook his head. "First of all, Miss—"

"Pennington."

"Pennington, really? Oh. I do remember your father. He's a world class clockmaker. But no"—he shook his head rapidly—"*first of all*, Miss Pennington, I did no such thing as rob your family's shop. And second of all, *that* is not my tree."

"I'm sorry, what? But the tree—I saw you out there—"

"Yes, confronting the dandy who appears to think other

people's hard-wrought ideas can simply be used for his own use. But the fool won't be winning the exhibition," he said scornfully. "He overreached, attempting to make his duplicate tree better than mine was, and now his mechanisms are all locked up." He laughed without humor. "Or maybe the tree got sick of his hideous waistcoat and the gears simply gave up."

"I—" Verity's mouth hung open, but it was devoid of words, much like her brain.

Marigold grabbed her arm. "Are you all right?"

"The man in the yellow waistcoat?" she said.

"Yes," Risewell said, "I met the scoundrel at last year's fair as well—right about when I met your father, if I recall."

Marigold bobbed on her heels. "Then—if I'm following this right—and Verity, you really should have told me. You know I love a good mystery—perhaps this yellow-waistcoated scoundrel is the one who broke into your shop?"

"If this one's telling the truth," Verity hedged, crossing her arms over her chest.

A waiter passed by offering a tray of lime pinwheel cookies, and Verity was sad to see him walk away.

"Of course, I am," Risewell exclaimed, crossing his own arms. "That Winch fellow is the one who stole my idea. Do you know how long it took to craft that tree? Each branch, each twig, each leaf? The amount of clockwork it took to give it motion? And I didn't even win last year," he said quieter, "so who knows why he chose my design to steal. Apparently, my cousins prefer lifelike figures. I never had a chance against that phoenix."

Verity sought his gaze, and a wave of apprehension flooded her. So he had lost to the beautiful phoenix sculpture last year. Now that she thought about it, she did recall reading about it in the paper. It was an admirable defeat; the phoenix was truly stunning. Sudden heat rushed to her cheeks, and she was immensely glad for her mask. She shifted, clenching her hidden fists behind her crossed arms. "Well, he stole plans for a very special clock from my father. Invaluable ones. I need them back."

"What do you expect me to do?" Risewell said, throwing his arms down and retreating closer to his dancer. "I've got a loose pinion to fix in her right shoulder before the judging commences. And besides, I've already tried to confront Winch. He claimed *I* copied *him*."

"Well, wouldn't the Speares believe you over him?" Verity said.

He *tsked*. "We're third cousins and barely know each other, so I doubt it."

Verity huffed, staring at the stationery mechanical dancer. Her right arm did look a little askew... "Does she dance? Truly?" she asked suddenly.

A smile came over Risewell's lips. "She does. But not gracefully if I don't fix this pinion. The arm'll throw off the entire balance system."

She cut her eyes toward Marigold, who glanced back at her meaningfully. Verity sighed again. "Look, I'm sorry I accused you," she said quietly. "But we thought you were the only one who knew about the plans. Do you think Winch overheard at last year's fair?"

Risewell sank down to retrieve his screwdriver and advanced upon his dancer, unscrewing the casing near the shoulder. "He spent plenty of time admiring my tree. I thought he was a painter or something—he had a sketchbook and everything. That scoundrel was merely drawing up schematics, more likely. Though, at least, he never figured out how to make the leaves fall and return to the tree. That had been my next improvement idea for it. And I think that's what's got his tree stalled right now."

Mouth open in wonder, Verity gazed out the balcony door, where the top of the tree was still visible. "I wonder if that's why he stole the plans from Father. The steam train clock is supposed to have pieces that move and return using a system of magnets."

The dancer's shoulder casing came off, and Risewell tucked the screws into his waistcoat pocket as he peered inside. "Look, it sounds like these plans are important to you, but I need to fix this. I doubt I'll ever get invited back to the Midsummer ball if this fails, distant relations to Lady Tania notwithstanding."

Verity gazed inside the dancer's shoulder cavity at the

wheels as she thought. Then a smile came over her, and she reached for Risewell's screwdriver. "I have an idea."

"Are you sure?" Marigold asked her for the tenth time as they hustled down the balcony steps and into the garden exhibits. The detestable tree rose up in front of them, but Winch was nowhere to be seen. Verity glanced around, then spotted the woman with long braided hair standing proudly beside the masterful waterfall sculpture. The wooden gears turned like interlocking waterwheels, moving the basins up and down to their own rhythm, playing the secret song of water.

"I'm sure," Verity said under her breath to her friend. "It's beautiful," she told the inventor, who smiled. "Have you seen Mr. Winch? The one with the tree?"

The woman narrowed her eyes and waved toward the rose garden. "I believe he went to the hedge maze."

"Perfect," Verity said, and led the way.

She averted her eyes as a black-clad figure in a butterfly mask stole into the shadows behind the tree.

"Well, William is nice," Marigold said in a quiet cheery voice as they entered the rose garden, their way lit by the leaf-encased lamps lining the side of the path.

"William?"

"Mr. Risewell!"

"Oh, yes," Verity said, her thoughts briefly flitting to

wonder what the rest of his face looked like under his mask to match the gold eyes.

Marigold smiled slyly at her. "It was nice of you to help fix his dancer."

"We needed him to sneak into Winch's things and look for the pilfered plans. It was the quickest way to get him to help. And it was just a pinion. I don't know why he was having so much trouble with it."

"Nerves, maybe," Marigold said. "Or, you know, he's not from a family where clockwork runs in his blood, where he eats, drinks, and breathes cogs and, well, pinions."

Verity shrugged, somewhat pleased.

The gate to the hedge maze stood wide open, the twining wrought iron inviting them inside. Verity suddenly wished the lights above it were ten times brighter, but at least she wasn't entering alone. She took Marigold's elbow, and together, they went inside.

"How far in do you think he is?" Marigold whispered as they faced a fork in the path right away.

"No idea. Left, do you think?"

Marigold shrugged.

Verity led the way. "He said something about a fox sculpture being at the center of the maze, though. I just hope this doesn't take forever. I don't want us to miss the whole evening because of this." She hustled down the verdant corridor, wondering if she was hearing the sound of the inventor's water sculpture, or if there was a fountain nearby.

"It'll give William plenty of time to find the stolen plans, anyway," Marigold said.

"Well, yes, but I wanted us to have fun tonight, it being your last—"

Marigold nudged her sharply with her elbow. "Would you stop that? I *am* having fun. Besides, even setting aside the fact that we *need* to recover these stolen plans which are integral to your father's success, this is a marvelous mystery. You couldn't pay for entertainment like this! We're on a hunt for a dastardly thief, to right a wrong done to my greatest friend and her family."

Verity chuckled. "I'm going to miss you," she said earnestly.

"And I you," Marigold said with relish. "But even though we'll be cut off from each other, we'll both grow new roots."

Verity pursed her lips. "Really?" she said in a low tone.

"Oh, you love me and my wordplay."

"I do," Verity admitted with another chuckle as they reached an intersection and chose the right path this time. They wandered for perhaps ten minutes before the sound of water grew stronger. "Do you think that's the center of the maze? Where else would they put a fountain, right?"

"Yes," Marigold agreed, "it's coming from over there, if we just go up this path—"

They turned the next corner and drew up quick—not two

feet from them stood Reginald Winch in his foppishly embroidered yellow waistcoat, gazing at the mechanical fox sculpture atop the small fountain. The fox's tail swished in a rolling movement of metal.

Winch turned, spotting them. "Ah! There you are, and you found your friend too." He bowed at the waist, and Verity noticed that hideous yellow lace lined his entire collar. She wrinkled her nose but schooled her expression into a polite smile as he straightened up. They had to keep him occupied so Risewell could search.

"I hope there's still time to help you with your invention?" she said, working hard to keep the disdain out of her voice. "You never told me the problem."

"Ah, yes," he said, rubbing his hands together. He took a half-step forward, gesturing at her face and said, "Well, your ingenious mask made me think of a possible solution—"

Without warning he lunged at her, ripping the mask off her face and darting back behind the fountain.

Verity reached forward but he lifted the mask and held it precariously between two fingers over the fountain's pool.

"Ah, ah, ah," he taunted. "Wouldn't want this finery ruined, would you? You'd be ejected from the ball immediately. And you'd ruin your night with your dear friend."

Verity drew a sharp breath in through her nose, her heart pounding furiously in her chest. "Give it back."

"Why would I?" he said shrewdly, and Verity noted all manner of attractiveness had gone from him. "I'm a dastardly thief, aren't I?"

Marigold and Verity shared a look, and Winch guffawed at them.

"The center of the maze is not the center at all," he said, "but quite at the beginning. It is rather ingenious, I must say."

"Give it back," Verity repeated. "That's my gr—well, it's none of your business what it is. Give it back!" Not only would the clockwork movement get flooded and risk rusting, but the varnish on the flowers and ivy would be no match for the plunge. She watched as the gold filigree slowly opened once more, exposing the delicate inner vines and gems.

"No," he said simply. "I've worked hard to get here, and I won't stop now. Your father's schematics were the only ones that offered a possible solution. My tree will blow Risewell's out of the water with what I've got planned.

"What you need to do if you want this mask back, Miss Pennington, is to explain the missing part of your father's schematics. He's been working on them for over a year—how is it missing the fine details of installing the going train?"

Verity furrowed her brows, suddenly missing the mask covering her emotions. "I—"

He let the mask slip in his fingers but caught it before it dropped.

"I don't know!" she shouted, though her outburst was out

of anger rather than confusion. Of course, she knew. Her father didn't need to write down his signature going train schematics. He could do them in his sleep. And so could she.

"You know," he said shrewdly.

She turned her face away. *Really wish I had that mask on,* she thought to herself.

"Fine," he said. "Maybe I'll learn the secret to my success by studying your mask; the movement is perfect, after all."

He went to touch one of the exposed cogs, and she shouted, "Wait!" Despite his evil smile, she went on, "Look, he didn't write it down because he didn't have to. It's kind of our family's signature clock movement, if you must know."

"Very well. Then you will accompany me to my exhibit and address the problem before the judging occurs." He paused. "*And,* if a certain inventor has been rifling through my things at your behest, neither of you will get what you're looking for."

That must mean he has the plans on him, she thought. *But how will I get them from him? And if I don't get my mask back, I'll be kicked out...*

Though the prospect of leaving the ball and finding Officer Credge or another constable was tempting, she didn't think she would be able to return. She wouldn't be able to improvise one mask at such short notice, let alone two. It was evident that the Speares wouldn't even let in the constabulary under their ridiculous rules. But she didn't know what to do.

She took a deep breath. Finally, she said, "Give me my mask then. I'll do it."

Winch shook his head, a horrible smile on his face. "No, not until you fix the tree."

Verity stiffened. "But how... If I'm seen without it—"

"If it's so simple—this signature setup of yours—then you should be able to fix it in no time. An incentive, let's call it."

Her breath burned as she sucked it in, and every fiber of her being wanted to reach out and strike him—or at the very least, stalk from the party and find a constable. But how could she prove Winch was the one who stole the plans? What if he didn't have them on his person? And even then, would a constable search him just over hearsay?

She shared a look with Marigold, whose eyes had lost their usual vibrance. Verity smiled sadly at her. "Fine. Under one condition: you give me my father's plans when I get it to work."

He frowned, considering. "Very well."

"Let's go." She jerked her chin at Winch and said, "But you're walking ahead of me."

IX

With Winch in front, and Marigold beside her, they exited the hedge maze. The lights lining the path through the rose garden seemed to beam up at her naked face like beacons, and she tried to keep her head down. She was sure if any of the servants—or worse, the Speare family themselves—saw her, she would be ejected. And though Marigold said she was having a good time before, the situation had taken a turn down a dark path.

Her grandmother's mask was tucked into an interior pocket of Winch's waistcoat, after Verity had pleaded with him to let her turn it off. Though she had spent several days of work on that mask, and was quite proud of it, at this point, all she wanted were those plans—and to get away from this swindler. It had been a fun ball while it lasted.

They reached the avenue of inventions in no time, Verity's nerves tenser than an overwound clock. William was nowhere to be seen; she could only hope that he had gone back to his mechanical dancer to await the judging, which was bound to be happening soon. Verity could see the beginnings of an enormous bonfire being set up in an open field at the other end of the exhibits. Surely once the decision was made, the Midsummer fires would be lit, and with the competition over, everyone could have a good time.

Verity no longer thought she would qualify for such fun. She had ruined the evening with Marigold. She wouldn't get her father's plans back unless she helped Winch. And she would hate herself if his tree won this year. What with the theme of this ball, it seemed a perfect fit. *That must be why he stole the idea from William*...but how had he known the theme in advance?

If she got it to work, with its leaves that could fall and return to the tree repeatedly, it might just be the winner. She stood frozen for a full minute when they reached his exhibit.

Marigold nudged her, and she jolted forward, retreating into the shadows near the trunk to hide her face. "What if you just say you lost your mask?" Marigold hissed, glancing at Winch's back as he stood near his open crates, casually inspecting them as he fiddled with his pocket watch chain.

"I don't know," Verity said, "but if I've gotten in this deep, I want those plans back. And my mask. I have to."

Marigold let out a shaky breath. "Are you all right by yourself here if I go? I have an idea."

Looking over at the nearby woman at the water exhibit and the other ball guests mingling in the area discussing the prospects of each invention, Verity nodded.

Maskless and now friendless, she located Winch's toolbox and identified the control panel in the tree's trunk. The metal access door was easy to find; it wasn't as flush with the bark as it should be, and she wasn't surprised at the poor handiwork. Winch was a charlatan and a thief. And he didn't deserve to win.

"Do you have a size fourteen and a size eleven wheel?" she asked him a few minutes later.

After rummaging in his crates, he came over with a jumbled handful. She resisted rolling her eyes and selected the ones she needed.

As her fingers brushed the wires inside the tree, the magnets pulled by the movement she was installing, a sinking feeling wove through her. She raised her eyes to look up at the branches. The leaves were stationary—for now—and the fairy lights scattered across the limbs were as picturesque as William's tree had been. What was she doing?

She couldn't let Winch win. He was a cheat. And a thief. He was the one who had slunk through her shop, her home, rifled through her father's things. Not William.

Her stomach roiling, she lifted the wire cutters. She stilled her shaking hand and clipped the main wire connected to the movement she had just installed. But she didn't clip it all the way; she left it hanging by a thread.

"Better be done soon," Winch hissed behind her. She jumped. "Lady Tania's just come out of the ballroom. She'll be heading this way in a minute."

She took one look at the functioning gears, then slammed the control box and put the screws back in. "Look for yourself," she said, nodding up.

His gaze darted between her and the leaves, then settled in the branches above as he watched the leaves and smaller branches begin to sway as if in a gentle breeze. "And the fall?"

"It's on a timer," she said through clenched teeth. "You don't want them all to drop at once, do you? Well? The plans? My mask?"

"You can have them after the judging," he said.

She opened her mouth to speak, her heart fit to burst with rage, but Lady Tania was now descending the stairs with her bevy of admirers and friends, and Winch's tree was the first exhibit right up front. Verity backed up, suddenly regretting using those wire cutters, and wondering just where in the solarbelt Marigold had gone. Her feet dragged through the short-cropped grass, trying to figure out where to go, or what to do.

A throat cleared behind her. As Verity turned, a woman gently took her arm and pulled her into the shadow behind the musical water sculpture. After a moment's confusion, Verity edged to the back of the exhibit, looking into the dark space in the shadow where the inventor stood. "Thank you," Verity whispered.

The woman nodded. "I knew there was something off about him. And I believe he took my spot. I was supposed to be at the bottom of the stairs."

Verity puffed a breath out of her nose in amusement as the woman stepped back out to the front of her exhibit. Verity listened to the sound of water falling as Lady Tania approached Winch, who was smoothing down his ridiculous waistcoat.

"Ah," Lady Tania said to her group, "How fitting for our theme, a great mechanical tree! But haven't I seen this before?"

Winch shook his head. "Not this tree, Lady Tania. This tree... It is...even more unique than it appears," he said, obviously trying to stall until the mechanical magic happened. Verity watched, clutching the folds of her golden dress, unsure exactly what would happen. She might have ruined her chance to get the plans and the mask back, but she knew deep down to her core that she couldn't help him.

Verity might have imagined it, but she thought she heard a light metallic sort of *tink* inside the tree, and a single leaf fell from the branch above Winch. He stepped aside, and the silver leaf fell to the grass. Nothing else happened. His mouth agape, he stared around as Lady Tania's group tittered.

"I see," she said, "Well, happy Midsummer to you, sir." She waved a green satin-gloved hand at her retinue to follow her on. Verity stood frozen as they inspected the water sculpture. They wouldn't be able to see her unless someone came around the back and looked directly into the shadows where she stood.

She watched Winch stand there as she lingered in the darkness. He strode over to the control panel and banged on it a few times before begrudgingly pulling the screwdriver out of a box.

How could she retrieve her mask now? At the very least, she knew where *that* was. But that would involve getting close to Winch again.

She was forestalled from making any kind of decision when she spotted a peculiar figure walking down the balcony stairs.

A man dressed like a constable—no, it was a real officer, she realized; that truncheon looked quite menacing—with a familiar brass mask adorned with metal leaves.

Verity blinked. Wasn't that...?

Behind the constable came Marigold, and a few paces behind her, William Risewell.

By the time Lady Tania's guests noticed the officer, he was already approaching Winch, who was staring into the depths of the control panel and cursing. The guests let out a few carefully crafted remarks, and a gasp or two. Lady Tania straightened—though Verity wasn't sure how exactly someone standing so straight could look even taller—and approached the constable.

"Good evening, sir," she said, nodding deeply at him. "Is there something I can assist you with? You don't look as if you've come for the bonfire."

"Regretfully, no, Lady Tania," the man said, and Verity realized it was Officer Credge. Verity gazed at Marigold in amazement. How had she realized? How had she known what to do?

And the mask Credge wore—it was definitely the one from William's dancer.

"I do apologize," Credge went on, "but Mr. Winch here is in possession of stolen items."

A lady in a finch mask let out a gasp worthy of the stage. Winch recoiled, puffing out his chest as he pulled in closer to the tree trunk.

"On what grounds do you make that claim?" Winch demanded.

"This is... highly irregular, officer," Lady Tania said tentatively. "Yet I must also ask the same question."

Officer Credge nodded, the strap of his helmet digging into the skin of his neck. "Among some other objects I suspect he has on his person, the waistcoat he wears matches the description of one taken from Hubert Danbury's house, which was broken into two days ago in search of sensitive plans involving clockwork." Winch blanched under his simple mask.

Lady Tania put a hand to her chest, letting it flutter there. "Thieving, sir?" she demanded. "And I don't suppose these plans you needed had anything to do with your exhibit tonight?"

Winch's mouth opened and closed as he glanced from Officer Credge to Lady Tania and back. At that moment, there was another *tink* from inside the tree trunk, and every leaf on the tree fell in a shimmering crash. Winch held his arms above his head, pelted with the harmless metal until at last only a handful of leaves remained on the tree.

Everyone stood quiet for several moments until Lady Tania cleared her throat. "It is obvious your lack of skill drove you to such measures," she said to Winch, wrinkling her nose. "And next time, perhaps don't pilfer such a distinct garment."

At that, Officer Credge came forward and took Winch forcefully by the elbow, pulling out a pair of shackles and leading him toward the balcony. Verity lurched forward, almost coming out of the shadows, but paused, not wanting to reveal herself to Lady Tania and her retinue. But Credge was hauling Winch away...and her mask...

She couldn't signal Marigold, who surely couldn't see her in this dark corner of the garden exhibits. There was nothing for it; she had to go.

As though not looking at Lady Tania and her group would

prevent them from seeing her, Verity quickly darted out from behind the water exhibit and across the path to the stairs, trying to catch up with Credge and Winch.

"Wait a moment," Lady Tania's voice rang out. "Who are you? And where is your mask?"

Verity spun on her heels, several stairs down from Credge and Winch.

From beside them, Marigold shoved her hand into the stolen yellow waistcoat which Winch had been forced to remove. When she pulled it out, revealing Verity's mask, the two girls met each other halfway on the stairs. Verity held it up. "Right here," she said. "It was another thing Winch stole. I was attempting to get it back when...when I realized he must have illicitly discovered your ball theme probably months ago, hence, the tree..."

"I see," Lady Tania said, then turned her face to Officer Credge. "Well, in that case, officer, whatever charges this rogue is being detained on, I want my own charges added to it, since trespass is the only way that could have happened. Even my own family did not know."

She pursed her lips. "And perhaps," she continued, making eye contact with Verity and her own followers, "Perhaps it wasn't the right choice to withhold the information. I had thought it a fun challenge, but I can see it has caused much distress for many, and even"—she looked pitifully on Winch—"desperate lawlessness."

Her speech was met with resounding applause, and after securing her mask, Verity joined in the clapping.

"Well, then," Lady Tania said, "the night is young. Let us see what else is in store! The final exhibit announcement will be in the ballroom before midnight, and then we will light the bonfire." Her final words summoned sparks of their own across those assembled, and Verity glanced over at the unlit bonfire with a grin.

More clapping broke out as Lady Tania led the crowd down the line to look at the other inventions.

Her heart thudding much like the percussion of the clapping below, Verity walked up the remaining steps to join Officer Credge.

"You're here!" Verity said. "How did you—"

"Your friend here told me you had caught the thief responsible for all the break-ins and brought me this mask," he said, pointing.

"Ah, yes," William interjected. "I'll be needing that back— they'll be judging the exhibits in the hall last, but..."

"Of course," Credge said, removing it and returning it to William. The chain of the shackle holding Winch's wrists together rattled. "I don't think anyone will stop me as I leave," he said.

A somewhat-deranged giggle escaped Verity, and Credge smiled.

"But how did you know about the waistcoat?"

It was Marigold who answered. "When I went back to ask William for the mask, those two boys from earlier were there, and it was them who recognized it."

Credge nodded, turning to glance up at the boys in question, who had appeared a few steps above. "I told Theo he would get into the ball with those masks. And he has the sharpest eye when it comes to fabrics. He recognized Mr. Danbury's coat immediately."

Theo ducked his head, and his partner nudged him with his elbow. "Well, it's not a subtle pattern, Father. Anyone could have recognized it."

Winch glared at them as Verity and Marigold snorted, and Officer Credge turned to leave.

"Oh! Wait!" Verity called at their retreating backs. "My father's plans," she said to Credge. "*He* still has them. Do you think..."

Credge frowned, then plunged a hand into the pockets of the yellow waistcoat, searching. Finally, Verity heard the sound of crinkling paper.

A surge of warmth flooded out from the center of her chest as he handed her the schematics, her father's handwriting as recognizable as her own. She took it with both hands and hugged it to her chest with a grin.

"Your mask came out exquisitely, by the way," Credge said. "A work of art worthy of this competition I might say."

"Oh, I doubt it," Verity said, blushing, "but thank you.

Thank you for everything."

"Is this... er... over?" William asked, waving the mechanical dancer's mask around vaguely. "I think the judges are heading back this way."

X

Verity ran her fingers along the edges of her mask to reassure herself, careful not to touch the exposed gears as they twirled in their constant dance. With the mask on her face, the plans in her pocket, and Marigold beside her, every bad feeling that had built up throughout the night dissipated as she walked through the doors into the ballroom, the facade of the hidden garden again a pleasant sight.

A lively waltz played, the quartet at one end of the ballroom under a towering trellis covered in what looked like wisteria vines. Twinkling lights hidden in the vines reflected in the high ceiling-to-floor windows behind them as the stage and trellis gently rotated on a massive wheel.

They followed William over to his dancer, where he

quickly snapped the mask back on and tied the decorative ribbon in place.

He took a step back, assessing his work, his hands clasped behind his back.

Verity smiled reassuringly at him, and to her surprise, he flashed a grin at her.

"I saw what you did to Winch's tree," he said, leaning in close. She caught the tang of lime on his breath. "I nearly collapsed in fits when that single leaf fell, and then the cascade..."

A giggle bubbled up in her throat, but she stifled it as soon as she saw Lady Tania's extravagant mask crest the top of the balcony stairs before any other part of her.

William stiffened, and Verity leaned into him and said, "I haven't seen her dance, but if she was made by you, I'm sure she's wonderful."

His lips parted, and then his attention was drawn to Lady Tania as she stepped forward. Verity did her best to sink back to the wall, not wanting to steal any attention from his exhibit. She watched with pride as he carefully positioned the dancer in the center of Lady Tania's onlookers and started the dancer's movement. As soon as he stepped back, the dancer began to spin on the spot, the casters sliding perfectly over the floor. Then the dancer let down an arm in a graceful arc, followed by the other. Each limb, each joint moved with as much grace as a live dancer. Though the mechanical dancer couldn't hear the music of the ballroom she danced in, it was as if it was being played just for her.

At one point, Verity glanced over at William, her amazement at the dancer transformed into amazement for William. He caught her eye and smiled shyly. Her breath hitched.

Lady Tania signaled for the quartet to halt and stepped forward.

The dancer continued on in silence only broken by the rolling of her wheels.

"Marvelous," Lady Tania said, and the crowd grew rapt in attention around her. "But your dancer is all alone. Does she not have a partner?"

William's eyes bulged momentarily. "I—"

Marigold looked over at him. "Can she? Have a partner, I mean."

He nodded woodenly but made no move to come forward.

"Can I?" Marigold said.

He nodded again.

Marigold stepped forward, her teal dress swishing about her feet.

She timed her movements with the dancer and joined in, grabbing the dancer's hand and following her lead.

Verity couldn't help but grin. She leaned into William, accidentally brushing his arm. Where she touched his skin, her own tingled. "I think you've just made Marigold's night."

"I think she made her own night," he said. "You two made everything right."

Marigold kept up with the dancer while the quartet played the next song, and finally Lady Tania called for a halt. William rushed forward and turned off the dancer's movement while Marigold stepped away amid a cacophony of applause.

Lady Tania stepped into the clearing beside the dancer, her turquoise and purple gown suddenly reminding Verity of a peacock. "Our garden that was once hidden has been discovered for what it truly is! And we have our clear winner of tonight's exhibits," she lifted an imperious hand to point at William's dancer.

Cheering alongside everyone else, Verity and Marigold grew ecstatic as they watched William accept the commendation. As he led the dancer back over to where they stood, Verity met his eyes and the sudden urge to rip his mask off struck her. She fought it, but just barely. The music struck back up, and the volume of the revelry seemed to escalate.

"Would you like to dance?" she asked instead, surprising herself.

His cheeks reddened. "No... I don't..."

"Really? But what about..." she glanced at his dancer.

He ducked his head. "I do appreciate the irony."

"Oh, all right, then I'll just—" She took a step back.

"No, wait." He reached out and took her hand. "Would you like to come watch the bonfire?"

It wasn't until midnight that she saw his face.

Revelers from all over the estate converged on the wide lawn where the Midsummer bonfire would be lit, only minutes from now.

"I still can't believe you did all that work on your mask just to get in here," William was saying as they found places near the front. Marigold had brought her new friends, Theo and his partner. A few of Lady Tania's staff were still arranging the logs and kindling, the anticipation in the crowd rising.

"Well," Verity began, "Marigold and I have been trying to get into the ball forever, so it was really for her. At first, anyway. And then I had to get my father's plans back, I had to find...you. Or so I thought," she added under her breath.

He chuckled. "Well, it seems to have worked out for you."

"I mean, I would have preferred I *didn't* have to go through all that with Winch and his copycat tree. I always loved yours, by the way," she blurted.

He ducked his head. "Thank you. I... um... I remembered you."

"Hmm?" she said, distracted now by the five torches approaching the bonfire, one of which was held by Lady Tania, surprising Verity.

"When you took your mask off," William said, "I remembered you from the Fawney Fair."

"Oh... um... really?"

His golden eyes met hers, sending a pleasant warmth through her body.

"Really. And I think it's only fair..." he said, lifting his mask to rest on the top of his head.

Her heart lifted as she raised her eyes to him, and though his face was revealed, she found herself staring straight into his eyes. Suddenly she wasn't sure she needed to breathe anymore.

Amid the crackling of the dry kindling as they lit the Midsummer fire, Verity—though her heart was racing—reached over and took William's hand, and to her surprise, he lifted it to his lips.

Verity, her gaze on the sparking bonfire, leaned into Marigold next to her, and said, "How about I write to you every *other* day?"

Marigold snorted and grabbed Verity's other hand. "Very well."

THE END

ALL HALLOWS AIRSHIP

CAZ COPPERSDOWN

I

A dry orange leaf skittered across her path as Caz Coppersdown stepped off the train and inhaled the unfamiliar scents of the countryside. A cloud of coal smoke wafted in her direction, cutting short her enjoyment of the dried leaves and a hint of baked apple. She coughed and clutched her carpetbag to her chest as she stepped away from the steam train and onto the small wooden platform.

Haversdale wasn't a busy stop, and only one other passenger departed the train after her, immediately striding off in the direction of the bakery from which that heavenly apple scent wafted. It was a quiet village, with just one row of quaint shops lining either side of the cobblestone street.

Caz wondered whether she would have time to pop into the

bakery before her aunt arrived to pick her up. She almost never got to go out and try the many bakeries and eateries back in Soldark. But for once, she was on her own, even if her parents had sent her to the countryside while they went on their business trip.

The steam train hissed, its gears and motors moving into motion. As it pulled away from the small platform, it revealed a black auto parked on the other side of the tracks. She didn't recognize the gentleman in black standing there, so she shrugged and tramped over toward the bakery. *Probably waiting for the next train*, she thought, but then she heard the man call, "Miss Caroline?"

She winced and turned toward him. "It's Caz," she said automatically.

He bobbed his head and touched the brim of his bowler cap. "Of course," he said. "My apologies. The dowager sent me to retrieve you. She's up to her elbows in the garden at the moment."

Caz raised her eyebrows as she pictured her famously wealthy great-aunt doing anything more than *stroll* through her gardens, but she headed toward the man and his auto just the same.

Recognizing the Daguerre house livery as she got closer, she let him secure her carpetbag, and give her a hand into the auto. She took great care getting into the pristine vehicle; even though her ankle boots were freshly polished and blackened, she still didn't want to scuff up her aunt's auto.

"There you are, Miss Caz," he said after she was settled.

"Thank you," she said. "And you are?"

He ducked his head, "Beg your pardon, ma'am. You can call me Grimlee. I'm the butler at Daguerre." He looked much older than her father, and she wondered if Grimlee had been working at Daguerre when her father came to visit as a boy. Caz had rarely left her own house until a few years ago, let alone been allowed to leave Soldark to visit her aunt's grand estate. She coughed into her gloved hand, a remnant of her childhood illness.

"Mind your skirts now." Grimlee shut the door and briskly went around to the other side.

She folded her gloved hands in her lap, unaccustomed to the silk. The gown she wore was much finer than she was accustomed to, though she still wore no corset to allow for easier breathing. Her gaze flicked out the window at the unfamiliar houses. Between the foreign scents, and the suddenly stifling neckcloth she wore... She wondered if this was all a mistake, accepting her aunt's invitation to her country home for the season. How was she to fit in? She ripped the kerchief from her neck and swiftly stuffed it in her deep dress pocket, taking calculated breaths.

But her parents had already sailed on the airship yesterday to the new copper mine in Angleshire for an inspection. And she had even less of a desire to spend the next month staring at rocks.

If only she could have remained in Soldark writing her first big story. But her parents didn't know about her newswriting ambitions and would never leave her in their grand estate unattended. She knew they were worried about her after a childhood spent in sickness, but that was years ago! And though she had to work to catch her breath sometimes, she could get along quite sufficiently by herself.

Grimlee got in and started up the auto, jerking her back into the moment. She clutched the seat as he brought the auto down the bumpy cobblestone streets of Haversdale, glad her stomach was empty for such a tumultuous drive. The streets of Soldark were much smoother, though she often walked or took the train now that her parents allowed her to leave the estate on the rare occasion. At first, she had had a hard time convincing them to let her go out on her own, but the doctor had said a little exercise would be good for her lungs, and her parents couldn't always accompany her. Her favorite outings were to the corner newsstand.

She eyed a pair of girls strolling down the sidewalk in extravagant dresses, their corsets cinched to perfection, coquettishly giggling behind fans as they watched a group of boys playing football on a nearby pitch. Caz rolled her eyes, though she wished she could get out and walk too. Just as she was wondering how much more bumping she could take, Grimlee turned the auto down a white gravel drive, which was measurably smoother.

As far as mansions went, Daguerre was a grand one.

Her home back in Soldark was quite large, she knew, and having grown up in the wood-paneled monstrosity, she found the Coppersdown estate to be comfortable, full of plush pillows on every chair, fresh candles twinkling from every sconce, tapestries from her parents' travels muffling the sounds of the city outside, and always brimming with the scent of fresh tea and whatever baked goods Mrs. Pratt was cooking up that day.

Caz had visited some other estates in Soldark as her parents mingled with the Grandvilles, the Danburys, and the Stonytons, but to her, all their mansions seemed cold: too big, too clean, and filled with meaningless artwork and decor.

Even from far down the drive, Daguerre's elaborate columns and copper fox statues looked elegant yet inviting. Shrubs and trees by the entrance looked a little overgrown, not like the perfectly manicured and managed nature she was used to in the city.

As they pulled up to the front door of Daguerre, Caz didn't know what to expect. She certainly didn't expect to see her great-aunt, dressed in a modest burgundy gown with black lace edging, stacking pumpkins on the doorstep with the help of a maid. There was dirt under her fingernails. Caz grinned and removed her satin gloves, stuffing them into her pocket before opening the door to the auto. Grimlee wordlessly brought her carpetbag around as Caz stepped forward. She took a deep breath of the country air, inhaling the unfamiliar yet alluring scents of nature.

Dowager Daguerre straightened, a calculating look in her eye as she smiled at her great-niece. "Go get the last four, will you, Marla, and then we can see if we need to buy extra from Shore. Caroline! Welcome to Daguerre."

"It's Caz," she blurted, and heat immediately rushed to her cheeks as she reached up to cover her mouth. Had she really just corrected her? "I'm sorry, Dowager."

Her great-aunt raised a single eyebrow—a feat Caz envied—and said, "What for? I would never wish to call you by a name you dislike. And as far as names go, you may call me Elmira. We are flesh and blood, by golly."

"I...all right," Caz said breathlessly, her cheeks still burning, though she was secretly pleased. Her aunt was *nothing* like the stuffy nobles in Soldark. Her opinion on the upcoming month shifted immediately to excitement.

"Grimlee, take her bag to her room. It's already prepared. That's all you brought?" she asked Caz.

"No, my trunk should be here this afternoon. At least, that's what my father said."

"Perfect," Elmira said crisply. "Now, I need your opinion on these pumpkins."

Caz grinned as her great-aunt picked up some wicked-looking shears and sliced off a few inches of the long stem on one of the bright orange gourds littering the mansion's doorstep.

Though she wasn't sure she'd find much action worthy of a gripping story she could write for the *Soldark Times*, perhaps the season in the country wouldn't be so boring after all.

II

ut *saints*, she was wrong. Anyone who spent five minutes with Great-Aunt Elmira soon became aware that she possessed the spirit of a much younger woman, with a sharp tongue and a sharper mind. Caz quickly became so enamored with her bold and brassy aunt that she wondered if she could write an article featuring the woman. *How to be More Like Elmira: Speak Your Mind or Mind your Business, a Widow's Tale*. She mused about it over breakfast the next morning, then snorted into her cup of tea at the ludicrous idea.

The itch to come up with a story worthy of attention of the *Times* still stung her though, and even though she now realized her time in the country might be entertaining, her aim to be hired as a journalist was growing more distant by the day. How was a formerly shut-in girl supposed to find something newsworthy all the way out here?

At least she had her great-aunt to distract her from her delayed dreams.

Yesterday, after her trunk arrived, Elmira had helped settle Caz into her second-floor suite, then took Caz on a tour of the estate, complete with commentary ranging from what she thought of the people in the village, stories from when Caz's father visited as a boy, and Elmira's favorite subject—the All Hallows Eve soiree she would be hosting at the end of the week.

When she showed her the empty pumpkin patch where Elmira had evidently harvested many of the gourds herself, her aunt nodded firmly and said, "We must go to Shore's tomorrow for more pumpkins. I didn't grow nearly enough. We had a spot of blight in the northeast corner of the garden. Lucky it didn't get all of them. And besides, we'll need more for the invitations."

And so, as soon as Caz finished her breakfast tea, her aunt, draped in another burgundy and black gown, this one with little black spiderweb designs embroidered across the bodice, guided her out the front door to where Grimlee stood waiting with the auto.

"What do you mean, for the invitations?" Caz inquired as they rumbled down the road. She groaned quietly as she glanced out the window at the cobblestones.

"I'd ask Grimlee to slow down, but that only makes it worse," Elmira said, interpreting Caz's discomfort. "Then you feel *each and every* bump. At least, when we go fast, the bumps go by faster."

Caz frowned. "I'll have to take your word for it."

Elmira guffawed and went on. "What I meant, speaking of the invitations, dear niece, is my accounting of the guest list was three short. I have only my own wits to blame. And so now I am three pumpkins short. But I certainly can't detract from the ones we need for decorations. There's barely enough as it is."

"What—"

"Ah, of course. You wouldn't know. It's become something of a legend in Haversdale, if I do say so. Every year when I throw the soiree, I deliver a pumpkin to the doorstep as an invitation. Sometimes I'll have Grimlee carve the time and date onto the pumpkin, or we'll include a paper invitation, rolled up and stuffed right into the pumpkin itself. Everyone knows who it's from."

Caz stared at her in appreciation for a moment, then realized she was picturing her great-aunt sneaking around at night, placing pumpkins on unsuspecting doorsteps.

"Wow," she said finally, thinking her aunt's "soiree" was probably something that would rival the balls and parties thrown in Soldark, judging from what she had already seen of the preparations.

She wondered if, perhaps, the soiree would be newsworthy enough for her story. She had certainly seen plenty of stories about the annual Midsummer Masquerade ball a few months ago in not only the *Soldark Times*, but in the *Sunbelt Chronicle* and the *Soldark Inquirer* too.

As fun and well thought out as it may be, did she really want to report on a party?

She shook her head. No, and even if the *Times* took it and hired her, she'd get stuck reporting on all the parties and events. Though she enjoyed attending the occasional ball, when she had the energy, she would much rather report on something more interesting.

But *what*?

All her life she had ravenously poured through any reading material she could get her hands on, being shut up in the estate all the time. And though she liked novels, what she most looked forward to was the newspapers her parents would get at the newsstands. Reading about what was going on in the world outside her door had always fascinated her. As she got older, she tried writing her own stories, but could never quite manage something so long as a novel. But she hadn't seriously considered writing her own news articles until recently, when the man who ran the newsstand by her house mentioned a friend of his was a journalist. And a fire had been lit. She went through stacks of empty journals, practicing her prose in her long hours at home.

Her first story had to be good, though. It had to be perfect, something people would actually *want* to read and that would leave them wanting more. And that would mean more stories she could write.

She gazed out the window of the auto and spied a lone airship in the sky. It wasn't too far away, so she could make out some details from the ground. It was nothing like the ones she had seen over Soldark, which had large enclosed gondolas for transporting lots of people. She didn't think this one would hold more than one person. And it had strange metallic fins on top of the balloon and jutting out from the sides of the gondola. It sailed through the pink morning clouds with a faint hum that reached her ears when the auto came to an abrupt halt outside a farm stand.

Caz distractedly watched the unusual airship as she stepped out of the auto and followed her aunt to a mound of pumpkins. Elmira began to instruct the farmer and Grimlee to load up what looked like a dozen or more of the orange gourds.

And that's when the nose of the airship dropped.

She paused with her hand on the farm cart as her aunt paid the farmer, Caz's breath coming fast. The airship was still diving. Was this normal? The airships over Soldark never behaved like this, not even when her father brought her to watch them land at the nearby airfield.

"Oh no," her aunt said from right beside her, a pumpkin under each arm, her mouth agape.

Grimlee *tsked*, his arms full of pumpkins. "I'm sorry, ma'am."

"*What?*" Caz demanded, confusion etching her face. "What is it?"

Just then, the airship leveled out, sailing upward again in a sharp curve. It continued to sail across the pink morning sky as if it hadn't almost just crashed.

"The airshow," Elmira said in disgust, placing the pumpkins into the back of the auto with a *thunk*.

"Oh," Caz said, still thoroughly confused, but glad she hadn't

witnessed an airship crash.

"They started it last year," Elmira explained as they got back into the auto a minute later. "It was quite popular. Ran all week. Popular enough that people left my soiree to watch the finale. I had hoped they wouldn't return this year. Or, at least, not during the week of All Hallows."

For a moment, Caz blinked at her aunt, at the uncharacteristic disappointment coursing through Elmira's features. But with Elmira's devotion to her party planning—Saints! Even planting and harvesting pumpkins herself—it was obvious that this event meant a lot to her. And it was coming to mean something to Caz too.

"I'm sorry," Caz said as the auto bumped over the cobblestones. She glanced out the back window, sure they would have lost some pumpkins. But no, Grimlee had covered them with a black canvas tarpaulin. "How about you tell me what you're doing with the invitations this year?"

Elmira gleamed and leaned forward, launching into a description of how she planned to carve out the inside of the pumpkins and put a candle in each one.

By the time they reached Daguerre, her aunt seemed her usual self, but as they unloaded the pumpkins onto the front steps, the sounds of another airship reached their ears. Elmira looked up at the sky with such animosity that Caz took a step back, glad her aunt had never pierced her with that look before—and hoped she never would.

III

The fire crackled as Caz lifted the carving knife, her hands and forearms covered in the guts of half a dozen pumpkins.

"That's marvelous," Elmira said, coming in with a large silver tray laden with steaming mugs and sweet orange bread.

Caz set down the knife and wiped her hands and arms with the damp towel her aunt had brought. She admired her work in the afternoon sunlight slanting through the large mullioned windows.

She never thought she'd be spending her time in the country learning to carve pumpkins, but it was still better than trekking through the copper mine and looking at rocks with her parents—who were always asking her if she needed to stop and take a rest or if the air was too stiff for her. But she was actually having *fun*.

Her first pumpkin was passable—a single, misshapen hole

through which the candlelight would shine. But after the first few, she had decided to try something more interesting.

"A cat?" Elmira said in admiration, handing her a mug.

"A black cat," Caz clarified. She inhaled the powerful scent of hot apple with spices.

"How can it be black, when it's carved out of a pumpkin!" Elmira jested.

Chuckling to herself, Caz put her lips to the mug and sampled its contents. The taste exploded on her tongue, and she took a large gulp. "This is amazing," she muttered. "What is it?"

"Hot apple cider with cinnamon and nutmeg," Elmira said, sipping her own with an indulgent smile. "It was Jack's favorite too."

Caz's gaze went to the portrait of Elmira's late husband over the fireplace, the Daguerre himself. His coal-black top hat shadowed his face, which sported a gray grizzled beard. He looked as wily and sharp as Elmira. She gave her aunt a sad smile. "It's fantastic. I can see why he liked it."

Elmira cleared her throat and set her own mug back on the tray. "Now, you're quite good at carving those pumpkins, dear niece, and I don't want you to think I'm putting you to work, but have you any interest in helping with the rest of the decorations?"

She couldn't tell if the heat in her cheeks was from Elmira's compliment or the warm cider. Pleased, she said, "Sure, I'd love to."

The scent of hearth fire and mulled spices drifted from the open doors of the modest ballroom when Caz entered an hour later after they cleaned up the pumpkin carving mess. Her eyes were immediately drawn upward to the swaths of sheer black fabric Grimlee and the maid Marla were draping from the silver gilt chandeliers, along with garlands of black and red silk flowers.

Grimlee descended from his ladder with surprising agility after securing his fabric and headed over to the wooden crates stacked by the doors where Caz and Elmira stood admiring the work.

"Wait until it's done," Elmira assured her, a bony hand on Caz's arm. "This is just the beginning."

The beginning was a cloud of realistic fabric bats suspended from the ceiling over the large fireplace, each suspended on a thread, bobbing in the heat wafting upward; portraits on the walls draped in the same sheer black fabric as if newly mourned; and pumpkins along with their trailing vines lining the walls, the yellowing leaves and dying vines pinned up on the walls as if they had grown there.

"Fantastic," Caz said, taking a step toward another portrait of the Daguerre. "Huh," she said, noticing through the sheer black drape an airship painted prominently in the background behind him.

A sharp crack drew her attention as Elmira took a crowbar to the lid of one of the wooden crates. Her aunt said, "It's almost suppertime. Why don't you take a look at the rest of the decorations tomorrow morning, and see if anything catches your fancy? Having a fresh eye might give us that new perspective."

"Sure."

The next morning, after a hearty breakfast that included

kippers and eggs, orange scones, and cold cider, Caz began inspecting the crates. Just as she was pulling out some elaborate lanterns with little golden bone details on the panes, Grimlee arrived with a silver tray. But it didn't bear any of that hot cider, much to Caz's disappointment. Instead, a single piece of paper: a telegram addressed to her.

Caz's heart skipped a beat, imagining something horrible had happened to her parents, an airship crash or worse, but as she picked it up and read the missive, her heart dropped far past her stomach in disappointment.

To: Ms. Caroline (Caz) Coppersdown
From: Mr. Edward Coppersdown

Landed at Angleshire mine successfully, but nothing to look at. Unexpected collapse the morning of our departure. Will take months to re-secure. No workers injured. We will return to the solarbelt and collect you from Daguerre on All Hallows Day. ~All our love.

Her mouth agape, she reread the telegram several times by the cold morning light twinkling in through the mullioned windows. She shivered, pulling her knit cardigan over her chest. But somehow, no matter how many times she reread it, the words remained the same.

So much for finding a big story here in the countryside. And so much for her newfound freedom outside of Soldark. At least she would get to stay for her aunt's soiree. But Caz had already grown to enjoy Daguerre and, more importantly, not being cooped up in her own home as she had been for the past seventeen years. But what she would miss most of all was her aunt.

Elmira strode into the ballroom with the clickety-clack of her sharp-heeled boots, startling Caz, who almost dropped the telegram. She fumbled with it and returned it to the tray Grimlee held, still politely waiting. "Sorry," she muttered to Grimlee.

Her aunt surveyed the ballroom with relish, her gaze roving over the crates. "Well, at least, all is going well in here, eh?" she said. "But I've just run out of crimson ink in my study—another errand in town."

"I'll go," Caz blurted.

Elmira looked her over, her eyes momentarily watching the retreating back of Grimlee with the bad news sitting primly on a platter as he left the room.

"Is something—"

"It's fine," Caz said. "Well... My parents are coming back early. All Hallows Day, they'll be here to collect me."

She turned her back on her aunt when her eyes burned with surprising emotion and pretended to study the bone lantern she had pulled out of the crate.

"I see. Well, that's disappointing."

Caz bit her lip. Why was she so upset? She hadn't even wanted to come out to the countryside. But now that her stay was coming to an abrupt end, she found she didn't want to leave.

"I'd quite been looking forward to having you for the next month," Elmira said. "Not much to do around here, and it's always the same company."

"I'm disappointed too," Caz admitted, waiting until the burning in her eyes had gone—there was no way she was going to cry over this and not in front of Elmira, certainly. "I'm used to the same company too," she joked feebly, turning around.

"Well, we must make the most of it," Elmira said. "Why don't I ask Grimlee to bring the car around so you can go to the stationery shop?"

Caz began to tidy up the crates she'd been poking through. "No, I'd like to walk if it's not too far."

Elmira gave her a knowing smile. "Why don't you get yourself something too? Watson's has an extensive selection. Just be sure to get a bottle of Crimson Cordial for me."

Caz nodded, a slight smile forming. Perhaps drowning her sorrows in purchasing new ink and paper would be just the thing she needed.

IV

By the time she reached the shops, Caz was beginning to regret her decision to turn down a ride in the auto, no matter how bumpy it might have been. Panting, she took refuge in the shadow of the bakery on the edge of the small village. When she was finally able to draw a deep enough breath, she straightened her orange-hued skirts and patted the purse in her pocket. Her parents had given her plenty of pocket money for her now-truncated trip to the country, and though she had no intention of spending it all in one go, she certainly felt entitled to a few items to commemorate her trip.

After taking a moment to pull her knit stockings back up where they belonged, she left the shadow of the bakery—vowing to grab some of the apple tarts on her way back to Daguerre.

Just as she was rounding the corner of the brick building, she ran right into someone.

"Oh!" she exclaimed, her breath getting knocked out of her. She doubled over at the unexpected loss of air.

"Miss, my apologies! Are you all right?" he said.

She straightened and held up a finger to indicate she merely needed a minute to resume normal operations. Finally, she said, "It's all right. I'm winded easily is all."

"I'm so sorry," the man said. "I shouldn't have been rushing down the sidewalk like that, I'm just supposed to be hanging up these flyers." He bent down and began to pick up the flyers Caz hadn't realized he dropped—each one scattering across the sidewalk like leaves, but instead of orange and red hues, these sheafs featured a skillfully inked airship. She sunk down automatically to help him, at the same time trying to inconspicuously steady her breathing.

"What's—oh," she said, picking up one and reading the words underneath the illustration. She looked up at the man's face for the first time. "This is for the airshow?"

He nodded, his eyes bright—which was quite noticeable since he had an imprint from some goggles around his eyes, dark shading of dirt and oil around the two circles on his skin. Said goggles perched atop his head, nestled in his windblown brown hair, the copper contraption glinting in the morning sun with a multitude of dials and knobs. "Yup," he said. "It's already up and running. Goes 'til Friday for the big finale!"

"I see," Caz said somewhat reluctantly, pulling her gaze away from his comely face. This fellow seemed perfectly nice, but she felt she should be offended on her aunt's behalf. Though, surely, he had nothing to do with scheduling the airshow this week...

She mustered a smile. "Well, good luck with it."

"Here," he said with a grin, thrusting a flyer into her hands. "It's going to be great fun. You should come by."

"Oh...uh...well, I'm staying with my great-aunt, and we have plans this week," she said, realizing she didn't want to offend him. "Are you... are you a pilot or something?" She idly stuffed the flyer into her dress pocket.

He nodded, a pleased smile curling his lips. "I'm flying the *Bressieux Mark II*, the featured airship for the grand finale. It's a recreation of the original *Bressieux*, flown by one of the greatest— but I'm sorry, I'm rambling."

"No, no, it's fine," she said with a light chuckle. "It sounds wonderful. You must be skilled to be flying in the finale."

He ducked his head. "Sometimes I think luck had something to do with it. But I've been working on airships since I was a kid."

"Well, I wish you good luck. And actually... it sounds quite..." Her eye caught on the stationery shop across the street, the quills and ink featured in the window. "*Newsworthy...*" Her heart leaped.

"I better go do my shopping," she said breathlessly.

He bobbed his head and said, "I should finish hanging these. My boss was a bit late on organizing the show this year, tied up with repairs and all." He gestured to the flyers. "It was nice running into you—" He froze, then laughed at her smirk. "Well, what I meant to say was, it was nice to *meet* you, and I'm sorry for running into you."

"It's quite all right," she said.

"I'm Hanson, by the way," he said. "Hanson McCleary."

"Caz. Coppersdown," she added with a bob of her head, uncharacteristically hoping he didn't recognize her family name. On the few occasions she met people in Soldark, they immediately changed their demeanor as they realized who they were talking to. There was a whole square named after her family, for sun's sake! But she felt as if she had done nothing to earn that recognition. Not yet anyway. Just because her grandfather had grown an efficient and prosperous copper enterprise didn't mean anyone should treat *her* differently.

But Hanson didn't blink an eye, merely smiled ruefully down at his flyers. "If you can get away, come see me at the airshow!"

"I'll...er...try!" She gave him a wave as she crossed the empty street, still not used to the non-existent traffic out here in the country. Her face inexplicably warming, she hurried across the cobblestones to the stationery store. She snuck a glance back at Hanson, who was busy tacking up a flyer to a fencepost by the train platform.

As the bell rang over the door to Watson's Stationery, her mind wandered to what Hanson said about the airshow, and the finale— it had actually sounded quite in line with something that would make a good story to submit to the *Soldark Times*, particularly about the finale, and some famous airship recreation.

She quickly found the Crimson Cordial ink, and began to peruse the diaries of blank paper with ornate silver-embossed covers. She quite fancied having a nice new blank diary to write in...

But could she, in good conscience, write a story about the airshow that so incensed Elmira?

Was it really newsworthy enough to disappoint her aunt like that? For she was sure Elmira would find out if she wrote an article on the despised event. What was that airship called again? And why had Hanson said it was so important?

She pulled the hastily crumpled flyer out of her pocket and read it closer this time. *The Bressieux Mark II—first time ever presented!—an accurate recreation of the famous airship flown by the greatest pilot in the history of the solarbelt, Jack Daguerre.*

The Crimson Cordial fell right from her hand. The glass shattered, and red ink splattered across her hem.

By the time she and the shopkeeper—Watson himself—cleared up the mess, the sky was glowing a dusky orange with the impending sunset. There was nothing they could do about her dress, which looked as if she had been splattered with blood in some gory accident—so all in all, she was not looking forward to walking all the way back to Daguerre, particularly when she knew how much the physical exertion would trouble her, let alone in her seemingly bloody state.

It was for this reason that her heart soared upon seeing a now-familiar black auto parked on the street corner by the bakery, with Grimlee standing idly by the driver's side. She checked the otherwise empty street before crossing and rushed to meet him. His placid face morphed into a look of horror, and she looked down at her ruined dress and chuckled.

"Had a little accident in the shop—Oh, no! Don't worry, it's just ink," she assured him.

He closed his gaping mouth and pressed a hand to his heart. "Thank the sun's rays! It looks like you've witnessed a murder!"

She stifled a chill as a sharp breeze rounded the corner of the bakery. "Fitting, no? It's almost All Hallows." She clutched her sweater around her torso to ward off the chill.

"You sound like your great-uncle," Grimlee said, looking almost pleased. "It was truly his favorite holiday—favorite season, to be sure."

Caz smiled, thinking back to the portrait of Jack Daguerre in the ballroom, where she had *definitely* seen an airship painted in the background, now that she thought of it. Why Elmira despised the airshow, she wasn't sure. Would Elmira know about the *Bressieux Mark II*, if this was the first time ever presented? A drop of guilt surged through her insides as she wondered again whether she could even write about the airshow now—or whether she *should*.

The guilt intensified as she wondered whether she should be the one to tell her aunt about the airship modeled after Jack's.

"Did you get everything you needed?" Grimlee asked her.

She opened her mouth to reply, but her gaze fell on the window of the bakery, the sun's orange rays glinting off of it. "Not quite. Do you mind waiting while I go get one of those pies?"

As she endured the bumping along the cobblestones, she tried to focus on the heavenly scent coming from the waxed paper box in her lap. But as she spotted an airship rising in the sky as they drove, her stomach swooped from more than just the turbulent ride.

V

lmira was stabbing pumpkins through the tines of the black wrought-iron fence, and she wasn't doing it gently.

As Caz got out of the auto, she saw the source of Elmira's anger: an elderly woman in a frilly puce dress, with a cane and an enormous black hat covered in all manner of decorations: a pumpkin made of straw, a felt bat, dried orange leaves, and what Caz suspected were real animal bones. Caz raised her eyebrows at the woman whose enthusiasm for the season might have just rivaled Elmira's. But the hat didn't seem to be the source of discontent.

"I told you. I don't truck with that nonsense—ah, dear Caz, you're back!" Elmira said, ushering her over with a wave of her bony arm.

Caz obeyed, still clutching the pie and the paper bag containing her new journal and the fresh bottle of Crimson Cordial.

The woman in puce let out a shriek.

Elmira demanded, *"What in the name of the spirits happened to you?"*

"Oh!" Caz said, "It's just ink!"

"You gave me such a fright," the other woman said, clutching her chest.

"I apologize," Caz said, "I dropped a bottle at the shop, and well…" She gestured to her hem.

Elmira began to chuckle. "Perhaps you should wear that dress to the soiree."

Caz grinned. "Perhaps."

"Ah," the woman interrupted, "Now, you might be interested, Miss… Caz, is it? I was just telling your great-aunt, I've offered my services as a medium to converse with the spirits on All Hallows—you know, when the veil is thin, it is easy to reach out and speak to those who have passed beyond—"

"We're not interested, Dolly," Elmira said.

Caz pressed her lips tight and nodded in agreement. There was no way she would do anything *but* agree, with that look on her aunt's face. And it was certainly not her place to decide.

Elmira stabbed another pumpkin onto a fence tine as if to run the point home.

But Dolly didn't seem put off in the least. She leaned heavily on her cane, and Caz noticed a black raven's head carved into the top.

"I have a feeling you'll change your mind one of these days," Dolly said, waggling a finger. She nodded at both of them, her hat wobbling precariously on her head but somehow remaining firm. "I'll see you on Friday, my dears!"

And off she went down the lane, disappearing into the bright orange afternoon sunlight and falling leaves.

Caz lifted her armful of purchases and said, "I've got the ink, do you need help with the rest of the invitations?"

Elmira stabbed the last pumpkin onto the fence with relish.

Grinning at the display, Caz said, "That looks wonderful."

Her aunt brushed her hands off on the white apron she had tied around her waist, but uncustomarily remained silent, now staring off down the lane, lost in thought.

"I got an apple pie," Caz volunteered, unsure what to do about her aunt's pensive mood. Pastries always cheered *her* up; Mrs. Pratt back home always kept a tray of baked goods on the counter in their spacious kitchen. And though Caz longed for some of their cook's best pumpkin scones at the moment, she was sure the apple pie would do just fine.

Elmira sighed, glanced at the speared pumpkins as if just noticing the job complete, then shook her head a little. "Come with me," she said. "I want to show you something."

They deposited Caz's purchases with Marla at the front door, and to Caz's surprise, Elmira took her around the back of the house to a large barn situated between the toolshed and the garage. Elmira took a key from a ribbon around her neck, a massive brass affair with ornate scrollwork, and inserted it into the lock on the barn. She pulled open the hinged doors with surprising strength, the cross-beamed doors swinging wide.

Darkness greeted them. Caz saw a massive looming shadow and took a step back. Elmira, though, stepped forward into the dark barn. The next moment, Caz heard a sure *thunk* of a metal switch, and gas lamps twinkled to life from the rafters, illuminating the barn with flickering yellow light.

Skeletal girders lined a rigid balloon in the unmistakable outline of an airship. The gondola, where passengers would stand, rested on a wooden platform, attached to a ramp that led into the barn. Weights, pulleys, gears, and levers lined the edges of the gondola, culminating in the front center in a highly-polished wooden helm. Caz's own feet led her closer without much thought. The gaslight flickered and danced over the airship, bringing shadows to life and making it look like it could take off at any moment.

Carved in intricate scrollwork across the bow of the gondola, in gilt letters, was the word *Bressieux.*

"Jack loved to fly," Elmira said quietly from beside her.

A knife in her heart, Caz turned to her aunt to see tears lingering in the corners of her eyes.

"Is that... is that why you hate the airshow so much?" Caz said in a small voice.

To her surprise, Elmira snorted. "No, not really. It's because, well, you might think me a silly old woman—"

"I would never!" Caz blurted. "You're the most amazing person

I've ever met!" she said, realizing as she said the words that it was true.

"Thank you, my dear. But it's because Jack also loved All Hallows, and celebrating the evening with our friends. The pumpkins, the decorations, the soiree, it all started with him."

"Oh, Elmira," Caz said, reaching out and taking her aunt's hand.

Elmira squeezed back with vigor and gave her a watery smile.

"Tell me more about Jack," Caz insisted.

Her aunt shivered, then pulled a black kerchief from her pocket to dab her eyes. "I'd love to. But let's do it over pie. We'd catch a death of cold out here once the sun goes down."

In front of the cozy hearth in the study, the remnants of Caz's second piece of pie strewn across her plate, Elmira's stories almost lulled her to a pleasant sleep. But her curiosity kept her awake, as Elmira spoke of trips to far off locations, fantastic journeys Jack would take her on when he wasn't busy breaking some new airship record. Of autumn nights walking by the river. Of the look on his face when he came home after a flight. When her aunt grew silent, Caz smiled and said, "It sounds like Jack really loved his airship and All Hallows, but I think most of all, he loved you."

VI

After dreams of flying an airship to far-off countries, Caz awoke with a plan. She just had no idea how to execute it.

A hot cup of tea was waiting for her when she came to the parlor for breakfast, and it did wonders to take off the morning chill that was already creeping in through the cuffs of her dress. She would have to grab a sweater or a shawl if she were to leave the house—she just needed to figure out how to get over to the airfield without Elmira or anyone knowing.

And that was going to be quite a feat if she wanted to make it by sundown without collapsing out of breath.

After seeing Elmira's face last night—darkened by the ghost

of the airship, then brightened by the stories by the hearth—a fire burned in Caz's chest at the insult to the Daguerres over the airshow and their even naming a ship after Jack's without her aunt's knowledge. For she was sure her aunt didn't know about the airshow finale—and she really didn't want to be the one to tell her about it.

She pressed her lips together as her aunt told her that she and Grimlee would be delivering the invitations late that evening. "It's only two days away—though it's just a formality. Surely everyone will know with the decorations going up."

Caz nodded, taking another sip of tea. "Of course. I mean, the pumpkins on the fence are a dead giveaway." She grinned.

Elmira eyed her over her own teacup—an orange bone porcelain affair with vines adorning the rim—and snorted. "You know, you're welcome to visit here anytime, Caz," her aunt said, surprising her.

"Oh." Caz flushed, pleased. "I'd love to, if my parents—"

Waving a hand as if swatting away a fly, Elmira said, "Phooey. You're old enough to decide. And I've got some words for my nephew when he comes on Saturday to pick you up. You've hardly had enough time to enjoy Haversdale at all! Are you sure they wouldn't let you stay longer?"

Her face flushing even deeper, Caz ducked her head. "I don't think they would come pick me up themselves if they were planning on letting me stay. It's all right. I'm used to it."

"Well, I'm not," Elmira went on. "You should be able to

make your own decisions. What will they do when you decide to get a job? Or an admirer?"

Unsure whether her face could get any hotter, Caz muttered, "I don't know."

Elmira crossed her arms over her umber-colored gown, with matching stitching across the bodice. "What *would* you like to do?"

"I..." Her gaze darted around the parlor, everywhere except her aunt's quizzical stare. "I want to be a journalist."

Finally, Caz looked at her aunt, who was now studying her in appreciation. "I see. And have you told your parents this?"

Caz took a large gulp of tea, which had luckily cooled down to a temperature where this action didn't burn her whole mouth. "I... have. And I wanted to get a job as a newsie, so I could make connections at the *Soldark Times*, but, well—"

"Hmm," her aunt said. "I suppose all that walking might not be advisable for you. That's why I sent Grimlee yesterday to pick you up, just in case."

"Thank you for that," Caz said. "I didn't think the village was that far, and I confess I was dreading the walk home."

"So, newsie is out," Elmira continued. "But how do you become a journalist?"

Caz wriggled in her seat, not used to all the interest—her parents usually brushed it off whenever Caz brought it up. "You could be a journalist yourself, with all these questions!" she chuckled.

Elmira raised a brow. "Perhaps you get it from me, then."

The thought warmed Caz's insides at the reminder that she shared lineage with this tenacious woman. "I need to write a story—probably more than one—and submit it to the paper. If the editors like it, they'll print it, and I'll have a foot in the door."

"Ah," Elmira said, leaning back in her chair, though her posture was as perfect as ever. "Any burgeoning story ideas in that head of yours?"

Caz shook her head sadly, draining the rest of her tea. Her stomach gave a little flip as she considered her intended destination for the day...and the fact that she would need to go behind her aunt's back to do it.

But she couldn't write a story about the *Bressieux* and the *Bressieux Mark II*, could she?

She shook her head violently. No. She wouldn't.

Her aunt took her vehemence for anger, and her expression softened. "You'll find something worthy of your writing, I'm sure of it."

Caz swallowed the lump in her throat. "Thank you."

She spent the morning digging through cobwebs—some real and others spun of silk—in the ballroom while her aunt finished the calligraphy on the invitations. While Grimlee and Marla were busy on the ladders hanging more black silk from the ceiling, Caz snuck outside to inspect something in the back. She returned with some freshly fallen orange and red leaves as an excuse should anyone notice her absence.

After they finished their afternoon tea, Caz broached the question she had been working on wordsmithing in her head all day. "I'd like to go into the village again. I didn't get to look at the other shops much, and I'm not really sure when I'll get to come back to Haversdale."

"I'll have Grimlee bring the auto around," her aunt suggested.

"Actually... when I was gathering some leaves outside, I noticed some bicycles in the garage?" she said. "I thought if I rode on the grass or the sidewalks, it would be preferable to bumping around in the auto," she said truthfully. Surely it would be easier on her lungs than walking.

But what she really didn't want was Grimlee or anyone else knowing her destination.

"Oh, sure," Elmira said easily, "You're welcome to borrow one. I'm too old for those now. Should have donated them to someone more sprightly years ago. I used to take your father and his cousins out on rides through the fields down by the river."

"Thank you," Caz said, her stomach doing a flip. The first stage of her plan, done.

"I'll ask Grimlee to check the tires for you."

Less than an hour later, Caz pedaled down the lane on her aunt's black bicycle, fresh air in the tires, and crisp autumn air whisking past her face. Large empty baskets sat astride the bicycle, and one in front, reminding Caz that she would need to actually stop in the village for another trinket or two to prove her cover story.

She squashed down the guilt at the white lie she had given her aunt. But really, it was for the best.

Stuffing her hand in her dress pocket as she glided down a hill of close-cropped grass just outside the village, she pulled out the flyer for the airshow, wondering just where the airfield was when she saw another airship chugging through the sky, nose-down.

"That's lucky," she breathed, pulling the bicycle onto the sidewalk near the train stop and getting a whiff of pure deliciousness from the bakery as she sped past. She followed the trajectory of the airship, which appeared to be coming in for a landing.

She barely had time to register more than a handful of the shop names before she had passed through the town entirely. *Not much to look at*, she noted. *At least I can stop on my way back.*

And it wasn't just for her cover story. She truly *didn't* want to leave Haversdale on Saturday, only to return to her sedentary life back at the estate in Soldark. Perhaps Elmira could convince her parents to let her visit again, but she didn't want to place all her hopes on that happening anytime soon.

Could she really go back to being stuck inside the estate, only dreaming of finding a story to write about?

I've got a story brewing right here, she thought to herself as she tracked the landing airship as it got lower and lower.

No, she told herself. *That's not why I'm going here.*

She spotted a wooden fence and an open gate with a sign on a post which read: *Eldrough's*. Two dirt tracks from all the autos going in and out made a perfect lane for her bicycle, and she slowly pedaled up to the gate, not at all winded.

Airships were parked all around the field—which looked to function as a cow pasture when not an airfield, judging by the cow patties in the corner—a variety of dirigibles, some with rigid balloons and large gondolas, and others with simple baskets and balloons only held open with hot air. Caz watched as one of the hot air balloons inflated before her eyes, and she dismounted from her bicycle and led it inside. A man at the gate cleared his throat, and she startled, swiveling her head to look at him standing beside the gate with his hand out.

She looked at him in question, and he nodded at a small hand-lettered sign tacked to the gate which read: *Admission: 5 coppers.*

"Oh, I'm not coming for the show," she said, "I just wanted to speak to one of the pilots."

He nodded at the sign again, bowler cap shading his eyes, "Sorry, miss, plenty of people come just to look at the ships and meet the pilots too. We gotta charge everybody the admission."

"All right," she said, shrugging, though she didn't want to financially support the airshow out of spite. She dug in her pocket and retrieved the coppers.

He slid them into a pouch at his belt with a nod of thanks and handed her a ticket with grimy hands. "Enjoy," he said with a grin that Caz could only describe as slimy.

"Thanks," she said, refraining from wrinkling her nose at him. Though she wanted to drop the ticket on the ground the first chance she got, she slipped it into her pocket instead, in case anyone was checking for them.

She walked beside her bicycle, wheeling it over to the long line of airships, wondering if she could identify the *Bressieux Mark II*. She had wanted to take another look at the original *Bressieux* this morning when she snuck out behind the mansion, but had forgotten about the lock on the barn doors. That was when she spotted the bicycles in the garage.

The sun hung low in the sky, painting the clouds with splashes of orange and red. She walked past the hot air balloon, which was mostly inflated now, and watched in amusement as two mechanics tossed tools and parts back and forth to one another from one of the airships, one of them in the gondola assumably fixing something, the other on the ground fetching and replacing things from a toolbox.

But as she rounded the next airship and recognized the skeletal girders wrapped in sheet metal of a familiar-looking rigid balloon, someone called from behind her, "Hey, miss!"

She whirled around, her auburn hair sailing off her shoulder. Almost fearing the grimy gatekeeper, she was relieved to see the handsome pilot, Hanson, striding up to her, a wrench in his hand.

"You came!" he said.

She pressed her lips together, trying to form a polite smile. "I did," she hedged. "I...um...had some questions for you."

"Well, come over here to the *Bressieux II* while I try and get this girder straight. I still can't take off, and I only have two days to get it in order. Alcide is going to wring my neck if we can't get it off the ground."

"Oh," she said, secretly hoping he couldn't get it fixed. "Who's Alcide?" she asked, unsure how to broach the subject she came to discuss. She had tried wordsmithing it in her head on the way over, but couldn't get it right.

"Manager of the airshow—my boss. It was his idea to recreate the *Bressieux,* but I wish he hadn't publicized it," he added in a mutter.

"Why not?"

Hanson lowered his voice. "I still haven't flown it. It's a beautiful recreation. He got the plans from the Air Museum—apparently the original ones were donated by the Daguerre himself—or, you wouldn't know..."

She drew herself up, "Actually, I would. He was my great-uncle."

He looked as if he'd been struck in the face with a hammer. She almost laughed.

"Really?" he finally said. "Did you know him? Did you ever

get to go in an airship with him?"

She shook her head, almost chuckling at the admiration on Hanson's face. "No. I never met him. I think I was just a few years old when he passed away, and I never even left the house until—" she flushed, then ducked her head. "Well, listen," she said, and cleared her throat. "I came here to ask you about the airship. I don't think you should fly it. It's insulting to the dowager Daguerre."

The name felt strange coming from her lips, but she thought it might carry more weight than *my aunt, Elmira.*

His mouth opened again in shock. "What? But why?"

"I... She..." Her stomach tightened as she fretted over what to say. Sudden doubt struck her. Would her aunt really want her here? She shook her head. She knew the answer to that question. "Listen, she holds an All Hallows soiree every year in Ja—in the Daguerre's honor. *In his honor.* And the airshow is right on—"

"Oh," Hanson said, his face falling. He licked his lips nervously. "But I have to, or Alcide will fire me. I mean"—he laughed nervously—"if I can't get it working, we won't fly it, but...he'd probably fire me, then, too," he added under his breath. He glanced up at the airship in worry.

Caz felt a pang of concern over his predicament. She should probably be talking to this Alcide person, but she had a bad feeling he was the grimy man at the gate, and somehow, she didn't think he would understand anything about the situation.

She puffed out her chest. *But if I'm to become a journalist, I'm going to have to ask the hard questions and track down the real story about things.* She glanced over at the gate, and her nose twitched.

"I'm sorry," she said, clasping both hands together. "I hope you don't lose your job. What's wrong with it?"

His face lit up, and he led her over to the side of the airship, where one of the girders fastening the gondola to the balloon had some bolts missing.

He tapped the girder with his wrench, making a *clang, clang, clang.* "Support girder's bent. Bolts won't even go back on."

"Oh," she said, taking a careful step forward. There were toolboxes and crates strewn about the ground beside the gondola, and a small box of pastries sitting on an upturned crate made her crack a smile. "From the village?" she inquired, nodding at the box.

Hanson grinned and nodded appreciatively. "Pumpkin scones with chocolate ganache. I got them this morning before I noticed the girder."

Her eyes must have lit up, because he immediately bent over and picked up the box. His hands were covered in what looked like ages of oil or grease, but it looked more like an aged patina, rather than the greasy hands of Alcide at the gate. They didn't even mar the perfect paper box.

"Here," he said. "Take one, I've got plenty."

"Oh, no, I couldn't," she waved him away, though one look at the open box and her mouth watered.

"Take them all, you can...erm...share them with your aunt. You know, I'd love to meet her, if she wasn't...if I... Is it truly offending her that we're going to fly a replica of the Daguerre's airship?"

Her mouth fell open. "Well, to be honest, she didn't—"

"Hanson!" someone called casually.

They both looked up from the pastry box. The mechanic on the airship next to them whistled, and Hanson said, "Alcide's probably coming—I should really—"

"Oh, sorry," she said.

"Here, take these," he said, thrusting the whole pastry box into her hands. "I'm really sorry if the airshow coincides with your aunt's party. If there was anything I could do...but I have to get this ship working."

"I understand," she said. "It's not your fault."

He gave her a careworn smile, and she began to wheel her bicycle away, not wanting to get him into trouble with his boss.

"Good luck," she said quietly as she wheeled away, pastry box in her front basket.

She heard someone bark Hanson's name as she walked to the next airship, pretending to take in the sights before turning her bicycle around and heading back for the gate. She snuck a glance at the *Bressieux Mark II* as she walked on by, but

Hanson and his boss were nowhere to be seen; the sound of shouting came from behind the gondola.

In the end, she didn't feel like stopping in the village, though she had plenty of time. The box of scones tucked into the bicycle basket made her stomach flip, but she wasn't sure if it was from guilt or flattery.

VII

Unfortunately, the way back was more uphill than she had reckoned.

A chill breeze rattled the trees, plucking a few dead leaves off and scattering them across her path on the side of the road. She could *see* Daguerre, since it was set on somewhat of a hill, but the distance she still had to go was making her breathless.

She dismounted from the bicycle and trudged up a slight incline. A road to her left caught her attention; it looked like a shortcut. She puffed out a tired breath and turned the bicycle down the dirt road on a whim. As long as she could still see Daguerre, there was no way she could get lost. She tightened her shawl about her shoulders and paused for a moment to tighten the clasp holding it together, a cloak pin her aunt had loaned her. It was steel, twisted into a circle, with a pin that stabbed through the knit fibers of her shawl. When turned, the steel circle butted up against the pin, holding it closed. But all the jolting on the bicycle had loosened the pin, so she turned it again tight.

The ground evened out, so she got back on the bicycle, her gaze landing on the parcel of scones tucked into the basket. Hanson had been so nice. Though she had first wanted to yell at him and tell him not to fly the airship, she couldn't. As she pedaled down the dirt lane in the evening gloam, she wondered again if she should tell Elmira about the *Bressieux Mark II*.

Her aunt was bound to find out somehow. If she came into the village and saw any of those flyers, for instance. *She must know*, Caz thought. *Surely! And if for some sun-forsaken chance she doesn't, I don't want to be the one to tell her.*

The path was now going slightly downhill, easing the burden on Caz's lungs. She heaved a sigh of relief as she glided down the road, eyes on Daguerre in the distance. A lone crow soared over the house, and Caz smiled, thinking how her aunt would probably be happy to see the bird, one so favorably featured in her decorations in the ballroom.

The thought of her aunt's party, and the care and love she put into honoring Jack and his love for the holiday made a warm burst of happiness dance in her core. All those stories by the fire about Jack's adventures on his airship—traveling up and down the solarbelt, even getting stranded for a month once in Adonia—filled Caz with joy. She didn't want to do anything to tarnish Jack's memory or Elmira's remembrance of him.

There was *no possible way* she could write an article about the *Bressieux Mark II* or the airshow. She would put the whole thing from her mind. She wouldn't mind running into Hanson again in the village—perhaps she would visit the bakery in the morning—but she wouldn't go to the airfield again. She would focus on spending time with her aunt, decorating for the soiree, and enjoying the party when it came. She would just have to find her big story when she returned to Soldark.

Her heart sank. There was no way she would find any news stories from behind those walls.

The sound of an airship puttered off in the distance, and Caz turned to look for it. Maybe it was the *Bressieux II* and Hanson had fixed it after all. At that moment, her cloak pin came undone, and her shawl slipped. Fearing it getting tangled in the pedals and wheels, Caz looked down, and her steering grew erratic.

She wobbled right off the road into a ditch, but managed to keep upright. She was now careening downhill into what looked like—to her horror—a graveyard.

Massive oak trees held vigil all around the burying ground, their burnt orange leaves casting the graveyard into a dusky gloom. Forgetting about the shawl, she desperately tried to brake, the looming headstones and markers coming up fast in the dim light.

But as she feared, the shawl got tangled in the wheels, and she toppled over, tumbling right into a holly bush next to an enormous mausoleum.

She lay panting in the bush for a minute, counting her blessings that she hadn't smashed headfirst into the stone mausoleum. The large columned building cast her and the holly bush into cold shadow.

She looked about, getting her bearings. A breeze rustled through the trees, making her shiver. She detangled the maroon shawl from the wheels and holly branches, and clutched it about herself, not even bothering to put the cloak pin back on. In fact, she didn't see it anywhere.

"Oh no," she cried, spotting the scones scattered across the dead leaves under the bush. With a frown, she gathered up the box and stuffed it into the bicycle basket, leaving the now-dirty scones for the birds.

After dragging the bicycle out of the bush, she searched in the darkening graveyard for her aunt's pin, but it was getting hard to see. Her heart suddenly pounding, she lifted her head in panic, searching for the hill where Daguerre stood. She couldn't see it. It had been visible only minutes ago as she glided down the road—

"Oh," she said, staring at the mausoleum no doubt blocking her view. "Oh, thank goodness!" she said as she rounded the front where she caught sight of Daguerre in the distance. As her eyes focused back on the mausoleum, she noticed the words carved into the stone on the lintel: *Daguerre.*

With a little gasp, she looked at the building with more interest. But it was getting darker by the second, and she still had to climb a slight hill to get back to the estate.

She turned away, but saw something glinting on the ground before her. It was her aunt's pin.

Her stomach flipped, and she picked it up, stuffing it hastily in a pocket. She went back to where the bicycle lay askew on the ground, not bothering to look around and see how the pin had somehow managed to get to the other side of the mausoleum from where she had careened through the graveyard.

With haste, she wheeled the bicycle around headstones and grave markers, not looking back at the mausoleum, her gaze firmly on the house ahead on the hill.

Her aunt's face was creased with worry when she answered the front door herself. Elmira didn't admonish Caz in the slightest, only said, "Come, I've a warm dinner ready for you, and we'll get you a nice warm bath. It's cold tonight, isn't it?"

Shivering, Caz agreed, though she shed her troublesome shawl at the coat stand in the doorway, vowing never to ride a bicycle with such precarious articles of clothing again.

After tidying herself up, she made her way to the dining parlor, where a soup of butternut squash greeted her, and she hastily tucked in.

"The secret is adding an apple," her aunt told her, ladling soup for herself from the tureen.

"An apple?" Caz asked incredulously, looking down at her soup.

"And the spices, of course."

Caz nodded, thoroughly enjoying the fare. A thick slice of fresh bread dipped in the soup warmed her more than the warm coals in the fire at the end of the room.

She said nothing of her trip except mourning the loss of the scones—though she didn't mention exactly how and where they had flown out of the bicycle basket—and was soon ready for the hot bath her aunt had suggested. Elmira excitedly told her of Grimlee's plans to deliver the pumpkin invitations tonight, and Caz warmed from the inside out at her aunt's happiness.

Inside her suite, she donned a clean robe and headed for the bathing room.

Black and white checkered tile spread across the floor, with a well-proportioned claw-footed tub in the center, and copper piping coming up through the floor tiles. The walls were painted a deep green color, with black and gold molding running along the tops and bottoms of each wall. Caz ran the bath and added some scented soap from a dish—something that smelled vaguely of cranberry.

Clutching the paperback book she brought from home, Caz

lowered herself into the piping hot water with a sigh. She quickly lost herself in cranberry bubbles and a plot of intrigue. It drove all thoughts of the *Bressieux*–One or Two–from her mind, and her haunting crash in the graveyard.

Clean, dry, and bundled up in her warmest woolen socks and dressing gown, she wriggled under the covers of the large four-poster bed. As she closed her eyes, she thought she heard the sound of an auto leaving the estate, and she smiled at the thought of the pumpkins no doubt loaded onto the back of it.

VIII

Her aunt was not in the parlor for breakfast. So Caz poured herself tea from the sideboard and waited at the table with her bowl of porridge, trying to catch Marla's eye as she went down the hallway.

By the time her second cup of tea was empty and she had just started on her cold porridge, Elmira breezed in, wearing a black dress with white stitching around the collar.

"So," her aunt said, pulling out the chair across from Caz and sitting down empty-handed, though she was sporting a bandage on her thumb, "tell me again how your trip went yesterday. Where did you say you went?"

Caz's heart hammered against her ribcage, traitorously beating too fast. "I..."

Elmira shook her head. "The airshow."

"How did you know?" Caz blurted.

"I don't have to be a journalist—just a part-time laundress." She lifted a slip of paper out of her pocket, and Caz was horrified to recognize it as her ticket from the airfield.

And even more horrifying was the illustration of the particular airship on said slip of paper.

Caz opened her mouth, but the words wouldn't come. Every nerve in her body seemed to melt right down to the floor through her shoes. *The ticket!* Her breathing shallow, she clenched the sides of her chair.

"I gave Marla the night off what with the soiree tomorrow night and figured I'd collect your dress for laundering—I noticed it looked a bit ruffled at dinner. And I found this," she added.

"I'm sorry—I didn't *want* to go, and I didn't want to give them any money, I—"

"Did you see it?" she said quietly, but she might as well have yelled it for all the impact it had on Caz. The illustration of the *Bressieux II* beamed up at them from the table as if illuminated by their attention. Caz was surprised Elmira *wasn't* yelling.

She hung her head. "I did, but only because I asked the pilot not to fly it."

The silence pressed in on her, and she risked a look at her aunt, who was gazing out the window.

"I'm sorry," Caz said again, seizing the opportunity. "I'm sorry I didn't tell you where I was going. I didn't want you to find out about the *Bressieux II*. I told the pilot not to fly it, because it was on All Hallows. And I thought you would be hurt if you knew—but he was having trouble fixing it anyway..." She rambled, anxiety flooding her chest. It had been so stupid to go to the airfield, and now she had gone and disappointed Elmira—would she even want Caz to come back and visit again after this?

Her aunt's demeanor changed, and her face visibly softened. "My dear, I was worried sick when it grew dark and you hadn't returned. If you had only asked, I would have had Grimlee drive you to the airfield."

"Really?" She deflated like a balloon, the anxiety in her chest releasing its terrible claws—most of the way.

"Of course. If that was what you wanted to do. But you needn't worry about my feelings, and you needn't confront unsuspecting pilots on my behalf—I *can* take care of myself, you know."

Caz pressed her lips tight. "I'm sorry," she whispered.

"I know you're used to being on your own at home and

your parents making all your decisions for you, but I don't need protecting the same as *you* don't need protecting. We can look out for ourselves, us gals."

A timid smile formed at Caz's lips, and she said, "All right." The claws finally released. She was still amazed that Elmira never lifted her voice, but she did seem more worried about Caz than actually disappointed in her.

"I appreciate you wanting to look out for me, but it will be all right." Elmira rose and went to the sideboard to pour them some tea. When she sat back down, she said, "Now, I would have understood if you wanted to write your big story about the airshow—but just to go tell them not to fly! Why, my dear, what*ever* were you thinking?"

Her face warmed, and she hid it behind a sip of tea. "You-you wouldn't mind if I wrote about the airshow?"

Elmira inhaled the steam circling off her teacup and sighed. "Of course not. You said you needed something big to write about. It's newsworthy, I suppose. Although, I don't think they'll have quite the attendance they hoped for, for the finale."

"Oh?" Caz asked, still reeling from the ups and downs of the conversation.

"I've already got over twenty responses to the invitations," Elmira said, a content smile returning to her face.

Caz's insides warmed at the direction the conversation had taken, as it steered away from her ridiculous trip yesterday to more pleasant matters.

"Twenty? Already?"

Elmira nodded.

Just then, a knock came at the door. A brief concern that her parents might be early flitted through Caz. But even if they were, she was sure between her and Elmira, they could convince them to let her stay for the All Hallows soiree at the very least.

"I'd better get that," Elmira said with a slight groan. "I gave Grimlee the morning off after such a late night, and Marla will be off too. Probably another invitation response. I *told* them to just leave them on the doormat," she muttered as she left the room.

Caz finished up her cold porridge. She heard the creak of the hinges as the heavy front door opened, and then the rumble of voices. Just as she was wondering if she should bring the bowls and teacups to the kitchen if Marla and Grimlee were both off, she heard the voices at the door grow louder— particularly her aunt's.

She hastened to the doorway of the dining parlor and poked her head out. At the front door stood an unfamiliar man in a constable's uniform. He was older-looking and wore a monocle firmly perched in front of one eye.

"You can come back when you have some proof!" her aunt shouted. "What a taradiddle!"

"Very well, ma'am," he said, and stepped back.

Elmira took advantage of his retreat from the door to slam it in his face.

Mouth agape, Caz started forward just as her aunt whirled around in a rage.

"What nonsense!" Elmira fumed, striding down the hallway.

Caz followed. "What is it?"

Elmira turned around so fast Caz had to stop in her tracks. "Something happened at the airfield last night. Vandalism. Arson. What have you. Either way, no one will be flying the *Bressieux Mark II* ever again."

"*What?* Wait, why was the constable *here*? They think—"

"That I did it? Yes." Her aunt was shaking in anger, or fear, she couldn't tell.

"Here," Caz said, "let's go." She guided her aunt to the study where the small hearth smoldered with coals, helped her aunt to a wing-backed chair, then went and stoked the coals into cheerful flame.

Elmira took a hearty glance at the portrait of Jack over the fireplace, then stared in silence at the fire. Unsure of what to say or do, Caz decided to go make some more tea.

While she was bustling about in the kitchen with a kettle, she heard a sound in the hallway.

By the time she came out, kettle still in hand, she spotted her aunt with a black traveling cloak and a wide-brimmed black hat on, opening the back door.

Elmira turned when she heard Caz's footsteps. "Ah, dear, I'm taking the auto to Mr. Harrington's—my lawyer, you see.

With the soiree tomorrow night, I cannot afford the constables banging down the door all day. Mr. Harrington will sort it out. Are you all right here? If you like, you could put the finishing touches on the candles in the ballroom."

Caz lowered the teakettle in surprise. "Oh, sure."

With a curt nod, Elmira whisked out the back door.

Eyebrows furrowed, Caz stared at the door after it slammed shut. "What was that all about? And I'm to stay here and set out candles?" she demanded of the empty house.

She stomped her boot, awakening a thin cloud of dust mites into the shaft of morning sunlight coming in through the window above the door. She stalked halfway to the ballroom when she realized she was still holding the teakettle. With a groan, she returned to the kitchen and decided to make herself that cup of tea, after all.

Putting the kettle back on the burner, she slumped against the long marble counter, arms crossed in thought. What in the sun's rays was going on?

What was it her aunt had said? That no one would be flying the *Bressieux Mark II* ever again. Vandalism—no, arson. That must mean... "Fire," she muttered, as the teakettle began to whistle shrilly.

And they thought the culprit was Elmira. It was nonsense, like Elmira said. She was an old woman—how could she possibly sneak into the airfield and set an airship aflame? Caz shook her head and poured the hot water into a teapot, the leaves swirling about the pot as she poured.

But she had seen her aunt do many things with surprising strength and agility belying her years. Stabbing pumpkins through the fence. Balancing on a ladder to adjust the bats above the fireplace in the ballroom. Carrying a large gaskin into the garage...

She shook her head violently. No, it was ludicrous. But Elmira and Grimlee had taken the auto last night...to deliver the invitations, of course.

It was all giving her a headache. She poured out some tea into one of the orange bone porcelain cups, with only a few bits of tea making it past the porcelain strainer in the pot.

She let out a small gasp. "Hanson," she said, her eyes bulging. Then she tried to wrack her brain to remember what her aunt and the constable had said—had anyone been hurt?

She was on her feet before she even thought it through. The bicycle was in the garage. She could take it to the airfield and look around. Perhaps she could sneak through the fence far away from the main gate to avoid Alcide—it was a cow pasture after all.

No. If the constables suspected Elmira of the arson, Caz shouldn't go anywhere near the airfield. And Caz had already been seen yesterday beside the ship in question. No wonder they thought it was Elmira.

A sharp pain seared through her skull as her headache bloomed into something worse. She sat back down and concentrated on her tea. "Ugh," she growled, wishing Elmira had stayed or, at the very least, taken Caz with her to the lawyer's.

The soiree was tomorrow night. If the constables found some evidence against Elmira—no, no, that wasn't possible! Elmira couldn't have done it!

Right?

She paused, setting her empty teacup down on the saucer with a clatter. "How can I even think that?" she muttered, gazing at the random pattern the tea leaves left at the bottom of the cup. She froze, suddenly realizing the tea leaves didn't look *quite* so random. She turned the cup in its saucer a quarter turn and inhaled sharply. Then she pushed the whole cup away.

But the image of a skull in soggy leaves was permanently etched in her brain.

Agitated, she fled from the kitchen to look for the candles. She stalked into the ballroom over to the remaining crates of decorations, wondering when Marla or Grimlee would be back, so she wasn't all alone in the mansion at least.

Around midday, when she had finally put out the last candle—blood red—into the final wall sconce, she heaved a sigh as she gazed around at the ballroom. The bats hanging from the ceiling were still. The fireplace was cold, the logs stacked and ready to light tomorrow night. Each sconce had either a pristine black, red, or white candle in it. She had chosen black for all of the bone lanterns she had selected from the decorations, which hung in one corner of the ballroom with a collection of animal bones—all of which Elmira assured her had been discovered naturally in the woods.

A loud thump made her jump about half a foot in the air. She whirled around, gaze searching the deserted ballroom. She chuckled nervously, eyeing the decorations, and shook her head at her silliness. She clutched her sweater around her tight—a black and silver one she thought she might want to wear to the soiree—and headed out to look for the source of the noise. The halls were empty—not counting the numerous fake pumpkins, stuffed crows, and bat sculptures that lined every surface or hung from the ceiling. A garland of red silk flowers led her down the quiet hall.

"Elmira?" she called, wondering if her aunt had come in through the back door near the kitchen. "Grimlee? Marla?"

When no one answered, she clutched her arms tighter about herself. She poked her head into the drawing room to look at the grandfather clock there. It was almost noon. Was Elmira still talking to her lawyer?

A bang came from the garage, and Caz stifled a gasp.

She crept down the hallway toward the back door, passing the deserted kitchen. She peered through the glass panes, her back pressed to the wall beside the door, but she didn't see anything in the gravel drive. Carefully, she turned the big brass knob and opened the back door. Her breathing shallow, she decided to head for the garage. Maybe Elmira and Grimlee had returned and needed her help with something.

But there was no auto in the garage. There was, however, a foot-wide crack between the garage doors. Careful to keep quiet on the gravel, Caz made for the door that was partially open. She felt silly, but she didn't want to look inside, so she swung the door wide in a quick motion instead.

A black cat streaked in front of her, knocking over a bucket on its way out.

"Oh!" Caz exclaimed, leaping back a step. She watched the retreating feline, then noticed the bicycle leaning against the wall in the garage had been knocked over as well. "That's what that bang was." Her heart relaxed back into its usual rhythm, not the frantically restricted beating it had been doing since she had first heard the noise from inside the empty mansion.

There were a few scone crumbs stuck in the wire basket, along with dried bits of ganache, and when Caz turned to see if the cat was still there, she was startled yet again to see it coming back over to her. There was ganache on its whiskers.

"Oh," she said again. "Um...are you hungry?"

It licked its lips and stared at the fallen bicycle. Caz stepped away. "I can go get you something so you don't have to nibble on old crumbs," she said quietly, wondering why she was talking to a cat.

Well, there's no one else around, she thought as she retreated into the house, shutting the door firmly behind her. She had no idea whose cat it was, but Elmira certainly hadn't mentioned one, and Caz didn't want it messing up the decorations.

She scrounged up a few things from the kitchen—a leftover crumpet, a small piece of ham, and some cheese—and brought them back outside. The cat was curled up in the wire basket, licking its lips.

"Here you go," Caz said, holding out the ham first. It didn't budge, just looked at her from the basket with an expression of disdain.

"How about this?" She offered the crumpet.

The cat lifted its head, but remained in the basket.

"Look, I think I might ride into town," she told the cat. "I'm going to need that bicycle, you know. Take this."

Still, it didn't move. "Fine, I'm picking it up," she warned. She snorted when it remained in the basket as she tilted it upright. The cat seemed to magically shift so it was upright at all times. It looked at her expectantly when she straddled the bicycle and arranged her skirts. "Here," she conceded, handing over the crumpet.

The cat swiped at it with its paw, causing the crumpet to land with it in the basket, where it began to nibble on it. It still had some chocolate ganache on its whiskers. Caz chuckled. "All right, little Ganache Whiskers," she said slowly. "Do you want to go into town?"

It ignored her.

"Looks like you get a free ride, then. I'm tired of hanging around here alone. I want to know what happened at the airfield. And I don't really want to be here if the constables come back looking for Elmira..." She trailed off, still in shock that anyone thought her aunt had caused the arson. The guilt for going to the airfield yesterday had grown immeasurably painful.

The cat seemed content even when she started pedaling, intent on the crumpet. Caz shrugged, and took the regular way into town, not wanting to repeat her ungainly crash in the graveyard—though, quite responsibly, she was wearing a tight-fitting sweater that wouldn't betray her this time. She decided she would wear it to the soiree; it would go well with the black dress she planned on wearing, the silver embroidery on the shoulders of the sweater almost looked like spiderwebs. She *had* saved the ink-splattered dress from laundering, but she thought it looked a bit *too* gruesome to wear to the party, so she would go with her original outfit as planned. She hadn't seen Elmira's outfit yet, but her aunt had been gushing about it since the day Caz arrived at Daguerre.

Caz sighed in worry as she reached the outskirts of town. Where *was* Elmira? Still at her lawyer's? What if he couldn't do anything to help her? Caz glanced in the direction of the airfield. What they would really need was some proof that Elmira was innocent.

Yes, that was it. Because Elmira *was* innocent. Meaning someone else was guilty.

She wished she could just go over to the airfield. But surely, the place would be crawling with the local constabulary, and she didn't want to make things look worse for her aunt.

She wheeled into town, her new feline friend still lounging in her basket and wondered how she could find evidence of wrongdoing if she couldn't even get to the airfield. Her gaze lit on the bakery, and the patrons gathered inside. Her chest swelled, and she smiled as she saw a familiar face.

"But first..." she said, angling the bicycle toward the stationery shop.

Five minutes later, she was striding across the street with another new blank journal and fountain pen in hand, wheeling her cat-filled bicycle beside her. You could never have too many notebooks, she thought, and she had left her other one at the mansion.

The tinkling of the bell overhead made the man at one of the small tables perk his head up, and Hanson turned. He was hunched over a small plate with a croissant on it, the pastry so large it barely fit on the decorative plate. He had been eating it in small bites, and Caz could see the chocolate filling from here. Her mouth watered. She cleared her throat and hefted up the blank journal.

With a glance out of the window at her bicycle propped against the shop front, and its curled-up cargo, Caz approached Hanson carefully.

"You," he said, though without any accusation or anger, either of which she had expected.

"You," she replied, attempting a smile. "I heard about the *Bressieux II*. Can I sit down?"

"Sure," he said, shrugging. He pulled off the end of his croissant and carefully ate it. He was devoid of any of his previous enthusiasm, and she now noticed his listless stare out the window.

"What happened?" She cracked open the new journal with satisfaction, smoothing the first blank page, full of possibilities. Her pen—the self-inking kind—hovered over the blank paper in anticipation.

"I..." He trailed off, sighed, then shook his head, now picking up a small porcelain cup filled with coffee.

She cocked her head to the side, and closed the notebook with a snap. Maybe this wasn't the time to find her story—poor Hanson looked as if he'd lost his favorite pet. "Are you all right?"

He breathed in deep over his foamy coffee, and seemed to gain some of his energy back. His eyes lit upon her, and something flipped in the region of her chest. "I'm fine. I wasn't anywhere near the explosion—"

"Explosion?" she demanded, jaw dropping.

"—but I'm out of a job now," he finished. "And I'll really never get to fly the *Bressieux II*."

"I–I'm sorry about that," she said earnestly. Her fingers itched for her notebook, though, and possible angles flitted through her head. *Explosion at Eldrough's Field: The True Story of the Doomed Airship.*

She shoved the headline out of her thoughts. "But can we go back to the part about an explosion? The constable said arson—"

"Constable?" he said, straightening his posture.

"Oh, um, one came to the house this morning."

His eyes narrowed over his coffee cup. "What for?"

"Well," she paused, her whole body flaming as she remembered her aunt chastising her for trying to solve her problems. Somehow she didn't think Elmira would want her sharing that horrible accusation either. But with Hanson's hopelessly curious expression, she knew it was too late. And, possibly, he could help. A journalist had to rely on her sources, after all. "My aunt was accused of the arson."

His face darkened.

"It wasn't her," Caz insisted, and she finally realized, she didn't actually believe her aunt *would* do that. Was she capable of it? Absolutely. She was a wily and strong old woman. But after spending all week with her, and watching her recount her favorite stories of her life with Jack, Caz knew Elmira to be an honorable and trustworthy person—though it was hard not to picture her taking revenge on the airshow and dousing the *Bressieux II* in gasoline and igniting it.

Elmira *could*, but she *didn't*. Caz was sure.

"Of course, it wasn't her," Hanson said. "Why would the constables accuse her of that? Jack Daguerre's widow destroying the airship constructed in his honor?"

"Well," Caz said, shifting uncomfortably in her seat. "Like I said yesterday, she wasn't too keen on the airshow happening, what with her soiree the same night as the finale."

He shook his head. "No, it couldn't have been her," he insisted vehemently.

"How do you know?" she said. He sounded so sure. She hadn't even been completely sure until just now, and it was *her* aunt.

"It must have been something I did when repairing it last night. I got kind of desperate," he said in a whisper.

Caz leaned forward, her hand reaching closer to him unconsciously. "Oh, no, I'm sure it wasn't—"

He shook his head violently, his words coming out in a rush. "My boss said he would fire me if I couldn't get the *Bressieux II* up and running for the finale. I couldn't get that girder to straighten out for the life of me. And all of the other mechanics were busy—the *Argyle* was about to take off, and there were some issues with the engine—so I unbolted the lifting-gas tank by myself so I could reach the girder better and I was finally able to get it bolted to the gondola. I thought I hooked the lifting-gas back up properly, but..." His face sank, and he took a draft of his coffee. "And now your aunt's been blamed?" He hung his head.

Her hand inched forward, and though her whole chest was aflame, she clasped his hand holding the coffee cup. He looked up at her, the ghost of sadness on his face flitting away. Then her chest tingled unpleasantly. She yanked her hand away just in time to cough into her elbow.

After her coughing fit had subsided, her face aflame, she cleared her throat and said, "I think I need one of those coffees."

She took some deep breaths as she waited at the counter for her coffee. The shopkeeper handed her the chocolate croissant she had ordered—Hanson's looked too good not to try one—and she idly turned to catch sight of the airship pilot to see if he was looking in her direction. Her hand still tingled warmly. But her stolen glance turned into a full-blown stare out the shop window when she spotted Grimlee striding down the sidewalk to the Daguerre's black auto parked across the street.

"I'll be right back," she told the shopkeeper, then repeated the same to Hanson as she dashed outside.

With a guttural meow, little Ganache Whiskers followed her as she raced across the street, and she laughed as she realized she was still holding the plate with the croissant on it. "This isn't for you," she told the cat at her heels.

"Grimlee!" she shouted, and he turned, face dour.

"Miss Caz," he said, his expression melting in relief. "I'm so glad you're here, I thought you were at the constabulary with Mrs. Elmira—"

"What's she doing at the constabulary?" she asked, almost dropping her croissant. The black cat perched hopefully next to her foot. "I thought she was at her lawyer's?" Caz's stomach hardened in fear.

Grimlee bobbed his head. "She was. I went back to Daguerre at lunch, and as I was sorting through the invitations on the front step, Mr. Harrington pulled up in his auto. He told me the constables had taken her down to the station while she was in town."

IX

Caz's jaw dropped. "But…what…what kind of proof did they find? They wouldn't have taken her in without…"

Shaking his head sadly, Grimlee said, "I don't know, miss."

"They'll have to release her, right?" Caz felt her eyes tearing up.

Grimlee pressed his lips together. Instead of answering her question, he said, "I better get back to Daguerre in case I need to take a message or Elmira calls for a ride. Mr. Harrington brought me over to his office to pick up the auto."

Caz bobbed her head, biting the inside of her lip. She waved farewell to Grimlee, dumbstruck, and crossed the empty street back to the bakery.

Suddenly a well of emotion gushed up inside her chest, and

it took all her strength to quash it down and keep from crying. This was all her fault. If only she hadn't gone to the airfield, arousing suspicions.

Still holding the plate with her croissant on it, she stood next to her bicycle for a minute, collecting her thoughts, and just trying to breathe.

The black cat rubbed at her ankles, and it made her chuckle a little. She broke off the end of the chocolate-filled croissant and offered it to him. "Shall I call you Ganache?" Caz said idly as the cat all but inhaled the piece of pastry, getting more of the chocolate on his whiskers.

A chiming bell awoke Caz from her reverie. She looked up in surprise to see Hanson there, carefully holding a porcelain cup of coffee out in front of him. Her heart leaped at the sight of him. Her encounter with Grimlee had all but chased her conversation with Hanson out of her head, and the memory of touching his warm hand...

"I didn't know if you were coming back in," he said, lifting the coffee. "Figured you'd want this."

It felt good to smile, and she accepted the cup, but now her hands were full of porcelain.

The cat had finished with his piece of croissant and was now rearing up on his hind legs to paw at her dress for more. Hands full, she shrugged and said, "I can't help you, Ganache."

Unamused, the cat continued to paw at her. "Argh," she muttered, looking for somewhere to put something down.

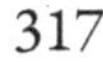

"Here," Hanson said, holding out a hand to take the coffee back. "I didn't realize you had your hands full out here."

She tore off a piece of the croissant for the cat and tossed it into her bicycle basket. "There, that should keep him occupied. Why don't we—" She nodded toward the bakery door, and they returned to their table inside.

With a content sigh, she set down her plate, and he returned her coffee. When she took a sip, it felt as if she sunk further into the cushioned chair in relief.

"So, is everything all right?" Hanson inquired, his eyes darting to look back out on the street.

"Oh, yes," she said. "Well, no, actually. My aunt's at the constabulary now."

Hanson's mouth popped open in surprise. At that, something inside Caz's chest snapped and she blurted, "This is all my fault!"

"What?" he exclaimed. "What do you mean? No. If *I* hadn't unbolted the lifting-gas—"

"I'm sure it wasn't your fault, Hanson. You've been working on airships *how long*?" she asked rhetorically.

He gave her a half shrug, though he looked somewhat pleased.

"What I meant was, I went down to the airfield yesterday, and asked you not to fly! Someone must have told the constables that, and it made them suspicious. I don't know if they found some other bogus evidence, though, since they took her into the station—"

Hanson huffed. "Well, I didn't tell anyone. I mean, Aberforth, the mechanic on the *Crooked Tankard* asked if you were a friend of mine, but I didn't tell him you were related to the Daguerres..." He trailed off, his face coloring.

Caz half smiled as she wondered what he *did* tell Aberforth about her, but she heaved a sigh and said, "I need to find some proof that my aunt is innocent."

She had left her blank journal on the table, and she now pulled it toward her, uncapping the pen.

As she began scribbling notes about her aunt, the mansion, and the distance to the airfield, Hanson leaned in for a closer look.

"Wow, you're really good at all those details," he said.

Her face warmed. "Oh...um...yes. I... I'm hoping to be a journalist someday." She continued to jot out notes about the airfield, and started doodling a little map of the path she had taken both to and from the airfield the other day. "Here. Can you tell me more about the airfield? How many airships there are, nearby buildings, or other entrances into the field?"

He cocked his head to the side with an amused grin. "You sure sound like a journalist."

"Did you get many visitors asking questions about the airshow?"

Shaking his head, he said, "No, but for other shows I've flown in, they usually like to interview the pilots. But Mr.

Alcide was late in organizing the show this year, so we didn't really get much publicity. He was busy trying to get the *Bressieux II* ready," Hanson said with a frown.

"Ah," Caz said, noticing the forlorn look in his eyes. "I…um…I'm hoping to be a journalist for the *Soldark Times*," she told him, hoping to change the subject from airships he would never get to fly, "but I haven't found a good story to write about just yet."

He twisted his frown into an ironic grimace. "Well, I think you've stumbled on a good one here."

"No, I just want to prove Elmira's innocent. This is personal reporting, you could say. At the very least, Elmira might still be detained for her soiree—and I told you how much it means to her—and at the worst…" she trailed off, not wanting to voice her concerns about wrongful imprisonment. What would the charge be for arson and destruction of property— one so costly as an airship?

"There's twenty airships," Hanson said, "Or—there were. Next to mine was the *Crooked Tankard*, and after that the *Locust…*"

And with his help, Caz began a rough map of the airfield on the next page.

After she finished with the map and her notes, she tapped the end of the pen against her lips in thought. She flipped back to the first page and perused her notes, still tapping the pen. She had eaten the rest of her croissant—Ganache had had enough pastries, she thought. Only a few drops of delicious coffee remained in her cup. Hanson had taken his goggles off his head, and his hair looked charmingly ruffled without them.

"Argh," Caz exclaimed with a glance out the shop window. She could tell the sun was on its way to setting, and she wasn't looking forward to another bicycle ride in near darkness. "I better get back to Daguerre," she said forlornly. "Though what we're going to do about those invitations piling up on the stoop, if we can't have the soiree..." She trailed off.

She was on her feet in a second. "The invitations!" she cried, capping her pen and stuffing it in her deep dress pocket along with the journal. "That's what Elmira was doing last night," she told Hanson. "Delivering the invitations to her party. Well, some of the party guests must have seen her, right? She should have a dozen alibis!"

His face cracked into a smile. "That's great!"

"Thanks for your help," Caz said, unsure how to say goodbye. She glanced at his hands, but that single hand-touch earlier felt like it had been a dream. Had she really even done that? She clutched her arms, rubbing her thumb along the knit sweater. "I better go..."

"Wait," he said as she turned around. "It's getting dark, let me at least walk with you."

Everything inside her melted as she realized that with all her being she had been hoping he would say those words. "Um, thank you," she squeaked.

Ganache was lounging in the bicycle basket when they came out into the dusky street, and he perked his little feline head up looking for treats. "No more," Caz told him, and he lowered his head again and feigned sleep. She snorted and picked up the bicycle, walking it in the direction of Daguerre, with Hanson on the other side.

A breeze rattled the trees along the lane, and several of them divested themselves of dry leaves, which rained down upon the two of them. Caz's heart was racing—not just because she finally thought of something that might help Elmira's case. She had suddenly run out of things to say to Hanson.

"So, um... What will you do now?" she asked him after they had left the village shops.

He whistled a low note. "I'm not sure. Alcide runs all the airshows out here in Haver County. Maybe I'll head to Soldark and get a job at the airyard servicing ships. I doubt they'd let a nobody like me fly right away, though."

"Oh," Caz said. "I'll be heading back to Soldark in a few days myself."

"You don't sound so happy about that."

She had to unclench her jaw to respond. "I thought I wouldn't even like it out here in the country—but my parents are coming back from their business trip early, and I find I don't want to go home. And now I don't even know if we'll get to have my aunt's party." She sighed, her heart constricting.

He brushed her shoulder lightly, and she looked up into his

eyes and away quickly as the thought of kissing him flitted through her head. Her cheeks flamed.

"We'll figure it out," Hanson said, looking similarly flushed. "I couldn't stand the thought of your aunt getting into trouble just because of the *Bressieux II*. Hey, do you want to take a break for a second?"

She didn't think her face could get any hotter. Was she really panting that badly? She thought she was being quiet about it, but they were going up a hill now, and it was getting harder to breathe in the cold air. "No, it's fine. I—this is how I... I was really sick when I was a child, and it's just hard for me to breathe sometimes still."

"Well, at least, let me push the bicycle," he offered. "That cat looks like it's had its fair share of pastries."

Snorting, she passed him the handlebars. Ganache let out a sleepy *mew*.

"Isn't that Daguerre up there?" he asked, nodding up at the mansion on the hill.

"Mmhmm," she said.

"Let's take the church road," he suggested, nodding at the dirt path that made her stomach sink. She could see the graveyard from here.

"Oh, um..."

"It'll be loads faster than taking Main Street." he said.

She eyed the mausoleum warily, but she had Hanson with her, and she wouldn't be careening down the hill this time, so she agreed. The quicker they got back to Daguerre, the better.

They passed the graveyard without incident, and were soon crunching up the gravel drive of the mansion. Lamps flickered from the front doors, their warm yellow light glinting off the twin copper fox statues and making shadows dance over the pumpkins piled around them. Caz directed Hanson around back to stow the bicycle in the garage, and let them in through the back door by the kitchen. Ganache lingered in the garage, tucking himself into a corner to continue his nap.

Hanson let out a low whistle. The hallway was dark, the only illumination coming from a lamp in the front foyer. They could only see the outlines of all the crows, skeletons, and bats lurking in the shadows. Instinctively, Caz reached out for Hanson's arm, since she knew the layout of the house better. Even through his rough coat, his arm felt warm to her touch, and sent a thrill down her spine.

Quite suddenly, piano music began playing, a haunting melody that cascaded through the house. Caz clutched Hanson's arm tighter and she let out a squeak.

"What—" she gasped.

"—is that?" Hanson finished her thought.

It was coming from the ballroom. She loosened her grip on his arm, though she was quite enjoying the closeness. He smelled of mechanical grease and apple pie, an odd-yet-intriguing combination.

They rounded the corner to the ballroom, and Caz saw the

fire was lit, making the bats dance in the air, floating on the updrafts wafting from the hearth. Grimlee sat at the grand piano, fingers gliding over the piano keys in surprising coordination and grace. Caz stood there with her mouth open, listening to the melody, never suspecting such music to come from the dour and restrained butler.

He nodded at Caz, and soon the song finished.

She clapped her hands in front of her mouth in awe. "That was amazing!" she cried, advancing into the dimly lit ballroom. She motioned for Hanson to follow.

Grimlee bowed his head. "Thank you, Miss Caz. I was practicing for tomorrow."

"Oh," she said, her stomach dropping. "Tomorrow. Yes. Any word from Elmira? Or the constables?"

"None whatsoever."

She puffed out a breath. "Well, we had an idea," she said. "Do you have all of the responses to the invitations? We thought the guests would be her alibi—did anyone come out to get their invitation in person?"

Grimlee rose from the piano bench and straightened his suit, motioning them out of the ballroom. "They're in the study," he said, leading them out. "And yes, of those I remember, the widow Madson, her sister Ginny, and then Dolly. I hadn't thought of that. I didn't think they would let me stand as a witness to her innocence, considering I'm in her employment and was the only other person out driving with her."

"That's ridiculous," Caz said, affronted. Though she supposed if *she* were in the constable's shoes, she would wonder whether both Elmira and Grimlee had committed the crime together. She whipped out her notebook when they entered the study and quickly wrote down the names Grimlee had told her.

Hanson lingered awkwardly by the door to the study.

"Oh," Caz said, waving him closer. "Grimlee, this is Hanson—"

"McCleary," Hanson supplied, coming forward and holding out his hand.

"He was the pilot for the..." Caz faltered. "For the, well..."

"*The Bressieux II*," Hanson said, unabashed. "Though, no longer."

"Indeed," Grimlee said. "Well, welcome to Daguerre, Mr. McCleary."

They set to work sorting through the pile of responses. Caz perched on the front of the wing-backed chair's cushion, comparing the responses to her growing list by the firelight. After a little while, Grimlee took it upon himself to light the gas lamps along the walls, making it much easier on Caz's eyes.

"Well, we've got a nice list here," she said after a hasty thirty minutes of checking off names. "Is it too late to go ask them to go down to the station? It sounds like Dolly is close by."

Both Hanson and Grimlee gave her guarded looks, and she huffed. "You mean to say we have to wait til morning? Will they really keep Elmira overnight?"

Hesitating, Grimlee wrung his hands. "I fear they would have phoned if Ms. Elmira needed a lift, and if she hasn't returned by now..."

Caz bit her lip at the anxiety swelling up her throat. Her poor aunt would be stuck in the station all night—alone—probably dreading being alone on All Hallows Eve. And, of course, wondering if the party would be canceled. Because it wasn't *just* a party, it was Elmira's annual tribute to Jack and the love they shared for the day when the veil between the living and the dead thinned. She glanced up at Jack's portrait and into the knowing look in his eyes.

"No," Caz said. "I have an idea—there's something we can do tonight."

X

"There," Caz said, tossing an envelope onto the widow Madson's front stoop. The envelope was covered in red splattered ink, courtesy of Crimson Cordial.

Inside the folded parchment, in her best hand, Caz had penned a different kind of invitation:

ACCUSATIONS MOST FOWL!
YOUR PRESENCE IS REQUESTED AT A HIGH-
STAKES GAME OF WHODUNNIT PRIOR TO THE
ALL HALLOWS EVE SOIREE. MEET AT THE
CONSTABULARY ON FRONT STREET ON THE
DAY OF ALL HALLOWS EVE TO PROCLAIM
YOUR TESTIMONY IN MRS. ELMIRA
DAGUERRE'S HONOR. THE FIRST TO WIN THE
GAME SHALL BE AWARDED A PRIZE.

She grinned at Hanson, who straddled a bicycle on Madson's driveway, while holding the handlebars of Caz's waiting bicycle. Ganache had yowled when the three of them went to retrieve the auto and bicycles before splitting up with the new invitations. Caz had rejected the idea of taking the auto, and Hanson had insisted on accompanying her.

A glass-paned lantern hung from one of his handlebars, and he steadied it again as she took back her bicycle. "Well, that's it," she said.

Far off, perhaps inside the Madson house, a clock chimed midnight. Caz pulled her sweater tighter around herself. "Let's get back—will you stay at Daguerre? Or—"

She stopped, realizing she had no idea where he even lived, or much else about him besides his airship aspirations, really.

"I'll take you back," he said. "I have a flat across town with my Da, but he probably thinks I'm working late again."

"Thank you," she said, her cold cheeks flushing. "I'd love to get back and have some mulled cider or something, after all of this."

He chuckled. "That sounds wonderful."

They pedaled down the lane, passing by an empty cornfield. Clouds rolled across the sky in the chill breeze, revealing the waxing moon.

"A favorite of Jack Daguerre, apparently," Caz said with a slight smile.

"Ah, even better."

"Was he really that famous of a pilot?" she burst, "That your boss would commission recreating his airship?"

She could see him smiling in the moonlight. "Maybe I'll have to take you to the Air Museum before you leave."

Her heart sank, seeming to leave her body altogether. And when she remembered it was now past midnight, and that she only had a little over twenty-four hours left in Haversdale, she gasped. But it wasn't the exertion of the pedaling that had her breathless. She snuck a glance at Hanson as they glided down the lane, the Daguerre mansion now looming up over the mostly barren pumpkin field at Shore's farm.

"I'm not sure I'll have time," she said, but quickly moved on. "Do you really think you'd come to Soldark like you said?"

She thought he shrugged, but it was hard to tell on a bicycle. "If I want to keep flying, I'll have to. But my Da..." he paused, glancing past the dark pumpkin patch. "I don't want to leave him either."

"I wouldn't mind some *more* time away from my parents," Caz groused. "I haven't even been here a week. I thought I'd have more time."

"I'm sorry," he said as they rounded the corner and pulled slowly onto the gravel drive, careful not to skid on the stones. They dismounted and walked the bicycles back around the mansion to the garage.

But Caz made no move to park them inside the garage, because she felt that when she did, Hanson would leave and she

330

didn't want him to just yet.

"It's all right," she told him, "I'm used to it. I've spent a lot of time at home."

"You were sick?" he asked, face wrinkled in concern.

She nodded once, shrugging. "I've grown out of it...mostly. But they still don't like me out of the house much—having worked so hard to keep me safe and alive and all, they never really stopped worrying about me." She smiled sadly, realizing the truth of it as she said it.

"Well, if I come to Soldark, you can show me—"

A loud clang came from the barn. Which was locked.

Goosebumps rose on Caz's neck and she turned to look at the big building. She brushed against Hanson as she turned, and he leaned close to whisper, "What is it?"

"I don't know," she breathed. "It's supposed to be locked."

What if the same arsonist who had blown up the *Bressieux II* had come looking for the original? The unpleasant thought snaked its way through her mind, making her stride forward. She couldn't let that happen. This was her uncle's airship.

"Wait," Hanson hissed, lurching after her and grabbing her hand. She clasped it back, firmly squeezing his somehow warm fingers. They were so solid against hers in the cold and dark, and she didn't want to let go.

One of the barn doors was open about a foot or so, and it was still dark inside. Caz remembered her aunt flicking a switch just inside the doors, so, still clutching Hanson's hand, she sidled through the opening and inched inside. She groped for the switch with her other hand in silence. Then finally, with a *thunk* of the metal switch, the barn was illuminated by half a dozen gas lamps.

Hanson uttered a soft gasp as the *Bressieux* emerged from the darkness. But there was no sign of arsonists, or ghosts even—the other absurd hypothesis of Caz's wild imaginings. They inspected the barn but saw no one, until, that is, they spotted Ganache atop the gondola, lounging right at the helm.

"What in sunspots are you doing in here?" Caz demanded. "And how did you even get in?"

Exasperated, she rushed back to the barn doors and inspected the lock. But there was no key and the lock hung open. "Now that's a mystery," she said, shaking her head. "Maybe Grimlee unlocked it," she added hopefully, glancing up at her uncle's airship.

Hanson was still gazing up at it, his eyes wide. Caz sidled back over to him. "Well, I'm glad you got to see it," she said.

He glanced down at her and gave her a smile, his ruffled hair looking charming in the dim light. "It's even better than I imagined. See where the spanners on the gondola connect to the engine? Flawless work. And the gear shift..."

She could tell he wanted to get closer, but there was no way she could grant him that permission. For that, she needed...

Elmira. A wave of apprehension flooded her as she wondered if her plan would work. She thought Elmira would approve of the way she handled it—she thoroughly recalled Elmira chastising her for trying to solve her problems, but Caz felt this was a little more important than hurt feelings and party attendance. This was about clearing Elmira's name and retrieving her from the constable's clutches.

A slow blink brought her back to her senses, and she wobbled a little on her feet. Hanson instinctively reached over and steadied her. "It's late," he said. "Well past midnight."

"I should get some sleep," Caz agreed. "With any luck, we've got a party to attend tonight. And you're invited, by the way—Elmira said I could have a guest if I made any new friends in town."

"That'd be great," he said, eyes dancing in the gaslight.

The pounding on her suite door woke her the next morning, and Caz jolted upright. She shook herself, blinking fast, and for a moment completely forgot where she was. This wasn't her bedroom at home.

She thrust her feet into the slippers beside the bed and quickly padded over to the door, wrenching it open.

There stood Elmira, looking only slightly ruffled in yesterday's dress.

Her aunt smiled, wrinkles creasing her face with joy. Caz squealed and launched herself into her aunt's arms. "You're here!" Caz cried. "What happened? They let you go!" She glanced at her windows, thinking it was still quite early for anyone to even open their invitations from last night.

Elmira clutched Caz's arm, and guffawed. "Ginny Madson beat down their door before dawn to testify to my innocence— to a crime she knew nothing about, I might add. But, by golly, she was a knowledgeable and reliable witness."

Caz's jaw dropped, and she burst into a fit of giggles. "It worked! I hope you don't mind, but—"

"Mind? I ran into Dolly as we entered the drive, and she took the liberty of showing me your marvelous invitation. I bet the rest are still lined up outside the station, hoping to win some prize—those poor constables. Between you and me, they deserve it. They had no right to hold me there like some delinquent."

Caz could picture a line of people forming, waiting their turn to defend Elmira—from what, they didn't know, but it was clear that most people in town would do anything for her should she ask.

"Well, maybe next year, I'll have to work in a little murder-mystery game to the soiree," Elmira said with a wink.

"Do you know who really did it?" Caz asked curiously, as they sat down to breakfast half an hour later. Caz sank happily into her chair, though it strangely felt as if they were missing someone, even though the breakfast was usually just the two of them.

"Not a clue," Elmira said, "but now I have to come up with some kind of prize for Ginny. I don't suppose you already had one in mind?"

Caz bit her lip and shook her head, holding in a chuckle. "I'm sorry. I thought the idea of a prize would entice people to go early."

"Too true," her aunt said, raising a cup of tea in a toast. "We'll figure out something. Now, we've got some preparations to finish up and not a moment to waste."

Caz smiled to herself as her aunt excitedly numbered off the final plans, bemoaning the time they had lost to the "airship arson incident" as she called it. And though she looked forward to the soiree, she couldn't stop wondering what had really happened with the *Bressieux II*.

As she waited for her aunt to find the correct paint to touch up the silver skeleton hands adorning the hearth in the ballroom, Caz went to go find her journal and make a few notes.

She was surprised she had stopped searching for her big story, but when it came down to it, she had been more concerned for Elmira's well-being than the chance of her writing being featured in the paper.

But now those gears were churning again.

Someone had blown up the *Bressieux II*. But why?

She began a rudimentary sketch of the original *Bressieux* while she waited for her aunt to return with the paint, her thoughts whirring. A thrill of electricity jolted through her when she thought back to the hours she had spent with Hanson, particularly close up in the barn, holding hands in the dark.

When Elmira came back in, Caz had an idea, but first...

"The barn was unlocked last night, do you know how—"

"Oh, yes. Grimlee told me," Elmira said, setting down the silver paint and some brushes on the stepstool by the hearth. "That cat keeps getting in there through a gap in the boards, so I told him to just unlock it and get him out."

"Oh," Caz said, chuckling. "All right. As long as little Ganache Whiskers didn't open it himself."

Elmira snorted. "Now, after this, I think we might be done!"

"Actually..." Caz said, a grin lighting up her face. "I've been thinking. It's completely up to you, but I had an idea that might help us draw out the real arsonist—and also a way to honor Jack and draw more excitement to the party."

"You're full of these ideas. At this rate, I'll need you for next year to top this party. Well, what is it?" Elmira demanded.

"We might need more ink."

XI

For the First Time in 15 Years,
the Bressieux Flies Again!

In Honor of Revered Airship Pilot,
Jack Daguerre, the Bressieux will be flown
as a one-time Event prior to the
All Hallows Eve soiree.
Gather at Shore's Pumpkin Patch
at Sunset to see this Marvel,
flown by the talented
Airship Pilot, Hanson McCleary!

The clatter of porcelain *clinked* across the bakery as Hanson's empty coffee cup shattered on the floor. "Y-you can't mean...you aren't serious..." he stuttered.

Caz held the flier out to him. He took it with a shaking hand.

"I-I get to fly it?" he said in a small voice. "This... This can't be real."

Nodding, Caz bent down and began to retrieve the pieces of the broken cup, which luckily only numbered a few. Hanson immediately joined her, taking one of her hands to stop her. He caught her eyes and looked deep into them. "This is the nicest thing—Thank you."

Her face lit up. "You're welcome," she said. "But it's not *just* a treat for you and for everyone to watch." She lowered her voice. "I'm hoping we draw out the real arsonist. They're bound to show up at Shore's. Then maybe we can figure out who it is."

He frowned in thought. "I suppose. We better make sure the *Bressieux* stays safe, though."

"Definitely," she agreed. "Grimlee is at the barn now, though you'll probably need to come help set up the balloon, I don't think he wanted to do that by himself. I guess he's been keeping it in working order all these years. And Farmer Shore offered to tow it over to the field with his tractor."

Hanson's face lit up. "I should probably go now. The flight's at sunset?"

She nodded, then handed the broken cup pieces over to the bakery owner with an apology and a few coppers.

"I just have to hang a few of these up first," she told Hanson, holding up the small stack of flyers she had painstakingly penned this morning.

Caz could feel her time in Haversdale ticking away as she hurried back to the mansion with Hanson at her heels. Her parents would be here tomorrow. She had yet to pack a single thing. When would she have the time? She wished she could stay all season long and spend more time with Elmira...and Hanson. At least she could stall by claiming she needed to finish packing.

When they got back to Daguerre, she thought Hanson would want to go straight to the barn, but he insisted on first going inside and personally thanking Elmira for the chance to fly the *Bressieux*. Blushing—truly blushing—Elmira clasped his hands.

"I don't think Jack would want it to rot away in the barn forever," she said, her voice wavering slightly as she gazed into the early afternoon sunlight peering through the window. "And today is the perfect day. He...he'll get to see it in the sky again."

Caz swallowed a lump in her throat and came forward to give her aunt a side hug. Whether the veil between the living and the dead was indeed thin on this night of all nights, she was positive that wherever he was, Jack would be watching out for them.

"Well, we're all ready in here," Elmira said, her voice steady again as she gestured around at the decorations. A silver skull grinned down on them from above the window. "Now why don't you get ready out there."

The sun hastened in its decline, casting red and orange hues over the nearly barren pumpkin patch. Only a few misshapen or small-sized gourds remained on the vines, leaving plenty of room for onlookers to gather. And gather they did, in a huge crowd, much bigger than the number of people invited to the soiree later. Caz was amazed at the number, considering the small number of flyers she had put up, and at such late notice.

But word must have flown around Haversdale, and the villagers who had intended on seeing the finale at the airfield must have gotten word and come here instead. Caz wondered what was going on at the airfield right now, but at one thought of Hanson's boss, she decided she didn't care.

This was for Jack. And Elmira. And Hanson.

Hanson...who suddenly appeared at her elbow, his goggles perched in his unruly hair, a grin of wild abandon plastered across his face.

"Aren't you supposed to be taking off soon?" Caz demanded.

"I am," he said, "but I wanted to tell you my old boss Alcide is here, and he doesn't look too happy."

"Well, that's too bad," Caz said, spotting the man in the crowd as Hanson pointed him out. Elmira came over then to wish Hanson good luck. The *Bressieux* stood waiting, its engine steadily idling. The crowd had gathered a respectable distance from the airship, *ooing* and *ahhing* over the elaborate wooden scrollwork on the gondola, and the sturdy frame that formed the ribcage of the rigid balloon. The helm gleamed in the light of the setting sun; Caz had been the one to polish it while Grimlee and Hanson made the other more mechanical preparations. It was stunning.

Caz's gaze slid unpleasantly to Hanson's former boss in the crowd, thinking he didn't deserve to be here to witness this. He edged around the crowd, and Caz hoped he was leaving. "Maybe if he didn't threaten to fire you over fixing the *Bressieux II*..." Caz trailed off. "Wait a minute," she said, putting a hand on his shoulder. "Did you *ever* get to fly the *Bressieux II*?"

Hanson shook his head sadly, though his gaze kept jumping back to the waiting airship in anticipation. "It was finished just in time for this year's show."

"Maybe it had *never flown*! Maybe it *never* worked!" Caz exclaimed. "And that's why you couldn't fix it!"

Elmira frowned, overhearing. "Are you saying he destroyed his own ship because it couldn't perform as promised? Well, and then there's insurance payouts..."

Caz nodded, and someone spit on the ground behind them.

"Not something you're like to prove," Alcide said, hands in his pockets. He jingled them, no doubt the coins from ticket sales.

"You," Caz said. "I don't think you're welcome here anymore."

"Ah, well, I didn't see anyone collecting tickets, so I'd say I'm about as welcome as anyone."

Caz glanced about the crowd, hoping to spot a constable— where were they when you needed one? But if there were any, she couldn't see them.

"Ah, you!" a voice cried from beside Elmira. It was Dolly, and she had that ridiculous hat perched on her head again, the crow eyeing them all beadily. "You have an aura about you that is beset with troubled souls," she intoned. "You must allow me to give you a reading. My work as a medium..." She was ramping up for a robustly one-sided conversation. She winked at Elmira and Caz as she led an uncomfortable-looking Alcide away.

Ginny Madson came up to Elmira then, elbowing her genially in the side. "You know, I would just love to head down to the constabulary before the soiree to testify again—I heard the whole thing, my dear. And I wouldn't even need a prize this time!"

Caz beamed at the older woman, and they all stared daggers after Alcide as he fled from the field, fighting off Dolly's offers for a spiritual reading.

As soon as the sun sank fully below the horizon—better visibility for the pilot and the onlookers, Hanson told her earlier—the engine roared to life under Hanson and Grimlee's hands as they revved it, much to the appreciation of the gathering crowd.

Caz didn't even notice the chill on her face as she watched Hanson concentrating on the gears at the helm, when suddenly the airship lifted off the ground as smoothly as a leaf caught by a breeze. And as the *Bressieux* sailed into the orange-hued sky, Caz reached down and clutched her aunt's bony hand. Though she didn't need to look, she could tell her aunt was smiling, and they both knew that Jack was watching. The airship flew higher and higher, silhouetted against the dusky sky.

That haunting melody floated out of the ballroom played on piano keys, as dozens of people gathered and talked and admired the mansion's decorations. The flight of the *Bressieux* was the topic of choice, as well as the disgrace of the airshow manager, who, according to Ginny and Dolly, was already in custody at the station.

After watching Hanson glide skillfully through the sky in the airship earlier, they had gone back and changed into their party attire. Grimlee and Hanson re-secured the *Bressieux* in the barn—triply locked this time against felines and felons. On a whim, Caz had opted for the ink-spattered dress with her black sweater, while Elmira graced the halls in a fabulous black and gold gown with silver spiderwebs embroidered all over it. She wore a gold and black hat perched jauntily on her head, with a menacing-looking felt spider sewn onto the side, which she told Caz had been a gift from Jack one All Hallows Eve.

Caz gazed into the ballroom, satisfaction burning in her belly. They had done it. They had pulled off Elmira's soiree, and even given the party guests more festivities to talk about all year long. And to top it all, the culprit behind the airship explosion had been apprehended. *That* would *make quite a good story*, Caz mused, her hand itching for that self-inking pen upstairs.

"That's going to be hard to beat next year," someone said from beside Caz. "*The Bressieux flies again*... I can just see it in the headlines at the newsstand."

Hanson wore a black half-mask that covered his eyes and his forehead, with large black horns curling back into his unruly hair. Caz's heart began racing, and she took a sharp breath. But something about what he said made her thoughts turn and whirl.

"Yes," she breathed, not taking her eyes off him. "Maybe you'll have to fly it again next year."

He pursed his lips in thought, then pulled her close to him. "Well, that depends."

"On...?" Suddenly she could barely breathe, but not because of her condition.

"On where you'll be. If you're in Soldark, then I hardly need

344

be here." His arms encircled her, and she all but melted from the warmth.

Breath surged into her lungs as she leaned forward, and her lips met his. Her fingers found his shoulders, hard with muscle under the black shirt he wore.

She pulled away, noting the grin on his devilishly handsome face. "I'll be wherever you'll be."

XII

"I'll be wherever *they* say," Caz grumbled the next morning, her stomach roiling as she spotted an unfamiliar auto in the drive from her window upstairs.

After the excitement and elation of last night, she had slept quite late, only to be awoken by the sound of the auto doors closing. She rubbed her eyes, gathering her things. She would pack after breakfast.

Memories of the soiree replayed in her head as she brushed her hair and pulled on thick woolen socks that slid up to her knees. Hanson in his black-horned mask dancing with her. Elmira laughing with Dolly and showing off the pumpkin carvings Caz had done to anyone who would look. Grimlee playing the piano, and even Marla joining him to sing a song in old Haveric that sounded beautiful even if Caz couldn't understand it. Sneaking out back with Hanson to give Ganache half a pumpkin tart. And another kiss, just inside the back door, before Hanson left.

They had exchanged addresses, and Caz had assured him she would write. But as she tromped down the stairs in her ankle boots—dressed for travel, as much as she resented it—sadness trickled through her. Would she really see him again? Would he really come to Soldark?

"Caz!" her mother called joyously from the bottom of the stairs, arms flung wide. Caz threw herself into them and then gave her father just as tight of a hug. Grimlee ushered them all into the dining parlor for breakfast, and Caz's nerves began buzzing, because she hadn't quite resigned herself to going home.

They were halfway through their porridge when Caz cleared her throat and pulled her notebook from her large dress pocket and set it on the table.

Elmira looked at it knowingly. "What are you writing, my dear?"

"A story," Caz declared. "A big one. Something that will get the attention of the editors at the *Soldark Times*, or the *Sunbelt Chronicle*, even."

"Oh?" her mother said, a forkful of kippers halfway to her mouth.

"Yes," Caz said, soldiering on. "But it's not done yet. I have quite a bit of research to do."

Her father clapped his hands together. "That's wonderful. I'm sure our library—"

"Actually, I need to stay in Haversdale to do the research."

"But we're going home today," her mother said, eyebrows pinched in genuine confusion.

Her parents looked more than confused. She had never so much as contradicted them before. Not when she asked to get a newsie job and they refused. Not when they told her she was to go to Daguerre for the season. Caz almost laughed at the looks on their faces, but one look at Elmira's proud expression gave her the courage to continue.

"I'd like to stay here for the remainder of the season, and Aunt Elmira has agreed. That was the plan, after all."

"I...well..." her father stuttered.

"I'll be finishing my story, and spending time with Elmira. I'm sure she'd love my help putting away the decorations."

"Of course, dear," Elmira said. "Though I think I'll leave them up for a few weeks yet," she added with a grin.

"It's settled then," Caz said in her most confident voice, "and I can even send my story off to Soldark by post."

Her mother gaped at her, but her father finally said, "Well, Caz, why not? As you said, that was the plan."

Caz nodded triumphantly and shared a look of joy with Elmira. Her heart leaped. She had done it, and they hadn't said no! Now, the possibilities of spending the season at Daguerre spread before her again, much like when she first arrived. But she had a story to write.

"What will the story be about?" her mother inquired as they finished up their tea.

"We heard in town about the airshow manager," her father began.

"I had considered that angle," Caz said. "But I had a better idea."

TWO WEEKS LATER

Caz hastened down the street on her bicycle, Ganache in her basket as usual. It had taken her a little longer than expected to finish her article—two trips to the Air Museum with Hanson and several long talks with her aunt—but only one week after posting it to the editor at the *Soldark Times*, she had gotten a positive response by telegram.

It was to be printed today. And there was only one place in Haversdale where the *Soldark Times* was delivered—a newspaper stand outside of Watson's Stationery.

Hanson met her there. Her eyes alight, she barely registered his arms as he flung them around her, surrounding her with warmth. The day had started off frigid; the trees had quickly lost all of their leaves these past few weeks, but the strength of the sunshine promised more warmth as it grew higher in the sky.

Her hand was shaking as she withdrew a copper to place into the coin slot of the newspaper stand. "Here, you do it," she told Hanson, and thrust her coin purse into his hands.

He deftly inserted the copper and retrieved a paper.

Her vision went blurry around the edges as she spotted the title of her story—on the front page, no less! Sure, it was on the bottom corner, but as she yanked the paper out of Hanson's hands and skimmed through it, she thought she might burst with happiness.

THE BRESSIEUX FLIES AGAIN!
THE LIFE AND AFTERLIFE OF CELEBRATED
AIRSHIP ENTHUSIAST JACK DAGUERRE
~ BY CAZ COPPERSDOWN ~

After purchasing five more—some for Elmira, a few for herself, and one for Hanson—she took Hanson's hand and they strode across the street to warm up in the bakery.

"I think I'll ask Elmira if she doesn't mind me coming back for Christmas," she told Hanson, still gazing lovingly at her headline on the paper as they sipped their coffees.

"I'm sure she'd love to have you," he said, and reached for her hand. "I wouldn't mind seeing you either."

"Are you enjoying your new job?"

"Which one?" he asked with a chuckle.

"Both. Either."

"Well, the Air Museum is great," he said. "But I have to say, I do enjoy driving up to Daguerre. Though if we could just keep that cat out of the barn, I wouldn't have to spend so much time sweeping cat hair off the *Bressieux*."

Caz snorted, glancing out the window at her bicycle where Ganache was curled up in a blanket she now kept in the basket. "I'm so glad," she said, "and I know you want to stay with your da. I'll miss you when I'm in Soldark, but I don't think I can quite convince my parents to let me move out to the country *just* yet."

"I'll miss you too. But you get to meet the editor of the *Times!* You'll have to tell me all about it when you come back."

"I will. I promise. I better get working on another story, though, and soon, if I want to keep my spot on the front page."

As they left the bakery, infused with warmth inside and out, Caz took a deep lungful of air, and though she could smell coal smoke on the wind from the trains that passed through the village, the breeze was also full of promise. Of mystery.

Of a thousand stories and a thousand memories.

She squeezed Hanson's hand and they headed back to Daguerre, to share her first real story, a tribute to a memory.

THE END

THE
CLOCKWORK
ICE DRAGON

AURELIA SUNDON

I

FOUR DAYS UNTIL CHRISTMAS

The snow began as Aurelia Sundon switched off all the gas lamps in her workshop, except the one over her drafting table. She paused at the window when she spotted the delicate white snowflakes drifting down from the dark sky.

They were the first snowflakes she had ever seen in her life.

Wide-eyed, she watched them drift onto the street below as she gnawed on the end of her pencil. She couldn't go outside and see them in person. Not yet.

However much she wanted to feel the snow on her face, she had work to do. She put her hand on the cold glass, seeing at once the drifting snowflakes and her pale reflection, her short dark hair that barely hid her ears and her curved button nose. She shivered, then took her hand off the glass, leaving a foggy imprint of her hand there. *How had it gotten cold enough to snow?* She had read nothing about this amazing winter phenomenon in the papers.

Shaking her head, she perched herself on her creaky stool, then sifted through the scraps of paper on her drafting table, each with a fragment of an idea on it that she had scribbled in her spare moments.

She was running out of time to finish her plans for her magnetic train. The City of Soldark's Magistrate of Invention had announced just two days ago that they would be open for submissions from non-union inventors, but only on Christmas Day. It was a once-in-a-lifetime chance. Why they picked Christmas of all days, Aurelia couldn't fathom, but ever since she had learned the news, she had started formulating her plan. She only had four days left.

Her mag-train would win the attention of the magistrate. It had to. It would revolutionize transportation from Soldark into the surrounding countryside, neighboring cities, and even the countries Aurelia had only heard of but never seen. Only people who could afford airship fare could ever get the chance to see the world outside of Soldark. She just had trouble finding enough time to put her dream onto paper and into metal.

Four days to create a working prototype. She crumpled up another botched drawing and tossed it on the floor, where it landed among the stacks of sheet metal, iron molds, her precious magnets, and spools of copper wiring. She gazed out at the snow, falling like bits of stuffing past her window. She still couldn't allow herself to stop working to go out and see it.

Just like her chance with the Magistrate of Invention, the snow was an extraordinary occurrence here in Soldark. Rather sensibly, she told herself, she would focus on her train, instead. At least she could watch the snow from the window.

She cursed her boss, Mr. Augur, at the metal foundry. Even though he knew she was submitting something to the Magistrate of Invention, he had been scheduling her for twelve-hour days all week. The only time she had for her project was when she *should* be catching up on sleep. But as always, she needed the money, so she couldn't pass up the work. Obviously, Mr. Augur didn't want to lose her. If she made it into the inventor's union, all kinds of job opportunities would open up for her. Better paying ones.

Aurelia sketched long into the night, occasionally glancing out her window to watch the snow piling up outside on the street. *Soon*, she kept promising herself, she would go out and see the snow. Soon, she would have a viable plan.

She couldn't see very well with just the one lamp, but she couldn't afford to keep all of the lights on all night. She could barely afford the rent on her workshop as it was. Most of her foundry wages went to her parents' house on the outskirts of the city, where her parents were trying desperately to keep their farm from falling into the ground—literally. Two months ago, the chicken coop had collapsed after a storm, and repairing it hadn't been cheap. If her parents lost the farm, they would have to move into the city, and it was likely that Aurelia would have to give up her workshop to make ends meet, and that would be the end of her inventing dreams.

Most nights when Aurelia worked too late—and tonight was looking like one of those nights—she would curl up on the cot she kept folded up under her drafting table. The few trains into the country didn't run past midnight. But she could change that.

The drawing was taking shape. She had already worked out the schematics in her head during the long hours at the foundry, and scribbled bits and pieces of the design—as she thought of them—onto scraps of paper she stuffed into her pockets. And she had even done some preliminary work on the train itself. She reached for the compass out of her pencil cup, telling herself she could go out and see the snow once she added the final touch: the wheels.

Of course, the idea of the mag-train was that it didn't need wheels; it would hover over the track. But by a stroke of incredible luck, she had acquired an old early-model steam train at a scrap metal auction several months back, and it had the most gorgeous wheels. The antique steam train had inspired her dream of the mag-train in the first place.

After she had stored it in her parents' barn, she had spent

days combing it for parts she could repurpose or sell. At first, that's all it was to her: a hunk of parts. But as she inspected it, she realized it was in pretty good shape for an antique that had sat in an auction yard for a few decades. And even though the wheels were heavy and would add unnecessary weight to the levitating train, the spokes were pristine, the bolts well-seated, and the treads suited to magnetizing. They would add flare if nothing else.

Eventually she realized the wheels would be the key to her invention. If she could use the same tracks as the steam trains, there would be no reason for the city of Soldark not to use her mag-train. It would be faster, and less likely to break down or need parts, and the best part was, since the wheels would levitate off the tracks, rain and dust and grime wouldn't affect them. *And snow*, she thought suddenly, tearing her gaze away from her design.

It was still snowing. She stood up and stretched, then gave her design one last glance: it was finished. There was only one hitch in her plan. She still needed the electricity.

She grabbed her coat off its peg by the door, and slipped out of her workshop, locking it behind her with a big brass key. She crept down the wooden staircase, careful to walk quietly past the other tenants' doors. Some, like her, slept nights in their shops, either because they were hard at work or just didn't have a home to go to. Not many who rented in this part of Soldark were lucky enough to be part of the inventor's union and got by from job to job.

Finally, she eased open the heavy door at the bottom of the stairs, and she breathed in the unfamiliar scent of snow in the night air. Her boots scuffed the pristine white flakes that had already piled up a half-inch or so on the sidewalk, covering up the grime that she knew lay underneath.

She held out her hand and watched as the snow fell on her palm, melting after an instant. She grinned, gazing up at the black night sky, where thousands of snowflakes drifted down toward the earth. She shivered, her forearms warm at least since she hadn't bothered to unlace her leather arm-warmers that kept her forearms free from pencil marks. Her coat was thin, not made for this temperature.

"What do you think?"

She whirled around and came face to face with Frederick Grandville, who rented one of the workshops on the floor beneath hers. He was the son of a wealthy businessman, and although he was quite handsome, Aurelia despised everything about him. She took a step away from him, crossing her arms over her middle as she took in his foppish appearance.

His chestnut hair was ruffled, which was quite unusual for him, and he'd crammed a brown top hat over it—something Aurelia found ridiculous. He was wearing his usual garb: the embroidered waistcoat underneath a fine brown coat, both tailored to fit his form perfectly. His golden eyes watched her keenly, and his mouth quirked up in a tantalizing smile.

"It's wonderful," Aurelia said coldly. She turned to go back inside, her magical moment in the snow dirtied by his pretentious presence.

"Wait, Aurelia," Frederick said, his smooth voice grating her nerves. "Don't leave because of me."

She rolled her eyes, fidgeting with the thin edge of lace poking out of her arm-warmers. "I don't do anything because of you. I need to get back to my workshop. I have plans that need finishing. Excuse me."

He didn't step aside, instead leaned against the door, still in her way. He crossed his arms over his chest, gazing at the snow. "Come on. I know you came out here to look at the snow. So did I. We don't even have to talk."

"Move aside."

"Aurelia," he pleaded, cocking his head and gazing at her under the rim of his top hat. "It's almost Christmas. Can't you be nice to me for once?"

Aurelia took a deep breath, looking up at the majestic sky and the twirling fall of snow. She leaned against the brick building, resolutely looking in the other direction. She *did* want to watch the snow.

"So..." he began.

"I thought you weren't going to talk?"

"Aurelia, come on!" He reached out and wrapped his hands around her forearms. She could almost feel his warmth. "When are you going to let this go? I had no idea I was up against you for the apprenticeship. You and I hadn't even talked in months."

She pulled her arms out of his grasp, and tried to shove past him to the door, but he planted himself in her way. "Why would you?" she scathed. "And once they saw your last name, it didn't matter who else applied for the apprenticeship, did it?" She took a step to her right, and he mirrored her.

His face crumpled. "That's what this is about?" he asked, aghast. "You think they gave it to me because of my father?"

"Of course they did. He owns the whole city." She tried to step to the left this time, but he moved that way too.

"He doesn't own it—he just powers it!"

"Same thing." She gave up trying to get around him and slumped against the brick wall again. *Maybe I can just ignore him,* she thought. *At least until he lets me inside so I can get some sleep before my shift tomorrow.* She stifled a yawn, then shivered. Her coat was really not made for this weather.

"So what do you think?" Frederick asked again, nodding at the falling flakes, as though he were solely responsible for the once-in-a-lifetime snowfall.

"I told you, it's wonderful," she said through grit teeth.

"I thought you'd like it."

"You're really full of yourself, you know that, right?"

He grinned at her, then stuck his hands in the pockets of his waistcoat. "It was very difficult."

"What was?"

"Getting it to snow."

She scoffed. "You didn't."

"I did."

Aurelia looked up to the heavens and breathed, "You're ridiculous. I don't believe you."

"I'll have to show you then. I'll have it back late tonight after its first voyage."

"*It*? What are you talking about?"

Frederick beamed, and Aurelia recognized the smile as one she used to enjoy before he went and betrayed her. She forced herself to look away, clenching her fists.

Words began to tumble out of Frederick's mouth in his excitement. "I told you: I got it to snow. It's my invention—my prototype to show to the inventor's union on Christmas. Did you hear they're accepting plans from non-union inventors?"

Aurelia closed her eyes briefly, trying to wrap her head around the idea that Frederick had made an invention that had made it snow here in Soldark, the place where it was always warm, and the sun shone year-round. Then she said in a near whisper, "Don't you dare. Don't you dare tell me you're submitting a plan to the inventor's union."

His face fell. "What? Why?"

"Why?" she scathed, then lowered her voice as a group of young laborers trotted down the sidewalk on their way to a late shift—or early shift, Aurelia had completely lost track of the time. "You've got an apprenticeship at Penydarren Place; you'll be able to get into the union in less than a year, guaranteed. What are you doing submitting plans now? Are you planning on ruining my submission for this too?"

"Ruining—What? What are you talking about?"

She threw her hands up. "I'm done talking to you Grandville. Step aside."

Frederick, mouth agape in confusion, didn't try to stop her as she shoved her way to the door.

"What am I talking about indeed," she muttered to herself once the door shut, drawing into the dim stairwell. She glanced back at Frederick through the glass paneled door. He was looking up at the snow falling from the sky. He muttered something to himself and then stalked off down the street, probably to drive home in his top-of-the-line motorcar he kept parked around the corner.

Aurelia scoffed then began trudging back up the staircase, making sure to give Frederick's workshop door a mean look as well, just to vent her feelings some more.

She curled up on the cot in her workshop, underneath a large sheet of canvas she had pulled off one of her train models. She couldn't even smell the oil on it, a scent which permeated the workshop anyway. She turned to watch the snow falling outside her window and drifted to sleep.

II

THREE DAYS UNTIL CHRISTMAS

It was still snowing the next morning.

An irritating buzz awoke Aurelia before dawn, the sound of the alarm she had rigged herself. She flung her hand out to stop it, groping around the edge of the drafting table above her. Finally, she laid her hand on the small contraption and flipped the switch over.

She shivered as she pulled back the canvas sheet. At least, she knew she would warm up at the foundry.

Twenty minutes later, she trudged down the lane through the thickening snow. She was glad for the black lace-up boots she wore; the snow had piled up to her ankles already. She didn't have anything warmer to wear than her usual nondescript brown trousers, long-sleeve burgundy undershirt, and brown leather vest. The brown coat was thin but better than nothing.

She thought back to her encounter with Frederick last night and scoffed, her breath clouding the air before her face. As if he knew enough to invent something that could create this. He was a hack, riding along his father's coattails, and always would be.

It snowed in plenty of places in the Galderon Republic, just never here in Soldark, the largest city at the heart of the solarbelt, where it was always sunny and warm. Aurelia didn't know how anyone lived with this freezing precipitation all the time like they did outside the solarbelt. She brushed some snowflakes out of her hair and her fingers came back glittering. It *was* pretty, though.

An intoxicatingly warm scent of hot coffee came over her at the next corner, where Max had parked his newsstand. She had known Max for a few years now, ever since she began renting her workshop space in the Brassborough neighborhood. He had given up the dream years ago of becoming a full-fledged inventor himself, so he ran a newsstand instead. And it wasn't just any newsstand.

Before Aurelia had met him, Max had crafted a first-class wheeled contraption that could hardly even be called a newsstand, it had so many bells and whistles on it—literally. There were bells and whistles at the front for when Max led the steam-powered cart down the street, to park at the next desirable corner. It would follow behind him all by itself as he gave it directions with an enormous control box that he kept slung by his side at all times.

In addition to its uncanny mobility, there were all kinds of compartments on the sides that opened up to display the day's papers—under glass, where a customer could press a button for their desired paper, and a chute would open up and provide them a freshly rolled-up copy. There was a variety of paperbacks for workers to tuck in their back pockets to read during breaks, and an array of snacks and drinks, all in their neat compartments. But today, he had hot coffee.

Aurelia drifted her way over to the newsstand behind some enthusiastic customers admiring Max's newest addition. He had rigged up an enormous metal urn to the corner of the cart, hot steam billowing from it and melting snowflakes on impact. Aurelia watched a customer hand over a copper coin, and Max took a paper cup from where he stood inside the cart, then placed it in a mechanical arm. He flipped a switch and the arm brought the cup over to the urn at the corner and began to fill it with hot coffee.

Impressed, Aurelia smiled at Max and glanced at the newspaper headlines behind glass as she waited her turn. *First Snow in Soldark in over 100 Years Baffles Weatherologists. SNOW, is it Good or Bad for Soldark?* Aurelia snorted.

"May I try a coffee please?" she asked when she got to the front of the line.

Max grinned at her. "Anything for my favorite inventor!" He inserted a paper cup into the mechanical arm and leaned his elbows on the tiny counter he stood behind. He adjusted his newsie cap, revealing short-cropped hair nearly the same color as his copper skin, which had faint lines around his eyes and mouth because he smiled so often.

"When did you do all this?" she asked in wonder, watching the mechanical arm up close. There were pistons and rods to make up the arm, with a clamp of sorts to hold the cup. What she couldn't figure out was how the urn began to pour coffee into the cup as soon as the cup was underneath the spout.

"Last night," Max said, shrugging. "Couldn't sleep, thought coffee would be a hit seller, and I was right."

Aurelia glanced back at the line forming behind her. He handed her the hot cup and her change. "And I thought *I* was up late," she said, breathing in the warm scent of the coffee. It was a rare treat; she didn't have too many coppers to spare even on paydays, and the cafes and eateries normally charged exorbitant amounts for the beverage.

"Working on your secret project again?" he asked, waggling his eyebrows at her.

A wide grin came across her face. "I finished all the calculations last night. Now I just need to find a power source."

Max scratched his stubbly chin. "And you won't ask—"

"Never. I can find someone other than the Grandvilles to ask for a handout." She huffed, her breath coming out in a cloud of steam. "I better get out of your line," she said, deciding not to tell him about her encounter with Frederick last night. She didn't feel the need to relive the experience.

"All right." Max shrugged. "But if it's going to cost you getting into the inventor's union, you might want to think about swallowing that pride of yours."

She glared at him over her steaming coffee cup. "What pride?" she said, chuckling. "I can get into the union all by myself, you watch me."

"I can't wait to see it in the papers," he replied, tipping his cap to her as she walked away.

III

After her twelve-hour shift at the foundry, Aurelia went straight to the train station. She counted out her coppers and saw she had enough for three trips to her parents' farm and back. After that, she'd have to wait until payday, and that wasn't until after Christmas. Mr. Augur had told them this morning that he wouldn't be providing any Christmas bonuses this year and wouldn't even pay them in advance before the holiday.

Not that Aurelia had complained out loud at the news. She could scrape by until after the holiday. Normally, when she ran out of money for train tickets, she'd just sleep in her workshop instead of going home for the night. But now it was just a matter of getting her train completed in time before the Magistrate of Invention sent out judges. She still couldn't believe they were doing it on Christmas Day.

She stepped onto the steam train, harried by the persistent snowflakes. It hadn't let up all day. While she had helped haul and pour giant vats of molten metal all day, she caught glimpses of it through the windows far up on the high walls of the foundry warehouse. She rolled her eyes again as she thought of what Frederick had said last night about the snow. It was just some fluke, some Christmas miracle like you read about in those two-penny paperbacks Max sold at his newsstand.

Normally, she hated taking the train right after her shift got out, when it was packed to the brim with workers heading outside the city, but she needed to get some measurements of the antique train before she brought over all her supplies and tools from the workshop. She wished her workshop were big enough, and that she had the means to bring the train there. It would make this fanciful Christmas deadline a little easier to meet. But she was lucky to even have her second-floor space at all.

As the train squealed to a stop at the small platform just outside city limits, Aurelia squeezed herself between the crush of commuters heading home and emerged onto the platform. The sun-beaten wooden planks of the platform were completely hidden by several inches of snow, and she had to brush off the wrought-iron railing as she descended. Luckily, her parents' farm was only a short walk from here, located in one of the older rural areas that the city hadn't had a chance to develop yet.

She nodded to the man in the small ticket booth at the bottom of the stairs, papers and paraphernalia stacked unceremoniously on wooden ledges behind the counter, a poor comparison to Max's remarkable newsstand. She wished she could have brought her parents some of Max's hot coffee, but she didn't know where his stand might have been after her shift, since he moved around throughout the day.

So she tromped through the snow down the country lane, a leather satchel at her side filled with her notebooks, blueprints, measuring tapes, rulers, and levels. She didn't appreciate the wind whipping snowflakes at her as it barreled across the Morrison's corn fields, which had long since been picked. She shrugged into her coat and ducked her head, wondering if she could find a hat or something at home for the trip back to the workshop.

Finally, she got some relief from the wind as she reached the edge of her parents' land, where a line of trees on either side of the lane offered some shelter. She wasn't looking forward to making this trip back later when it would be properly dark. Even now, she couldn't see the sun, blocked as it was by the snow and clouds.

Two beams of light came at her from the eerie darkness down the lane, accompanied by the chugging sound of an automobile. She darted to the side of the road before it whizzed by her.

She turned to watch it drive off, skidding a little on the slippery dirt track, but she had no idea whose auto it might have been. Her parents didn't often get visitors. She just hoped that it wasn't the bank again. A week before Christmas was surely not the time to be making house calls to lean on mortgagees behind on payments.

The tire tracks provided an easier path to walk in, and it wasn't long before the huge old farmhouse loomed up out of the snowy gloom. The front porch light flickered, illuminating the covered wrap-around deck that was sagging only a little in front of the door. Lights were on all over the house, in fact, upstairs and downstairs, which she found unusual. Her parents were normally very responsible with the gas, and only lit the rooms they absolutely needed to. Electric lights out in the country were harder to come by, and so gas was still cheaper out here.

She followed the tire tracks, which went nearly up to the door, and then the footprints in the snow, until she reached the warmth and light of the porch. The warm scent of freshly baked bread invited her in, and the heavy door creaked as she entered. She drew a deep breath once she got inside and went straight to the fireplace in the sitting room to the left.

Her hands already warming in front of the fire, she heard her father's voice drift down from upstairs. "Is that you, Aurelia?"

"Yes, I'm in the sitting room!" she called back. "I just came to take some measurements, and then I have to get back to the workshop before the last train goes through."

The stairs creaked as her father descended. She turned to warm her backside as he came into the sitting room. There were dark shadows under his eyes and a frown on his sun-weathered face.

"What's wrong?" she asked. "Who came in the auto?"

Her father sank into an old wingback chair beside the fire. "That was Doctor Abbeysworth. Your mother isn't feeling well again."

"What? I thought that medication the doctor gave her last year was working?" Aurelia took off her leather satchel and sank into the other wingback, her train plans forgotten for the moment.

"It might be the sudden cold," her father said, staring into the flickering flames before him. "That's what the doctor said. Or, well, the shock."

"Shock? What do you mean, shock?"

"Well..." he said, frowning. "The snow. Our crops are well on their way to dying. They're buried in snow, and they won't survive the temperature much longer."

Aurelia gasped. "All of them?"

"All of them."

She closed her eyes for a moment. She hadn't noticed anything wrong with the fields as she'd trudged down the lane, blocked by the trees as they were. If her parents couldn't harvest and sell their turnips, broccoli, and cabbages at the winter markets, they would be in even more dire straits than they already were.

"Don't mention it to your mother again when she wakes up," he said. "We can't have her worrying, not when she's feeling so poorly. The doctor gave her a dose of something strong before she left and prescribed a higher dose of the daily treatment too."

Aurelia took a deep breath, hearing his words add up in her mental ledger of their predicaments. The crops were a devastating subtraction. The higher dosage, another.

"Do you need help with the measurements?" her father asked, his gray eyes lighting up despite the new shadows underneath them.

She shook her head. "No, you stay inside with Mother. Can I borrow a hat?"

As soon as she reached the barn where her train was stored, she paused against the big open doorframe and caught her breath. She only had an hour to take all the measurements and get back to the train platform before the last train went by. If she missed it, she would have to stay at the farm overnight, and she was planning on doing a lot more work before tomorrow's shift at the foundry.

Suddenly her invention's importance towered over her, much like the enormous antique sitting in the dark barn. If her project was picked by the Magistrate of Invention, not only would she be given inventor's union status, but she would receive the prize being offered up: enough money to buy a new farm or fix up the old one; she'd take either.

But before, it had been something she had *wanted*. Now it was something she needed.

She got to work.

She pulled out her headlamp—several weeks' worth of pay, but worth it—and cranked the gear on the side for a few minutes. A light blared out of the bulb, and she strapped the lamp to her forehead. Even if there were enough lights in the barn to illuminate the train, she wasn't about to waste a whiff of her parents' precious gas.

The headlamp threw the train into view in bits and pieces, making drastic shadows as she moved her head and looked it over. It wasn't an entire train, of course, but the front cab, which contained the conductor's controls and the boiler, and one short car attached behind it that would normally haul coal and water. The only place for a passenger right now was in the driver's cab up front, but she didn't need to show the Magistrate of Invention how it would carry passengers. She only needed to show them that it worked.

And once she finished rigging up all the new parts to the train, all she needed was power.

But the amount she would need was exponential and couldn't be generated by the train's boiler alone. She would just have to figure it out while she installed the new parts.

Her beam of light focused on the connecting rods down by the wheels. Those, she needed to lock so the wheels wouldn't turn once the train was hovering magnetically above the track. And when the magnets weren't being powered, the train would be able to rest perfectly on the tracks like it did now. She pulled her plans out of her satchel along with a measuring tape.

Next, she focused her beam on the tracks the train sat on, which ran out of the barn and connected to an old Soldark Line that was abandoned years ago. This was the other reason her project was a perfect idea. She already had the tracks—which she had tripped over and played on endlessly as a kid—so she could test out the train easily without interfering with any active tracks. A few years back, she had even rigged up a farm cart to the tracks so her father could carry heavy equipment down to some of the fields that the abandoned line ran past. She had always been fascinated by trains. But that cart moved by ways of pumping a seesaw-like arm by hand.

She was glad she had already installed the magnets on the tracks a few weeks ago, since now the tracks outside were getting covered in snow. But a little snow wouldn't stop it from levitating, and she did at least have the short length of track inside the barn that was clear. It was certainly enough to experiment on.

She brushed her hand over the frontmost wheel, then yanked it back, burned by the cold. She brought her fingers before her mouth and breathed on them. For a second, she thought of going back inside the house to get a pair of gardening gloves, but hoped she wouldn't be out here long enough to warrant them. Her heavy-duty leather work gloves were back in her workshop in the city. She would have to remember to bring them when she came back tomorrow. If it was still cold and snowing, that is. It was strange not seeing the sun, and even more, she missed the warmth.

Her mother was still sleeping when Aurelia went back inside the house. Aurelia tiptoed over to her bed and gave her a kiss on the forehead before leaving. She tried not to think of how clammy and feverish her mother's forehead felt as she headed back down the creaky stairs, but surely the doctor's new medicine would help. It had the last time.

"Here," her father said, coming out of the sitting room with a pair of gardening gloves, a slouchy hat that might have once been gray, and a swath of burgundy velvet she could use as a scarf. Aurelia thought the velvet might have been a decorative drape from across the back of one of the chairs, but it was warm and soft, and she didn't care.

"Thanks," she said, putting it all on. "I-I'm sorry about the vegetables," she told her father. His gray eyes darted away for a second, then locked back on hers.

"It's certainly not your fault," he said, the sun-kissed wrinkles around his eyes deepening. He straightened his gray button-up shirt—about as dressed up as her father ever got, probably for the doctor's sake—and cleared his throat. "We'll be fine. Everyone will be fine."

She nodded, her throat constricting as she thought of her mother in bed upstairs and the crops dying outside. "I should get back to the workshop. This train isn't going to win in the state it's in right now."

A smile warmed her father's face, and he flicked the tip of her cap. "That's the spirit I want to hear. You'll do wonders as a union inventor."

"All I really want is the prize," she admitted.

He shrugged. "That wouldn't hurt, but with union status, you'll be well employed for the rest of your life."

She smiled. "I better hurry. I'm definitely not walking back to the city in this weather."

IV

As she rode the last train back to Soldark, Aurelia leaned heavily on the brass armrest beside her, worrying about her parents, the farm, and her invention. Her foot beat out a ceaseless rhythm, crossed at the ankle over her knee. It was as if she had drunk another jolt of Max's coffee; she was so wired, despite the approach of midnight and the pleasant but normally soporific dim lights in the nearly empty train car.

There was no way now she could think of asking her father to borrow any coppers for train tickets, so she only had two trips she could take to the farm and back. And one of them would be to meet the judge on Christmas Day. She would have to make all of her adjustments in one night, since the next few days leading up to Christmas she was working twelve-hour shifts at the foundry. By a stroke of luck—certainly not out of her boss's good nature—she would have the days between Christmas and the Dawn of the New Year off. It would be a wonderful time to rest. But it taunted her that she had so much free time to look forward to once the judging was over. If only she had as much time leading up to the Magistrate of Invention's deadline.

But she had to make it work, not just for her own sake, but her parents'. If they lost the farm, they'd have to move to the city, and her father would get stuck working in a factory just like Aurelia—but she was young, she didn't mind the back-breaking labor. Her father had run the farm since his own father had willed it to him, sure, but farm work was different. Soldark's factories were run by tyrannous overseers who barely let their workers take breaks and were more concerned about output than safety. Aurelia was careful at the foundry, but who knows what kind of job her father would secure—if he were even able to get one?

And her mother... She sighed as she watched the huge snowflakes speed past outside in the dark, illuminated only by the train's lamp.

Her mother had been doing poorly ever since last year. But Doctor Abbeysworth had prescribed her some morphine and another concoction that seemed to make the condition improve. Aurelia hoped it wasn't this blasted cold that had sunken both her mother's health, and the profits of the farm all in one go.

When she got back to the Brassborough neighborhood, the snow had piled up halfway to her knees. It had been wonderful at first, but when was it going to stop? The city was having a hard time clearing it off the streets and sidewalks, she had read in someone's discarded *Soldark Afternoon Times* on her ten-minute lunch break that afternoon. The automobiles couldn't even pass down most streets without skidding, and there had been a record number of accidents.

She had to yank hard on the door open to the stairs that led up to her workshop. The door carved a flat arcing path in the snow that had piled up in front of the stoop. She shook herself once she was indoors, brushing the snow out of her hair and off her borrowed scarf.

As she began to climb up to her second-floor workshop, her stomach dropped unpleasantly, as if she had missed a step. The lights were on in Frederick Grandville's workshop, she could see them shining brightly through the wavy glass window on his door.

She narrowed her eyes at the perfect little brass sign he had mounted beside the doorframe, *Frederick Grandville the Third, Inventor*. She stared at it for a moment, her eyes boring into the little screws holding the sign in place, her gut churning.

She couldn't ask him.

But she needed power. She only had three days until Christmas, when the judge would meet her at the farm. And the last thing in the republic she wanted other than embarrassing herself as a failed inventor, was to let down her parents now. She let out an irritated breath and put her hand on the doorknob.

It turned on its own, and she jumped back.

Frederick stood in the doorway, just as shocked as she was. She pretended to adjust her scarf as she mounted the next stair.

"Aurelia," he said, reaching out to try and catch her arm. She grabbed for the unreliable railing instead. "I've been waiting for you all night. I have to talk to you."

Her heart thudded. The words *I have to talk to you too,* burned her tongue, but she didn't say them.

"Something's wrong," he blurted, tucking his hands into the pockets of his blue and silver brocade waistcoat. For the first time, she recognized the manic look on his face. His eyes were darting all around, and his hair was ruffled as if he had been running his hands through it.

She took another step up, facing him. "What?"

He glanced through the foggy glass window leading outside, and said, "It won't stop."

"What won't stop?" she asked, becoming annoyed. She had work to do, cutting electrical wire and packing up the electromagnets to bring back to the farm. If she wasn't going to ask him now, she needed to get some work done before catching a few hours' sleep.

"It won't stop snowing."

"Well, yes, I noticed," she said. "It's a little inconvenient, but it's fairly nice for the season anyway. What, are you worried you'll be snowed in here and can't get home to the family estate?"

"No," he said, reaching out and grabbing her arm with both hands. "It's not that. I told you—I made it snow. And it won't stop."

Aurelia pulled away from him and flung her hands up in exasperation. "What in the sun-drenched republic are you talking about? I thought you were just joking about making it snow."

He shook his head. "It's my invention for Christmas Day. I did a test run last night, when you and I met outside. But it was supposed to come back. It didn't come back."

"What didn't come back?"

"The clockwork ice dragon."

V

Aurelia insisted Frederick come up to her second-floor workshop and explain while she got down to work. As she compared her new measurements to her blueprints, he told her about his invention.

"You converted an airship into something to make it snow?" she clarified for perhaps the third time. "And you made it look like a dragon?"

"Yes," he admitted. "The gears at the base of the wings actually help power—"

"And it's stuck up there right now?" she interrupted around the pencil in her mouth as she stared at the blueprints. She tweaked one of the numbers, neatly crossing off her original calculation.

"Yes, and it won't respond to the emergency return signal I worked into it," he said. "It was supposed to come back after the test last night—three hours. I've tried boosting the signal, but it's still up there, churning up the clouds and dropping the temperature."

The pencil fell from Aurelia's mouth and clattered across the floor as the realization came to her.

"You!" she pointed a finger at him as she advanced upon him. She stopped half-way when she almost ran into a stack of crates holding her magnets. "You're the reason my parents' crops are dead! The reason my mother's health suddenly declined! And you thought you could just do whatever you wanted to the weather?"

The finger she was still pointing at him was shaking. She lowered it.

"I...Aurelia, I'm so sorry. Is your mother all right? I didn't know."

Her chest tightened, and she didn't reply, afraid her words would come out high-pitched and pitiful. She turned around and grabbed a spool of wire, then stuffed it into a crate of magnets. Her wire-cutters were next. Then her toolbelt.

"I didn't know," Frederick said softly, placing a hand on her arm.

She pulled away. "Don't touch me, Grandville. I should go to the police right now and report you for meddling with the weather and causing so many catastrophes. Have you even read the papers? Seen how many automobile accidents there've been?"

"Please, I need your help."

"Help?" She scoffed. "Why would I ever help you? Why don't you just go to your father and ask him to help you out of this mess?"

"I can't," he said in a strangled sort of voice. "No one will help me."

"What about your friends at the Arts Bank Club, you know plenty of top inventors."

Frederick seemed to shrink in on himself, and he found a closed crate to sit on. "They're not my real friends. I don't really have any to be honest. They'd probably turn me in faster than you for this invention gone wrong. And none of them know I'm trying to get into the inventor's union this way. They'd resent me for it. They all earned their place through merit, they'd say."

Aurelia fiddled with the toolbelt still in her hands, carefully rolling it up so nothing fell out of its many leather pockets. She hadn't known that. Frederick always seemed surrounded by friends and lackeys, on the rare occasion she ran into him.

"But what about your father?" she asked again. She bent down and stowed the toolbelt in the nearest crate bound for the farm.

His eyes widened. "I can't tell him I made a mistake," he said incredulously.

"Oh, please," she said, turning away and digging through a metal cabinet beside her drafting table. "He thinks the world of you. He'll help you."

"I-I can't ask him."

Aurelia pulled out her torque gun and a container of heavy bolts to go with it, then turned to Frederick. "You didn't tell him you're competing either, did you?"

He dropped his face into his hands and shook his head.

Aurelia wrinkled her face in surprise. She watched him rub his eyes for a moment, and memories of what the two of them used to be like together threatened to wash over her. The way he always asked how her day was—*No*. It was over between them, even before he betrayed her, then stole that apprenticeship from her.

She crossed her arms over her chest. "Fine, I'll help you."

He jerked his head up. "Really?"

"Really. But you are going to do something for me in return."

VI

After her shift, Aurelia hastily stopped by her workshop to lug all her crates down the stairs and onto a handcart. She pulled the handcart through the snow to the nearest train station. Now gray and dirty, the snow had lost its wonder—mostly because of what had happened to her parents and now because she was going to have to help Frederick when she was supposed to be working on her own invention. The many footprints throughout the day had packed the snow down some, but lugging the handcart over the uneven frozen path wasn't easy.

She barely made it onto the next train and had to shove her way in with the cart, earning many irritated grunts and glances from her fellow passengers. She kept her eyes forward and didn't acknowledge any of them. She breathed in the smell of home from her borrowed scarf, and used her grip on the cart to catch her balance when the train began to move.

Fresh tire tracks led down the lane to her parents' house, making it easier to pull the heavy cart. After switching hands yet again, she finally spotted the porch light in the snowy gloom. She puffed out a sigh of relief and trudged on.

A newer model automobile sat in front of the house, and Aurelia wondered why the doctor was here again. She left the cart out in the snow and rushed up to the front door, her heart racing.

When she opened the door, she came face to face with Frederick.

"Oh, it's you. I thought the doctor—" Aurelia spotted her father over Frederick's shoulder, standing awkwardly in the doorway to the sitting room.

"I'll get that cart for you, Aurelia," Frederick offered.

"No, leave it, it's going to the barn," she said, knowing he was just trying to butter her up since she had agreed to help him.

Frederick dawdled over by the front door instead, fiddling with the pockets of his waistcoat, burgundy and gold today.

Aurelia ignored him and strode over to her father. "How's Mother doing today?"

Her father gave her a wan smile. "Better. Definitely better. She was awake all day, though, so she went to bed early."

"Good."

"And what's—" Her father began quietly, eyeing Frederick by the door.

"Er...he's helping me power the train."

"Really?" Her father's eyes widened. "What made you change—"

"I'll tell you later. We should probably get to work," she said louder, including Frederick in the conversation. Aurelia squeezed her father's shoulder before heading out the door with Frederick.

Outside in the snow, she grabbed the handle of the cart before Frederick could and wheeled it around his automobile.

"I didn't know you had your own auto," she said, fighting to pull the cart through the deep snow and heading to the barn, a short distance from the right side of the house. Her footsteps from yesterday had already filled in.

"It's not mine. I borrowed it."

She scoffed. "Why can't you just borrow an airship to go get your clockwork ice dragon to come down?"

"I did ask," he said defensively, "but no one will let me take one alone and certainly not in this weather."

"This weather," she muttered incredulously under her breath. "And whose fault is that?"

"I can hear you, you know."

"Good."

"Aurelia, can we just be civil for once? I came to you asking for help because you're a brilliant inventor and a kind person. You can go back to hating me in peace when we're done. We've both had rough patches when we've been there for each other."

Aurelia bristled as they came under the shelter of the barn. "I don't want to talk about any of that. Let's just get to work."

She brought the crates over beside her train and ran a gloved hand lovingly over the front wheel. Success was in sight. She knew it. She would get her power.

"Wait, I thought we were going to figure out how to bring the clockwork dragon down first?" Frederick asked as she pulled out her torque gun and bolts.

"I only have tonight to make the rest of the adjustments before the judging on Christmas. I've barely had any time to work on it since they announced the contest. We can talk while I work."

For a second, he smiled—at some old memory perhaps—then furrowed his brow. "But Aurelia, we have to stop the snow. The city is in a panic. Autos are barely able to move—I was lucky there were some chains in the garage to rig onto my tires to even make it out here. People are freezing, and the crops—"

He stopped talking at her icy glare.

"Well, what do you want me to do?" she asked. "I can secure these bolts while we talk." Already hooked up to the pneumatic line in the barn, she revved the torque gun. It roared as loud as a buzz saw.

She winced. "Ok, I'll just run these wires then."

"What about tomorrow? Can't you work on it then?"

"I can't—I don't have the—tonight's the only night I have. I thought we came here so you could help hook up the electricity?"

"What, do you have a night shift on Christmas Eve or something?" he prodded.

"I can't afford another train ticket!" she burst. "Okay? So can we get on with this?"

His face fell. "Oh. Oh, I'm sorry, I shouldn't have—"

"That's right. you shouldn't have. Did you even bring anything to hook up the electrical? Or was that just another empty promise?"

He tucked his hands in his waistcoat pockets and cleared his throat. "No, I didn't, sorry. I thought we'd figure out the ice dragon tonight, and we could do the train's electrical tomorrow. The snow's only going to keep piling up."

Aurelia rolled her eyes.

He continued, "But-but I can give you train fare or drive you out here tomorrow to finish your invention, even. It's the least I can do for causing you so much grief with this snowstorm."

She let out an exasperated sigh. "Fine. But I'm still running these wires."

Even if she didn't take Frederick's money, maybe she could borrow a few coppers from Max. She could pay him back next week—either with her wages, or, she hoped, the prize money. She hated asking favors from Max, but she didn't really have many other friends.

"So why is it still up there?" she asked, clipping a wire and jerking her head up to the sky. "Hasn't it run out of fuel yet? What's it running on?"

"Well, it's steam and coal powered like the original airship I converted, but the clockwork wings and workings I added allow it to keep operating once it gets going. They recharge it, in a way, with their movement."

"And you think you rigged the timer wrong to come back?"

"I must have," he said, shrugging.

She nodded. He was remarkably unashamed of his failure, at least to her, anyway. She was sure his father could have figured out a solution with all his resources at Grandville Electric. But she did understand Frederick's desire to remain anonymous about creating this devastating storm. The papers would drag him—and his father's company—through the mud if they ever found out who caused it.

"The clockwork... it's run with electricity generated by the steam engine?"

"Yes, that's the problem. If it were only steam powered, it would have run out of fuel by now."

She nodded again, looking down at the wire in her hands, her thoughts churning. "The train I'm working on is going to channel a lot of electrical energy through the magnets in order to make the train levitate off the tracks. I wonder... Have you ever heard of an electromagnetic pulse?"

His eyes widened. "Yes," he said slowly. "If we could even pull it off, wouldn't it short out everything powered by electricity in all of Soldark?"

She shrugged, then climbed up into the train cab with her measured wire pieces in hand. She hoisted herself into the conductor's cab and pulled open the control panel she had already begun work on a few weeks ago. "It would depend on the force of the pulse, but it would short some things, I'm sure. Wouldn't that be an acceptable trade to get this snow to stop?"

"But we might get discovered that way—I mean, *I* might get discovered," he corrected, seeing her sharp glare as she looked up from the control panel, wire cutters in hand.

With everything hooked up to the panel, she began to run the wires carefully inside the cabin. It didn't need to look too pretty for the test run, but she didn't want the judge tripping on them or anything. She began to bundle them along one wall, tucking them around the large bolts that secured outer panels and windows.

"So, do you know how to make an electromagnetic pulse or what?" Frederick demanded, poking his head into the cab.

She smiled where she crouched, tucking the ends of the wires through a small hole that led outside, where they would connect to the coal cart. "Maybe."

"Let's get on with it! Maybe the city won't care if they lose power for a short time, if this abominable storm stops. They might not even figure out it was me. And half of Soldark still runs gas lamps and heat anyway."

"I know how to make it happen," she said, still trying to jam the wires into the small hole she had drilled a while back, "but I don't think we should leave the radius of the thing up to chance. Having the pulse wide enough to reach the ice dragon might shut down *the whole city*, Frederick. I know dumping snow on all those poor people wasn't a problem for you, but—"

"I didn't mean for it to be this much!" He lurched up the steep steps into the cab, coming too close to her. "Let me help you with that."

"Fine," she snapped, dodging around him and getting out of the cab, clinging to the handle as she practically leapt to the ground. "Pass them through and I'll pull from the other side."

He passed her one wire at a time, and she pulled them as far as they could comfortably go, leaving a nice gap over the connector between cars. She began to connect them to the secondary panel in the coal car.

"I want to find a way to focus the pulse, if we're going to do this," she said.

"And then we can use it to stop the ice dragon?"

"Yes. I accidentally stumbled across the pulse when I made the miniature prototype for the train. Shorted everything in my workshop and actually fried a few things permanently. That's why we can't just let it go off and possibly affect the whole city.

Entire electrical systems and units could be permanently damaged. And your father's company..." she trailed off, knowing that would convince him.

"Huh," he said thoughtfully from the other car. "Wait a minute! When was this? That you accidentally released a pulse?"

Aurelia felt her cheeks warm. "Um, about a month ago. Why?"

"That was you?" he cried. "I fried my best amp meter! I was working on the ice dragon in my workshop. I thought there was something wrong with the wiring for weeks."

"Sorry," she said, though she wasn't really. It wasn't like Frederick couldn't afford twenty more amp meters from his apprenticeship wages. "But we have a solution to your ice dragon problem now, so you should be thanking me for frying your meter." She smirked, then hopped down from the coal car.

"We need to get to work attaching and hooking up the magnets. That's the last thing I need to do."

"But what about the electromagnetic pulse? The ice? I thought we had agreed to tackle my problem first."

She handed him a crate of her precious magnets, copper wire wrapped around iron tubes, which she would run electricity through in order to create the magnetic fields. When placed opposingly—on the bottom of the locked wheels, and on the track—the electromagnets *should* cause the train to levitate.

"Well lucky for you," she said, "my invention is actually the solution to your problem, once everything is hooked up. And we'll need to move the train out of the barn—I don't want anything exploding in here when we set off the pulse."

"Do you think that's likely?" he said, grunting at the weight of the crate.

"I don't want to chance it. We'll need to hook up the magnets, then the electrical. So it looks like we'll definitely have to come back here tomorrow. You didn't have any Christmas Eve plans, did you?"

"Not since the snow wouldn't stop," he said bitterly.

"Well, we'll solve both our problems now. Finish my train. Stop your storm." She began pointing out where the magnets would go, where she had carefully marked them previously with some red paint. He followed her directions and began bringing the magnets to the designated spots for her to attach.

As she revved the torque gun, her eyes fell on an old paper coffee cup lying on the ground after one of her previous nights of work. "I think I know who we can ask about focusing the pulse beam."

VII

THE DAY BEFORE CHRISTMAS

By some miracle, her boss let them off work two hours early—though, of course, it had less to do with care for his workers than a desire to get home to the delicious meal his wife was making that he had bragged about all day.

A thrill ran through Aurelia as she clocked out, the timeclock stamping her card with a resounding *thud* when she pulled the lever. She was free for a little over a week, until the Dawn of the New Year. And tonight, she and Frederick would hook up her train. The judge would come tomorrow, and one way or another, it would be over.

She pulled the letter from the Magistrate of Invention out of her pocket again, already worn from handling it all day ever since she had gotten it in the post this morning at her workshop. It confirmed her appointment with the judge, at half past nine on Christmas morning. She still couldn't believe they were working on Christmas Day. It was just about the most inconvenient day to get anything done—not to mention ruining any holiday plans people might have.

The city had managed to clear the roads a little better today for the autos, but hadn't bothered with the sidewalks, so Aurelia walked in the street, a cheerful bounce in her step.

She was on her way to meet Frederick at Max's cart. Before her shift this morning, she had told Max she needed to speak with him, and asked where his cart would be when she got out of work. Since she had left the foundry two hours early, she hoped she could still find Max's cart and not waste the extra time she had been given. At least, she knew where he would be two hours from now.

By some luck, Frederick was already waiting at the corner of Solastra Street and Anville Lane where they had agreed. He was leaning against a black wrought-iron lamppost, reading a folded newspaper. Perhaps he had gotten out of work early too.

It was unusual spending so much time with him after their years apart. He had even bought her a cup of Max's coffee this morning while they had made the plans to meet this afternoon.

He didn't look ruffled in the slightest since she last saw him, after his day apprenticing down at Penydarren Place, the most well-known workshop full of Soldark's leading inventors. He wore a gaudy red and green brocade waistcoat today, with the chain of a watch dangling from one pocket. A black bowler cap protected his hair from the snow, and he had a cup of coffee in his hand. His eyes glinted at her from under the brim of his bowler cap as she trudged through the dirty and uneven snow at the side of the road.

She was glad for the cold for once, the hat and scarf hiding her rumpled hair and sweaty clothes after a long day of work. With how busy she'd been, she hadn't even had a chance to wash her clothes for a few days. *Well, I can take a nice long bath tomorrow as a treat*, she told herself. That is, if they hadn't blown out the electricity in all of Soldark and on the chance that her parents had enough heating gas to spare.

The enticingly warm scent of Frederick's coffee wafted toward her, and she wondered where he had gotten it.

"You're early," she said, finally reaching the corner.

An auto blew by them, somewhat out of control on the still icy roads. Frederick pulled her out of the way.

"Oh!" she yelped, the auto careening behind her as Frederick pulled her close to his chest.

A hot sensation, then cold, seeped down her pant leg. She backed away and looked down to see his coffee had spilled on both of them.

"Oh no," Frederick said, his hands raised helplessly. "I'm so sorry! Are you all right?"

"Yes, yes, I'm fine. Thank you for that. Not for spilling

coffee on me—the other thing."

"Of course," he replied.

"Where'd you get the coffee anyway?" She glanced down at the wet stain and shrugged; she didn't have anything to wipe it dry with anyway.

"Max's," he said. "You know, I've never really talked to him much before. He's a keen fellow."

"You found his cart already?"

He nodded, peering into his coffee cup and finding he still had some left. "My boss gave us a half day. So I wandered around the area to see if I could find him. He's just down at Coppersdown Square right now."

"Well, let's go then. Did you take your auto?" She started walking and he followed. Her boots crunched through the gritty snow still left on the street as they walked along the side. Aurelia kept her ears peeled for any more approaching autos.

"I left it parked at the square," he said. "We can drive to the farm right after. That is, if that's all right with you."

She nodded. A cramped auto ride cooped up with him would be better than taking the train at least.

Coppersdown Square was filled with people and more filled with holiday cheer. Tents and carts had been brought in by vendors like Max, selling food, gifts, and knick-knacks for the last-minute holiday shoppers.

The square was surrounded by four clock towers, one at each corner, each telling a different figure. One told the time, another the temperature, another the date, and the fourth had something to do with astrology—Aurelia didn't really know what that one was.

A covered walkway ran around the edge, filled with vendors who didn't have a tent or anything to cover their goods from the persistent snow, Aurelia suspected. They had tables laid out with metal figurines, pocket watches, jewelry, and plenty of food. The smell of sweet cinnamon and clove assailed her nose, and she wondered where it was coming from.

Max's cart was right under the tower that told the temperature. Aurelia shuddered as she read the pearlescent clock face. Never in her life had she seen the temperature this low.

Max was in his element. He had rigged up a second urn on the other corner of the cart, and he was filling up cups of coffee left and right. His line wove in front of several other vendors.

Aurelia's face fell. Maybe they would have to wait until later when they were originally supposed to meet Max to even speak with him. He couldn't possibly have time to explain what she needed to know. A selfish thought of taking the time to explore the holiday market passed through Aurelia's head, but she pushed it aside. She had so much work to do.

If they didn't stop the snow soon, the regular trains might stop running. She knew the city was doing their best to try and clear the snow from the train tracks, but the ones leading out into the countryside probably weren't a priority. And soon, there would be nowhere to put the snow they managed to clear from the roads, and no one would be able to drive their autos anywhere. With Aurelia's luck, the judge wouldn't even make it out to the farm. They had to stop this infernal snow.

The newscart operator waved Aurelia over when he spotted her in the crowd. She came over and lifted a gloved hand in greeting.

"Hey," Max said, his face alight at all the excitement. He shifted his newsie cap to let some cool air hit his short-cropped hair. "Isn't this great? Really get a feel for the Christmas spirit," he said, grinning as he handed someone two cups of coffee.

"I'm sorry we're early," Aurelia said. "We'll just meet you later like we planned."

Max waved her words aside and reached behind him after taking his next customer's order. He handed her a sheet of paper that had more than one coffee stain on it, among the notes and drawings he had done. "I don't know why you're interested in how the coffee urn detects movement with a focused beam, but I'm happy to help with your invention. I had some downtime before I brought the cart to the square." He grinned and handed her a cup of coffee with a wink. "On the house. Merry Christmas, Aurelia."

"Merry Christmas to you too," she said, her face lighting up in a grin as she clutched the paper to her chest. "And thank you! I'll let you know how it all goes!"

He cheerfully waved her off, and she got out of the way of

his paying customers. She clutched the notes and coffee as she walked back to where Frederick stood beside an old-fashioned candlemaker's stand.

She eyed the candles for a second as she walked over, thinking her mother would love them. The pretty colored wax poured into unique glass containers was exactly something her mother would like. But she didn't go over for a closer look. Even assuming Frederick might drive her out to the farm tomorrow, too, she didn't have enough coppers for anything like that.

"He made us some notes," she told Frederick, holding up the paper.

"Perfect. We can get a head start. I parked my auto just around the block."

Aurelia sipped her coffee as they walked to the auto and was surprised to taste a hint of cinnamon and clove. It was delicious and warmed her like nothing else.

Frederick opened the passenger door for her, and she gave him a look before getting in.

"What?" he asked when he got in the driver's seat.

"Nothing. Do you have everything you need to hook up the electrical this time?"

"Yes," he said, "I loaded everything up this morning. We'll be pulling off the Grandville Electric grid, but I don't think anyone will notice. And if they do, I'll put it under my account."

He started the auto with a chugging roar and pulled out onto the icy road.

"Be careful," Aurelia warned him, clutching her coffee to keep it from spilling as he pulled the auto into the next lane. "No one seems to want to drive slowly in this mess."

"It's not as if I've ever driven in snow before," he said. "It's the first time Soldark's had snow in a hundred years, remember?"

She scoffed. "Yes, and I think I remember why. Something to do with an overly ambitious inventor going way too far with an invention he didn't even need to make."

"I wouldn't say I'm *overly* ambitious. Perhaps just the normal amount. And what do you mean an invention I didn't need to make? Who really needs a reason to invent something?"

She took a sip of her coffee, regretting bringing it up. The cinnamon and clove wove through her senses on the way down. "Well, you don't really need to enter this competition, do you? You'll get into the inventor's union soon enough on your own merits, what with your position at Penydarren Place and all."

Frederick didn't say anything for a few minutes as they drove out of city limits. "People keep saying that, but I haven't done anything to draw the eye of the master inventors, no matter how hard I try. I'll never get enough notoriety to join the union at this rate. I think they just like having cheap apprentices around to do their busy work. You were better off striking out on your own."

She turned to look at him incredulously. "I didn't strike out on my own because I *wanted to*, I was up for that same apprenticeship you don't even value! Remember?"

"Not really," he admitted, his hands sliding to a different position on the steering wheel. "I didn't know you were in the running at the time. When I found out after... I mean, I felt bad that you didn't get it, but you don't really resent me for winning it, do you? Is that why you haven't spoken to me in seven years? You're upset about *that*?"

She flumped back into the seat, her coffee almost gone already. She looked down into the cup and said, "That's not it, and you know it."

The ride turned even bumpier as they reached the country lane leading past the Morrisons' farm, and soon after, her parents' fields. She looked out the windows at the dead crops and didn't say anything further. She finished her coffee, the dregs bitter. She felt slightly ill after not eating for a few hours, but the coffee had been worth it.

When they got closer to the house, Aurelia saw an auto pulled up in front again. *Not again.* Her heart dropped to her stomach. This couldn't be good news.

She didn't say anything when Frederick put his auto in park, just ripped open the latch and bolted from the car. She shoved her way through the thick snowdrifts as fast as she could up to the porch, then ran inside the house.

"Father?" she called, her hand on the banister at the bottom of the stairs. Her heart was thudding. Was it the doctor's auto? Had something happened?

Her father appeared at the top of the stairs, with her mother leaning on his arm. Aurelia couldn't repress the sigh of relief at the wonderful sight of her mother out of bed. The doctor was just behind them as they all came down the creaking stairs.

Aurelia heard Frederick silently enter the house, then wander into the sitting room out of the way.

"Mother," she said, "you're looking so well. Should you be out of bed?"

"Do you think Doctor Abbeysworth would be letting me if I shouldn't?" her mother replied with a smile. She looked thinner and paler than usual, but her face was glowing with health. She was wearing her holiday nightgown, embroidered at the ends of the long white sleeves and hem with holly leaves and berries.

Aurelia pulled her mother into a one-armed hug when she reached the bottom. She smiled at her father and the doctor, not sure what to say. She never felt comfortable talking about her mother's health in front of her.

The doctor saved her from asking what she wanted to know. "The new medication is working wonders for your mother," she said, closing up the handles of her black leather bag with a *snap*. She adjusted the cravat at her throat then checked her pocket watch. "Sometimes these things just need adjusting. Well, good luck tomorrow, Aurelia; your parents told me all about your invention."

Warmth spread to her cheeks and Aurelia said, "Thank you Doctor Abbeysworth. And thank you for taking care of my mother." She stuck her hand out to shake, and the doctor bid them farewell and went out into the snowy night.

Her mother smiled at her, then glanced into the sitting room where Frederick stood by the fire, adeptly staying out of the family discussion. "The doctor said it might not even have been the cold, since it's still so cold and I'm feeling better already."

"That's great," Aurelia replied truthfully. She would never, *ever*, forgive Frederick if something terrible had happened to her mother because of his idiotic invention. The crops were bad enough.

"Is that Frederick Grandville?" her mother asked. "You know, your father and I haven't had dinner yet. We could all sit down together for a Christmas Eve dinner. Wouldn't that be nice?"

Aurelia's face crumpled. "I'd love to, Mother, truly, but Frederick and I have a lot of work to do tonight on the train. The judge is coming at nine-thirty tomorrow morning."

And she wasn't really sure she wanted to sit down to dinner with just Frederick and her parents. It screamed of an intimacy they no longer had, and she was still seething from their conversation on the way over. How could he not remember what had driven them apart. The promise he had broken.

"Well, you get to work then," her mother said, chucking her on the shoulder. I'll send your father out with some turkey sandwiches when it's done roasting."

"Thanks," Aurelia said, unable to keep from smiling. "Frederick, let's get out to the barn while there's still a little light out."

With a few polite words to her parents, Frederick followed her outside. It was slow going through the ever-increasing snow, and Aurelia was glad to get into the barn where she stomped off her boots.

Frederick rigged up a control panel and began running a line to the Grandville Electric box out by the Soldark Line tracks, just a little farther off from the abandoned track. He came in and out of the barn a few times while Aurelia finished up modifications on the train.

She was again glad she had already installed the magnets on the train tracks a while back; there was no way she could get to them easily now. Her fingers were already half-frozen as she finally finished. She flexed her hands inside her leather gloves to try and warm them.

The wheels were locked, the magnets in place, cables run to each. Now all she needed was the power to charge them. Once the current was live, the magnetic field generated by each electromagnet would create enough lift to levitate the train. Then, the magnets installed in the tracks would help push and pull it forward depending on the polarity of the magnets.

That was the idea anyway. She just hoped all of her calculations were correct, and the magnetic fields were large enough to lift the heavy antique. She had gutted plenty of unneeded parts and sold them for scrap, but the construction of the train was quite solid.

She sat down on an empty crate and pulled out her headlamp and Max's notes to study.

Finally, Frederick came back in, and he clapped his hands. "It should be ready," he told her. "Let me just check the readings down on this end before I flip the switch."

He brought a handheld meter to the control panel he'd set up on a stack of crates just inside the barn door. Wires snaked from the brass box, while switches, buttons, and knobs decorated the top. He checked a few wires with his meter and turned to Aurelia who had just come up behind him. "I think we're ready. Any progress on the focusing beam?"

"Yes," she said, pointing to part of Max's diagram. "See here where the detection beam connects to the urn? The beam isn't the same as what we need to do, but the theory helps. See how he did the wiring?"

"Oh," Frederick said, leaning in close. "But how will we use the train to generate the pulse beam?"

"The train will act as the transformer since it's going to have the power running through it and the magnets, but we'll need to add a set of antennas on top, and a couple of capacitors to focus the magnetic field into a beam shape."

They got to work. Frederick brought out a few wind-up lights much like Aurelia's headlamp, but these looked more like old-fashioned lanterns, which he placed on the top of the train car where they would be working. Aurelia's father brought them some turkey sandwiches with cranberry jam, and some hot chocolate.

Aurelia was itching to turn on the electricity and try the mag-train out, but there would be time enough for that once they finished the focusing beam. She certainly didn't want to have to get up on top of the train outside in the snow to rig everything up. So they stayed in the barn and finished the adjustments. Once the electromagnetic pulse generator was all set, they could move the train out and aim it at the sky, where the clockwork ice dragon circled Soldark.

Straddling the train car, an almond cookie in her mouth as she fiddled with the three antennas, Aurelia nearly jumped out of her skin at a roaring sound from above.

She looked up at the barn's ceiling, wondering if the clockwork dragon was somehow already falling down upon them. But no, glancing at the side of the barn, she could see through the gaps in the planks that snow was falling in an avalanche from the roof.

"Wow," Frederick said, glancing up at her, pliers in hand.

"I know," she said around the last bite of her cookie. "Hey, I think I'm done with the antennas. How about you?"

"Done."

"Ready to power it up?" she asked, grinning. She couldn't wait to flip the switch and turn on her train after all the planning and accumulating parts with her measly wages. Her ticket into the union.

"I guess."

"You guess?" she asked incredulously. "We're done! We'll bring down the clockwork ice dragon, no one will be the wiser, and my train will work just in time. What's the matter with you?"

"I just..." He put down the pliers and looked her right in the eyes. "What you said earlier. About us. The reason you stopped wanting to see me. I feel as if I did something wrong."

Aurelia's chest burned, first in anger. *How could he possibly forget? He doesn't even know what he did?*

And then her cheeks flamed in embarrassment. *He doesn't remember. Had she misinterpreted what had happened? Had she been holding a grudge for all these years for nothing?*

"I—You—" She huffed, her breath coming out in a cloud between them. "You promised me something, and you went back on that promise."

He frowned. "What promise?"

"I don't really want to talk about this. Can we just turn on the train?" she pleaded.

Scooting closer, down the top of the train car, he shook his head. "What promise?"

She looked up at the ceiling, as if the right words might be up there somewhere, might fall on her like an avalanche of snow. "Fine. You promised you'd never make me feel bad about being—well, poor, when we were dating. And on your eighteenth birthday, you held a party at your parents' estate."

"Right..." he said, clearly not remembering what had happened.

"And I came and met your parents and friends from home and more family, your cousins..." she paused, hoping he might jump in and stop her. But unfortunately, she had to continue to explain the scene that had repeated in her head for seven years, whenever she felt down about herself.

She didn't look at him.

"Well, once I was alone, two of your cousins cornered me in the back gardens. One of them kicked me down to the ground, and the other shoved mud in my face. They told me you didn't want me there, that you were embarrassed I had even come." She lowered her voice in mortification. "It was a formal event, remember? And you know I've never owned formal clothes in my entire life. Then I had to run all the way home."

She felt a hand on her chin, and she looked up, startled. She hadn't heard him come any closer.

"I never knew about that," he said. "I swear. I never even *thought* those words about you. And I certainly didn't say anything of the sort to my cousins."

Her chest swelled, but she was not about to start crying. The tears might freeze to her face.

He cocked his head. "I always wondered why you left early that night. I had been meaning to give you a gift, and then I never saw you again, never heard back when I tried to send you telegrams or letters even."

Flashes of torn up letters and telegrams flew threw her mind, along with the memory of dumping a whole box of them into the fire, unopened.

Another roaring sound from above intruded. Aurelia looked around to see where the snow was sliding, and then she saw movement outside the open barn doors. The snow was coming off the front of the house now, dropping straight onto Frederick's auto, which was parked outside the front door.

She gasped, and Frederick turned to see his auto buried in several days' accumulation.

Aurelia took the distraction to slide over the side of the train car and lower herself down, wedging her boots into crevices and grabbing rods and bolts for handholds until she got back down to the ground. She wandered over to the doorway to get a better look at the buried auto. It was getting harder to see the house from here; the snow was coming down thick and fast.

Frederick wasn't far behind her. "Ah, oh well. We can worry about that later." He shrugged.

Aurelia went over to the electric control panel Frederick had set up, still not looking at him. Since he had been the one to configure the panel, she wasn't sure what everything did yet. Her finger hovered over a switch she thought might be the one to turn on the power to everything.

"Wait, Aurelia," he said from behind her. She didn't turn. "I'm sorry my cousins did that to you back then—and I really had no idea. I didn't know what I did wrong. And then the next year I heard I beat you out of the apprenticeship, and I... I guess I've chalked it up to that this whole time."

Her voice was a little wobbly when she said, "Well, the apprenticeship situation didn't help matters. Can we just do this?"

"I want—" he began.

A screeching noise met their ears. This wasn't more snow falling from roofs. It was coming from much higher up.

Aurelia darted just outside the door, gazing up at the clouds. It seemed like it was coming from up there. "The clockwork dragon," she breathed. "Is that it? What in the republic is that noise?"

"I've no idea," Frederick replied beside her. "It sounds mechanical. I wonder if something's jammed. There certainly seems to be a lot more snow than before," he said loudly. Between the wind and the screeching, it was getting hard to hear anything else.

"Quick, let's turn the beam on," he said.

"No, we have to pull the train out first. I'm not risking anything happening to the barn, and it'll have a clearer shot out in the open."

"All right."

They rushed back to the control panel, and Frederick's finger went to the big brass lever at the bottom right. Then he said, "Do you want to do the honors?"

She grinned and stepped forward. "Absolutely." She clutched the lever and flipped on the power.

A loud hum came from the train, filling the barn with even more noise than what was going on outside.

"Is it working?" she asked, almost afraid to go and see.

He said nothing, only pointed.

She ran over to inspect it. The wheels, locked in place and their electromagnets firmly bolted to the bottoms, were hovering nearly a foot off the track. "Wow," she whispered. "I didn't think it would go that high. That's...incredible. Did you send more power to it than I had in my calculations?"

Frederick came over with a mischievous grin. "I might have."

"What?" she yelped, lurching backward. "You could have fried everything! I calculated the exact amount we needed—I've tested it small-scale dozens of times."

For a minute they both just stared at the gap between the wheels and the track, a wonder of electromagnetic energy that had seemed almost impossible. Like magic, if there was such a thing.

"It looks good to me," Frederick said.

"Well, I'll let you get in it first and see if you get electrocuted. Now I don't know if I can trust your wiring."

He continued grinning and reached out to touch the handrail. He grasped it firmly, then pulled himself up and into the cab. "Aren't you coming on for the first voyage?"

She followed him in, hurling herself upward into the cab, now a foot higher than it was before. She couldn't tell if she was imagining the feeling of floating as she planted her boots on the cab floor. He moved aside so she could get to the conductor's control panel.

"Here we go," she said, her heart racing as she pushed the lever forward that would direct the magnets' poles to begin pulling the train from the front and pushing from the back.

The movement was smooth, unlike anything she had ever experienced on the Soldark Line's steam trains.

They began to glide forward, but when they reached the barn door opening, where snow was piled upon the track, they slowed to a stop.

VIII

"No!" Aurelia shouted, slamming her fist on the side of the cab. Without any clear thought, she shoved past Frederick and swung herself down and out. She stared at the front of the train.

The snow was much too high. Even a foot off the ground was not enough, and for all she knew, the accumulation was interfering with the magnetic fields. She came around the front, sinking into the cold snowdrifts. Then she had an idea.

"Back it up a bit!" she called to Frederick, who had remained in the cab, his face frozen, unsure what to do next. "Pull the lever back."

She raced over to her toolbox and pulled out her torque gun. "Now come give me a hand! This is going to be heavy."

Revving the torque gun, she unbolted the large pilot mounted at the front of the train, its pointed front designed to deflect obstacles in front of it down the track. But now the track was much lower, and the pilot wasn't able to clear anything from up so high.

They both grunted at the weight of the pilot as it came loose. Aurelia turned to grab her headlamp from a nearby crate and jammed it on her head, glad it still had a charge. She stared at the front of the train, looking for places to re-mount it. She gazed into the guts of the train, not sure if this would work or not.

"There!" Frederick said, pointing. "And along there! Here—" He lifted the pilot and got it close to where they could mount it, low enough to plow aside the snow.

Aurelia used one hand to help line up the pilot with the bolt holes, and the other hand to rev up her torque gun, bolting the thing in place while Frederick held it up. The sound of the torque gun drowned out the screeching from outside, and the howling of the storm.

Finally, they got it in place, about a foot lower from where it started. She and Frederick looked at each other, their eyes wide in excitement. Without a word, they both headed back into the cab, and Aurelia jammed the lever forward.

They glided into motion, gathering speed as they went. The pilot plowed the snow aside, clearing the track as they went. It was difficult to pull back on the lever to slow down—not because anything was wrong with it, but because she wanted to keep racing down the track. She could try *that* later, when they had stopped the clockwork ice dragon and stopped the snow from burying them here out in the middle of the countryside.

The train emerged into the open field before it. Aurelia and Frederick were pelted with snow coming in from the side of the conductor's cab. The screeching above had turned into a keening whine coming from the clouds, and the white flakes were still coming down thick and fast.

Reaching the middle of the field, a good distance from both the house and barn, Aurelia pulled the lever all the way back. Slowly, the magnetic poles allowed it to stop.

"All right," she said, a little breathless. "Are you ready to generate the pulse?"

Frederick nodded. "And you're sure it won't power down the train or fry it?" he asked.

"The pulse will focus in a beam, upwards. And I'm pretty sure we'll get the clockwork dragon—it feels like it's right above us."

"Wait a minute," Frederick said. "It's just going to fall out of the sky, right?"

Aurelia's jaw fell, and she closed her mouth. "What if it falls on the house? What if it's not even near here and kills some unsuspecting people?"

Frederick slapped a hand to his forehead. "Gah! I'm such an idiot for inventing this thing! I can't do anything right!"

"Frederick! Frederick, just stop and think for a moment," she said, grabbing hold of his arms and shaking him a little. "All right, so it's going to fall out of the sky," she said, trying to jumpstart some ideas in either of them. "We need to control the landing. Let's think."

Frederick closed his eyes, thinking hard. "Assuming the pulse doesn't kill the train—"

"Don't you dare say that! The train will be fine. It has to be fine."

"All right, all right. The train will be fine. What if we reverse all the electromagnets after the beam goes off—and pull everything down to the track? How big is the track? How far did you run the magnets?"

Aurelia gasped. "It's not huge—it runs from the barn out and along these two fields, where it used to connect to the old Soldark Line. But the tracks aren't even connected anymore. I ran the magnets as far as I could go. We could! We could do it!"

"Lucky my auto's buried in snow," Frederick said.

"What? Why?"

"Well, when we reverse all the magnets—instead of the flux push and pull pattern you've got running through the track now, it'll pull a lot of metal toward the track, probably even the auto if it weren't buried."

She snorted out a giggle. "Let's do this!"

"Wait," Frederick said, looking down at the controls. "We can generate the pulse beam from here—but your track's master electromagnetic system is rigged up in the barn. I'll have to go back—you generate the pulse, and then I'll flip the magnets, all right?"

"All right," she said, glancing at the distance to the barn, a blizzard crossing the field between. "Don't walk on the tracks, remember? And I'll signal you with my headlamp as soon as I've run the pulse."

"Just be careful, all right?" he said, one hand on the railing as he readied to hop out of the cab. "The clockwork dragon will hopefully get pulled down to the track—but it could be any part of the track. So keep an eye on the sky—you won't be able to move the train."

"Got it," she said, nodding.

"Thank you." He caught her gaze and stared fiercely at her. "For everything. Soldark would be buried without your help."

"It's not over yet, Grandville," she said, her finger on the pulse beam's lever.

He ducked his head. "I know, but we've almost done it. And I'm sorry you ever believed that I thought less of you. I never knew what came between us, and I'm sorry you thought I broke that promise. I would never."

She shivered in the cold cab as a gust of wind pelted her with more snow. Her eyelids fluttered as the flakes assailed her, and suddenly Frederick was standing right in front of her.

"Thank you," he said, and leaned down to kiss her.

Her eyes closed and she shivered again, but not from the cold wind. A warmth began at her lips and spread down to her chest, to her fingertips. She breathed in his scent—so familiar, yet at the same time so foreign. It had been seven years.

Knees beginning to weaken, she kissed him back fiercely, then broke apart. "We've got more pressing matters," she said, pointing up at the sky, where the keening had returned to a loud screeching. "Maybe we'll have more time for that later."

A haphazard grin spreading across his face, he leapt out of the cab and went as fast as he could through the snowdrifts; in some places it rose up to his hips, but others were ankle-high thanks to the wind.

Aurelia licked her lips, just as more snow pelted at her from the cab window, and the taste of winter flicked across her tongue. She took a steadying breath as she watched Frederick get closer to the barn.

"Oh, right," she muttered, then fumbled with her headlamp, still attached to her head. She yanked it off and cranked the reel so it would have more of a charge. By the time Frederick got to the barn, it was ready. She gave him the count of two minutes after he got inside—the control panel was right inside the door; he should have plenty of time to get ready— and then she flipped the lever for the electromagnetic pulse beam.

A hum sounded throughout the train cab, louder than the gentle hum of levitation, louder than the screeching above. The beam was working—running anyway.

Headlamp in hand, she flashed it toward the barn, angling the light back and forth. Then, without warning, the train dropped to the tracks.

She threw her hands out to grab hold of anything to catch her balance at the jarring landing. Her teeth chattered together, not from the cold. Frederick had reversed the polarity.

All that was left to do was wait for the clockwork menace to fall.

She closed her eyes for a second. And just like that, the screeching in the clouds stopped.

Aurelia opened her eyes and went to the open cab door. Clutching the handlebar, she leaned out of the train and looked up.

Snow whirled around her, the wind still barreling across the open field. She couldn't tell, but it looked like it could be thinning.

And then she heard a whistling sound. Eyes wide, she searched the skies. Where was it? Should she get out of the train? Would she be safer inside it? She would *kill* Frederick if this thing demolished her invention, just when she had gotten it to work.

A cloud drifted away, and she saw it in the newly revealed moonlight. The clockwork ice dragon was falling, sinking and breaking through clouds, snowflakes fluttering in its wake.

And it was heading right for the barn.

IX

"Frederick!" she shouted, leaping down from the cab, her legs sinking into the snow. She fought her way through the drifts, stumbling, pushing. The beam of her headlamp wove in a drunken pattern across the snowy field as she lurched across.

It was as if all noise had ceased. No humming, no screeching, no howling wind. Just the blessed silence of the last of the snowflakes drifting peacefully down to the earth.

The dark shadow that was the clockwork dragon dropped faster toward the old barn. "Frederick!" she screamed at the top of her lungs, not sure if he could hear her despite the seeming lack of sound. "Frederick!"

She stumbled and fell into a snowdrift. By the time she clawed her way back out, she looked up in time to see the clockwork dragon crash into the barn.

In the vacuum of silence, the crash filled the frozen world

around her. Wooden beams splintering, shattering, crashing. The sound of metal crumpling as it all came apart. It went on and on as pieces of the barn collapsed onto the clockwork contraption that had destroyed it.

She continued trudging toward the barn, as if she moved through cold molasses.

Everything was suddenly and completely still. The snow had stopped, the final flakes settled. The barn, which was now piles of timber, lay like an open wound in the snowy white field. And in the middle of it all, the clockwork ice dragon lay, the canvas stretching over the wings torn, gears and rods sticking out in all directions. Aurelia could see what looked like the head of the dragon sticking up, steam issuing from its open mouth as it breathed its last.

"Frederick," she mumbled, her lips numb with cold. Her legs, just as numb, could barely make it through the last of the snow.

She sunk down to her knees when she saw him, not even feeling the cold wetness pressing through her trousers. He was kneeling beside the clockwork dragon, hand stroking the face of it, talking to himself—or it.

"Frederick!" she shouted, getting to her feet again. "You're all right!"

He turned, a sheepish grin on his face as he dropped his hand from the face of the dragon.

"I didn't see you leave the barn! How are you all right?"

"I thought I should get away from the track, so I got out right after I flipped the polarity."

She puffed out a breath and closed her eyes for a second, the adrenaline washing out of her.

He took one last look at the broken dragon, still issuing steam from its mouth, then turned and enveloped her in a hug. He smelled of the cold, and electricity, and a familiar scent she couldn't place.

He pulled away and looked at her, cradling her face in his gloved hands. "We did it! We did it!" He leaned his forehead against hers, and she closed her eyes, suddenly exhausted.

The last hour or so had been a terrible mess of storm, and sound, and terror. When she looked up, he opened his eyes, too, and their lips met as one final snowflake drifted down from the heavens.

X

CHRISTMAS DAY

At nine-thirty the next morning, Aurelia stood at the front porch of her parents' house, watching the judge approach down the lane in his auto.

The sun was shining again.

The snow that had covered Frederick's auto had been cleared, and both the auto and Frederick were gone before Aurelia even woke up. He had accepted Aurelia's father's offer to sleep on the settee in the sitting room, and Aurelia had collapsed into her bed upstairs well past midnight, fully clothed. She had managed to shuck off her soaking wet boots, at least.

With no idea where Frederick had gone, Aurelia had tromped out to what used to be the barn that morning to check on the train. She had woken before sunup with a terrible thought—what had happened to the control panel inside the barn? Lurching out of bed, she had jammed her boots on and hurried downstairs and outside.

After fiddling with the levers, she realized the control panel was still intact. But she also suspected that Frederick had been out here before she awoke, since planks had been shifted aside, and fresh shoe prints had led to the panel. And she noticed that the pulse beam antenna had been removed from the train too.

She had barely glanced at the ruins of the clockwork ice dragon before heading over to the train. After making sure that that, too, was operational, she went back inside the house and had a surprisingly normal breakfast with her parents. They chatted over coffee and cinnamon rolls as Aurelia anxiously waited for nine-thirty.

And now, here came the judge. His auto was even more expensive-looking than Frederick's. An older gentleman stepped from the passenger seat, putting on a top hat and pulling out a cane with an emerald topper. The driver, a boy Aurelia's age, remained in the auto.

"Leland Cornwall," the gentleman said, holding out his hand to her.

She shook it, reminding herself to keep her grip firm. "Aurelia Sundon. It's nice to meet you, Mr. Cornwall. Thank you for coming out all this way and on Christmas."

"Of course, of course. Not as if I had a choice. The Office of the Magistrate pulls all the strings, my dear. So here I am." He shrugged.

She smiled, immediately liking the older man. He had a monocle perched in one eye, and the red and green cravat at his throat was tasteful and not gaudy for the holiday.

"Let me bring you around to where my invention is," she said, "but first, would you like any coffee? Tea? Cinnamon rolls?"

"No, thank you. That's quite kind. I've four more stops to make today unless you're the clear winner. I've, at least, got the authority to induct any inventors I see fit, even if I didn't get to make up any of the rules for this competition."

A shiver ran through her, and for once it had nothing to do with the cold. She was so close, she could taste it. She relished the sunshine that shone down upon them as she led him behind the house to where she had left the train. The paths they had worn to and from the barn were becoming slushy and muddy.

"Marvelous," Cornwall said in awe as they rounded the corner. The train was levitating a foot off the track, looking for all the world as if she had done magic to it instead of all the careful scientific calculations. Or at least, that's how she thought of it. She had decided to turn everything on before the judge arrived, just for this purpose.

"Let me show you how it moves," she said, and sprung toward the conductor's cab. She launched herself up into the high cab and readied herself in front of the controls. Peeking her head out of the cab window, she saw Cornwall pull a small notebook from his coat pocket and begin writing in it.

She waited until he looked up before she moved the lever.

Slowly at first, the train began to move down the track toward the barn, the pushing and pulling of the electromagnets levitating her along.

"Wonderful!" Cornwall called. She could hear him chuckling as she passed him, and the smile grew wider on her face. She had it. It was in the bag.

But as she approached the barn, she heard the sound of clanking metal, and then—astonishingly—wheels creaking. *Was something wrong with the train?* She hadn't felt it drop down to the tracks.

Then she looked out the window and saw a large truck and crane approaching down the side of the field toward the ruins of the barn. *What was going on?*

She pulled the lever back and slowed down the train, sure the demonstration had been enough to impress Cornwall.

When she hopped down, Cornwall wasn't even looking at his notepad, merely staring at the train.

"So what do you think?" she couldn't help but ask.

"Well done, Ms. Sundon! Why, I think—"

The crane and truck were close now, their mechanical jangling loud as they approached the barn.

Much to her surprise, Frederick came out of the passenger side of the truck when it parked.

"I'm so sorry," she told Cornwall. "Would you excuse me for a moment?"

He waved her away, "Not at all, not at all. I'd like to get a closer look inside—may I?"

"Please," she said, and lent her arm to help him up into the high cab.

She strode over to Frederick and hissed, "What are you doing? The judge is here!"

"I'm sorry," he said, glancing back at where Cornwall stood inside the train cab, investigating the control panel. "I tried to get them here before the judge arrived to clean this mess up. But you have no idea how hard it was to convince them I was serious."

"Well, it's Christmas Day, you dolt. Did you pull them away from their families?"

"What? No, of course not. No, they were on duty already. They just didn't think I meant I wanted to clean up a whole barn in one morning, plus haul out a large piece of machinery, on today of all days."

The two men who had come with the truck and crane were now staring at the piece of machinery in question, the remains of the clockwork dragon. A limp and broken wing stuck up from the pile, gears sprawled across the planks of wood, the head visible even from where Aurelia stood. And then she noticed Frederick must have moved the pulse beam antenna from the train over near the dragon; it leaned against its damaged chest.

"Ah, Mr. Grandville," Cornwall said as he joined them. "I'm scheduled to judge your invention at four this evening. I don't suppose—"

Frederick smiled and shook Cornwall's hand as if he already knew him well. Frederick glanced at Aurelia and then at the dragon.

Her stomach lurched. *He wasn't going to steal her judge, now, was he? She was this close!*

His dragon was in ruins, but he had moved the pulse beam antenna over here...

"Looks like you'll finish with your judging early today, then," Frederick told him. "I'm out of the running. Behind me is the failure that was my invention."

Aurelia's heart fluttered and she let out a breath.

"Oh, my dear boy, my judging today is done already. I have my clear selection right here," Cornwall said, and clapped a hand on Aurelia's shoulder.

For a second, she didn't register the words.

Then her eyes bulged. "Really? Really?"

"Yes, really," Cornwall said, adjusting his monocle as he peered back to where her train still levitated off the humming tracks. "That is the most innovative invention I've seen in a very long time. Now I can go back to the Magistrate of Invention and tell them doing this on Christmas was an abomination of protocol." He lowered his voice, "The union reps forced a vote that we open up a contest this year for anyone in Soldark, and the higher-ups wanted to weed out sub-par inventors from applying. They seemed to think a last-minute Christmas deadline would result in fewer applicants."

Aurelia stifled a gasp. *So that was why.*

"When I tell them what you have here," Cornwall continued, "They'll regret looking down on candidates who don't show the 'right' career path or what have you."

She glanced at Frederick. The surprise at this information was evident on his face too.

"Well, congratulations," Cornwall said, shaking her hand again. "Welcome to the inventor's union, Ms. Sundon. I'll send along a courier with your prize money this afternoon, and all of the glorious paperwork we need you to fill out. Once you've joined the union, you'll have all kinds of opportunities. Just don't apply for management," he added in a stage whisper. "They make you work on Christmas."

A giggle burst from her throat, and she wanted to fling her arms around the old man and hug him, but she instead offered him coffee again, or more time to look at the train.

He shook his head and straightened his top hat before making his way back to his auto. Before he rounded the corner of the house he called out, "If you need anyone to consult on getting patents for your marvelous invention, please, get in touch, Ms. Sundon. I'd love to see more of your inventions."

"I will!" she called, raising a hand in farewell.

She was grinning from ear to ear when she turned back to Frederick, who was watching the two workers make a plan for the barn cleanup.

"You didn't have to do this," she said, wondering how much it cost to rent a crane and hire the men to operate it.

"I kind of did," he replied. "Soldark would be buried in snow without you. The least I can do is replace your family's barn. Besides, I need to get my clockwork dragon back to my workshop."

"You're not going to—"

"No, no. Never again will I meddle with the weather. And besides, it was fried, remember? I just want to scrap the parts."

"Good," she said.

He slipped his hand into hers, and she felt a small box there when he pulled away.

"What's this?"

"For you. Merry Christmas."

"Oh, Frederick, you didn't have to—when did you even—"

Her protests were interrupted when his lips met hers. They were warm and sweet and tasted of ginger.

"I've wanted to give that to you for a long time," he said. "Go ahead."

She pulled the lid off the small nondescript brown box. Inside were a pair of earrings. But not just any earrings. "The dragon earrings!" She gasped. "From the Fawney Fair we went to the last summer of school! How do you even have these?"

He shrugged and tucked his hands into his waistcoat pockets. He'd done away with the gaudy red and green, and today was wearing a more mellow brown and gold waistcoat to match his brown pants and bowler cap. "I told you, I've had it for a long time. I was going to give them to you that night...of the party," he ended awkwardly.

"Oh," she said, poking a finger into the small box and touching the earrings amid the wood shaving padding. Made of real silver with actual emeralds for eyes, the dragons hung from the earring posts by their claws, their wings spreading wide, and tails curling down at the bottom. She had thought they were marvelous that day at the fair with Frederick. But she had never been able to afford anything like them in her life.

Frederick cleared his throat, and she looked up. "They were kind of the inspiration for..." He nodded to the clockwork dragon.

"No," she said. "Really? But why the snow?"

"Well... Don't laugh, but I... wanted to impress you. You know I rented that workshop space in your building to try and speak to you again."

She shifted on her feet and glanced back down at the dragon earrings. She had wondered why he had rented a space in that part of town, when he could easily have a workspace at home in his father's estate.

"I... don't know what to say," she admitted.

"Say you like the earrings? Say you'll come back to my house for Christmas dinner?"

She chuckled. "I have grand plans today, Frederick. They involve a bath, and filling my face with as much Christmas dinner as I possibly can, and celebrating with my parents about the prize the train has won us."

"Well, I could help with the dinner part," he said, "but I'll leave you to your grand plans here. I was planning on riding back with the clockwork dragon once they've extricated it. I'll have builders out here as soon as the ground looks good enough to pour new foundation posts. It's a mix of ice and mud at the moment," he said, looking down at his shiny brown shoes that were covered in mud and slush.

"Thank you," she said, pulling him into a hug as she slipped the earrings into her pocket. "For the barn, for everything—well, no, not for almost ruining my invention and dumping all that snow on us, but, you know."

He smirked. "I guess I got your attention with the dragon after all."

She punched him lightly on the shoulder. "Never go to those lengths again to get anyone's attention. Your ideas are dangerous."

A grin lit up his face. "Well, as long as I have you to save me from myself..." he murmured, pulling her back into his arms.

"Within reason," she agreed.

THE END

Epilogue

"Next stop, University of Soldark!" the ticket collector called as he walked down the aisle of the gently rocking train car. Mae Wright straightened her collar as Robyn nudged her, pointing out the window.

The university came into view around the bend, its grand buildings revealed behind the brick structures on the left side of the tracks.

Mae grinned as the small train stop came into view. Standing on the simple wooden platform was Robyn's boyfriend, Theo, whom they had come to support at the annual Invention Gala, hosted by the Magistrate of Invention. Though the title of the event merely suggested inventions, Theo's fashion line was to be featured in an art gala portion of the evening.

"You know," Robyn said, grinning as the train brakes squealed, "I still think you should teach sewing at the University.

You're loads better than Theo's professors."

Mae chuckled, swatting imaginary dirt from her tidy maroon skirt, the prototype of one of the new styles she sold in her shop. "Oh, I'm quite happy living my double life as a seamstress and a costumer, thank you very much. I don't need to add yet another project."

Robyn waggled his eyebrows at her. "Maybe you just don't want to be training the competition, eh?"

As the train shuddered to a halt and they headed for the exit, Mae snorted. "Hardly. It's not as if I can clothe the entirety of Soldark. And you know I don't consider Theo to be competition! I'd hire him in the shop the second he graduates, if he didn't want to go off on his own and start a clothing line."

"He is rather stubborn," Robyn agreed, greeting the boy in question with a kiss on the cheek.

"You talking about Des?" Theo quipped, with a knowing smirk at Mae. "It couldn't possibly be anyone else, I am sure."

With a sly chuckle his only reply, Robyn slipped his fingers into Theo's waiting hand.

"You look positively dashing," Mae said to Theo, following the pair down the sidewalk leading to the University. Theo had designed the suit himself, of a high-quality brown tweed, the waistcoat boasting the delicate chain of a pocket watch. Mae admired the cut of the collar; though men's suits weren't often in her inventory, perhaps a more subtle look could be adapted to dresses...

"Hey," Robyn interjected, "That's my line."

"Well, you were too slow," Mae ribbed, tossing aside all thoughts of work. She was here to have fun, not spend the night dreaming up dress designs—a directive Des had given her before heading for the train. He knew how her brain wouldn't stop working sometimes.

"Oh, Theo," Mae began, "Des said he was sorry he couldn't make it; he and Charlie will probably be stuck in the theater until late tonight; there's a wiring problem in the lighting grid, and we've got a matinee tomorrow."

Theo nodded, and led them past the trees lining the sidewalk, their leaves just beginning to turn orange. His pace notably slowed as they rounded the corner of the Grand Hall, where the gala and exhibition would take place. She thought she understood his hesitation; everything he had worked on for so long; on display for the higher-ups at the University, and the Magistrate of Invention to see. A night that could decide the fate of his career.

Robyn leaned into Theo's shoulder and murmured something Mae couldn't hear. Theo's back straightened. He hitched up his smile, and led them inside.

Verity Pennington clutched her best friend Marigold's arm as they walked the perimeter of the Grand Hall, admiring the inventions, art, and fashion on display. "This is almost as good as the Masquerade," Verity murmured. "The first year, anyway, this last summer was all right."

"Just all right?" Marigold said with a snort, "You were too busy admiring one particular corner of the Speare estate where a certain inventor was concerned—"

"William needed help placing pinions on his second dancer! And it's not my fault he was posted up by the buffet table. What else was there to see?"

A chuckle, almost like chiming bells, rang from her best friend, and Verity clutched her arm even tighter. "I'm so glad you enrolled too," Verity said in earnest. "And we couldn't very well have attended university together if you'd moved to Corbright."

Marigold nodded seriously. "I thank my lucky stars every day that my mom's family decided to move closer to us, rather than the opposite. Something about not wanting to uproot young flowers before their roots are established, I believe they said..."

Verity let the flower pun go with a shake of her head.

"Anyway," Marigold continued, "I'm only taking a few classes, as you very well know. Not all of us can afford full tuition."

Verity jabbed Marigold with her elbow as they sailed past the art exhibit, admiring the paintings and lithographs, but also the frames surrounding the artwork. Many of them were painted wood, carved with whorls and fleurs, deep valleys of shadow, and high peaks of glinting gold paint. Verity sighed. "It's not all it's cracked up to be, you know. How would you like waking up before dawn to learn calculus? But if you want to suffer with me, you could always design a float for the spring festival or something to get the money!"

A giggle escaped Marigold as she snatched a glass of apple cider from a roving server's tray.

"Hey," Verity hissed, "Grab me one next time, won't you?"

"Sorry, he was too fast. And I'm not in the float business," Marigold said, taking a sip of her cider and handing Verity the glass.

Verity accepted the offering and took her own sip. It had a delightful addition of spices and wasn't too sweet; crisp and refreshing as the apple it came from. "But you could win something like that—that theater did, with your flowers!"

"And I told you, that woman shared some of her winnings with us afterward! That's half the reason I can even take these classes," Marigold said with a bemused smile. "But you think I'm going to go to the trouble of constructing a vehicle that can roll by Coppersdown Square, complete with some clever theme? Nah, I'll leave that to you engineers."

Verity straightened her shoulders, hiding a small grin. She was quite pleased she had been accepted into the college of engineers at the University. Her entire family was *more than* pleased at her acceptance.

She had gotten in on the merits of her own invention—with miniscule workings as small as a watch, her portfolio project had been a small mechanical dancer that wove around a magnetic board. She would never forget the warm look on William's face when she told him of the idea of the miniature dancer.

Her breath caught as she saw the man in question striding toward them, two ciders in hand. "There you two are! Did you see the weatherbird over there? I was just talking to the inventor." He handed one of the glasses to Verity. She enthusiastically sampled her own cider, watching him out of the corner of her eye.

"Is that what took you so long?" Marigold griped good-naturedly. "Talking the inventor's ear off?"

William ducked his head. "Hey, she's a union inventor; I'll do what I can to get in. But no, she uh—heard about my dancers at the masquerade and wanted to ask me about them."

"Really?" Verity demanded with interest, putting a hand on William's forearm. "That's wonderful. So, you're acquainted with a union inventor now. You'll be in the union in no time," she added sagely.

"Sun's light willing," he said bracingly. "Hey, is that the Coppersdowns?"

They turned to gaze at the entrance, and saw the copper mogul and his willowy wife enter, preceded by their daughter. Auburn of hair, and clutching a notebook to her chest with vigor, the girl surveyed the room with a keen eye.

Caz Coppersdown stepped into the Grand Hall and inhaled the ghost of a scent of machine grease, mixed with something she thought was oil paint. Giving a quick wave to her parents, she set off about the large room, surveying the mix of inventions and art—but sunspots, it was hard to tell which was which sometimes.

A title for a news article floated to her mind, and she grinned, staring at a mechanical vase which had water trickling artfully down its sides to where it pooled at the base before cycling through the pot again. *Art Meets Innovation at the Annual Invention Gala.* It would do for a start—until she found a more unique angle to the evening, that is. She always liked to infuse her stories with a human element. Perhaps a personal story from one of the inventors. She knew it would come to her as the night wore on.

But, she had to remind herself, she wasn't only here to write a news article. Though the *Soldark Times* accepted nearly every article she submitted to them, she was only a freelance journalist. What she really wanted to do was get to know some of her fellow students. In every letter Aunt Elmira sent, she kept asking if Caz had any new university friends.

Her correspondence with Elmira was a writing endeavor she treasured more than her dozen articles published in the *Times*. She kept all her aunt's letters bound in a thick notebook, complete with copies of her own letters, for cataloging purposes. In the back of her mind, she thought maybe someday she could turn it all into a book. Though her own letters were mediocre of wit, Elmira's verbosity shone through each parchment, down to the saucy remarks about the denizens of her hometown Haversdale, to the deeply profound ruminations on everything from politics and art, to life itself.

She sighed, missing Daguerre, her little country home away from home. She had already bought her train tickets for All Hallows—and alerted her professors that she would be taking off two weeks from school for personal reasons—to celebrate with Elmira. Though she would rather stay longer, Elmira herself put her foot down when it came to Caz's studies. At least Caz could visit the little suburb any weekend she liked. She already had a few trips planned with Hanson, though he insisted on coming to Soldark as often as not. Elmira preferred to stay in Haversdale, and Caz treasured her solo visits out into the countryside.

Caz's gaze was drawn to the largest invention, a great mechanical beast of a thing—not a literal beast like some of the metal objects sitting on plinths and podiums around the hall, but a massive column of metal pipes and gears. She couldn't quite tell its purpose. She strode toward its place of prominence at the opposite side of the hall, rolling her pen between her fingers.

Aurelia Sundon crossed her arms across her chest, shooting a playfully annoyed look at Frederick. He stood beside his massive power converter, one hand slipped dashingly into his waistcoat pocket.

A smirk grew on her face. "You know, Fred," she called from her post beside her invention, "You don't have to make things bigger to be better." She made a show of gazing up at the mechanical monolith.

He shook himself out of a reverie. "Says the woman whose first union invention was an entire train."

"It wasn't the entire train, and you know it. It was two cars."

"Well, not all of us can rein it in like you, Aurelia," he said, nodding at her weatherbird. "I heard Mr. Cornwall helped you get your patent for that already?"

She nodded, a grin rising to her lips.

He gazed at her. "I expect you'll be getting a lot of telegrams from the city—and all across the Galderon Republic—after this, my dear."

Her face flooded with warmth and she blinked rapidly, turning away to look at her invention. Inspired by Frederick's failed clockwork ice dragon last winter, Aurelia never could turn her thoughts away from the weather. Her clockwork bird was not only beautiful—a happy byproduct of mechanics—but successfully measured the wind currents and air pressure. The Magistrate of Invention had invited her to display it tonight for the students, and she couldn't pretend she wasn't proud of it. It had been a lot of work.

A younger girl with bright auburn hair approached, tilting her head as she gazed up at Frederick's power converter.

Aurelia hitched up a smile. Being in the union had never-ending perks, it seemed, but also came with responsibilities, like enticing young inventors into swelling its prestigious ranks, and displaying their worth to the city.

The girl's head tilted back down as she read the placard in front of Frederick's invention. "Ah, Grandville, is it?" the girl said with some familiarity, holding out her hand. "I'm Caz Coppersdown, I—"

Frederick grasped her hand, and grinning, said, "Of course I remember you! Though you don't always attend our parties, your parents speak highly of you."

Caz smiled, turning toward Aurelia, and reading the placard in front of the weatherbird.

Frederick said, "Aurelia's is much more interesting." He nodded toward the weatherbird. "You should interview her."

"Interview?" Aurelia said, balking. She could talk barometers and bearings with other engineers all day, but...

Caz gave a demure chuckle. "Don't worry," she said, cutting a stern glance at Frederick. "I'm not here to interview anyone—necessarily. I write for the *Soldark Times*, sometimes," she added at Aurelia's confused expression.

"Don't think I didn't recognize your name in the paper," Frederick said to Caz with a grin.

"Oh, I see," Aurelia said. "But aren't you a student here?" Aurelia added, crossing her arms in the other direction.

"I am," Caz offered. "I just write on the side, when I can. But for the sake of conversation… Can you tell me how your invention works? On or off the record."

Frederick edged close, so their arms were touching.

"Sure," Aurelia said. "It all started with that freak snowstorm last winter. I thought for the sake of my family's crops, it might be worthwhile to come up with a kind of indicator for bad weather…"

Aurelia warmed up to the conversation the more she talked about the weatherbird. Since Caz wasn't scribbling in her notebook like Aurelia imagined a journalist would, she was quite liking the attention on the invention. Plenty of engineers had come up to talk nuts and bolts, but Caz's interest was more about the impact it would make.

"Is that the famous playwright Ms. Coppersdown?" a voice called from a few paces away.

Caz turned, pale face flaming as she whirled around to face a pair of boys heading over to them.

Aurelia recognized one of them as an actor from the Proserpina Theater. The woman who designed their marvelous costumes trailed after them like a proud older sister.

"Oh, sorry," the boy who had spoken said to Aurelia. "Name's Robyn, and this is Theo, and Mae." The boy introduced as Theo was sporting a gold ribbon on his lapel, perhaps the prize from the art show.

"Aurelia," she said.

"Frederick," he offered.

Robyn's eyes widened as he spotted the remainder of Frederick's name on his placard. "Sorry for interrupting. We'll just—"

"Oh no, please," Aurelia insisted. "What was that about a playwright?"

Caz's pale skin still blushed a pretty cherry under her freckles. "That would be me, yes."

Robyn came forward and clapped her on the back, face alight with mischief. "Miss Coppersdown wrote the summer play at the Proserpina! To rave reviews, I might add."

Frederick had put a finger over his mouth as if in thought, then pointed at Robyn. "Ah, yes, you played the young Daguerre!"

Robyn gave a mock bow, all uncertainty vanished. "At your service."

Aurelia wracked her brain, twitching her fingers in their crossed position. "I don't remember that one."

"You were on an airship to Angleshire, my dear. For the conference."

"Oh, right." Aurelia rolled her eyes.

"The trials of union inventors," Frederick sighed in a stage-whisper. "Always gallivanting off to foreign countries to be congratulated on their brilliance."

Aurelia uncrossed her arms and lightly punched his shoulder. "You were invited, too, if I recall!"

Frederick's gaze slid away with a mischievous grin. "Well, I had prior engagements."

"Tickets to the theater?" Aurelia said, eyebrow raised.

"I don't recall anymore," he said loftily. She knew that twinkle in his eye.

"I think you owe me a cup of coffee," she said.

"Gladly, my dear," he said, glancing at his pocket watch. "I could use one myself."

The theater crowd had withdrawn during their good-natured ribbing to further inspect Frederick's invention, massive in its brilliance as it was.

Caz, however, came closer to Aurelia as Frederick departed. Aurelia wasn't sure if she was excited or resigned at the sight of the notebook Caz had begun scribbling in.

"This won't be painful, I promise," Caz said. "You already told me pretty much everything I need."

"Oh," Aurelia replied in relief. Between that and the cup of coffee she knew would be forthcoming, the evening had lost its burdensome edge. A waft of autumn air came in through the open door and circled the hall, bringing with it the scent of crushed leaves. "I'd much rather be curled up in my workshop, sketching away at my drafting table, on nights like tonight, you know," she told Caz, who smiled.

"I feel the same way about my writing desk sometimes," Caz said.

The conversations in the Great Hall were interrupted by a loud *clang* that echoed deafeningly through the hall.

All faces turned to look at Frederick's invention, and consequently, at Aurelia standing right beside it.

"You've got to be kidding me," she said, resigned. Frederick was nowhere in sight.

"What was that?" Caz said, positioning herself ever-so-slightly with Aurelia between her and the invention.

Aurelia didn't blame her. The power converter Frederick had developed for the family electric company was a prototype for a new kind of power harnessed by the sun and converted to steam.

"It shouldn't even be working now," Aurelia said, glancing up at the glass-paneled ceiling of the hall. "There isn't any sunlight anymore."

Conversations around them resumed at an uneasy clip, though Aurelia remained stock still, hoping Frederick would be on his way back soon. Apparently, she chose the worst time to request a coffee.

Another loud *clang* sounded, this one a slightly different tone.

Voices in the crowd hissed uneasily as gazes turned their way. Caz took another step back, scribbling furiously in her journal. Aurelia groaned. She should probably do something before Frederick's invention's gears started turning, possibly exploding all over the place. She would never let him live down that clockwork ice dragon. But she didn't really know much about this power converter.

She spotted a familiar man in the crowd nearby. She darted forward and tugged on his sleeve. "Hey, William Risewell, right?"

The man perked up, his gaze going to the power converter. "R-right." He glanced uncertainly at the black-haired girl next to him.

"Is this the inventor you told me about?" the girl hissed.

Aurelia forced down a smirk as she towed Risewell and his date over to the power converter.

"You told me you were familiar with backwards engineering and cyclical power structures, right?"

"Oh," Risewell said, eyes widening. "Yes?"

They stopped in front of the control box at the head of the power converter. Aurelia glanced around the hall, but there was still no Frederick striding toward them with a rakish expression on his handsome face, hands full of delicious cups of coffee, and brain full of solutions to this mess.

"Is it a yes or a no?" Aurelia tried to infuse a little more calm into her voice, with mixed results.

Risewell's date piped up, "Yes. I mean, we can take a look, right?"

Aurelia eyed the girl with interest. "Who're you?"

"Verity Pennington," she said succinctly. Aurelia thought the name sounded familiar—something to do with a masterful clock the Grandvilles had bought.

"Let's look," Aurelia agreed.

Jiggling the control panel open, Aurelia moved a few wires aside, wishing she had acquainted herself with the steam and solar monolith a bit better. But she had spent countless days over the last few months traveling with her weatherbird to test it out in different altitudes and climates.

Clockwork peeked out from behind the wires, gears spinning daintily in their precision. Aurelia's brow wrinkled.

Verity poked her head around the man and gasped. "Oh!"

"What is it?" Aurelia demanded.

Another *clang* sounded, much louder, causing everyone around the mechanical monolith to duck.

Except Verity. She gazed into the guts of the clockwork and pulled the smallest screwdriver Aurelia had ever seen from her skirt pocket.

Aurelia's eyes widened as the girl fearlessly inserted the screwdriver into the inner workings of the control panel. Risewell had wisely stepped aside, letting Verity work.

Caz had crept close behind Aurelia, hands with her journal and pen draped at her side. The theater crowd stared openmouthed at the clockmaker braving the contraption.

It seemed as if everyone in the hall held their breath, with only a few errant sounds of clockwork and bubbling water coming from other inventions in the exhibition.

Verity jiggled her screwdriver in a way one really shouldn't jiggle a screwdriver.

"Are you sure—" Aurelia began, panicked gaze searching for Frederick.

"I need something small to stick in here," Verity said with a huff, glancing about.

"Smaller than that?" Risewell said. He patted his pockets, but came up with nothing. Aurelia, too, had no tools.

Mae, the costumer from the theater, stepped up. "Will this do?"

Aurelia had to squint to see what she was holding between two pinched fingers—a silver sewing pin.

Verity snatched it and turned back to the control panel. "Thanks," she murmured, eyes focused on the clockwork.

Aurelia held her breath, waiting for another clang, or an eruption of clockwork.

Finally, Verity withdrew her screwdriver and the pin, and said, "There!"

Another *clang* sounded. Aurelia ducked with the rest of them, until she noticed an array of lights at the top of the invention had brazed bright at the sound, illuminating the hall against the ever-darkening windows.

"Is—is that it?" Aurelia said.

Risewell grinned and squeezed Verity around the shoulders, their grins matching.

"I don't know much about power converters, but I do know clockwork," Verity said. "The spread wasn't hitching properly." Her gaze wandered up to the bright lights atop it. "My guess would be it completed its power cycle—it stopped getting sunlight—and it tried to switch to conversion mode, but couldn't make the connection."

"Ah, I thought that might be the problem," a voice said from the crowd. Aurelia's nose was assailed with the scent of cinnamon-spiced coffee.

"Frederick!" she exclaimed. "We had to look—I think everyone thought it was going to blow the room to pieces," she said in an undertone as he approached.

"Quite understandable," he replied in her ear, causing a shiver to run down her spine. She accepted the coffee cup with a warm smile that wasn't just from the beverage.

"Brilliant work," Frederick told Verity. "Are you a student here?"

Verity grinned, glancing at a curly-haired girl just behind her. "Just enrolled."

"Well," Frederick said, smiling up at the blazing lights indicating his power converter was doing its job, "I think you have a brilliant future."

THE END

ACKNOWLEDGEMENTS

I am humbled to thank the following people who made this book happen: Scott Casey, David Green, Nord, Karen Delton, Karyne Norton, Dave Pergola, Jenna, David Trotter, Amy Campbell, Vancil Clayton Thomas, Hannah Conrad, Raven Oak, Sara Lawson, Billye Herndon, Benjamin Thomas, Heather Hyatt, Eerie Ventures Ltd., Spencer, Alex Grade, A. L. Lorensen, Katelyn, Carly Arave, Tiffany Smith, Robin Busch, Thona Bitzer, Emma, Megan, Kenyon Wensing, Lyle Martin, GrokTheGolem, Daniel Kenner, Dayenne, Andie, Deborah O'Carroll, Rottis, Vicky Salas, Maria Foronda, Nicholas Kendall Whittington, Alastair, Olia Baghdanov, Dr. Charles Elbert Norton III, Seamus Sands, Colin Letch, John Valeri, Ika, Bradley Hamm, Shanon Brown, Amanda Eschmeyer, Gregory Panjian, Courtney, Gabrielle Wright, Marie, Kimberly Grymes, Kelsey Stenberg, Jo Anderson, Esa Eriksson, Katherine Malloy, Alexandrea Oliver, Ari, Karen Bulgarelli, Samantha McCulloch, Valerie Lily, Pesti Boglárka, Agnes Jankiewicz, Brittney, Vaceran, jerome, Alexandra Corrsin, Sophia Hernandez, Alex Hux, Nicholle Taurins, Avery Moore, Finley Wilson, Chelsea Rogers, Angela Chen, Rachel Rener, Tereasa Liberty, Kariss Peterson, Anj, Sydney Baker, thomas knowles, MaeNadlen, Cathrine Bonham, Rebecca, Alexandrine Dube, and Alex Drummer.

I would also like to thank my husband Jeff for all his support as I go on this spectacular journey that is publishing. To my boys: I love seeing the world through your eyes, and hope you always follow your biggest dreams.

To Benjamin Thomas, Ben Daniels, and Kimberly Grymes, who are not only friends but amazing writers. Thank you for being there for the celebrations and commiserations.

And to all the readers: I am honored that you picked this book up and allowed me to take you to a place near and dear to me. Soldark will always be here to welcome you back with its quirky clockmakers, ambitious inventors, and dreams to follow. Until next time.

-Liz

ABOUT THE AUTHOR

Liz Delton writes and lives in New England, with her husband and sons. She studied Theater Management at the University of the Arts in Philly, always having enjoyed the backstage life of storytelling.

World-building is her favorite part of writing, and she is always dreaming up new fantastic places.

She loves drinking tea and traveling. When she's not writing or reading, you can find her baking in the kitchen, out in the garden, or narrating books on her podcast, Fictional Bookshop.

Visit her website at **LizDelton.com**

ALSO BY LIZ DELTON

SEASONS OF SOLDARK
Spectacle of the Spring Queen
The Mechanical Masquerade
All Hallows Airship
The Clockwork Ice Dragon

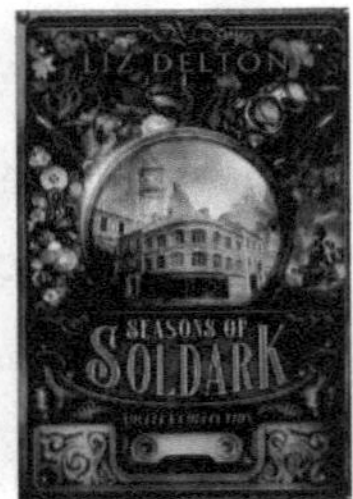

EVERTURN CHRONICLES
The Alchemyst's Mirror

REALM OF CAMELLIA
The Starless Girl
The Storm King
The Gray Mage
The Starlight Dragon
The Rogue Shadow

FOUR CITIES OF ARCERA
Meadowcity
The Fifth City
A Rift Between Cities
Sylvia in the Wilds

WRITER'S NOTEBOOKS
Writer's Notebook
Teen Writer's Notebook
Guided Writer's Notebook